Orlando

Orlando
A BIOGRAPHY

VIRGINIA
WOOLF

Annotated and with an introduction
by Maria DiBattista

Mark Hussey, General Editor

A Harvest Book • Harcourt, Inc.
Orlando Austin New York San Diego London

For information about permission
to reproduce selections from this book,
write to Permissions, Houghton Mifflin Harcourt
Publishing Company, 215 Park Avenue South,
New York, New York 10003.

www.hmhco.com

Library of Congress Cataloging-in-Publication Data
Woolf, Virginia, 1882–1941.
Orlando: a biography/Virginia Woolf; annotated and with an introduction
by Maria DiBattista; Mark Hussey, general editor.—Annotated ed., 1st ed.
p.   cm.—(A Harvest Book.)
Includes bibliographical references.
1. Transsexuals—Fiction.   2. Nobility—Fiction.   3. Sex role—Fiction.
4. England—Fiction.   I. DiBattista, Maria, 1947–   II. Hussey, Mark, 1956–   III. Title.
PR6045.O72O7   2006
823'.912—dc22   2005037769
ISBN 978-0-15-603151-6

Text set in Garamond MT
Designed by Cathy Riggs

Printed in the United States of America

First edition
DOC 20 19 18 17 16 15 14 13

CONTENTS

Orlando

VIRGINIA WOOLF

VIRGINIA WOOLF was born into what she once described as "a very communicative, literate, letter writing, visiting, articulate, late nineteenth century world." Her parents, Leslie and Julia Stephen, both previously widowed, began their marriage in 1878 with four young children: Laura (1870–1945), the daughter of Leslie Stephen and his first wife, Harriet Thackeray (1840–1875); and George (1868–1934), Gerald (1870–1937), and Stella Duckworth (1869–1897), the children of Julia Prinsep (1846–1895) and Herbert Duckworth (1833–1870). In the first five years of their marriage, the Stephens had four more children. Their third child, Virginia, was born in 1882, the year her father began work on the monumental *Dictionary of National Biography* that would earn him a knighthood in 1902. Virginia, her sister, Vanessa (1879–1961), and brothers, Thoby (1880–1906) and Adrian (1883–1948), all were born in the tall house at 22 Hyde Park Gate in London where the eight children lived with numerous servants, their eminent and irascible father, and their beautiful mother, who, in Woolf's words, was "in the very centre of that great Cathedral space that was childhood."

Woolf's parents knew many of the intellectual luminaries of the late Victorian era well, counting among their close friends novelists such as George Meredith, Thomas Hardy, and Henry James. Woolf's great-aunt Julia Margaret Cameron was a pioneering photographer who made portraits of the poets Alfred

Tennyson and Robert Browning, of the naturalist Charles Darwin, and of the philosopher and historian Thomas Carlyle, among many others. Beginning in the year Woolf was born, the entire Stephen family moved to Talland House in St. Ives, Cornwall, for the summer. There the younger children would spend their days playing cricket in the garden, frolicking on the beach, or taking walks along the coast, from where they could look out across the bay to the Godrevy lighthouse.

The early years of Woolf's life were marred by traumatic events. When she was thirteen, her mother, exhausted by a punishing schedule of charitable visits among the sick and poor, died from a bout of influenza. Woolf's half sister Stella took over the household responsibilities and bore the brunt of their self-pitying father's sorrow until she escaped into marriage in 1897 with Jack Hills, a young man who had been a favorite of Julia's. Within three months, Stella (who was pregnant) was dead, most likely from peritonitis. In this year, which she called "the first really *lived* year of my life," Woolf began a diary. Over the next twelve years, she would record in its pages her voracious reading, her impressions of people and places, feelings about her siblings, and events in the daily life of the large household.[1]

In addition to the premature deaths of her mother and half sister, there were other miseries in Woolf's childhood. In autobiographical writings and letters, Woolf referred to the sexual abuse she suffered at the hands of her two older half brothers, George and Gerald Duckworth. George, in one instance, explained his behavior to a family doctor as his effort to comfort his half sister for the fatal illness of their father. Sir Leslie died

---

[1]Woolf's early diary is published as *A Passionate Apprentice: The Early Journals, 1897–1909,* edited by Mitchell A. Leaska. A 1909 notebook discovered in 2002 has been published as *Carlyle's House and Other Sketches,* edited by David Bradshaw (London: Hesperus, 2003).

from cancer in 1904, and shortly thereafter the four Stephen children—Vanessa, Virginia, Thoby, and Adrian—moved together to the then-unfashionable London neighborhood of Bloomsbury. When Thoby Stephen began to bring his Cambridge University friends to the house on Thursday evenings, what would later become famous as the "Bloomsbury Group" began to form.

In an article marking the centenary of her father's birth, Woolf recalled his "allowing a girl of fifteen the free run of a large and quite unexpurgated library"—an unusual opportunity for a Victorian young woman, and evidence of the high regard Sir Leslie had for his daughter's intellectual talents. In her diary, she recorded the many different kinds of books her father recommended to her—biographies and memoirs, philosophy, history, and poetry. Although he believed that women should be "as well educated as men," Woolf's mother held that "to serve is the fulfilment of women's highest nature." The young Stephen children were first taught at home by their mother and father, with little success. Woolf herself received no formal education beyond some classes in Greek and Latin in the Ladies' Department of King's College in London, beginning in the fall of 1897. In 1899 she began lessons in Greek with Clara Pater, sister of the renowned Victorian critic Walter Pater, and in 1902 she was tutored in the classics by Janet Case (who also later involved her in work for women's suffrage). Such homeschooling was a source of some bitterness later in her life, as she recognized the advantages that derived from the expensive educations her brothers and half brothers received at private schools and university. Yet she also realized that her father's encouragement of her obviously keen intellect had given her an eclectic foundation. In the early years of Bloomsbury, she reveled in the opportunity to discuss ideas with her brother Thoby and his friends, among whom were Lytton Strachey, Clive Bell, and

E. M. Forster. From them, she heard, too, about an intense young man named Leonard Woolf, whom she had met briefly when visiting Thoby at Cambridge, and also in 1904 when he came to dinner at Gordon Square just before leaving for Ceylon (now called Sri Lanka), where he was to administer a far-flung outpost of the British Empire.

Virginia Woolf's first publications were unsigned reviews and essays in an Anglo-Catholic newspaper called the *Guardian,* beginning in December 1904. In the fall of 1906, she and Vanessa went with a family friend, Violet Dickinson, to meet their brothers in Greece. The trip was spoiled by Vanessa's falling ill, and when she returned to London, Virginia found both her brother Thoby—who had returned earlier—and her sister seriously ill. After a misdiagnosis by his doctors, Thoby died from typhoid fever on November 20, leaving Virginia to maintain a cheerful front while her sister and Violet Dickinson recovered from their own illnesses. Two days after Thoby's death, Vanessa agreed to marry his close friend Clive Bell.

While living in Bloomsbury, Woolf had begun to write a novel that would go through many drafts before it was published in 1915 as *The Voyage Out.* In these early years of independence, her social circle widened. She became close to the art critic Roger Fry, organizer of the First Post-Impressionist Exhibition in London in 1910, and also entered the orbit of the famed literary hostess Lady Ottoline Morrell (cruelly caricatured as Hermione Roddice in D. H. Lawrence's 1920 novel *Women in Love*). Her political consciousness also began to emerge. In 1910 she volunteered for the movement for women's suffrage. She also participated that February in a daring hoax that embarrassed the British Navy and led to questions being asked in the House of Commons: She and her brother Adrian, together with some other Cambridge friends, gained access to a secret warship by dressing up and posing as the Emperor of Abyssinia and his retinue. The "Dreadnought Hoax" was front-page news, complete with photographs of the phony Ethiopians with flowing robes, blackened faces, and false beards.

To the British establishment, one of the most embarrassing aspects of the Dreadnought affair was that a woman had taken part in the hoax. Vanessa Bell was concerned at what might have happened to her sister had she been discovered on the ship. She was also increasingly worried about Virginia's erratic health, and by the early summer 1910 had discussed with Dr. George Savage, one of the family's doctors, the debilitating headaches her sister suffered; Dr. Savage prescribed several weeks in a nursing home. Another element in Vanessa's concern was that Virginia was twenty-eight and still unmarried. Clive Bell and Virginia had, in fact, engaged in a hurtful flirtation soon after the birth of Vanessa's first child in 1908. Although she had been proposed to twice in 1909 and once in 1911, Virginia had not taken these offers very seriously.

Dropping by Vanessa's house on a July evening in 1911, Virginia met Leonard Woolf, recently back on leave from Ceylon. Soon after this, Leonard became a lodger at the house Virginia shared with Adrian, the economist John Maynard Keynes, and the painter Duncan Grant. Leonard decided to resign from the Colonial Service, hoping that Virginia would agree to marry him. After some considerable hesitation, she did, and they married in August 1912.

By the end of that year, Woolf was again suffering from the tremendous headaches that afflicted her throughout her life, and in 1913 she was again sent to a nursing home for what was then called a "rest cure." In September of that year, she took an overdose of a sleeping drug and was under care until the following spring. In early 1915 she suffered a severe breakdown and was ill throughout most of the year in which her first novel was published.

Despite this difficult beginning, Virginia and Leonard Woolf's marriage eventually settled into a pattern of immense productivity and mutual support. Leonard worked for a time for the Women's Cooperative Guild, and became increasingly involved with advising the Labour Party and writing on international politics, as well as editing several periodicals. Virginia began to establish herself as an important novelist and influential critic. In 1917 the Woolfs set up their own publishing house, the Hogarth Press, in their home in Richmond. Their first publication was *Two Stories*—Leonard's "Three Jews" and Virginia's experimental "The Mark on the Wall." They had decided to make their livings by writing, and in 1919, a few months before Woolf's second novel, *Night and Day,* was published, they bought a cottage in the village of Rodmell in Sussex. After moving back into London from Richmond in 1923, Woolf would spend summers at Monk's House, returning to the social whirl of the city in the fall.

"The Mark on the Wall" was one of a number of what Woolf called "sketches" that she began to write around the time she and Leonard bought their printing press. *Night and Day* was the last of her books to be published in England by another press. In 1919 Hogarth published her short story *Kew Gardens,* with two woodcuts by Vanessa Bell, and two years later came *Monday or Tuesday,* the only collection of her short fiction published in Woolf's lifetime. Her next novel was *Jacob's Room* (1922), a slim elegy to the generation of 1914, and to her beloved brother Thoby, whose life of great promise had also been cut short so suddenly. Woolf had written to her friend Margaret Llewelyn Davies in 1916 that the Great War, as it was then called, was a "preposterous masculine fiction" that made her "steadily more feminist," and in her fiction and nonfiction she began to articulate and illuminate the connections between the patriarchal status quo, the relatively subordinate position of women, and war making. Thinking about a novel she was calling "The Hours," Woolf wrote in her diary in 1923 that she wanted to criticize "the social system." Her inclusion in the novel of a shell-shocked war veteran named Septimus Warren Smith would confuse many of the early reviewers of her fourth novel, *Mrs. Dalloway* (1925), but others recognized that Woolf was breaking new ground in the way she rendered consciousness and her understanding of human subjectivity.

By the time she wrote *Mrs. Dalloway,* Woolf was also a sought-after essayist and reviewer who, like many of her celebrated contemporaries, was staking out her own particular piece of modernist territory. The Hogarth Press published radical young writers like Katherine Mansfield, T. S. Eliot, and Gertrude Stein. Approached by Harriet Shaw Weaver with part of the manuscript of James Joyce's *Ulysses* in 1918, the Woolfs turned it down. Their own small press could not cope with the long and complex manuscript, nor could Leonard Woolf find a commercial printer willing to risk prosecution for obscenity by producing it. In 1924 the Hogarth Press became the official English publisher of the works of Sigmund Freud, translated by Lytton Strachey's brother James. Woolf's own literary criticism was collected in a volume published in 1925, *The Common Reader*—a title signaling her distrust of academics and love of broad, eclectic reading.

The staggering range of Woolf's reading is reflected in the more than five hundred essays and reviews she published during her lifetime. Her critical writing is concerned not only with the canonical works of English literature from Chaucer to her contemporaries, but also ranges widely through lives of the obscure, memoirs, diaries, letters, and biographies. Models of the form, her essays comprise a body of work that has only recently begun to attract the kind of recognition her fiction has received.

In 1922 Woolf met "the lovely and gifted aristocrat" Vita Sackville-West, already a well-known poet and novelist. Their close friendship slowly turned into a love affair, glowing most intensely from about 1925 to 1928, before modulating into friendship once more in the 1930s. The period of their intimacy was extremely creative for both writers, Woolf publishing essays such as "Mr. Bennett and Mrs. Brown" and "Letter to a Young Poet," as well as three very different novels: *To the Lighthouse* (1927), which evoked her own childhood and had at its center the figure of a modernist woman artist, Lily Briscoe; *Orlando* (1928), a fantastic biography inspired by Vita's own remarkable family history; and *The Waves* (1931), a mystical and profoundly meditative work that pushed Woolf's concept of novel form to its limit. Woolf also published a second *Common Reader* in 1932, and the "biography" of *Flush,* Elizabeth Barrett Browning's dog (1933). She went with Sackville-West to Cambridge in the fall of 1928 to deliver the second of the two lectures on which her great feminist essay *A Room of One's Own* (1929) is based.

As the political situation in Europe in the 1930s moved inexorably to its crisis in 1939, Woolf began to collect newspaper clippings about the relations between the sexes in England, France, Germany, and Italy. The scrapbooks she made became the matrix from which developed the perspectives of her penultimate novel, *The Years* (1937), and the arguments of her pacifist-feminist polemic *Three Guineas* (1938). In 1937 Vanessa's eldest son, Julian Bell, was killed serving as an ambulance driver in the Spanish Civil War. Woolf later wrote to Vanessa that she had written *Three Guineas* partly as an argument with Julian. Her work on *The Years* was grindingly slow and difficult. Ironically, given Woolf's reputation as a highbrow, it became a bestseller in the United States, even being published in an Armed Services edition. While she labored over the novel in 1934, the news came of the death of Roger Fry, one of her oldest and closest friends and the former lover of her sister, Vanessa. Reluctantly, given her distaste for the conventions of biography, Woolf agreed to write his life, which was published in 1940.

In 1939, to relieve the strain of writing Fry's biography, Woolf began to write a memoir, "A Sketch of the Past," which remained unpublished until 1976, when the manuscripts were edited by Jeanne Schulkind for a collection of Woolf's autobiographical writings, *Moments of Being.* Withdrawing with Leonard to Monk's House in Sussex, where they could see the German airplanes flying low overhead on their way to bomb London, Woolf continued to write for peace and correspond with anti-war activists in Europe and the United States. She began to write her last novel, *Between the Acts,* in the spring of 1938, but by early 1941 was dissatisfied with it. Before completing her final revisions, Woolf ended her own life, walking into the River Ouse on the morning of March 28, 1941. To her sister, Vanessa, she wrote, "I can hardly think clearly any more. If I could I would tell you what you and the children have meant to me. I think you know." In her last note to Leonard, she told him he had given her "complete happiness," and asked him to destroy all her papers.

BY THE END of the twentieth century, Virginia Woolf had become an iconic figure, a touchstone for the feminism that revived in the 1960s as well as for the conservative backlash of the 1980s. Hailed by many as a radical writer of genius, she has also been dismissed as a narrowly focused snob. Her image adorns T-shirts, postcards, and even a beer advertisement, while phrases from her writings occur in all kinds of contexts, from peace-march slogans to highbrow book reviews. That Woolf is one of those figures upon whom the myriad competing narratives of twentieth- and twenty-first-century Western culture inscribe themselves is testified to by the enormous number of biographical works about her published in the decades since her nephew Quentin Bell broke the ground in 1972 with his two-volume biography of his aunt.

Argument continues about the work and life of Virginia Woolf: about her experience of incest, her madness, her class attitudes, her sexuality, the difficulty of her prose, her politics, her feminism, and her legacy. Perhaps, though, these words from her essay "How Should One Read a Book?" are our best guide: "The only advice, indeed, that one person can give another about reading is to take no advice, to follow your own instincts, to use your own reason, to come to your own conclusions."

—MARK HUSSEY, GENERAL EDITOR

CHRONOLOGY

Information is arranged in this order: 1. Virginia Woolf's family and her works; 2. Cultural and political events; 3. Significant publications and works of art.

1878   Marriage of Woolf's parents, Leslie Stephen (1832–1904) and Julia Prinsep Duckworth (née Jackson) (1846–1895). Leslie Stephen publishes *Samuel Johnson,* first volume in the English Men of Letters series.
England at war in Afghanistan.

1879   Vanessa Stephen (Bell) born (d. 1961). Edward Burne-Jones paints Julia Stephen as the Virgin Mary in *The Annunciation.* Leslie Stephen, *Hours in a Library,* 3rd series.
Somerville and Lady Margaret Hall Colleges for women founded at Oxford University.
Anglo-Zulu war in South Africa.

1880   Thoby Stephen born (d. 1906).
William Gladstone becomes prime minister for second time. First Boer War begins (1880–81). Deaths of Gustave Flaubert (b. 1821) and George Eliot (b. 1819). Lytton Strachey born (d. 1932).
Fyodor Dostoyevsky, *The Brothers Karamazov.*

1881　　Leslie Stephen buys lease of Talland House, St. Ives, Cornwall.

　　　　　Cambridge University Tripos exams opened to women. Henrik Ibsen, *Ghosts;* Henry James, *The Portrait of a Lady, Washington Square;* Christina Rossetti, *A Pageant and Other Poems;* D. G. Rossetti, *Ballads and Sonnets;* Oscar Wilde, *Poems.*

1882　　Adeline Virginia Stephen (Virginia Woolf) born January 25. Leslie Stephen begins work as editor of the *Dictionary of National Biography (DNB)*; publishes *The Science of Ethics.* The Stephen family spends its first summer at Talland House.

　　　　　Married Women's Property Act enables women to buy, sell, and own property and keep their own earnings. Triple Alliance between Germany, Italy, and Austria. Phoenix Park murders of British officials in Dublin, Ireland. James Joyce born (d. 1941). Death of Charles Darwin (b. 1809).

1883　　Adrian Leslie Stephen born (d. 1948). Julia Stephen's *Notes from Sick Rooms* published.

　　　　　Olive Schreiner, *The Story of an African Farm;* Robert Louis Stevenson, *Treasure Island.*

1884　　Leslie Stephen delivers the Clark Lectures at Cambridge University.

　　　　　Third Reform Act extends the franchise in England. Friedrich Engels, *The Origin of the Family, Private Property and the State;* John Ruskin, *The Storm-Cloud of the Nineteenth Century;* Mark Twain, *The Adventures of Huckleberry Finn.*

1885   First volume of Leslie Stephen's *Dictionary of National
        Biography* published.
        Redistribution Act further extends the franchise in En-
        gland. Ezra Pound born (d. 1972); D. H. Lawrence born
        (d. 1930).
        George Meredith, *Diana of the Crossways;* Émile Zola,
        Germinal.

1887   Queen Victoria's Golden Jubilee.
        Arthur Conan Doyle, *A Study in Scarlet;* H. Rider Hag-
        gard, *She;* Thomas Hardy, *The Woodlanders.*

1891   Leslie Stephen gives up the *DNB* editorship. Laura
        Stephen (1870–1945) is placed in an asylum.
        William Gladstone elected prime minister of England a
        fourth time.
        Thomas Hardy, *Tess of the D'Urbervilles;* Oscar Wilde,
        The Picture of Dorian Gray.

1895   Death of Julia Stephen.
        Armenian Massacres in Turkey. Discovery of X-rays
        by William Röntgen; Guglielmo Marconi discovers
        radio; invention of the cinematograph. Trials of Oscar
        Wilde.
        Thomas Hardy, *Jude the Obscure;* H. G. Wells, *The Time
        Machine;* Oscar Wilde, *The Importance of Being Earnest.*

1896   Vanessa Stephen begins drawing classes three after-
        noons a week.
        Death of William Morris (b. 1834); F. Scott Fitzgerald
        born (d. 1940).
        Anton Chekhov, *The Seagull.*

1897   Woolf attends Greek and history classes at King's College, London, and begins to keep a regular diary. Vanessa, Virginia, and Thoby watch Queen Victoria's Diamond Jubilee procession. Stella Duckworth (b. 1869) marries Jack Hills in April, but dies in July. Gerald Duckworth (1870–1937) establishes a publishing house.
Paul Gauguin, *Where Do We Come From? What Are We? Where Are We Going?;* Bram Stoker, *Dracula.*

1898   Spanish-American War (1898–99). Marie Curie discovers radium. Death of Stéphane Mallarmé (b. 1842).
H. G. Wells, *The War of the Worlds;* Oscar Wilde, *The Ballad of Reading Gaol.*

1899   Woolf begins Latin and Greek lessons with Clara Pater. Thoby Stephen goes up to Trinity College, Cambridge University, entering with Lytton Strachey, Leonard Woolf (1880–1969), and Clive Bell (1881–1964).
The Second Boer War begins (1899–1902) in South Africa. Ernest Hemingway born (d. 1961).

1900   Woolf and Vanessa attend the Trinity College Ball at Cambridge University.
Deaths of Friedrich Nietzsche (b. 1844), John Ruskin (b. 1819), and Oscar Wilde (b. 1854).
Sigmund Freud, *The Interpretation of Dreams.*

1901   Vanessa enters Royal Academy Schools.
Queen Victoria dies January 22. Edward VII becomes king. Marconi sends messages by wireless telegraphy from Cornwall to Newfoundland.

1902   Woolf begins classics lessons with Janet Case. Adrian
Stephen enters Trinity College, Cambridge University.
Leslie Stephen is knighted.

Joseph Conrad, *Heart of Darkness;* Henry James, *The
Wings of the Dove;* William James, *The Varieties of Religious
Experience.*

1903   The Wright Brothers fly a biplane 852 feet. Women's
Social and Political Union founded in England by Em-
meline Pankhurst.

1904   Sir Leslie Stephen dies. George Duckworth (1868–
1934) marries Lady Margaret Herbert. The Stephen
children—Vanessa, Virginia, Thoby, and Adrian—move
to 46 Gordon Square, in the Bloomsbury district of
London. Woolf contributes to F. W. Maitland's biography of her father. Leonard Woolf comes to dine before
sailing for Ceylon. Woolf travels in Italy and France.
Her first publication is an unsigned review in the
Guardian, a church weekly.

"Empire Day" inaugurated in London and in Britain's
colonies.

Anton Chekhov, *The Cherry Orchard;* Henry James, *The
Golden Bowl.*

1905   Woolf begins teaching weekly adult education classes at
Morley College. Thoby invites Cambridge friends to
their home for "Thursday Evenings"—the beginnings
of the Bloomsbury Group. Woolf travels with Adrian to
Portugal and Spain. The Stephens visit Cornwall for the
first time since their mother's death.

Revolution in Russia.

Albert Einstein, *Special Theory of Relativity;* E. M. Forster, *Where Angels Fear to Tread;* Sigmund Freud, *Essays in the Theory of Sexuality;* Edith Wharton, *The House of Mirth;* Oscar Wilde, *De Profundis.*

1906   The Stephens travel to Greece. Vanessa and Thoby fall ill. Thoby dies November 20; on November 22, Vanessa agrees to marry Clive Bell.
Deaths of Paul Cézanne (b. 1839) and Henrik Ibsen (b. 1828). Samuel Beckett born (d. 1989).

1907   Woolf moves with her brother Adrian to Fitzroy Square. Vanessa marries Clive Bell.
First Cubist exhibition in Paris. W. H. Auden born (d. 1973).
Joseph Conrad, *The Secret Agent;* E. M. Forster, *The Longest Journey;* Edmund Gosse, *Father and Son;* Pablo Picasso, *Demoiselles d'Avignon.*

1908   Birth of Vanessa Bell's first child, Julian. Woolf travels to Italy with Vanessa and Clive Bell.
Herbert Asquith becomes prime minister.
E. M. Forster, *A Room with a View;* Gertrude Stein, *Three Lives.*

1909   Woolf receives a legacy of £2,500 on the death of her Quaker aunt, Caroline Emelia Stephen. Lytton Strachey proposes marriage to Woolf, but they both quickly realize this would be a mistake. Woolf meets Lady Ottoline Morrell for the first time. She travels to the Wagner festival in Bayreuth.
Chancellor of the Exchequer David Lloyd George (1863–1945) introduces a "People's Budget," taxing

wealth to pay for social reforms. A constitutional crisis ensues when the House of Lords rejects it. Death of George Meredith (b. 1828).

Filippo Marinetti, "The Founding and Manifesto of Futurism"; Henri Matisse, *Dance.*

1910   Woolf participates in the Dreadnought Hoax. She volunteers for the cause of women's suffrage. Birth of Vanessa Bell's second child, Quentin (d. 1996).

First Post-Impressionist Exhibition ("Manet and the Post-Impressionists") organized by Roger Fry (1866–1934) at the Grafton Galleries in London. Edward VII dies May 6. George V becomes king. Death of Leo Tolstoy (b. 1828).

E. M. Forster, *Howards End;* Igor Stravinsky, *The Firebird.*

1911   Woolf rents Little Talland House in Sussex. Leonard Woolf returns from Ceylon; in November, he, Adrian Stephen, John Maynard Keynes (1883–1946), Woolf, and Duncan Grant (1885–1978) share a house together at Brunswick Square in London.

Ernest Rutherford makes first model of atomic structure. Rupert Brooke, *Poems;* Joseph Conrad, *Under Western Eyes;* D. H. Lawrence, *The White Peacock;* Katherine Mansfield, *In a German Pension;* Ezra Pound, *Canzoni;* Edith Wharton, *Ethan Frome.*

1912   Woolf leases Asheham House in Sussex. Marries Leonard on August 10; they move to Clifford's Inn, London.

Captain Robert Scott's expedition reaches the South Pole, but he and his companions die on the return journey. The *Titanic* sinks. Second Post-Impressionist Exhibition, for which Leonard Woolf serves as secretary.

Marcel Duchamp, *Nude Descending a Staircase;* Wassily Kandinsky, *Concerning the Spiritual in Art;* Thomas Mann, *Death in Venice;* George Bernard Shaw, *Pygmalion.*

1913 *The Voyage Out* manuscript delivered to Gerald Duckworth. Woolf enters a nursing home in July; in September, she attempts suicide.

Roger Fry founds the Omega Workshops.

Sigmund Freud, *Totem and Taboo;* D. H. Lawrence, *Sons and Lovers;* Marcel Proust, *Du côté de chez Swann;* Igor Stravinsky, *Le Sacre du printemps.*

1914 Leonard Woolf, *The Wise Virgins;* he reviews Freud's *The Psychopathology of Everyday Life.*

World War I ("The Great War") begins in August. Home Rule Bill for Ireland passed.

Clive Bell, *Art;* James Joyce, *Dubliners;* Wyndham Lewis et al., "Vorticist Manifesto" (in *Blast*); Gertrude Stein, *Tender Buttons.*

1915 *The Voyage Out,* Woolf's first novel, published by Duckworth. In April the Woolfs move to Hogarth House in Richmond. Woolf begins again to keep a regular diary. First Zeppelin attack on London. Death of Rupert Brooke (b. 1887).

Joseph Conrad, *Victory;* Ford Madox Ford, *The Good Soldier;* D. H. Lawrence, *The Rainbow;* Dorothy Richardson, *Pointed Roofs.*

1916 Woolf discovers Charleston, where her sister, Vanessa (no longer living with her husband, Clive), moves in October with her sons, Julian and Quentin, and Duncan Grant (with whom she is in love) and David Garnett (with whom Duncan is in love).

Easter Rising in Dublin. Death of Henry James (b. 1843).

Albert Einstein, *General Theory of Relativity;* James Joyce, *A Portrait of the Artist as a Young Man;* Dorothy Richardson, *Backwater.*

1917 The Hogarth Press established by Leonard and Virginia Woolf in Richmond. Their first publication is their own *Two Stories,* with woodcuts by Dora Carrington (1893–1932).

Russian Bolshevik Revolution destroys the rule of the czar. The United States enters the European war.

T. S. Eliot, *Prufrock and Other Observations;* Sigmund Freud, *Introduction to Psychoanalysis;* Carl Jung, *The Unconscious;* Dorothy Richardson, *Honeycomb;* W. B. Yeats, *The Wild Swans at Coole.*

1918 Woolf meets T. S. Eliot (1888–1965). Harriet Shaw Weaver comes to tea with the manuscript of James Joyce's *Ulysses.* Vanessa Bell and Duncan Grant's daughter, Angelica Garnett, born; her paternity is kept secret from all but a very few intimates.

Armistice signed November 11; Parliamentary Reform Act gives votes in Britain to women of thirty and older and to all men.

G. M. Hopkins, *Poems;* James Joyce, *Exiles;* Katherine Mansfield, *Prelude* (Hogarth Press); Marcel Proust, *À l'ombre des jeunes filles en fleurs;* Lytton Strachey, *Eminent Victorians;* Rebecca West, *The Return of the Soldier.*

1919   The Woolfs buy Monk's House in Sussex. Woolf's second novel, *Night and Day,* is published by Duckworth. Her essay "Modern Novels" (republished in 1925 as "Modern Fiction") appears in the *Times Literary Supplement; Kew Gardens* published by Hogarth Press.
Bauhaus founded by Walter Gropius in Weimar. Sex Disqualification (Removal) Act opens many professions and public offices to women. Election of first woman member of Parliament, Nancy Astor. Treaty of Versailles imposes harsh conditions on postwar Germany, opposed by John Maynard Keynes, who writes *The Economic Consequences of the Peace.* League of Nations created. T. S. Eliot, "Tradition and the Individual Talent," *Poems;* Dorothy Richardson, *The Tunnel, Interim;* Robert Wiene, *The Cabinet of Dr. Caligari* (film).

1920   The Memoir Club, comprising thirteen original members of the Bloomsbury Group, meets for the first time. *The Voyage Out* and *Night and Day* are published in the United States by George H. Doran.
Mohandas Gandhi initiates mass passive resistance against British rule in India.
T. S. Eliot, *The Sacred Wood;* Sigmund Freud, *Beyond the Pleasure Principle;* Roger Fry, *Vision and Design;* D. H. Lawrence, *Women in Love;* Katherine Mansfield, *Bliss and Other Stories;* Ezra Pound, *Hugh Selwyn Mauberley;* Marcel Proust, *Le Côté de Guermantes I;* Edith Wharton, *The Age of Innocence.*

1921   Woolf's short story collection *Monday or Tuesday* published by Hogarth Press, which will from this time publish all her books in England. The book is also published in the United States by Harcourt Brace, which from now on is her American publisher.

Aldous Huxley, *Crome Yellow;* Pablo Picasso, *Three Musicians;* Luigi Pirandello, *Six Characters in Search of an Author;* Marcel Proust, *Le Côté de Guermantes II, Sodome et Gomorrhe I;* Dorothy Richardson, *Deadlock;* Lytton Strachey, *Queen Victoria.*

1922 *Jacob's Room* published. Woolf meets Vita Sackville-West (1892–1962) for the first time.

Bonar Law elected prime minister. Mussolini comes to power in Italy. Irish Free State established. British Broadcasting Company (BBC) formed. Discovery of Tutankhamen's tomb in Egypt. Death of Marcel Proust (b. 1871).

T. S. Eliot, *The Waste Land;* James Joyce, *Ulysses;* Katherine Mansfield, *The Garden Party;* Marcel Proust, *Sodome et Gomorrhe II;* Ludwig Wittgenstein, *Tractatus Logico-Philosophicus.*

1923 The Woolfs travel to Spain, stopping in Paris on the way home. Hogarth Press publishes *The Waste Land.*

Stanley Baldwin succeeds Bonar Law as prime minister. Death of Katherine Mansfield (b. 1888).

Mina Loy, *Lunar Baedeker;* Marcel Proust, *La Prisonnière;* Dorothy Richardson, *Revolving Lights;* Rainer Maria Rilke, *Duino Elegies.*

1924 The Woolfs move to Tavistock Square. Woolf lectures on "Character in Fiction" to the Heretics Society at Cambridge University.

The Labour Party takes office for the first time under

the leadership of Ramsay MacDonald but is voted out within the year. Death of Joseph Conrad (b. 1857).

E. M. Forster, *A Passage to India;* Thomas Mann, *The Magic Mountain.*

1925 *Mrs. Dalloway* and *The Common Reader* published. Woolf stays with Vita Sackville-West at her house, Long Barn, for the first time.

Nancy Cunard, *Parallax;* F. Scott Fitzgerald, *The Great Gatsby;* Ernest Hemingway, *In Our Time;* Adolf Hitler, *Mein Kampf;* Franz Kafka, *The Trial;* Alain Locke, ed., *The New Negro;* Marcel Proust, *Albertine disparue;* Dorothy Richardson, *The Trap;* Gertrude Stein, *The Making of Americans.*

1926 Woolf lectures on "How Should One Read a Book?" at Hayes Court School. "Cinema" published in *Arts* (New York), "Impassioned Prose" in *Times Literary Supplement,* and "On Being Ill" in *New Criterion.* Meets Gertrude Stein (1874–1946).

The General Strike in support of mine workers in England lasts nearly two weeks.

Ernest Hemingway, *The Sun Also Rises;* Langston Hughes, *The Weary Blues;* Franz Kafka, *The Castle;* A. A. Milne, *Winnie-the-Pooh.*

1927 *To the Lighthouse,* "The Art of Fiction," "Poetry, Fiction and the Future," and "Street Haunting" published. The Woolfs travel with Vita Sackville-West and her husband, Harold Nicolson, to Yorkshire to see the total eclipse of the sun. They buy their first car.

Charles Lindbergh flies the Atlantic solo.

E. M. Forster, *Aspects of the Novel;* Ernest Hemingway, *Men without Women;* Franz Kafka, *Amerika;* Marcel

Proust, *Le Temps retrouvé;* Gertrude Stein, *Four Saints in Three Acts.*

1928   *Orlando: A Biography* published. In October, Woolf delivers two lectures at Cambridge on which she will base *A Room of One's Own.* Femina-Vie Heureuse prize awarded to *To the Lighthouse.*
The Equal Franchise Act gives the vote to all women over twenty-one. Sound films introduced. Death of Thomas Hardy (b. 1840).
Djuna Barnes, *Ladies Almanack;* Radclyffe Hall, *The Well of Loneliness;* D. H. Lawrence, *Lady Chatterley's Lover;* Evelyn Waugh, *Decline and Fall;* W. B. Yeats, *The Tower.*

1929   *A Room of One's Own* published. "Women and Fiction" in *The Forum* (New York).
Labour Party returned to power under Prime Minister MacDonald. Discovery of penicillin. Museum of Modern Art opens in New York. Wall Street crash.
William Faulkner, *The Sound and the Fury;* Ernest Hemingway, *A Farewell to Arms;* Nella Larsen, *Passing.*

1930   Woolf meets the pioneering composer, writer, and suffragette Ethel Smyth (1858–1944), with whom she forms a close friendship.
Death of D. H. Lawrence (b. 1885).
W. H. Auden, *Poems;* T. S. Eliot, *Ash Wednesday;* William Faulkner, *As I Lay Dying;* Sigmund Freud, *Civilisation and Its Discontents.*

1931   *The Waves* is published. First of six articles by Woolf about London published in *Good Housekeeping;* "Introductory Letter" to *Life As We Have Known It.* Lectures to London branch of National Society for Women's Service on "Professions for Women." Meets John Lehmann (1907–1987), who will become a partner in the Hogarth Press.

Growing financial crisis throughout Europe and beginning of the Great Depression.

1932 *The Common Reader, Second Series* and "Letter to a Young Poet" published. Woolf invited to give the 1933 Clark Lectures at Cambridge, which she declines.

Death of Lytton Strachey (b. 1880).

Aldous Huxley, *Brave New World*.

1933 *Flush: A Biography,* published. The Woolfs travel by car to Italy.

Adolf Hitler becomes chancellor of Germany, establishing the totalitarian dictatorship of his National Socialist (Nazi) Party.

T. S. Eliot, *The Use of Poetry and the Use of Criticism;* George Orwell, *Down and Out in Paris and London;* Gertrude Stein, *The Autobiography of Alice B. Toklas;* Nathanael West, *Miss Lonelyhearts;* W. B. Yeats, *The Collected Poems.*

1934 Woolf meets W. B. Yeats at Ottoline Morrell's house. Writes "Walter Sickert: A Conversation."

George Duckworth dies. Roger Fry dies.

Samuel Beckett, *More Pricks Than Kicks;* Nancy Cunard, ed., *Negro: An Anthology;* F. Scott Fitzgerald, *Tender Is the Night;* Wyndham Lewis, *Men Without Art;* Henry Miller, *Tropic of Cancer;* Ezra Pound, *ABC of Reading;* Evelyn Waugh, *A Handful of Dust.*

1935 The Woolfs travel to Germany, where they accidentally get caught up in a parade for Göring. They return to England via Italy and France.

1936 Woolf reads "Am I a Snob?" to the Memoir Club, and publishes "Why Art Today Follows Politics" in the *Daily Worker*.

Death of George V, who is succeeded by Edward VIII, who then abdicates to marry Wallis Simpson. George VI becomes king. Spanish Civil War (1936–38) begins when General Franco, assisted by Germany and Italy, attacks the Republican government. BBC television begins.

Djuna Barnes, *Nightwood;* Charlie Chaplin, *Modern Times* (film); Aldous Huxley, *Eyeless in Gaza;* J. M. Keynes, *The General Theory of Employment, Interest and Money;* Rose Macaulay, *Personal Pleasures;* Margaret Mitchell, *Gone with the Wind.*

1937 *The Years* published. Woolf's nephew Julian Bell killed in the Spanish Civil War.

Neville Chamberlain becomes prime minister.

Zora Neale Hurston, *Their Eyes Were Watching God;* David Jones, *In Parenthesis;* Pablo Picasso, *Guernica;* John Steinbeck, *Of Mice and Men;* J. R. R. Tolkien, *The Hobbit.*

1938 *Three Guineas* published.

Germany annexes Austria. Chamberlain negotiates the Munich Agreement ("Peace in our time"), ceding Czech territory to Hitler.

Samuel Beckett, *Murphy;* Elizabeth Bowen, *The Death of the Heart;* Jean-Paul Sartre, *La Nausée.*

1939   The Woolfs visit Sigmund Freud, living in exile in London having fled the Nazis. They move to Mecklenburgh Square.

Germany occupies Czechoslovakia; Italy occupies Albania; Russia makes a nonaggression pact with Germany. Germany invades Poland and war is declared by Britain and France on Germany, September 3. Deaths of W. B. Yeats (b. 1865), Sigmund Freud (b. 1856), and Ford Madox Ford (b. 1873).

James Joyce, *Finnegans Wake;* John Steinbeck, *The Grapes of Wrath;* Nathanael West, *The Day of the Locust.*

1940   *Roger Fry: A Biography* published. "Thoughts on Peace in an Air Raid" in the *New Republic.* Woolf lectures on "The Leaning Tower" to the Workers Educational Association in Brighton.

The Battle of Britain leads to German night bombings of English cities. The Woolfs' house at Mecklenburgh Square is severely damaged, as is their former house at Tavistock Square. Hogarth Press is moved out of London.

Ernest Hemingway, *For Whom the Bell Tolls;* Christina Stead, *The Man Who Loved Children.*

1941   Woolf drowns herself, March 28, in the River Ouse in Sussex. *Between the Acts* published in July.

Death of James Joyce (b. 1882).

Rebecca West, *Black Lamb and Grey Falcon.*

INTRODUCTION
BY MARIA DIBATTISTA

Genesis

ORLANDO IS THE wayward child born of Virginia Woolf's fanciful imagination. Like many an unruly offspring, it was a puzzle to its mother, an oddity to its contemporaries, and a curiosity to succeeding generations of readers. After the formally traditional but spiritually restless works of her apprentice years, *The Voyage Out* (1915) and *Night and Day* (1919), Woolf had delivered, with astounding and increasing confidence, three novels in which she fashioned a modernist "method" to rival James Joyce's "mythic method" as a way "of giving a shape and a significance to the immense panorama of futility and anarchy which is contemporary history."[1] *Jacob's Room* (1922), *Mrs. Dalloway* (1925), and *To the Lighthouse* (1927) all were fictions that responded in different but complementary ways to the fact that in or about December 1910, as Woolf proclaimed in drastic but earnest overstatement, human character changed ("Mr. Bennett and Mrs. Brown" 320). That change was magnified into historic, indeed catastrophic, proportions during the First World War, in which an estimated eight to nine million lost their lives. Writing in 1923, Woolf surveyed the postwar world and reported how it struck a contemporary like herself: "A shift in the scale — the war, the sudden slip of masses held in position for ages — has shaken the fabric from top to bottom . . ." ("How It Strikes a Contemporary" 357).

Woolf thought hard and continuously about the gravity, the scale, and the impact of these changes, and about the need for new literary forms to confront and interpret them. She was in the vanguard of a new generation of novelists for whom the traditional conventions of the novel no longer served to represent modern realities: the crumbling of established social and political orders, the sexual disquiet and jagged nerves, the moral revolt and cultural revolutions, the agitation for rights long denied, freedom unreasonably curbed or stupidly repressed. In "Modern Fiction," an early and influential manifesto of her aesthetic principles, Woolf argued that "the quality which distinguishes the work of several young writers, among whom Mr James Joyce is the most notable, from that of their predecessors" was their "attempt to come closer to life, and to preserve more sincerely and exactly what interests and moves them, even if to do so they must discard most of the conventions which are commonly observed by the novelist" (150). This was all very serious business, and this essay, like many of her critical reflections from this period, adopts a suitably grave, if generally optimistic, tone in considering whether the art of fiction will be "renewed and her sovereignty assured" ("Modern Fiction" 154). Woolf herself, meanwhile, is privately convinced of her achievement and can feel the future germinating within her. "I have made my method perfect," she writes in December 1926 as she is completing revisions of *To the Lighthouse*, "& it will now stay like this, & serve whatever use I wish to put it to" (*Diary* 3: 117). She feels the incipient pull of a new artistic "wish"—to write a "semi mystic very profound life of a woman, which shall all be told on one occasion; & time shall be utterly obliterated" (*Diary* 3: 118).

And then comes *Orlando*, a "joke" from beginning to end. A joke made without apology and pursued defiantly to the last page of the novel's recorded time, midnight on the eleventh of October, 1928, presumably the day, if not the exact time, on which the book is published (*Orlando* 241). Woolf's haunting vision of a semi-mystic, very profound life of a woman is displaced by an irreverent, often coarse, and occasionally trivial life of a man who becomes a woman. The mystic project to condense time into a single epiphanic occasion temporarily disappears into a distended and episodic narrative spanning three centuries. It will rematerialize later as *The Waves* (1931), a novel that disperses its mystical moments across the lifetime of its central characters. Still, Woolf's original hope to write a narrative in which time would be utterly obliterated is fulfilled in *Orlando,* but in an implausibly ironic form. *Orlando* obliterates time not by transcending it but by blithely ignoring its power to limit the life of its hero or end that of its heroine. Regarded in this light, *Orlando* may seem a major detour in Woolf's quest for an expressive form that will capture "the essence of reality" (*Diary* 3: 113) that hovers on a horizon just beyond her imaginative grasp.

Woolf shows no evident signs of distress over this time-consuming digression into fantasy. She actually cherishes *Orlando* as a writer's holiday from the "serious poetic experimental books whose form is always so closely considered" (*Diary* 3: 131). She is happy to be writing something that is *not* serious or closely considered but droll and reckless. "I have written this book quicker than any other," she notes in her diary, "[and] it is all a joke; & yet gay & quick reading I think; a writers holiday. I feel more and more sure that I will never write a novel again" (*Diary* 3: 177). Poetic seriousness is undone by the gaiety of parody and satire; exactness gives way to an irresponsible freedom in writing about things not as they are but as they might be. Rather than attempting to come closer to human life, as a proper modernist should, Woolf seems eager to distance herself from it. Death, that hard, impinging fact of human life that had cut short the promise of Jacob Flanders in *Jacob's Room,* intruded on Mrs. Dalloway's party, and in *To the Lighthouse* surprised Mrs.

Ramsay during her sleep, her daughter Prue in childbirth, and her son Andrew on the battlefields of France, ceases to enthrall her imagination. Besides *Night and Day, Orlando* is the only one of her fictions where death does not figure as a central presence and fact of her narrative, and the only one where death doesn't seem even a remote possibility for a protagonist who is more than three hundred years old at book's end.

The first glimmerings of *Orlando*'s deathless narrative appeared to Woolf's imagination as a "Defoe narrative for fun," to be called "The Jessamy Brides," which she envisioned as a satire centering on "[t]wo women, poor, solitary at the top of a house" (*Diary* 3: 131). The proposed title, which couples *Jessamy,* a slang term for perfumed, foppish, or simply naive manhood,[2] with *Brides,* a more genteel word that carries romantic suggestions of unsullied maidenhood, indicates the satiric vein Woolf hoped to pursue. She seems to be looking for a way to write outside or beyond the stylistic proprieties of her more "seriously considered" novels. She appears eager to admit, as she will in *Orlando,* all variety of human speech and expression into her fiction: slang and oaths as well as the euphemisms of the Court, the witticisms of the salon and coffeehouses; the jargon of the professions—maritime, diplomatic, and legal—but also the gibberish of lovers, their endearments, pet names, and the cipher language, like "Rattigan Glumphoboo" (208), they devise to indicate complicated emotional states known only to each other. She welcomes the prospect of self-mockery, especially as applied to her "own lyric vein." She will "suggest" (*Diary* 3: 131) rather than declare her heroine's Sapphism, perhaps in order to avoid the public fate of Radclyffe Hall's *The Well of Loneliness,* the lesbian novel tried and convicted as an obscene libel the same year *Orlando* was published.[3]

The "whole fantasy" she had conceived for "The Jessamy Brides," in which "no attempt is to be made to realise the character," never materializes, however, in its projected form (*Diary* 3: 131). As *Orlando* begins to gestate, there appears to be *every* attempt to realize character, and not just any character, but the creative, Sapphic, seductive character of Vita Sackville-West, writer, noblewoman, friend, and, on and off since 1925, Woolf's lover. The diary entry that records this change in the nature of the "fun" she envisages begins on a note of dejection. When an acquaintance, Philip Ritchie, dies at the pitifully young age of twenty-eight, Woolf notes her reactions with her customary pitiless candor: "I think for the first time I felt this death leaves me an elderly laggard; makes me feel I have no right to go on; as if my life were at the expense of his" (*Diary* 3: 156). Yet immediately her mood changes. Her survivor's guilt yields to the survivor's gladness in the life that is left to her to enjoy, explore, understand, represent. Her mind turns to a more immediate concern about whether to buy a house she and Vita had seen.

The very incongruity of her thoughts prompts her to note "the strength & vividness of feelings which suddenly break & foam away" (*Diary* 3: 156). Out of these more buoyant and vivid feelings comes a new literary idea:

> One of these days, though, I shall sketch here, like a grand historical picture, the outlines of all my friends. . . . It might be a way of writing the memoirs of one's own times during peoples lifetimes. It might be a most amusing book. The question is how to do it. Vita should be Orlando, a young nobleman. There should be Lytton. & it should be truthful; but fantastic. (*Diary* 3: 156–57)

The changes in subject and perspective accumulate with surprising consequences. A book that was to have no character was becoming a book to commemorate character. A book that would satisfy her desire to escape and obliterate time now promises to contain the very substance and temper of her times. Ritchie's death and her consciousness of time, her own time in particular, subtly infuse her conception of an amusing, truthful Defoe narrative and transpose it into the register of a grand and fantastic joke.

Not everyone got the joke, or liked it, but few could resist or deny its charm. *Orlando* became the most popular of her books to date, selling six thousand copies and going into a third edition two months after its publication.[4] Suddenly, the reigning Sibyl of Bloomsbury culture, the high priestess of modernism, was an entertaining madcap who had taken leave of her senses, writing an amusing but feigned biography of an Elizabethan nobleman of the sixteenth century who changes sex (without benefit of surgical intervention or psychological counseling) in the eighteenth and seems to be at her sexual and imaginative peak in the twentieth. Reviewers, both those who were friendly and those predictably unsympathetic to her literary views and methods, were not sure what to make of such a startling, if admittedly witty, performance. The American poet and critic Conrad Aiken, who found *Orlando* "exceedingly, not to say disconcertingly clever," predicted that readers would be unsure "whether to regard it as a biography, or a satire on biography; as a history, or a satire on history; as a novel, or as an allegory" (Aiken 234). He put an end to their uncertainty by pronouncing the generically puzzling work a *"jeu d'esprit"* that Woolf "had taken a shade too far towards an arid and ingenious convention" (Aiken 235). Yet what Aiken determines to be a work of literary burlesque, Desmond MacCarthy, who is thanked in *Orlando*'s acknowledgments, just as emphatically pronounces "a pure romance." *Orlando,* he enthuses, is "a wonderful phantasmagoria, in which imagination has all its own way and all matter-of-factness is exorcised from the start; in which, not without frequent flashes of laughter at her own extravagance, the writer combines images and historic facts, possibilities, and impossibilities, reflections upon history and manners with scenes from a dream-world" (MacCarthy 225).

The combinatory magic of *Orlando,* in which fact and fancy, dream and history indiscriminately mix and alter each other, dismayed as many of its readers as it enchanted. The novelist Elizabeth Bowen, revisiting *Orlando* in 1960 on the occasion of a paperback reissue, remembers how her generation, then the "young generation" of modernists, "scented the book as a transgression" (Bowen 131). Bowen relates how the serious young artists of the twenties, who venerated Woolf for "sublimating personality into poetry," felt Woolf had desecrated the sacred precepts of her art by writing a thinly disguised fictional biography of her intimate, Vita Sackville-West. They perceived the book Woolf had hoped would "revolutionize biography in a night" (*Letters* 3: 429) not as a bold innovation but as a reactionary swerve into coterie art. Personality was not sublimated but exhibited in the self-satisfied and flattering form of a roman à clef: "Inspired by a romantic friendship, written for the delectation of the romantic friend," Bowen recalls feeling, "it was likely to be fraught with playful allusion" (131). To be inspired by friendship may be forgiven, but to produce a work for the private "delectation" (the "hauteur" conveyed by that word!) of a lover violated all canons of modernist impersonality. In Bowen's youthful opinion, the offense of writing a work inspired and destined to be savored by a circle of intimates was compounded by the self-delighted face *Orlando* turned to its larger audience of common readers.

Bowen's youthful chagrin at her idol's distressing lapse into literary frivolity was countered by Winifred Holtby's more appreciative view of the highly expressive uses to which Woolf put her gift for fantasy. Holtby, whose wonderfully perceptive, even prescient, book was the first full-scale study of Woolf written during her lifetime, demonstrated the ways in which *Orlando* was not a scandalous departure or a disappointing aberration but a fiction that elaborated and refined a gift for caricature and exaggeration already evident in her more "serious" books. "That Mrs Woolf should write a fantasy," Holtby insisted, "was not at all surprising":

> She had already, in *A Society*, shown how well she could design a light-hearted squib. In *To the Lighthouse* she had enjoyed Mrs. Ramsay's gift of extravagant speech. Mrs. Ramsay cried that she would not keep dinner waiting for the Queen of England, "not for the Empress of Mexico." It was, after all, only going one step further to make Orlando actually late for dinner with a Queen. Mrs. Woolf had in *A Society* described the girl Rose going aboard one of his Majesty's ships disguised as an Ethiopian prince; it was only one step further to make the woman Orlando actually to have been British Ambassador at Constantinople. She had, in all her books, played with the notion of time and its importance. In *Mrs. Dalloway* the whole significance of fifty years had been gathered into twenty-four hours; it was only going one step further, in *Orlando*, to spread the experience of some forty years out over three centuries. (162)

Holtby's critical view is not just among the first but among the most satisfying accounts of *Orlando*'s imaginative genesis, reminding us, as she does, that *Orlando* exhibits the same disposition to exaggerate and comically distort reality that helped sustain the party spirit of *Mrs. Dalloway* and lift the anxious spirits of *To the Lighthouse*. (It is, after all, the comically inappropriate "What beautiful boots!" that relieves Lily Briscoe's dumb distress before Mr. Ramsay's importuning grief and allows her to resume her painting in the final panel of *To the Lighthouse* [157].)

Orlando is a fiction that is best regarded, then, as Holtby regards it—as "one step further" in Woolf's creative drive to overcome the constraints, including those originating within her own mind, that would impede her imaginative encounter with reality. It may be a spirited escapade, a writer's holiday from the matter-of-fact, but its liberties in expression and experiments in form are continuous with the masterworks that preceded it. The great Argentine modernist Jorge Luis Borges indeed considered *Orlando,* which he translated into Spanish, as Woolf's "most intense work and one of the most singular and maddening of our age" (92). *Orlando* is only apparently a changeling; in truth it belongs to the same great family of fantastic fictions that bear the genetic imprint of Woolf's literary genius. In her diary, Woolf speculated that "there are offices to be discharged by talent for the relief of genius: meaning that one has the play side; the gift when it is mere gift, unapplied gift; & the gift when it is serious, going to business. And one relieves the other" (*Diary* 3: 203). *Orlando* is the gift Woolf's talent makes to her own genius. Such gifts are serious business, as *Orlando,* that long, at times bad, joke, joco-seriously demonstrates.

Vita and Harold

ONE OF the offices that talent can discharge is to relieve genius of the "musts" of the novel, which, as Elizabeth Bowen remarked, bored Virginia Woolf (134). Talent cannot ignore or dispense altogether with these "musts," but it can show genius how to have fun with them. The fun starts even before *Orlando* properly begins, in its preface, in Woolf's comically profuse acknowledgments of the "many friends [who] have helped me in writing this book." One name, however, is conspicuously missing—its dedicatee, Vita Sackville-West. This odd, even

glaring oversight—the first of many embarrassing lacunae in a
book full of blanks and all variety of narrative omissions—
might be excused on the ground that the book is a portrait of
Vita and so an acknowledgment writ large of Woolf's debt to
her. While this reasoning may exculpate Woolf of the charge of
ingratitude, it leaves her open to renewed objections that *Orlando* does not amount to much more than a clever insider's joke
for the benefit of the Bloomsbury coterie. It might be more
prudent to dismiss this excuse as a transparent alibi, one inade-
quate to absolve Woolf for having borrowed—without explicit
attribution—Vita's character and ransacked her writing, especially *Knole and the Sackvilles,* Vita's history of her family and its
ancestral home, published in 1922. Woolf not only confiscated
the grounds and furnishings of Knole in her description of Orlando's estate but commandeered incidents from the annals of
the Sackville family history to tether her flight of fantasy to the
firm ground of historical fact: the visit of Queen Elizabeth to
Knole, the travels to Turkey, the irregular union with a gypsy, a
legal suit to determine who should inherit Knole.

Given the extent and narrative importance of these personal allusions to the Sackville family history, Woolf's forgetting—or is it her refusal?—to name Vita in the preface seems
to make a statement of quite a different sort. It is a sign of how
completely she had assimilated Vita's historical existence to her
imaginary biography of a fictional character named Orlando.
The photographs of Vita that are meant to represent Orlando
on her "return to England" from Constantinople, as she is said
to appear "about the year 1840," and "at the present time," are
a measure of how thoroughly her identity had been assimilated
into Woolf's imaginary creation and subordinated to Woolf's
determination to reinvent the novel in the guise of a realistically
fanciful biography.

Acting as midwife for this fantastic birth was *Some People,* an unusual memoir written by Vita's husband, Harold Nicolson, which Woolf reviewed in 1927, in the midst of writing *Orlando. Some People* is an engaging collection of anecdotal portraits "of real people in imaginary situations and imaginary people in real situations" (qtd. Nigel Nicolson, "Introduction" vii). Some People Nicolson describes are famous and retain their name, like Lord Curzon; Some People are obscure and so have less need of an imaginary or protective cover, like Nicolson's governess, Miss Plimsoll. Some People are metamorphosed into characters with names and habits Max Beerbohm might have invented (but did not), like Lambert Orme, who was modeled after the novelist Ronald Firbank. Nicolson's refusal to distinguish his real acquaintances from his imaginary ones, what actually took place from what, given such a character, *could* have taken place (and, presuming it had, would provide an even better clue to their character), appealed immensely to Woolf. She praised the book as an example of the "new" biography, pioneered by Lytton Strachey's *Eminent Victorians* (1918) and *Queen Victoria* (1921), that made original and exciting "use [of] the novelist's art of arrangement, suggestion, dramatic effect to expound the private life" ("New Biography" 234).

Woolf was perfectly aware that the collaboration between the biographer and novelist is not always an easy, or even a cordial, one. She acknowledges the intrinsic antagonisms that might jeopardize their collaboration at the very start of her essay. Quoting the biographer Sir Sidney Lee to the effect that the art of biography entails the "truthful transmission of personality," Woolf remarks that

> no single sentence could more neatly split up into two
> parts the whole problem of biography as it presents itself

to us today. On the one hand there is truth; on the other there is personality. And if we think of truth as something of granite-like solidity and of personality as something of rainbow-like intangibility and reflect that the aim of biography is to weld these two into one seamless whole, we shall admit that the problem is a stiff one and that we need not wonder if biographers have for the most part failed to solve it. ("New Biography" 229)

Orlando is Woolf's outlandish solution to the biographer's problem of welding the rainbow and granite, the aura of personality and the truth of fact. It is a solution fashioned in response to her belief that "the life which is increasingly real to us is the fictitious life; it dwells in the personality rather than in the act" (234). This is an amazing, one could even say preposterous, claim, and one can readily pity the biographer who is made responsible for adhering to its precepts. Nevertheless, this is the task she appoints to the biographer she creates to narrate *Orlando*. Whenever the truth of fact and truth of fiction are on the verge of destroying each other, the rainbow-like intangibles of personality triumph over the granite-like solidity of truth. Does Orlando fall into a deep sleep that lasts for days and weeks? However dubious the medical facts, such trancelike states are a necessity of his personality. Does Orlando change from a man into a woman? In the regime of fact, such a metamorphosis would be violently rejected as outright fantasy, but the truth of Orlando's sexual identity dwells in his fictitious "personality." The normally circumspect biographer is so overwhelmed by the force of Orlando's sexual personality that he drowns out the realist's expostulations with trumpets blasting forth "The Truth and nothing but the Truth!" (99)—turning historic and legal fact's own formula for incontestable reality against itself.

Vita made such an irresistible subject for Woolf's satire because she answered in crucial ways to Woolf's literary sense of what a personality *is*. Woolf wrote Vita that the book to come would be "all about you and the lusts of your flesh and the lure of your mind" (*Letters* 3: 429), imperious passions and seductive charms to which she had already succumbed. But it was a rather different sort of power, one might call it Vita's *historic* personality, that seems to have attracted Woolf to Vita as a subject for fictionalized biography. That attraction is evident in Woolf's account of a visit to Knole she made in mid-January of 1927. She records in her diary how she had seen Vita

> stalking in her Turkish dress, attended by small boys, down the gallery, wafting them on like some tall sailing ship—a sort of covey of noble English life: dogs walloping, children crowding, all very free & stately: & [a] cart bringing wood in to be sawn by the great circular saw. . . . They had brought wood in from the Park to replenish the great fires like this for centuries: & her ancestresses had walked so on the snow with great dogs bounding by them. All the centuries seemed lit up, the past expressive, articulate; not dumb & forgotten; but a crowd of people stood behind, not dead at all; not remarkable; fair faced, long limbed; affable; & so we reach the days of Elizabeth quite easily. . . . One had a sense of links fished up into the light which are usually submerged. Otherwise no particular awe or any great sense of difference or distinction. They are not a brilliant race. (*Diary* 3: 125)

Viewed impartially through the lens of facts uncompromising, the Sackvilles register as an unremarkable, if affable, family. What compels Woolf's novelistic attention is the power of

Vita's personality to evoke a *fictitious* idea of British nobility, an idea she then exploits to explore the expressive, articulate past. Vita's historic personality would be especially appealing to a writer who had argued in "How It Strikes a Contemporary" that the moderns were "sharply cut off from our predecessors" and "perhaps too vividly conscious of the present" (236). Whatever value — and it is not negligible — *Orlando* possesses as a historical novel that re-creates the past derives in large part from the details she learned from Vita about the clothes worn, the rooms appointed for royal and private use, the furnishings and utensils, the food consumed, the retinue of servants employed, and the pattern of life pursued at Knole. But it was in scrutinizing the portraits of succeeding generations of Sackvilles that Woolf most vividly imagined herself going back in time, reaching, quite easily as she says, the days of Elizabeth, where *Orlando* in fact begins.

What Woolf does not record in her musings about the Knole family portraits is that Vita viewed her ancestors precisely in the same light. Woolf's sense of Vita's "excellence as a subject" (*Letters* 3: 429) imaginatively conforms to Vita's own valuation of her Sackville ancestry: "Such interest as the Sackvilles have," she writes in *Knole and the Sackvilles,* "lies, I think, in their being so representative. From generation to generation they might stand, fully equipped, as portraits from English history" (28). Orlando's life span does not seem so inordinately long if he, then she, embodies a succession of representative English types, each of whom, as Vita proposed, might stand "as the prototype of his age, and at the same time as a link to carry on, not only the tradition but also the heredity of his race." Surveying the ancestral portraits hanging in the gallery of Knole, Vita reconstructs the genetic and historic links that united the first "grave Elizabethan, with the long, rather melancholy face" to his grandson, "the Cavalier by Vandyke hanging in the hall," who in turn is linked to the "florid magnificent Charles, fruit of the Restoration, poet and patron of poets, prodigal, jovial, and licentious," who in his turn is linked to "the beautiful sensitive face of the gay and fickle duke, spoilt, feared and propitiated by the women of London and Paris, the reputed lover of Marie Antoinette." The family chain breaks off with the fourth Duke of Dorset, a friend of Byron's, who was "the last direct male of a race too prodigal, too amorous, too weak, too indolent, and too melancholy" (28–29). These racial attributes—prodigality, amorousness, weakness, indolence, and melancholy—are recombined in different proportions in a female descendant who, as a fictional personality named Orlando, will successively incarnate various Sackvilles in her long and adventurous life.

It is not love that chooses to represent Vita this way. It has been one of the sentimental commonplaces attaching to *Orlando* criticism that it is "the longest and most charming love letter in literature" (Nicolson, *Portrait* 202). So Nigel Nicolson, Vita and Harold's son, characterized this fanciful biography of his mother. Sons may be forgiven for exaggerating both the intensity and duration of the ardor their mothers inspire and may be further forgiven for mistaking the literary form such ardent affection might take. Readers most likely will experience the book differently. Certainly some of its most interested readers did. Vita herself wrote Woolf after first reading the book praising her for having "invented a new form of Narcissism,—I confess,—I am in love with Orlando—this is a complication I had not foreseen" (*Letters of Vita Sackville-West* 289). One wonders exactly what Vita saw mirrored in the anamorphic lens of Woolf's art. Vita's mother was outraged by what she saw. So distressed was she that she wrote J. L. Garvin, editor of the *Observer,* pleading with him not to review the book. "'Love is slipping off one's petticoats' . . . All that is so coarse and will be so shocking to the middle classes, mostly. . . . I have spent years, *hiding* what Harold and Vita really are. I am sorry to confess it.

And it makes it twice as dreadful now and such food for indecent gossip" (qtd. Glendinning 206). What Harold and Vita
"really are" is in fact exposed in the great sexual recognition
scene that concludes Orlando's search for life and a lover:
"'You're a woman Shel!' she cried. 'You're a man, Orlando!' he
cried" (184). The gratifying ecstasies of transgender identification are not, however, what an aristocrat jealous of the family
honor might immediately appreciate. Vita's mother had ob-
jected to Woolf's portraying her daughter as a sexual adventuress, which in fact she plausibly can be said to have been. But
what she did catch was a certain ruthlessness, even cruelty, in
the subordination of Vita to Woolf's artistic design.[5] What made
Vita excellent as a novelistic subject of a mock biography is precisely what disqualified her as an artist of the first rank—what
I have been calling her historic personality.

In an essay dating to this period called, in fact, "Personalities," Woolf remarks that "the people whom we admire most as
writers, then, have something elusive, enigmatic, impersonal
about them":

> They rise slowly to their heights; and there they shine.
> They do not win fame directly, nor are they exposed to the
> alternations of praise and blame which rise from the pas-
> sion and prejudices of our hearts. In ransacking their
> drawers [as Woolf had figuratively ransacked Vita's] we
> shall find out little about them. All has been distilled into
> their books. The life is thin, modest, colourless, like blue
> skimmed milk at the bottom of the jar. It is the imperfect
> artists who never manage to say the whole thing in their
> books who wield the power of personality over us. (171)

The perfect artist is Shakespeare, who appears in *Orlando* as a
nondescript, shabbily dressed man who is oblivious of his sur-

roundings and, indeed, of his physical self. He is not named in the book, but we know who he is, such is the charisma of the perfect, if unassuming, genius figured in his globed eyes and transfixed gaze as he rolls "some thought up and down, to and fro in his mind till it gathered shape or momentum to his liking" (17). It is only the imperfect artist who wields the power of personality over us, as Woolf shows by giving us a portrait of Orlando as a young, then mature, man-woman of modest gifts. *Orlando* is hardly a flattering portrait drawn by a besotted lover. Not only does Woolf refuse to endow Vita's family with a distinction it lacks; she declines to flatter a talent that does not impress her. Rather, she portrays Orlando as a distinctly modern type—the person of artistic temperament with questionable artistic talent. To Vita, Woolf would write: "The danger for you with your sense of tradition and all those words—a gift of the Gods though—is that you help this too easily into existence. . . . I mean I think there are odder, deeper, more angular thoughts in your mind than you have yet let come out" (*Letters* 3: 321). But privately she is more candid and more generous to those qualities in Vita's art that do attract, if not enthrall, her: "Vita's prose is too fluent. I've been reading it, & it makes my pen run. . . . But she is very skilful & golden voiced" (*Diary* 3: 126).

Woolf's complex representation of Vita as a ravishing historic personality (the rainbow) melded with a limited talent (the granite) may explain how *Orlando,* which began by reimagining Vita as a transhistorical representative of her family, race, and even species, evolved into a self-portrait. Woolf had foreseen this as one of the consequences of the "new biography." In her review of *Some People,* she remarked how Nicolson "is as much the subject of his own irony and observation" as his real and imaginary subjects. "Indeed," she concluded, "by the end of the book we realize that the figure which has been most completely and most subtly displayed is that of the author" (233).

Woolf and Fantasy

ORLANDO IS A writer's biography in a double sense, both of them fun and serious at the same time. It is a mock biography of a friend with literary ambitions but no genius, and of a genius who is the subject of her own irony and observation. The first biography depends on Vita's personality. The second and complementary one depends, paradoxically, on Woolf's sublimating her personality in the modern manner. She did so by devising a dutiful, at times harried and befuddled, persona to serve as Orlando's biographer. Woolf's personified narrators eventually will prove better suited to her polemical and argumentative rather than fictional works. In *A Room of One's Own* and then in *Three Guineas,* Woolf will expose the speaking "I" as "only a convenient term for somebody who has no real being" (*A Room* 4), and decline to speak as her own "authorial" self except to introduce her argument and provide it with a peroration. The major part of her reflections in *A Room* on the relation between women and fiction, economic independence and female creativity, are attributed to a speaker variously named Mary Beton, Mary Seton, or Mary Carmichael. In the fictions written after *Orlando,* Woolf resumes speaking in the narrative voice she perfected in *To the Lighthouse,* the voice of an anonymous, impersonal narrator who passes in and out of the minds of the novel's characters with consummate ease, never disclosing who she is or what she has come for. *Orlando,* with the possible exception of *Flush* (1933), whose biographer possesses the enviable ability to enter the consciousness of another species, is the only one of her major imaginative works that plays with the biographer-narrator as a harried character in his—for there can be no doubt of his sex—own right.

This biographer is often perplexed but never negligent in recording facts and events that he does not for a moment understand, much less believe. Although *Orlando* begins on a note of dashing certainty—"He—for there could be no doubt of his sex, though the fashion of the time did something to disguise it—" (11)—that interjection increasingly comes to appear the desperate ploy of a biographer trying to head off trouble at the start. What reader, after all, would protest that Orlando was not male just one word into the book? From this point on, challenges to the biographer's assertions and tests of his documentary skills mount up with comic rapidity. The biographer's hope that he never need "invoke the help of novelist or poet" is dashed when he turns his gaze from Orlando's shapely legs, handsome body, and candid face, features that augur a life spent going from "deed to deed, from glory to glory, from office to office," to his less reassuring traits—his clumsy gait and violent mood swings and, most upsetting of all, a head full of "that riot and confusion of the passions and emotions which every good biographer detests" (12–13).

Orlando proves a difficult subject in other ways. He spends too much time writing, leaving the biographer literally passing the time: "It was now November. After November, comes December. Then January . . ." and so on until the next November "with a whole year accomplished" in half a dozen lines. Orlando's observations, what he thinks and what he writes (or fails to write), bore his biographer, who quickly dismisses them as so many tired clichés: "he saw—but probably the reader can imagine the passage which should follow and how every tree and plant in the neighbourhood is described first green, then golden . . ." (72). Finally arrives the moment when the biographer must surrender all claim to certainty and authority over truth. Faced with the demand that life yield its meaning, the biographer "must go and say straight out to the reader who waits a tiptoe to hear what life is—Alas, we don't know" (200). Given the number and comic nature of these difficulties, it is with some surprise that one finds the eminent biographer Leon Edel, author of a magisterial five-volume life of Henry James, embracing *Orlando* in a book that explores the tradition and conventions of literary biography. "*Orlando,*" he writes, in a section devoted to the shaping presence of time in biographical narratives, "is in reality neither a literary joke nor entirely a novel: it belongs to another genre. It is a fable—a fable for biographers" (139).

The word *fable* speaks to the presence and allure of "the rainbow," the aura of personality that biography ideally should transmit, even if a biography devolves into a displaced and discreet form of autobiography, as *Orlando* eventually does. If *Orlando* commemorates Vita's historic personality, it simultaneously emanates Woolf's literary personality. We get our first glimpse of this personality in the preface. In evoking the "illustrious" names of her predecessors, Woolf is also tracing her own literary genealogy. Unlike Vita, Woolf is free to select her ancestors and fashion an artistic lineage according to the character of her own mind. The preface shows her to be quite selective in this regard. She only takes time to mention "Defoe, Sir Thomas Browne, Sterne, Sir Walter Scott, Lord Macaulay, Emily Brontë, De Quincey, and Walter Pater,—to name the first that come to mind." In *being* the first to come to mind, these writers sketch out a coherent, if irregular, line of literary styles, beginning with the matter-of-fact realism of Defoe and concluding with the refined aestheticism of Pater, author of "imaginary portraits" of historic figures. Their names, however casually summoned, define a genealogical arc that encompasses the many "phases of fiction"—the different literary styles, genres, and modes—that make up Woolf's eccentric literary history.

The term "phases of fiction" is the title of an essay that preoccupied Woolf during the writing of *Orlando.* The essay is as important as "The New Biography" for understanding what inspired, or provoked, Woolf's bold experimentation with biogra-

phical and novelistic conventions. Most notably, Woolf adopts
the permeable concept of "phase" in the place of the more rigid
and constraining idea of genre or mode, apparently in an attempt to escape the burden of reading historically, or even crit-
ically. In tracking the different phases of fiction through its
various avatars and permutations, she feels obliged "to read only
for interest and pleasure, and, at the same time, to comment . . .
upon the nature of the interest and the pleasure" she finds (93).
She turns first to the Truth Tellers, among whom Defoe "is easily the English chief" (95), whose fictions persistently iterate
"the very facts that most reassure us of stability in real life, upon
money, furniture, food until we seem wedged among solid objects in a solid universe" (95); the Romantics, whom she introduces by excerpting a passage from Sir Walter Scott's *The Bride
of Lammermoor,* attract her mind by "the force the romantic ac-
quires by obliterating facts" (108) so that "other shapes become
apparent and other senses are roused" (108). In the Romantics,
she notes that "the dark and the distance actually seem to be
adding themselves to that other more truthful scene which we
still hold in mind, and to be giving it completeness" (104). Next
she seeks out the Character-Mongers, who satisfy our desire for
"a sense of walls and towns about us, with their lights and their
characters after the silence of the wind-blown heath" (110), and
after them, the Psychologists, who seek to illumine the mind
within rather than the world without. These phases are not organized according to a hierarchy of value or a sequence of historical development. Nevertheless, the last two phases seem to
satisfy her mercurial mind as no others quite do. These are the
phases over whom the Satirists and the Fantastics, then the
Poets, preside.

It is toward the ranks of Satirists, Fantastics, and their kindred Poets that Woolf's writing gravitates. Two eccentric figures
attract her to this company as kindred spirits: Sir Thomas

Browne and Laurence Sterne. Her esteem for Browne as the writer who in his "immense egotism has paved the way for all psychological novelists, autobiographers, confession-mongers, and dealers in the curious shades of our private life" ("Elizabethan Lumber Room" 45) is such that she makes reading him one of the central episodes in Orlando's young life. Through Browne, Orlando discovers an entirely unknown world that lies within, not outside, the mind. This inward turn exasperates his biographer, but it is crucial preparation for the metamorphosis to come. Yet if Browne shows Woolf the way into the mind, it is Sterne who shows her how to explore and describe that fantastic inner world she encounters there. Even though Sterne is never mentioned or quoted in *Orlando,* his spirit pervades the novel, haunts its prose, and affects its form. The blank "space . . . filled to repletion" (186), the narrative gaps and omissions, the capricious fairy-tale ending are signs of his benign and generative influence, just as the fantasy of an impossibly extended life is a concave mirror reflecting Tristram Shandy's abbreviated one. Woolf always approved and admired the liberties Sterne took "with grammar and syntax and sense and propriety and the long-standing tradition of how a novel should be written" ("'Sentimental Journey'" 78).

That she took those liberties as licensing her own extravagances in *Orlando* can be demonstrated by a little experiment: transposing and cross-checking Woolf's description of Sterne's writerly personality in *A Sentimental Journey* against her own in *Orlando.*

With the first words—"They order, said I, this much better in France" ["He—for there could be no doubt of his sex, though the fashion of the time did something to disguise it . . ."]—we are in the world of *Tristram Shandy* [*Orlando*]. It is a world in which anything may happen. We hardly know what jest, what jibe, what flash of poetry is not going to glance suddenly through the gap which this astonishingly agile pen has cut in the thick-set hedge of English prose. Is Sterne [Woolf] himself [herself] responsible? . . . The jerky, disconnected sentences are as rapid and it would seem as little under control as the phrases that fall from the lips of a brilliant talker. The very punctuation is that of speech, not writing, and brings the sound, the associations, of the speaking voice with it. ("'Sentimental Journey'" 79)

The family likeness is striking, both in style — the jesting sentences and the poetic flights — and in the willingness to let anything in the world that can happen, happen. E. M. Forster was the first to notice this likeness and proposed that Woolf, like Sterne, was best approached as a fantasist. Woolf and Sterne, he observed, "start with a little object, take a flutter from it, and settle on it again. They combine a humorous appreciation of the muddle of life with a keen sense of its beauty. There is even the same tone in their voices — a rather deliberate bewilderment, an announcement to all and sundry that they do not know where they are going" (36–37).

Gynomorphosis

Of course both Sterne and Woolf only look as if they do not know where they are going. Their itineraries may seem more improvised than in fact they are, because it is less a place than a state of mind that their narratives seek out. Still, readers looking for the "love interest or catastrophe in the accepted style" ("Modern Fiction" 150) of the traditional novel might be disappointed by *Orlando*. They should take warning from the abrupt

and shocking image that introduces us to its hero. A young
Elizabethan nobleman slices away at the head of a Moor, shriveled and debased into a plaything. In a single swoop of the pen,
the tradition of chivalric romance, summoned by the very name
of Orlando and its illustrious literary pedigree—Ariosto's *Orlando Furioso* and the exiled prince from Shakespeare's *As You
Like It*—is dealt a fatal blow. The curse of Empire, the corrupt-
ing lust for assertive action, the simultaneously ennobling and
debasing cult of heroic manhood are caricatured in the fantasy
combats of a young boy. Orlando's "fun" is a deceptively innocent figure for the deadly intentions of Woolf's satire—to
mount her own play-assault on the human head, where the most
fantastic notions of reality, honor, privilege, history, literature
are conceived, lodged, and defended.

Evidence of this intention is scattered throughout *Orlando*,
in references to the skulls that litter the vaults of Orlando's estates and the traitor's heads adorning the gates of Temple Bar, in
indirect allusion to the untimely death of Aethelbert, the decap-
itated Anglo-Saxon king who is the subject of one of Orlando's
bombastic tragedies, and in direct allusions to the historic be-
headings of Mary, Queen of Scots and of King Charles I. Woolf
even includes, in the form of a parlor witticism, the legend of
Saint Denis, the bishop who, undeterred at having his head
chopped off, picked it up, resumed walking, and continued
preaching (147). These severed heads are grim reminders of the
historical events and legends that exist outside Woolf's central
fantasy, but may also be said to necessitate it. Orlando's proto-
Romantic faith that one knows the world and oneself through
imagination is a fantasy not so much debunked as disciplined by
his disillusioning encounters with the indifferent laws of Nature,
the brutal realities of history, and the disobliging thoughts and
character of other people. The first lesson his imagination learns
is that "nature and letters seem to have a natural antipathy; bring

them together and they tear each other to pieces" (14). Having learned that "Green in nature is one thing, green in literature another" (14), he nevertheless persists in his belief that poets, "those instinct with such divine thoughts must . . . have aureoles for hair, incense for breath and roses must grow between their lips" (61) until "the mean figure" (63) of Nicholas Greene and later the misshapen one of Alexander Pope disabuse him.

Nevertheless, Orlando cannot withstand actual encounters with reality unassisted by imagination. When Sasha, his first passionate love, deserts him, he falls into a trancelike sleep that lasts a week. Caught up in a bloody insurrection in Constantinople, he falls into another trancelike sleep, from which he emerges a woman—a scandal the novel cannot and does not want to live down. The scandal of Orlando's metamorphosis into a woman is Woolf's most violent assault on the reader's consciousness. We might be willing to suspend belief, as Orlando suspends his waking consciousness, long enough to pretend that Orlando could live more than three hundred years, but probably not that he could change his sex after a good long sleep. What, then, to make of this outrageous transformation that exhausts all funds of belief? Do we read Orlando's change of sex as a formal protest against his sexual nature? There is nothing in Orlando's previous history that suggests that he has been restless or unhappy with his assigned sex. He loves indiscriminately in the "low style"—seeking out loose women boldly prowling the London docks, "marrying" a gypsy, to name just two episodes in his happily promiscuous life—and poetically in the "high style," sublimating his attraction to highborn women in sonnets addressed to Clorinda, Favilla, Euphrosyne, and conceiving a grand and violent passion for a Russian princess. Disappointment either with sex or with sexuality hardly explains Orlando's metamorphosis. There is not a single suggestion that his change of sex fulfills a yearning or "corrects" a genetic miscoding. Orlando's transformation at the age of thirty into a woman is presented as a "simple" narrative fact by his biographer, but it is embraced by Woolf as a poetic principle. Let us name this principle after the experience in which it is first and literally embodied: gynomorphosis.

Gynomorphosis, the transformation of male bodies and masculinist fictions into their equivalent—but different—female counterparts, answers to Woolf's desire for new narrative forms, that is, with new ways of understanding our human existence in time. Just as Orlando's change of sex might have altered his future but not "their"[6] identity, so the resulting change does not jeopardize *Orlando*'s identity as a legitimate fiction. Woolf's gynomorphic fiction does not eradicate but internalizes the self-actualizing, often violent movements and actions of traditional narrative. As Orlando's increasingly savage and exasperated assaults on the Moor's head dramatize, the epic and chivalric traditions devoted to the chronicling of heroic deeds and public glory have exhausted their authority, not to mention their charm, for the moderns. Woolf is even more explicit in the manuscript version of *Orlando,* which suggests that the chivalric code of violent action can persist only in the form of sadistic rages.[7] But Woolf seems more interested in demonstrating that excitement also attaches to violence that occurs *inside* the human head. Soon after Orlando leaves off his quixotic games, the biographer mounts "up the spiral stairway into his brain," where he confronts a quite different scene of violence—"that riot and confusion of the passions and emotions which every good biographer detests" (13).

Initially, all the active mental processes that distract Orlando and detain him in the company of his thoughts are figured, pejoratively, as feminine, in keeping with a rhetorical tradition that Woolf literalizes in her allegorical fantasies. Memory, for example, is figured in the homely guise of a seamstress, "and a capricious one at that" (58). Orlando's biographer feels it necessary to apologize for the odd, disconnected, agitated, and often uncouth piecework of effeminate Memory: "Instead of being a single, downright, bluff piece of work of which no man need feel ashamed, our commonest deeds are set about with a fluttering and flickering of wings, a rising and falling of lights" (58). Manliness is also undone when the "hussy, Memory, and all her ragtag and bobtail" revives the image "of a shabby man with bright eyes" (60) who becomes the fixed object of Orlando's fascinated, inward gaze. These meditative, visionary pauses, the biographer complains, "are our undoing": "It is then that sedition enters the fortress and our troops rise in insurrection" (60). This assault on the hegemony of male narrative is as comical as Orlando's earlier assault on a shriveled head, but because the attack consists in mental maneuvers, the invaders are harder to repel. Orlando's biographer, apparently abandoning all hope for his hero's masculine honor, records how a succeeding pause proves fatal, as "into the breach thus made, leap[s] Ambition, the harridan, and Poetry, the witch, and Desire of Fame, the strumpet; all joined hands and made of his heart their dancing ground" (60). The epic riot and upheaval in Orlando's own mind are the insurgent phases of Woolf's gynomorphic revolution against the actions and values of traditional male narrative. Gynomorphosis does not so much denature or desex these allegorical figures of Female Ambition, Poetry, and Fame, as rehabilitate and ennoble them. And it is equally busy expelling from its mental precincts Modesty, Chastity, and Purity, those idealizations of femininity that have shadowed, when they have not actively inhibited, women's creativity.

We can detect the subtle workings of Woolf's gynomorphic imagination in those nondramatic pauses in which epically significant actions allegedly occur. The biographer frequently complains of those moments of inaction in which nothing and yet everything happens. Eventually, even he realizes that he must

not only wait out these momentary halts in his narrative but try
to justify them. "As this pause was of extreme significance in his
history, more so, indeed, than many acts which bring men to
their knees and make rivers run with blood, it behooves us to ask
why he paused . . ." (58). The almost parenthetical casualness of
the biographer's claim should not blind us to its momentous-
ness. This claim will be elaborated much more straightforwardly
and impatiently in *A Room of One's Own*. Reflecting on the obvious fact that the "values of women differ very often from the
values which have been made by the other sex," Woolf immediately objects that

> it is the masculine values that prevail. Speaking crudely,
> football and sport are "important"; the worship of fash-
> ion, the buying of clothes "trivial." And these values are
> inevitably transferred from life to fiction. This is an im-
> portant book, the critic assumes, because it deals with
> war. This is an insignificant book because it deals with the
> feelings of women in a drawing-room. A scene in the
> battlefield is more important than a scene in a shop—
> everywhere and much more subtly the difference of value
> persists. (73)

In *Orlando,* Woolf not only parodies male values but relocates
them within the realm of thinking, dreaming, feeling, imagin-
ing, where they await their transfiguration. If a scene in the battle-
field is more important than a scene in a shop, then she will
oblige her readers by staging the riot of Orlando's mind as an
insurrection and his poetic yearnings as female marauders. If
football and war are more important than fashion, she will introduce her hero playing at war as if it were a sport. But she will
also insist on the primacy of her own values by calling attention
to her hero's clothes before anything else about him is revealed.

Clothes are invested with extraordinary novelistic value in *Orlando*. The history of Orlando's sexual and social identity is inseparable from the history of his, then her, attire. You know who Orlando is and when he, then she, is living by what he, then she, is wearing: doublet and hose, jerkin and knee breeches, morning suit, frock coat, and sponge-bag trousers; dresses of various lengths and comfort; satin bodices, corsets, crinolines, free-flowing skirts. In her final avatar, Orlando slips out of her skirt into "a pair of whipcord breeches, and leather jacket" (230). "There is much to support the view," the biographer reports, "that it is clothes that wear us and not we them; we may make them take the mould of arm or breast, but they mould our hearts, our brains, our tongues to their liking" (138). Readers persuaded of the view that clothes mold our hearts, brains, and tongues, hence affect what we feel, think, or speak, will be delighted by a book that is as observant of changes in sartorial as it is of changes in literary styles. Some might even express a professional interest in the intimate and reciprocal relation between clothes and self-image. When, for example, the fashion designer Karl Lagerfeld was asked who his favorite hero of fiction was, he named Orlando.[8]

There is much, however, to support the contrary view that clothes do not mold the man (and may indeed disguise the actual woman beneath). This view eventually is promoted to a novelistic truth, one Orlando's biographer does not overstate or underplay: "It was a change in Orlando herself that dictated her choice of a woman's dress and of a woman's sex" (139). This change in Orlando, his gynomorphosis as I have been calling it, is only a means, however, at getting at a truth so elemental that neither sex can fully embody or represent it: "Different though the sexes are, they intermix," asserts the biographer in matter-of-fact tones so rare in this fiction. "In every human being a vacillation from one sex to the other takes place, and often it is only the clothes that keep the male or female likeness, while underneath the sex is the very opposite of what it is above" (139). Clothes adorn and may even mold the external surfaces of human life, but they are unreliable indications of what may exist underneath.

We are given a final glimpse of what lies beneath the surface of consciousness and of traditional narrative when the biographer peers one last time into "the back of [Orlando's] brain": "everything was partly something else, and each gained an odd moving power from this union of itself and something not itself so that with this mixture of truth and falsehood her mind became like a forest in which things moved; lights and shadows changed, and one thing became another" (237). The fantasy that begins with a young boy battering a head concludes by looking within the depths of the mind, a realm of continual metamorphosis in which one thing becomes another thing, identities change or are exchanged, and even truth can mix with falsehood without sacrificing its essential nature. This is the world beneath the surface of the world in which we catch glimpses of what Woolf came to call "the essence of reality" (*Diary* 3: 113).

All joking aside, *Orlando* is a quest for that reality.

NOTES

[1]So T. S. Eliot proclaimed, in his famous review of Joyce's *Ulysses*. See his "*Ulysses,* Order, and Myth." In *Selected Prose of T. S. Eliot.* Edited by Frank Kermode. New York: Harcourt Brace Jovanovich, 1975: 177.

[2]The *Oxford English Dictionary* (OED), citing the associations of *Jessamy* with sex-linked characteristics, cites J. Hawkesworth, writing in the *Adventurer,* October 20, 1753, who places Jessamy on the lower end of an eight-scale progression from immature or undeveloped masculinity to full-blooded, self-assertive manhood: "You have frequently used the terms Buck and Blood, . . . but you have not considered them as the last stages of a regular procession . . . the scale consists of eight degrees; Greenhorn, Jemmy, Jes-

samy, Smart, Honest Fellow, Joyous Spirit, Buck, and Blood. *Ibid.* 177 My labour . . . recommended me to the notice of the ladies, and procured me the gentle appellation of Jessamy." The OED also gives us a truncated speculation of Mrs. J. West's *Infidel Father* I. 88, that also links Jessamy to gender reversals: "If men became Jessamys, and Women Amazons. *Ibid.* I. 296."

³Hermione Lee's reading of *Orlando* emphasizes the repressive presence of an invisible censor on the writing and final shape of the novel. Lee argues: "Through its fantasy and jokiness, *Orlando* escapes the public suppression which *The Well of Loneliness* notoriously encountered in the same year." She then details some of the more telling excisions from the manuscript version, including "references to Sappho, to Orlando's lusts and her love affairs with women" (Lee 517).

⁴"L. has just been in to consult about a 3rd edition of Orlando. This has been ordered; we have sold over 6000 copies; & sales are still amazingly brisk— 150 today for instance; most days between 50 and 60; always to my surprise" (*Diary* 3: 212).

⁵Noted by Hermione Lee: "Lady Sackville, for all her frantic paranoia, may have been right to accuse the book of cruelty. There is parody in it, as well as affectionate celebration" (Lee 515).

⁶Woolf deliberately shifts from the masculine singular to the third-person plural immediately after Orlando's change of sex. "Orlando," she writes, "had become a woman—there is no denying it. But in every other respect, Orlando remained precisely as *he* had been. The change of sex, though it altered *their* future, did nothing whatever to alter *their* identity" (102, emphasis mine).

⁷"And then leaping high [into the] air & holding the sword in both hands he would strike so viciously that [the] a little bit of the leathery skin would be sliced through: of such rages the shattered head bore many tokens." The excised passage continues in this vein, describing Orlando's desire to see the battered Moor's skull suffer (Moore 309).

⁸"Proust Questionnaire," *Vanity Fair,* September 2005: 402.

WORKS CITED

Aiken, Conrad. Review of *Orlando* in *Dial,* February 1929. In *Virginia Woolf: The Critical Heritage.* Edited by Robin Majumdar and Allen McLaurin, 234–36. Boston: Routledge, 1975.

Borges, Jorge Luis. "Virginia Woolf: A Capsule Biography." In *Borges: A Reader.* Edited by Emir Rodriguez Monegal and Alastair Reid, 91–92. New York: Dutton, 1981.

Bowen, Elizabeth. "Afterword" to *Orlando.* In *The Mulberry Tree.* Edited by Hermione Lee, 131–36. San Diego: Harcourt, 1986. Originally published in 1960.

Edel, Leon. *Literary Biography.* Bloomington: Indiana University Press, 1973.

Forster, E. M. *Aspects of the Novel.* New York: Harcourt, 1954.

Glendinning, Victoria. *Vita: The Life of V. Sackville-West.* New York: Knopf, 1983.

Holtby, Winifred. *Virginia Woolf: A Critical Memoir.* Chicago: Academy Press, 1978. Originally published in 1932.

MacCarthy, Desmond. Review of *Orlando. Sunday Times,* October 14, 1928. In *Virginia Woolf: The Critical Heritage.* Edited by Robin Majumdar and Allen McLaurin, 222–26. Boston: Routledge, 1975.

Moore, Madeline. "Virginia Woolf's *Orlando*: An Edition of the Manuscript." *Twentieth Century Literature* 25: 3–4 (Fall–Winter 1979): 303–55.

Nicolson, Nigel. "Introduction." In *Some People,* by Harold Nicolson. New York: Atheneum, 1982.

———. *Portrait of a Marriage.* New York: Atheneum, 1973.

Sackville-West, Vita. *Knole and the Sackvilles.* London: Lindsay Drummond Ltd., 1949. Originally published in 1922.

———. *The Letters of Vita Sackville-West to Virginia Woolf.* Edited by Louise DeSalvo and Mitchell Leaska. New York: William Morrow, 1985.

Woolf, Virginia. "The Elizabethan Lumber Room." In *The Common Reader.* First Series. Edited by Andrew McNeillie, 39–47. San Diego: Harcourt, 1984. Originally published in 1925.

———. "How It Strikes a Contemporary." In *The Essays of Virginia Woolf.* Vol. 3. Edited by Andrew McNeillie, 353–60. San Diego: Harcourt, 1988.

———. "Modern Fiction." In *The Common Reader.* First Series. Edited by Andrew McNeillie, 146–54. San Diego: Harcourt, 1984. Originally published in 1925.

———. "Mr. Bennett and Mrs. Brown." In *Collected Essays of Virginia Woolf.* Vol. 1, 319–37. New York: Harcourt, 1967.

———. "The New Biography." In *Collected Essays of Virginia Woolf.* Vol. 4, 229–35. New York: Harcourt, 1967.

———. "Personalities." In *The Moment and Other Essays,* 167–72. New York: Harcourt Brace Jovanovich, 1974. Originally published in 1948.

———. "Phases of Fiction." In *Granite and Rainbow,* 93–145. New York: Harcourt Brace Jovanovich, 1975. Originally published in 1958.

————. *A Room of One's Own.* Annotated and with an introduction by Susan Gubar. Orlando: Harcourt, 2005.

————. "The 'Sentimental Journey.'" *The Second Common Reader.* Edited by Andrew McNeillie, 78–85. San Diego: Harcourt, 1986. Originally published in 1932.

————. *To the Lighthouse.* Annotated and with an introduction by Mark Hussey. Orlando: Harcourt, 2005.

Orlando as a Boy

Orlando

A BIOGRAPHY

To V. Sackville-West

PREFACE

MANY FRIENDS *have helped me in writing this book. Some are dead and so illustrious that I scarcely dare name them, yet no one can read or write without being perpetually in the debt of Defoe, Sir Thomas Browne, Sterne, Sir Walter Scott, Lord Macaulay, Emily Brontë, De Quincey, and Walter Pater,— to name the first that come to mind. Others are alive, and though perhaps as illustrious in their own way, are less formidable for that very reason. I am specially indebted to Mr. C. P. Sanger, without whose knowledge of the law of real property this book could never have been written. Mr. Sydney-Turner's wide and peculiar erudition has saved me, I hope, some lamentable blunders. I have had the advantage — how great I alone can estimate — of Mr. Arthur Waley's knowledge of Chinese. Madame Lopokova (Mrs. J. M. Keynes) has been at hand to correct my Russian. To the unrivalled sympathy and imagination of Mr. Roger Fry I owe whatever understanding of the art of painting I may possess. I have, I hope, profited in another department by the singularly penetrating, if severe, criticism of my nephew Mr. Julian Bell. Miss M. K. Snowdon's indefatigable researches in the archives of Harrogate and Cheltenham were none the less arduous for being vain. Other friends have helped me in ways too various to specify. I must content myself with naming Mr. Angus Davidson; Mrs. Cartwright; Miss Janet Case; Lord Berners (whose knowledge of Elizabethan music has proved invaluable); Mr. Francis Birrell; my brother, Dr. Adrian Stephen; Mr. F. L. Lucas; Mr. and Mrs. Desmond Maccarthy; that most inspiriting of critics, my brother-in-law, Mr. Clive Bell; Mr. G. H. Rylands; Lady Colefax; Miss Nellie Boxall; Mr. J. M. Keynes; Miss Violet Dickinson; the Hon. Edward Sackville West; Mr. and Mrs.*

St. John Hutchinson; Mr. Duncan Grant; Mr. and Mrs. Stephen Tomlin; Mr. and Lady Ottoline Morrell; my mother-in-law, Mrs. Sidney Woolf; Mr. Osbert Sitwell; Madame Jacques Raverat; Colonel Cory Bell; Miss Valerie Taylor; Mr. J. T. Sheppard; Mr. and Mrs. T. S. Eliot; Miss Ethel Sands; Miss Nan Hudson; my nephew, Mr. Quentin Bell (an old and valued collaborator in fiction); Mr. Raymond Mortimer; Miss Emphie Case; Lady Gerald Wellesley; Mr. Lytton Strachey; the Viscountess Cecil; Miss Hope Mirrlees; Mr. E. M. Forster; the Hon. Harold Nicolson; my sister, Vanessa Bell — but the list threatens to grow too long and is already far too distinguished. For while it rouses in me memories of the pleasantest kind it will inevitably wake expectations in the reader which the book itself can only disappoint. Therefore I will conclude by thanking the officials of the British Museum and Record Office for their wonted courtesy; my niece Miss Angelica Bell, for a service which none but she could have rendered; and my husband for the patience with which he has invariably helped my researches and for the profound historical knowledge to which these pages owe whatever degree of accuracy they may attain. Finally, I would thank, had I not lost his name and address, a gentleman in America, who has generously and gratuitously corrected the punctuation, the botany, the entomology, the geography, and the chronology of previous works of mine and will, I hope, not spare his services on the present occasion.

V. W.

CONTENTS

ILLUSTRATIONS

CHAPTER ONE

HE—FOR THERE could be no doubt of his sex, though the fashion of the time did something to disguise it—was in the act of slicing at the head of a Moor which swung from the rafters. It was the colour of an old football, and more or less the shape of one, save for the sunken cheeks and a strand or two of coarse, dry hair, like the hair on a cocoanut. Orlando's father, or perhaps his grandfather, had struck it from the shoulders of a vast Pagan who had started up under the moon in the barbarian fields of Africa; and now it swung, gently, perpetually, in the breeze which never ceased blowing through the attic rooms of the gigantic house of the lord who had slain him.

Orlando's fathers had ridden in fields of asphodel, and stony fields, and fields watered by strange rivers, and they had struck many heads of many colours off many shoulders, and brought them back to hang from the rafters. So too would Orlando, he vowed. But since he was sixteen only, and too young to ride with them in Africa or France, he would steal away from his mother and the peacocks in the garden and go to his attic room and there lunge and plunge and slice the air with his blade. Sometimes he cut the cord so that the skull bumped on the floor and he had to string it up again, fastening it with some chivalry almost out of reach so that his enemy grinned at him through shrunk, black lips triumphantly. The skull swung to and fro, for the house, at the top of which he lived, was so vast that there seemed trapped in it the wind itself, blowing this way, blowing that way, winter or summer. The green arras with the hunters on it moved perpetually. His fathers had been noble since they had been at all. They came out of the northern mists wearing coronets on their heads. Were not the bars of darkness in the room, and the yellow pools which chequered the floor, made by the sun falling through the stained glass of a vast coat of arms in the window? Orlando stood now in the midst of the yellow body of an heraldic leopard. When he put his hand on the window-sill to push the window open, it was instantly coloured red, blue, and yellow like a butterfly's wing. Thus, those who like symbols, and have a turn for the deciphering of them, might observe that though the shapely legs, the handsome body, and the well-set shoulders were all of them decorated with various tints of heraldic light, Orlando's face, as he threw the window open, was lit solely by the sun itself. A more candid, sullen face it would be impossible to find. Happy the mother who bears, happier still the biographer who records the life of such a one! Never need she vex herself, nor he invoke the help of novelist or poet. From deed to deed, from glory to glory, from office to office he must go, his scribe following after, till they reach what ever seat it may be that is the height of their desire. [Orlando, to look at, was cut out precisely for some such career. The red of the cheeks was covered with peach down; the down on the lips was only a little thicker than the down on the cheeks. The lips themselves were short and slightly drawn back over teeth of an exquisite and almond whiteness. Nothing disturbed the arrowy nose in its short, tense flight; the hair was dark, the ears small, and fitted closely to the head. But, alas, that these catalogues of youthful beauty cannot end without mentioning forehead and eyes. Alas, that people are seldom born devoid of all three; for directly we glance at Orlando standing by the window, we must admit that he had eyes like drenched violets, so large that the water seemed to have brimmed in them and widened them; and a brow like the swelling of a marble dome pressed between the two blank medallions which were his temples. Directly we glance at eyes and forehead, thus do we rhapsodise. Directly we glance at eyes and forehead, we have to admit a thousand disagreeables which it is the aim of every good biographer to ignore. Sights disturbed him, like that of his mother, a very beautiful lady in green walking out to feed the peacocks with Twitchett, her maid, behind her; sights exalted him—the birds and the trees; and made him in love with death—the evening sky, the homing rooks; and so, mounting up the spiral stairway into his brain—which was a roomy one— all these sights, and the garden sounds too, the hammer beating, the wood chopping, began that riot and confusion of the passions and emotions which every good biographer detests. But to continue—Orlando slowly drew in his head, sat down at the table, and, with the half-conscious air of one doing what they do every day of their lives at this hour, took out a writing book labelled "Æthelbert: A Tragedy in Five Acts," and dipped an old stained goose quill in the ink.

Soon he had covered ten pages and more with poetry. He was fluent, evidently, but he was abstract. Vice, Crime, Misery were the personages of his drama; there were Kings and Queens of impossible territories; horrid plots confounded them; noble sentiments suffused them; there was never a word said as he himself would have said it, but all was turned with a fluency and sweetness which, considering his age—he was not yet seventeen—and that the sixteenth century had still some years of its course to run, were remarkable enough. At last, however, he came to a halt. He was describing, as all young poets are for ever describing, nature, and in order to match the shade of green precisely he looked (and here he showed more audacity than most) at the thing itself, which happened to be a laurel bush growing beneath the window. After that, of course, he could write no more. Green in nature is one thing, green in literature another. Nature and letters seem to have a natural antipathy; bring them together and they tear each other to pieces. The shade of green Orlando now saw spoilt his rhyme and split his metre. Moreover, nature has tricks of her own. Once look out of a window at bees among flowers, at a yawning dog, at the sun setting, once think "how many more suns shall I see set," etc., etc. (the thought is too well known to be worth writing out) and one drops the pen, takes one's cloak, strides out of the room, and catches one's foot on a painted chest as one does so. For Orlando was a trifle clumsy.

He was careful to avoid meeting anyone. There was Stubbs, the gardener, coming along the path. He hid behind a tree till he had passed. He let himself out at a little gate in the garden wall. He skirted all stables, kennels, breweries, carpenters' shops, wash-houses, places where they make tallow candles, kill oxen, forge horseshoes, stitch jerkins—for the house was a town ringing with men at work at their various crafts—and gained the ferny path leading uphill through the park unseen. There is perhaps a kinship among qualities; one draws another along with it; and the biographer should here call attention to the fact that this clumsiness is often mated with a love of solitude. Having stumbled over a chest, Orlando naturally loved solitary places, vast views, and to feel himself for ever and ever and ever alone.

So, after a long silence, "I am alone," he breathed at last, opening his lips for the first time in this record. He had walked very quickly uphill through ferns and hawthorn bushes, startling deer and wild birds, to a place crowned by a single oak tree. It was very high, so high indeed that nineteen English counties could be seen beneath, and on clear days thirty, or forty perhaps, if the weather was very fine. Sometimes one could see the English Channel, wave reiterating upon wave. Rivers could be seen and pleasure boats gliding on them; and galleons setting out to sea; and armadas with puffs of smoke from which came the dull thud of cannon firing; and forts on the coast; and castles among the meadows; and here a watch tower; and there a fortress; and again some vast mansion like that of Orlando's father, massed like a town in the valley circled by walls. To the east there were the spires of London and the smoke of the city; and perhaps on the very sky line, when the wind was in the right quarter, the craggy top and serrated edges of Snowden herself showed mountainous among the clouds. For a moment Orlando stood counting, gazing, recognising. That was his father's house; that his uncle's. His aunt owned those three great turrets among the trees there. The heath was theirs and the forest; the pheasant and the deer, the fox, the badger, and the butterfly.

He sighed profoundly, and flung himself—there was a passion in his movements which deserves the word—on the earth at the foot of the oak tree. He loved, beneath all this summer transiency, to feel the earth's spine beneath him; for such he took the hard root of the oak tree to be; or, for image followed image, it was the back of a great horse that he was riding; or the deck of a tumbling ship—it was anything indeed, so long as it was hard, for he felt the need of something which he could attach his floating heart to; the heart that tugged at his side; the heart that seemed filled with spiced and amorous gales every evening about this time when he walked out. To the oak tree he tied it and as he lay there, gradually the flutter in and about him stilled itself; the little leaves hung; the deer stopped; the pale summer clouds stayed; his limbs grew heavy on the ground; and he lay so still that by degrees the deer stepped nearer and the rooks wheeled round him and the swallows dipped and circled and the dragon-flies shot past, as if all the fertility and amorous activity of a summer's evening were woven web-like about his body.

After an hour or so — the sun was rapidly sinking, the white clouds had turned red, the hills were violet, the woods purple, the valleys black — a trumpet sounded. Orlando leapt to his feet. The shrill sound came from the valley. It came from a dark spot down there; a spot compact and mapped out; a maze; a town, yet girt about with walls; it came from the heart of his own great house in the valley, which, dark before, even as he looked and the single trumpet duplicated and reduplicated itself with other shriller sounds, lost its darkness and became pierced with lights. Some were small hurrying lights, as if servants dashed along corridors to answer summonses; others were high and lustrous lights, as if they burnt in empty banqueting-halls made ready to receive guests who had not come; and others dipped and waved and sank and rose, as if held in the hands of troops of serving men, bending, kneeling, rising, receiving, guarding, and escorting with all dignity indoors a great Princess alighting from her chariot. Coaches turned and wheeled in the courtyard. Horses tossed their plumes. The Queen had come.

Orlando looked no more. He dashed downhill. He let himself in at a wicket gate. He tore up the winding staircase. He reached his room. He tossed his stockings to one side of the room, his jerkin to the other. He dipped his head. He scoured his hands. He pared his finger nails. With no more than six inches of looking-glass and a pair of old candles to help him, he had thrust on crimson breeches, lace collar, waistcoat of taffeta, and shoes with rosettes on them as big as double dahlias in less than ten minutes by the stable clock. He was ready. He was flushed. He was excited. But he was terribly late.

By short cuts known to him, he made his way now through the vast congeries of rooms and staircases to the banqueting-hall, five acres distant on the other side of the house. But half-way there, in the back quarters where the servants lived, he stopped. The door of Mrs. Stewkley's sitting-room stood open—she was gone, doubtless, with all her keys to wait upon her mistress. But there, sitting at the servant's dinner table with a tankard beside him and paper in front of him, sat a rather fat, rather shabby man, whose ruff was a thought dirty, and whose clothes were of hodden brown. He held a pen in his hand, but he was not writing. He seemed in the act of rolling some thought up and down, to and fro in his mind till it gathered shape or momentum to his liking. His eyes, globed and clouded like some green stone of curious texture, were fixed. He did not see Orlando. For all his hurry, Orlando stopped dead. Was this a poet? Was he writing poetry? "Tell me," he wanted to say, "everything in the whole world"—for he had the wildest, most absurd, extravagant ideas about poets and poetry—but how speak to a man who does not see you? who sees ogres, satyrs, perhaps the depths of the sea instead? So Orlando stood gazing while the man turned his pen in his fingers, this way and that way; and gazed and mused; and then, very quickly, wrote half-a-dozen lines and looked up. Whereupon Orlando, overcome with shyness, darted off and reached the banqueting-hall only just in time to sink upon his knees and, hanging his head in confusion, to offer a bowl of rose water to the great Queen herself.

Such was his shyness that he saw no more of her than her ringed hand in water; but it was enough. It was a memorable hand; a thin hand with long fingers always curling as if round orb or sceptre; a nervous, crabbed, sickly hand; a commanding hand; a hand that had only to raise itself for a head to fall; a hand, he guessed, attached to an old body that smelt like a cupboard in which furs are kept in camphor; which body was yet caparisoned in all sorts of brocades and gems; and held itself very upright though perhaps in pain from sciatica; and never flinched though strung together by a thousand fears; and the Queen's eyes were light yellow. All this he felt as the great rings flashed in the water and then something pressed his hair—which, perhaps, accounts for his seeing nothing more likely to be of use to a historian. And in truth, his mind was such a welter of opposites—of the night and the blazing candles, of the shabby poet and the great Queen, of silent fields and the clatter of serving men—that he could see nothing; or only a hand.

By the same showing, the Queen herself can have seen only a head. But if it is possible from a hand to deduce a body, informed with all the attributes of a great Queen, her crabbedness, courage, frailty, and terror, surely a head can be as fertile, looked down upon from a chair of state by a lady whose eyes were always, if the waxworks at the Abbey are to be trusted, wide open. The long, curled hair, the dark head bent so reverently, so innocently before her, implied a pair of the finest legs that a young nobleman has ever stood upright upon; and violet eyes; and a heart of gold; and loyalty and manly charm—all qualities which the old woman loved the more the more they failed her. For she was growing old and worn and bent before her time. The sound of cannon was always in her ears. She saw always the glistening poison drop and the long stiletto. As she sat at table she listened; she heard the guns in the Channel; she dreaded—was that a curse, was that a whisper? Innocence, simplicity, were all the more dear to her for the dark background she set them against. And it was that same night, so tradition has it, when Orlando was sound asleep, that she made over formally, putting her hand and seal finally to the parchment, the gift of the great monastic house that had been the Archbishop's and then the King's to Orlando's father.

Orlando slept all night in ignorance. He had been kissed by a queen without knowing it. And perhaps, for women's hearts are intricate, it was his ignorance, and the start he gave when her lips touched him that kept the memory of her young cousin (for they had blood in common) green in her mind. At any rate, two years of this quiet country life had not passed, and Orlando had written no more perhaps than twenty tragedies and a dozen histories and a score of sonnets when a message came that he was to attend the Queen at Whitehall.

"Here," she said, watching him advance down the long gallery towards her, "comes my innocent!" (There was a serenity about him always which had the look of innocence when, technically, the word was no longer applicable.)

"Come!" she said. She was sitting bolt upright beside the fire. And she held him a foot's pace from her and looked him up and down. Was she matching her speculations the other night with the truth now visible? Did she find her guesses justified? Eyes, mouth, nose, breast, hips, hands—she ran them over; her lips twitched visibly as she looked; but when she saw his legs she laughed out loud. He was the very image of a noble gentleman. But inwardly? She flashed her yellow hawk's eyes upon him as if she would pierce his soul. The young man withstood her gaze, blushing only a damask rose as became him. Strength, grace, romance, folly, poetry, youth—she read him like a page. Instantly she plucked a ring from her finger (the joint was swollen rather) and as she fitted it to his, named him her Treasurer and Steward; next hung about him chains of office; and bidding him bend his knee, tied round it at the slenderest part the jewelled order of the Garter. Nothing after that was denied him. When she drove in state he rode at her carriage door. She sent him to Scotland on a sad embassy to the unhappy Queen. He was about to sail for the Polish wars when she recalled him. For how could she bear to think of that tender flesh torn and that curly head rolled in the dust? She kept him with her. At the height of her triumph when the guns were booming at the Tower and the air was thick enough with gunpowder to make one sneeze and the huzzas of the people rang beneath the windows, she pulled him down among the cushions where her women had laid her (she was so worn and old) and made him

bury his face in that astonishing composition—she had not
changed her dress for a month—which smelt for all the world,
he thought, recalling his boyish memory, like some old cabinet
at home where his mother's furs were stored. He rose, half suffocated from the embrace. "This," she breathed, "is my victory!"—even as a rocket roared up and dyed her cheeks scarlet.

For the old woman loved him. And the Queen, who knew
a man when she saw one, though not, it is said, in the usual way,
plotted for him a splendid ambitious career. Lands were given
him, houses assigned him. He was to be the son of her old age;
the limb of her infirmity; the oak tree on which she leant her
degradation. She croaked out these promises and strange dom-
ineering tendernesses (they were at Richmond now) sitting bolt
upright in her stiff brocades by the fire which, however high
they piled it, never kept her warm.

Meanwhile, the long winter months drew on. Every tree in
the Park was lined with frost. The river ran sluggishly. One day
when the snow was on the ground and the dark panelled rooms
were full of shadows and the stags were barking in the Park, she
saw in the mirror, which she kept for fear of spies always by
her, through the door, which she kept for fear of murderers always open, a boy—could it be Orlando?—kissing a girl—who
in the Devil's name was the brazen hussy? Snatching at her
golden-hilted sword she struck violently at the mirror. The glass
crashed; people came running; she was lifted and set in her chair
again; but she was stricken after that and groaned much, as her
days wore to an end, of man's treachery.

It was Orlando's fault perhaps; yet, after all, are we to blame
him? The age was the Elizabethan; their morals were not ours;
nor their poets; nor their climate; nor their vegetables even.
Everything was different. The weather itself, the heat and cold
of summer and winter, was, we may believe, of another temper
altogether. The brilliant amorous day was divided as sheerly from

the night as land from water. Sunsets were redder and more intense; dawns were whiter and more auroral. Of our crepuscular half-lights and lingering twilights they knew nothing. The rain fell vehemently, or not at all. The sun blazed or there was darkness. Translating this to the spiritual regions as their wont is, the poets sang beautifully how roses fade and petals fall. The moment is brief they sang; the moment is over; one long night is then to be slept by all. As for using the artifices of the greenhouse or conservatory to prolong or preserve these fresh pinks and roses, that was not their way. The withered intricacies and ambiguities of our more gradual and doubtful age were unknown to them. Violence was all. The flower bloomed and faded. The sun rose and sank. The lover loved and went. And what the poets said in rhyme, the young translated into practice. Girls were roses, and their seasons were short as the flowers'. Plucked they must be before nightfall; for the day was brief and the day was all. Thus, if Orlando followed the leading of the climate, of the poets, of the age itself, and plucked his flower in the window-seat even with the snow on the ground and the Queen vigilant in the corridor, we can scarcely bring ourselves to blame him. He was young; he was boyish; he did but as nature bade him. As for the girl, we know no more than Queen Elizabeth herself did what her name was. It may have been Doris, Chloris, Delia, or Diana, for he made rhymes to them all in turn; equally, she may have been a court lady, or some serving maid. For Orlando's taste was broad; he was no lover of garden flowers only; the wild and the weeds even had always a fascination for him.

Here, indeed, we lay bare rudely, as a biographer may, a curious trait in him, to be accounted for, perhaps, by the fact that a certain grandmother of his had worn a smock and carried milk-pails. Some grains of the Kentish or Sussex earth were mixed with the thin, fine fluid which came to him from Normandy. He held that the mixture of brown earth and blue blood was a good one. Certain it is that he had always a liking for low company, especially for that of lettered people whose wits so often keep them under, as if there were sympathy of blood between them. At this season of his life, when his head brimmed with rhymes and he never went to bed without striking off some conceit, the cheek of an innkeeper's daughter seemed fresher and the wit of a gamekeeper's niece seemed quicker than those of the ladies at Court. Hence, he began going frequently to Wapping Old Stairs and such places at night; wrapped in a grey cloak to hide the star at his neck and the garter at his knee. There, with a mug before him, among the sanded alleys and bowling greens and all the simple architecture of such places, he listened to sailors' stories of hardship and horror and cruelty on the Spanish main; how some had lost their toes, others their noses — for the spoken story was never so rounded or so finely coloured as the written. Especially he loved to hear them volley forth their songs of the Azores, while the parrakeets, which they had brought from those parts, pecked at the rings in their ears, tapped with their hard acquisitive beaks at the rubies on their fingers, and swore as vilely as their masters. The women were scarcely less bold in their speech and less free in their manners than the birds. They perched on his knee, flung their arms round his neck and, guessing that something out of the common lay hid beneath his duffle cloak, were quite as eager to come at the truth of the matter as Orlando himself.

Nor was opportunity lacking. The river was astir early and late with barges, wherries, and craft of all description. Every day sailed to sea some fine ship bound for the Indies; now and again another blackened and ragged with hairy unknown men on board crept painfully to anchor. No one missed a boy or girl if they dallied a little on the water after sunset; or raised an eyebrow if gossip had seen them sleeping soundly among the treasure sacks safe in each other's arms. Such indeed was the adventure that befell Orlando, Sukey, and the Earl of Cumberland. The day was hot; their love was active; they had fallen asleep among the rubies. Late that night the Earl, whose fortunes were much bound up in the Spanish ventures, came to check the booty alone with a lantern. He flashed the light on a barrel. He started back with an oath. Twined about the cask two spirits lay sleeping. Superstitious by nature, his conscience laden with many a crime, the Earl took the couple—they were wrapped in a red cloak, and Sukey's bosom was almost as white as the eternal snows of Orlando's poetry—for a phantom sprung from the graves of drowned sailors to upbraid him. He crossed himself. He vowed repentance. The row of alms houses still standing in the Sheen Road is the visible fruit of that moment's panic. Twelve poor old women of the parish to-day drink tea and to-night bless his Lordship for a roof above their heads; so that illicit love in a treasure ship—but we omit the moral.

Soon, however, Orlando grew tired, not only of the discomfort of this way of life, and of the crabbed streets of the neighbourhood, but of the primitive manners of the people. For it has to be remembered that crime and poverty had none of the attraction for the Elizabethans that they have for us. They had none of our modern shame of book learning; none of our belief that to be born the son of a butcher is a blessing and to be unable to read a virtue; no fancy that what we call "life" and "reality" are somehow connected with ignorance and brutality; nor, indeed, any equivalent for these two words at all. It was not to seek "life" that Orlando went among them; not in quest of "reality" that he left them. But when he had heard a score of times how Jakes had lost his nose and Sukey her honour—and they told the stories admirably, it must be admitted—he began to be a little weary of the repetition, for a nose can only be cut off in one way and maidenhood lost in another—or so it seemed to him—whereas the arts and the sciences had a diversity about them which stirred his curiosity profoundly. So, always keeping them in happy memory, he left off frequenting the beer gardens and the skittle alleys, hung his grey cloak in his wardrobe, let his star shine at his neck and his garter twinkle at his knee, and appeared once more at the Court of King James. He was young, he was rich, he was handsome. No one could have been received with greater acclamation than he was.

It is certain indeed that many ladies were ready to show him their favours. The names of three at least were freely coupled with his in marriage — Clorinda, Favilla, Euphrosyne — to give them the names he called them in his sonnets.

To take them in order; Clorinda was a sweet-mannered gentle lady enough;—indeed Orlando was greatly taken with her for six months and a half; but she had white eyelashes and could not bear the sight of blood. A hare brought up roasted at her father's table turned her faint. She was much under the influence of the Priests too, and stinted her underlinen in order to give to the poor. She took it on her to reform Orlando of his sins, which sickened him, so that he drew back from the marriage, and did not much regret it when she died soon after of the small pox.

Favilla, who comes next, was of a different sort altogether. She was the daughter of a poor Somersetshire gentleman; who, by sheer assiduity and the use of her eyes had worked her way up at court, where her address in horsemanship, her fine instep, and her grace in dancing won the admiration of all. Once, however, she was so ill-advised as to whip a spaniel that had torn one of her silk stockings (and it must be said in justice that Favilla had few stockings and those for the most part of drugget) within an inch of its life beneath Orlando's window. Orlando, who was a passionate lover of animals, now noticed that her teeth were crooked, and the two front turned inward, which, he said, is a sure sign of a perverse and cruel disposition in woman, and so broke the engagement that very night for ever.

The third, Euphrosyne, was by far the most serious of his flames. She was by birth one of the Irish Desmonds and had therefore a family tree of her own as old and deeply rooted as Orlando's itself. She was fair, florid, and a trifle phlegmatic. She spoke Italian well, had a perfect set of teeth in the upper jaw, though those on the lower were slightly discoloured. She was never without a whippet or spaniel at her knee; fed them with white bread from her own plate; sang sweetly to the virginals; and was never dressed before mid-day owing to the extreme care she took of her person. In short, she would have made a perfect wife for such a nobleman as Orlando, and matters had gone so far that the lawyers on both sides were busy with covenants, jointures, settlements, messuages, tenements, and whatever is needed before one great fortune can mate with another when, with the suddenness and severity that then marked the English climate, came the Great Frost.

The Great Frost was, historians tell us, the most severe that has ever visited these islands. Birds froze in mid-air and fell like stones to the ground. At Norwich a young countrywoman started to cross the road in her usual robust health and was seen by the onlookers to turn visibly to powder and be blown in a puff of dust over the roofs as the icy blast struck her at the street corner. The mortality among sheep and cattle was enormous. Corpses froze and could not be drawn from the sheets. It was no uncommon sight to come upon a whole herd of swine frozen immovable upon the road. The fields were full of shepherds, ploughmen, teams of horses, and little bird-scaring boys all struck stark in the act of the moment, one with his hand to his nose, another with the bottle to his lips, a third with a stone raised to throw at the raven who sat, as if stuffed, upon the

hedge within a yard of him. The severity of the frost was so extraordinary that a kind of petrifaction sometimes ensued; and it
was commonly supposed that the great increase of rocks in
some parts of Derbyshire was due to no eruption, for there was
none, but to the solidification of unfortunate wayfarers who had
been turned literally to stone where they stood. The Church
could give little help in the matter, and though some landown-
ers had these relics blessed, the most part preferred to use them
either as landmarks, scratching posts for sheep, or, when the
form of the stone allowed, drinking troughs for cattle, which
purposes they serve, admirably for the most part, to this day.

But while the country people suffered the extremity of want,
and the trade of the country was at a standstill, London enjoyed
a carnival of the utmost brilliancy. The Court was at Greenwich,
and the new King seized the opportunity that his coronation
gave him to curry favour with the citizens. He directed that the
river, which was frozen to a depth of twenty feet and more for
six or seven miles on either side, should be swept, decorated and
given all the semblance of a park or pleasure ground, with arbours, mazes, alleys, drinking booths, etc., at his expense. For
himself and the courtiers, he reserved a certain space immediately opposite the Palace gates; which, railed off from the public
only by a silken rope, became at once the centre of the most brilliant society in England. Great statesmen, in their beards and
ruffs, despatched affairs of state under the crimson awning of
the Royal Pagoda. Soldiers planned the conquest of the Moor
and the downfall of the Turk in striped arbours surmounted by
plumes of ostrich feathers. Admirals strode up and down the
narrow pathways, glass in hand, sweeping the horizon and telling
stories of the north-west passage and the Spanish Armada.
Lovers dallied upon divans spread with sables. Frozen roses fell
in showers when the Queen and her ladies walked abroad.
Coloured balloons hovered motionless in the air. Here and there

burnt vast bonfires of cedar and oak wood, lavishly salted, so
that the flames were of green, orange, and purple fire. But however fiercely they burnt, the heat was not enough to melt the ice
which, though of singular transparency, was yet of the hardness
of steel. So clear indeed was it that there could be seen, con-
gealed at a depth of several feet, here a porpoise, there a floun-
der. Shoals of eels lay motionless in a trance, but whether their
state was one of death or merely of suspended animation which
the warmth would revive puzzled the philosophers. Near London Bridge, where the river had frozen to a depth of some
twenty fathoms, a wrecked wherry boat was plainly visible, lying
on the bed of the river where it had sunk last autumn, overladen
with apples. The old bumboat woman, who was carrying her
fruit to market on the Surrey side, sat there in her plaids and farthingales with her lap full of apples, for all the world as if she
were about to serve a customer, though a certain blueness about
the lips hinted the truth. 'Twas a sight King James specially liked
to look upon, and he would bring a troupe of courtiers to gaze
with him. In short, nothing could exceed the brilliancy and gaiety of the scene by day. But it was at night that the carnival was
at its merriest. For the frost continued unbroken; the nights were
of perfect stillness; the moon and stars blazed with the hard fix-
ity of diamonds, and to the fine music of flute and trumpet the
courtiers danced.

Orlando, it is true, was none of those who tread lightly the
coranto and lavolta; he was clumsy; and a little absent-minded.
He much preferred the plain dances of his own country, which
he had danced as a child to these fantastic foreign measures. He
had indeed just brought his feet together about six in the evening
of the seventh of January at the finish of some such quadrille or
minuet when he beheld, coming from the pavilion of the Muscovite Embassy, a figure, which, whether boy's or woman's, for
the loose tunic and trousers of the Russian fashion served to

disguise the sex, filled him with the highest curiosity. The person, whatever the name or sex, was about middle height, very
slenderly fashioned, and dressed entirely in oyster-coloured velvet, trimmed with some unfamiliar greenish-coloured fur. But
these details were obscured by the extraordinary seductiveness
which issued from the whole person. Images, metaphors of the
most extreme and extravagant twined and twisted in his mind.
He called her a melon, a pineapple, an olive tree, an emerald,
and a fox in the snow all in the space of three seconds; he did
not know whether he had heard her, tasted her, seen her, or all
three together. (For though we must pause not a moment in the
narrative we may here hastily note that all his images at this time
were simple in the extreme to match his senses and were mostly
taken from things he had liked the taste of as a boy. But if his
senses were simple they were at the same time extremely strong.
To pause therefore and seek the reasons of things is out of
the question.) . . . A melon, an emerald, a fox in the snow—so
he raved, so he called her. When the boy, for alas, a boy it must
be—no woman could skate with such speed and vigour—swept
almost on tiptoe past him, Orlando was ready to tear his hair
with vexation that the person was of his own sex, and thus all
embraces were out of the question. But the skater came closer.
Legs, hands, carriage, were a boy's, but no boy ever had a mouth
like that; no boy had those breasts; no boy had those eyes which
looked as if they had been fished from the bottom of the sea.
Finally, coming to a stop and sweeping a curtsey with the utmost grace to the King, who was shuffling past on the arm of
some Lord-in-waiting, the unknown skater came to a standstill.
She was not a handsbreadth off. She was a woman. Orlando
stared; trembled; turned hot; turned cold; longed to hurl himself through the summer air; to crush acorns beneath his feet;
to toss his arms with the beech trees and the oaks. As it was, he
drew his lips up over his small white teeth; opened them per-

haps half an inch as if to bite and shut them as if he had bitten. The Lady Euphrosyne hung upon his arm.

The stranger's name, he found, was the Princess Marousha Stanilovska Dagmar Natasha Iliana Romanovitch, and she had come in the train of the Muscovite Ambassador, who was her uncle perhaps, or perhaps her father, to attend the coronation. Very little was known of the Muscovites. In their great beards and furred hats they sat almost silent; drinking some black liquid which they spat out now and then upon the ice. None spoke English, and French with which some at least were familiar was then little spoken at the English Court.

It was through this accident that Orlando and the Princess became acquainted. They were seated opposite each other at the great table spread under a huge awning for the entertainment of the notables. The Princess was placed between two young Lords, one Lord Francis Vere and the other the young Earl of Moray. It was laughable to see the predicament she soon had them in, for though both were fine lads in their way, the babe unborn had as much knowledge of the French tongue as they had. When at the beginning of dinner the Princess turned to the Earl and said, with a grace which ravished his heart, "Je crois avoir fait la connaissance d'un gentilhomme qui vous était apparenté en Pologne l'été dernier," or "La beauté des dames de la cour d'Angleterre me met dans le ravissement. On ne peut voir une dame plus gracieuse que votre reine, ni une coiffure plus belle que la sienne," both Lord Francis and the Earl showed the highest embarrassment. The one helped her largely to horse-radish sauce, the other whistled to his dog and made him beg for a marrow bone. At this the Princess could no longer contain her laughter, and Orlando, catching her eyes across the boars' heads and stuffed peacocks, laughed too. He laughed, but the laugh on his lips froze in wonder. Whom had he loved, what had he loved, he asked himself in a tumult of

emotion, until now? An old woman, he answered, all skin and
bone. Red-cheeked trulls too many to mention. A puling nun.
A hard-bitten cruel-mouthed adventuress. A nodding mass of
lace and ceremony. Love had meant to him nothing but sawdust
and cinders. The joys he had had of it tasted insipid in the extreme. He marvelled how he could have gone through with it
without yawning. For as he looked the thickness of his blood
melted; the ice turned to wine in his veins; he heard the waters
flowing and the birds singing; spring broke over the hard win-
try landscape; his manhood woke; he grasped a sword in his
hand; he charged a more daring foe than Pole or Moor; he dived
in deep water; he saw the flower of danger growing in a crevice;
he stretched his hand—in fact he was rattling off one of his
most impassioned sonnets when the Princess addressed him,
"Would you have the goodness to pass the salt?"

He blushed deeply.

"With all the pleasure in the world, Madame," he replied,
speaking French with a perfect accent. For, heaven be praised,
he spoke the tongue as his own; his mother's maid had taught
him. Yet perhaps it would have been better for him had he never
learnt that tongue; never answered that voice; never followed
the light of those eyes. . . .

The Princess continued. Who were those bumpkins she
asked him, who sat beside her with the manners of stablemen?
What was the nauseating mixture they had poured on her plate?
Did the dogs eat at the same table with the men in England?
Was that figure of fun at the end of the table with her hair rigged
up like a Maypole (une grande perche mal fagotée) really the
Queen? And did the King always slobber like that? And which
of those popinjays was George Villiers? Though these questions
rather discomposed Orlando at first, they were put with such
archness and drollery that he could not help but laugh; and as
he saw from the blank faces of the company that nobody un-

derstood a word, he answered her as freely as she asked him, speaking, as she did, in perfect French.

Thus began an intimacy between the two which soon became the scandal of the Court.

Soon it was observed Orlando paid the Muscovite far more attention than mere civility demanded. He was seldom far from her side, and their conversation, though unintelligible to the rest, was carried on with such animation, provoked such blushes and laughter, that the dullest could guess the subject. Moreover, the change in Orlando himself was extraordinary. Nobody had ever seen him so animated. In one night he had thrown off his boyish clumsiness; he was changed from a sulky stripling, who could not enter a ladies' room without sweeping half the ornaments from the table, to a nobleman, full of grace and manly courtesy. To see him hand the Muscovite (as she was called) to her sledge, or offer her his hand for the dance, or catch the spotted kerchief which she had let drop, or discharge any other of those manifold duties which the supreme lady exacts and the lover hastens to anticipate was a sight to kindle the dull eyes of age, and to make the quick pulse of youth beat faster. Yet over it all hung a cloud. The old men shrugged their shoulders. The young tittered between their fingers. All knew that Orlando was betrothed to another. The Lady Margaret O'Brien O'Dare O'Reilly Tyrconnel (for that was the proper name of Euphrosyne of the Sonnets) wore Orlando's splendid sapphire on the second finger of her left hand. It was she who had the supreme right to his attentions. Yet she might drop all the handkerchiefs in her wardrobe (of which she had many scores) upon the ice and Orlando never stooped to pick them up. She might wait twenty minutes for him to hand her to her sledge, and in the end have to be content with the services of her Blackamoor. When she skated, which she did rather clumsily, no one was at her elbow to encourage her, and, if she fell, which she did rather heavily, no one raised her to her feet and dusted the snow from her petticoats. Although she was naturally phlegmatic, slow to take offence, and more reluctant than most people to believe that a mere foreigner could oust her from Orlando's affections, still even the Lady Margaret herself was brought at last to suspect that something was brewing against her peace of mind.

Indeed, as the days passed, Orlando took less and less care to hide his feelings. Making some excuse or other, he would leave the company as soon as they had dined, or steal away from the skaters, who were forming sets for a quadrille. Next moment it would be seen that the Muscovite was missing too. But what most outraged the Court, and stung it in its tenderest part, which is its vanity, was that the couple was often seen to slip under the silken rope, which railed off the Royal enclosure from the public part of the river and to disappear among the crowd of common people. For suddenly the Princess would stamp her foot and cry, "Take me away. I detest your English mob," by which she meant the English Court itself. She could stand it no longer. It was full of prying old women, she said, who stared in one's face, and of bumptious young men who trod on one's toes. They smelt bad. Their dogs ran between her legs. It was like being in a cage. In Russia they had rivers ten miles broad on which one could gallop six horses abreast all day long without meeting a soul. Besides, she wanted to see the Tower, the Beefeaters, the Heads on Temple Bar, and the jewellers' shops in the city. Thus, it came about that Orlando took her into the city, showed her the Beefeaters and the rebels' heads, and bought her whatever took her fancy in the Royal Exchange. But this was not enough. Each increasingly desired the other's company in privacy all day long where there were none to marvel or to stare. Instead of taking the road to London, therefore, they turned the other way about and were soon beyond the crowd among the frozen reaches of the Thames where, save for sea birds and some old country woman hacking at the ice in a vain attempt to draw a pail full of water or gathering what sticks or dead leaves she could find for firing, not a living soul ever came their way. The poor kept closely to their cottages, and the better sort, who could afford it, crowded for warmth and merriment to the city.

Hence, Orlando and Sasha, as he called her for short, and because it was the name of a white Russian fox he had had as a boy—a creature soft as snow, but with teeth of steel, which bit him so savagely that his father had it killed—hence they had the river to themselves. Hot with skating and with love they would throw themselves down in some solitary reach, where the yellow osiers fringed the bank, and wrapped in a great fur cloak Orlando would take her in his arms, and know, for the first time, he murmured, the delights of love. Then, when the ecstasy was over and they lay lulled in a swoon on the ice, he would tell her of his other loves, and how, compared with her, they had been of wood, of sackcloth, and of cinders. And laughing at his vehemence, she would turn once more in his arms and give him, for love's sake, one more embrace. And then they would marvel that the ice did not melt with their heat, and pity the poor old woman who had no such natural means of thawing it, but must hack at it with a chopper of cold steel. And then, wrapped in their sables, they would talk of everything under the sun; of sights and travels; of Moor and Pagan; of this man's beard and that woman's skin; of a rat that fed from her hand at table; of the arras that moved always in the hall at home; of a face; of a feather. Nothing was too small for such converse, nothing was too great.

Then, suddenly Orlando would fall into one of his moods of melancholy; the sight of the old woman hobbling over the ice might be the cause of it, or nothing; and would fling himself face downwards on the ice and look into the frozen waters and think of death. For the philosopher is right who says that nothing thicker than a knife's blade separates happiness from melancholy; and he goes on to opine that one is twin fellow to the other; and draws from this the conclusion that all extremes of feeling are allied to madness; and so bids us take refuge in the true Church (in his view the Anabaptist) which is the only harbour, port, anchorage, etc., he said, for those tossed on this sea.

"All ends in death," Orlando would say, sitting upright, his face clouded with gloom. (For that was the way his mind worked now, in violent see-saws from life to death stopping at nothing in between, so that the biographer must not stop either, but must fly as fast as he can and so keep pace with the unthinking passionate foolish actions and sudden extravagant words in which, it is impossible to deny, Orlando at this time of his life indulged.)

"All ends in death," Orlando would say, sitting upright on the ice. But Sasha who after all had no English blood in her but was from Russia where the sunsets are longer, the dawns less sudden, and sentences often left unfinished from doubt as to how best to end them—Sasha stared at him, perhaps sneered at him, for he must have seemed a child to her, and said nothing. But at length the ice grew cold beneath them, which she disliked, so pulling him to his feet again, she talked so enchantingly, so wittily, so wisely (but unfortunately always in French, which notoriously loses its flavour in translation) that he forgot the frozen waters or night coming or the old woman or whatever it was, and would try to tell her—plunging and splashing among a thousand images which had gone as stale as the women who inspired them—what she was like. Snow, cream, marble, cherries, alabaster, golden wire? None of these. She was like a fox, or an olive tree; like the waves of the sea when you look down upon them from a height; like an emerald; like the sun on a green hill which is yet clouded—like nothing he had seen or known in England. Ransack the language as he might, words failed him. He wanted another landscape, and another tongue. English was too frank, too candid, too honeyed a speech for Sasha. For in all she said, however open she seemed and voluptuous, there was something hidden; in all she did, however daring, there was something concealed. So the green flame seems hidden in the emerald, or the sun prisoned in a hill. The clearness was only outward; within was a wandering flame. It came; it went; she never shone with the steady beam of an Englishwoman—here, however, remembering the Lady Margaret and her petticoats, Orlando ran wild in his transports and swept her over the ice, faster, faster, vowing that he would chase the flame, dive for the gem, and so on and so on, the words coming on the pants of his breath with the passion of a poet whose poetry is half pressed out of him by pain.

But Sasha was silent. When Orlando had done telling her that she was a fox, an olive tree, or a green hill-top, and had given her the whole history of his family; how their house was one of the most ancient in Britain; how they had come from Rome with the Caesars and had the right to walk down the Corso (which is the chief street in Rome) under a tasselled palanquin, which he said is a privilege reserved only for those of imperial blood (for there was an orgulous credulity about him which was pleasant enough) he would pause and ask her, Where was her own house? What was her father? Had she brothers? Why was she here alone with her uncle? Then, somehow, though she answered readily enough, an awkwardness would come between them. He suspected at first that her rank was not as high as she would like; or that she was ashamed of the savage ways of her people, for he had heard that the women in Muscovy wear beards and the men are covered with fur from the waist down; that both sexes are smeared with tallow to keep the cold out, tear meat with their fingers and live in huts where an English noble would scruple to keep his cattle; so that he forebore to press her. But on reflection, he concluded that her silence could not be for that reason; she herself was entirely free from hair on the chin; she dressed in velvet and pearls, and her manners were certainly not those of a woman bred in a cattle shed.

What, then, did she hide from him? The doubt underlying the tremendous force of his feelings was like a quicksand beneath a monument which shifts suddenly and makes the whole pile shake. The agony would seize him suddenly. Then he would blaze out in such wrath that she did not know how to quiet him. Perhaps she did not want to quiet him; perhaps his rages pleased her and she provoked them purposely—such is the curious obliquity of the Muscovitish temperament.

To continue the story—skating farther than their wont that day they reached that part of the river where the ships had anchored and been frozen in midstream. Among them was the ship of the Muscovite Embassy flying its double-headed black eagle from the main mast, which was hung with many-coloured icicles several yards in length. Sasha had left some of her clothing on board, and supposing the ship to be empty they climbed on deck and went in search of it. Remembering certain passages in his own past, Orlando would not have marvelled had some good citizens sought this refuge before them; and so it turned out. They had not ventured far, when a fine young man started up from some business of his own behind a coil of rope and saying, apparently, for he spoke Russian, that he was one of the crew and would help the Princess to find what she wanted, lit a lump of candle and disappeared with her into the lower parts of the ship.

Time went by, and Orlando, wrapped in his own dreams, thought only of the pleasures of life; of his jewel; of her rarity; of means for making her irrevocably and indissolubly his own. Obstacles there were and hardships to be overcome. She was determined to live in Russia, where there were frozen rivers and wild horses and men, she said, who gashed each other's throats open. It is true that a landscape of pine and snow, habits of lust and slaughter, did not entice him. Nor was he anxious to cease his pleasant country ways of sport and tree planting; relinquish his office; ruin his career; shoot the reindeer instead of the rabbit; drink vodka instead of canary, and slip a knife up his sleeve — for what purpose, he knew not. Still, all this and more than all this he would do for her sake. As for his marriage with the Lady Margaret, fixed though it was for this day sennight, the thing was so palpably absurd that he scarcely gave it a thought. Her kinsmen would abuse him for deserting a great lady; his friends would deride him for ruining the finest career in the world for a Cossack woman and a waste of snow — it weighed not a straw in the balance compared with Sasha herself. On the first dark night they would fly north; thence to Russia. So he pondered; so he plotted as he walked up and down the deck.

He was recalled, turning westward, by the sight of the sun, slung like an orange on the cross of St. Paul's. It was blood red and sinking rapidly. It must be almost evening. Sasha had been gone this hour and more. Seized instantly with those dark forebodings which shadowed even his most confident thoughts of her, he plunged the way he had seen them go into the hold of the ship; and, after stumbling among chests and barrels in the darkness, was made aware by a faint glimmer in a corner that they were seated there. For one second, he had a vision of them; saw Sasha seated on the sailor's knee; saw her bend towards him; saw them embrace before the light was blotted out in a red cloud by his rage. He blazed into such a howl of anguish that the whole ship echoed. Sasha threw herself between them, or the sailor would have been stifled before he could draw his cutlass. Then a deadly sickness came over Orlando, and they had to lay him on the floor and give him brandy to drink before he

revived. And then, when he had recovered and was sat upon a
heap of sacking on deck, Sasha hung over him, passing before
his dizzied eyes softly, sinuously, like the fox that had bit him,
now cajoling, now denouncing, so that he came to doubt what
he had seen. Had not the candle guttered; had not the shadows
moved? The box was heavy, she said; the man was helping her
to move it. Orlando believed her one moment—for who can
be sure that his rage has not painted what he most dreads to
find?—the next was the more violent with anger at her deceit.
Then Sasha herself turned white; stamped her foot on deck; said
she would go that night, and called upon her Gods to destroy
her, if she, a Romanovitch, had lain in the arms of a common
seaman. Indeed, looking at them together (which he could
hardly bring himself to do) Orlando was outraged by the foul-
ness of his imagination that could have painted so frail a creature in the paws of that hairy sea brute. The man was huge;
stood six feet four in his stockings; wore common wire rings in
his ears; and looked like a dray horse upon which some wren or
robin has perched in its flight. So he yielded; believed her; and
asked her pardon. Yet, when they were going down the ship's
side, lovingly again, Sasha paused with her hand on the ladder
and called back to this tawny wide-cheeked monster a volley of
Russian greetings, jests, or endearments, not a word of which
Orlando could understand. But there was something in her tone
(it might be the fault of the Russian consonants) that reminded
Orlando of a scene some nights since, when he had come upon
her in secret gnawing a candle end in a corner, which she had
picked from the floor. True, it was pink; it was gilt; and it was
from the King's table; but it was tallow, and she gnawed it. Was
there not, he thought, handing her on to the ice, something rank
in her, something coarse flavoured, something peasant-born?
And he fancied her at forty grown unwieldy though she was
now slim as a reed, and lethargic though she was now blithe as

a lark. But again as they skated towards London such suspicions melted in his breast, and he felt as if he had been hooked by a great fish through the nose and rushed through the waters unwillingly, yet with his own consent.

It was an evening of astonishing beauty. As the sun sank, all the domes, spires, turrets, and pinnacles of London rose in inky blackness against the furious red sunset clouds. Here was the fretted cross at Charing; there the dome of St. Paul's; there the massy square of the Tower buildings; there like a grove of trees stripped of all leaves save a knob at the end were the heads on the pikes at Temple Bar. Now the Abbey windows were lit up and burnt like a heavenly, many-coloured shield (in Orlando's fancy); now all the west seemed a golden window with troops of angels (in Orlando's fancy again) passing up and down the heavenly stairs perpetually. All the time they seemed to be skating on fathomless depths of air, so blue the ice had become; and so glassy smooth was it that they sped quicker and quicker to the city with the white gulls circling about them, and cutting in the air with their wings the very same sweeps that they cut on the ice with their skates.

Sasha, as if to reassure him, was tenderer than usual and even more delightful. Seldom would she talk about her past life, but now she told him how, in winter in Russia, she would listen to the wolves howling across the steppes, and thrice, to show him, she barked like a wolf. Upon which he told her of the stags in the snow at home, and how they would stray into the great hall for warmth and be fed by an old man with porridge from a bucket. And then she praised him; for his love of beasts; for his gallantry; for his legs. Ravished with her praises and shamed to think how he had maligned her by fancying her on the knees of a common sailor and grown fat and lethargic at forty, he told her that he could find no words to praise her; yet instantly bethought him how she was like the spring and green grass and rushing waters, and seizing her more tightly than ever, he swung her with him half across the river so that the gulls and the cormorants swung too. And halting at length, out of breath, she said, panting slightly, that he was like a million-candled Christmas tree (such as they have in Russia) hung with yellow globes; incandescent; enough to light a whole street by; (so one might translate it) for what with his glowing cheeks, his dark curls, his black and crimson cloak, he looked as if he were burning with his own radiance, from a lamp lit within.

All the colour, save the red of Orlando's cheeks, soon faded. Night came on. As the orange light of sunset vanished and was succeeded by an astonishing white glare from the torches, bonfires, flaming cressets, and other devices by which the river was lit up the strangest transformation took place. Various churches and noblemen's palaces, whose fronts were of white stone showed in streaks and patches as if floating on the air. Of St. Paul's, in particular, nothing was left but a gilt cross. The Abbey appeared like the grey skeleton of a leaf. Everything suffered emaciation and transformation. The sounds too seemed closed and concentrated. As they approached the carnival, they heard a deep note like that struck on a tuning-fork which boomed louder and louder until it became an uproar. Every now and then a great shout followed a rocket up into the air. Gradually they could discern little figures breaking off from the vast crowd and spinning hither and thither like gnats on the surface of a river. Above and around this brilliant circle like a bowl of darkness pressed the deep black of a winter's night. And then into this darkness there began to rise with pauses, which kept the expectation alert and the mouth open, flowering rockets; crescents; serpents; a crown. At one moment the woods and distant hills showed green as on a summer's day; the next all was winter and blackness again.

The Russian Princess as a Child

By this time Orlando and the Princess were close to the Royal enclosure and found their way barred by a great crowd of the common people, who were pressing as near to the silken rope as they dared. Loth to end their privacy and encounter the sharp eyes that were on the watch for them, the couple lingered there, shouldered by apprentices; tailors; fishwives; horse dealers; cony catchers; starving scholars; maid-servants in their whimples; orange girls; ostlers; sober citizens; bawdy tapsters; and a crowd of little ragamuffins such as always haunt the outskirts of a crowd, screaming and scrambling among people's feet—all the riff-raff of the London streets indeed was there, jesting and jostling, here casting dice, telling fortunes, shoving, tickling, pinching; here uproarious, there glum; some of them with mouths gaping a yard wide; others as little reverent as daws on a house-top; all as variously rigged out as their purse or stations allowed; here in fur and broadcloth; there in tatters with their feet kept from the ice only by a dishclout bound about them. The main press of people, it appeared, stood opposite a booth or stage something like our Punch and Judy show upon which some kind of theatrical performance was going forward. A black man was waving his arms and vociferating. There was a woman in white laid upon a bed. Rough though the staging was, the actors running up and down a pair of steps and sometimes tripping, and the crowd stamping their feet and whistling, or when they were bored, tossing a piece of orange peel at the actors which a dog would scramble for, still the astonishing, sinuous melody of the words stirred Orlando like music. Spoken with extreme speed and a daring agility of tongue which reminded him of the sailors singing in the beer gardens at Wapping, the words even without meaning were as wine to him. But now and again a single phrase would come to him over the ice which was as if torn from the depths of his heart. The frenzy of the Moor seemed to him his own frenzy, and when the Moor suffocated the woman in her bed it was Sasha he killed with his own hands.

At last the play was ended. All had grown dark. The tears streamed down his face. Looking up into the sky there was nothing but blackness there too. Ruin and death, he thought, cover all. The life of man ends in the grave. Worms devour us.

> Methinks it should be now a huge eclipse
> Of sun and moon, and that the affrighted globe
> Should yawn—

Even as he said this a star of some pallor rose in his memory. The night was dark; it was pitch dark; but it was such a night as this that they had waited for; it was on such a night as this that they had planned to fly. He remembered everything. The time had come. With a burst of passion he snatched Sasha to him, and hissed in her ear, "Jour de ma vie!" It was their signal. At midnight they would meet at an inn near Blackfriars. Horses waited there. Everything was in readiness for their flight. So they parted, she to her tent, he to his. It still wanted an hour of the time.

Long before midnight Orlando was in waiting. The night was of so inky a blackness that a man was on you before he could be seen, which was all to the good, but it was also of the most solemn stillness so that a horse's hoof, or a child's cry, could be heard at a distance of half a mile. Many a time did Orlando, pacing the little courtyard, hold his heart at the sound of some nag's steady footfall on the cobbles, or at the rustle of a woman's dress. But the traveller was only some merchant, making home belated; or some woman of the quarter whose errand was nothing so innocent. They passed, and the street was quieter than before. Then those lights which burnt downstairs in the small, huddled quarters where the poor of the city lived moved up to the sleeping-rooms, and then, one by one were extinguished. The street lanterns in this purlieus were few at most; and the negligence of the night watchman often suffered them to expire long before dawn. The darkness then became even deeper than before. Orlando looked to the wicks of his lantern, saw to the saddle girths; primed his pistols; examined his holsters; and did all these things a dozen times at least till he could find nothing more needing his attention. Though it still lacked some twenty minutes to midnight, he could not bring himself to go indoors to the inn parlour, where the hostess was still serving sack and the cheaper sort of canary wine to a few seafaring men, who would sit there trolling their ditties, and telling their stories of Drake, Hawkins, and Grenville, till they toppled off the benches and rolled asleep on the sanded floor. The darkness was more compassionate to his swollen and violent heart. He listened to every footfall; speculated on every sound. Each drunken shout and each wail from some poor wretch laid in the straw or in other distress cut his heart to the quick, as if it boded ill omen to his venture. Yet, he had no fear for Sasha. Her courage made nothing of the adventure. She would come alone, in her cloak and trousers, booted like a man. Light as her footfall was, it would hardly be heard, even in this silence.

So he waited in the darkness. Suddenly he was struck in the face by a blow, soft, yet heavy, on the side of his cheek. So strung with expectation was he, that he started and put his hand to his sword. The blow was repeated a dozen times on forehead and cheek. The dry frost had lasted so long that it took him a minute to realise that these were raindrops falling; the blows were the blows of the rain. At first, they fell slowly, deliberately, one by one. But soon the six drops became sixty; then six hundred; then ran themselves together in a steady spout of water. It was as if the hard and consolidated sky poured itself forth in one profuse fountain. In the space of five minutes Orlando was soaked to the skin.

Hastily putting the horses under cover, he sought shelter beneath the lintel of the door whence he could still observe the courtyard. The air was thicker now than ever, and such a steaming and droning rose from the downpour that no footfall of man or beast could be heard above it. The roads, pitted as they were with great holes, would be under water and perhaps impassable. But of what effect this would have upon their flight he scarcely thought. All his senses were bent upon gazing along the cobbled pathway—gleaming in the light of the lantern—for Sasha's coming. Sometimes, in the darkness, he seemed to see her wrapped about with rain strokes. But the phantom vanished. Suddenly, with an awful and ominous voice, a voice full of horror and alarm which raised every hair of anguish in Orlando's soul, St. Paul's struck the first stroke of midnight. Four times more it struck remorselessly. With the superstition of a lover, Orlando had made out that it was on the sixth stroke that she would come. But the sixth stroke echoed away, and the seventh came and the eighth, and to his apprehensive mind they seemed notes first heralding and then proclaiming death and disaster. When the twelfth struck he knew that his doom was sealed. It was useless for the rational part of him to reason; she might be late; she might be prevented; she might have missed her way. The passionate and feeling heart of Orlando knew the truth. Other clocks struck, jangling one after another. The whole world seemed to ring with the news of her deceit and his derision. The old suspicions subterraneously at work in him rushed forth from concealment openly. He was bitten by a swarm of snakes, each more poisonous than the last. He stood in the doorway in the tremendous rain without moving. As the minutes passed, he sagged a little at the knees. The downpour rushed on. In the thick of it, great guns seemed to boom. Huge noises as of the tearing and rending of oak trees could be heard. There were also wild cries and terrible inhuman groanings. But Orlando stood there immovable till Paul's clock struck two, and then, crying aloud with an awful irony, and all his teeth showing, "Jour de ma vie!" he dashed the lantern to the ground, mounted his horse and galloped he knew not where.

Some blind instinct, for he was past reasoning, must have driven him to take the river bank in the direction of the sea. For when the dawn broke, which it did with unusual suddenness, the sky turning a pale yellow and the rain almost ceasing, he found himself on the banks of the Thames off Wapping. Now a sight of the most extraordinary nature met his eyes. Where, for three months and more, there had been solid ice of such thickness that it seemed permanent as stone, and a whole gay city had stood on its pavement was now a race of turbulent yellow waters. The river had gained its freedom in the night. It was as if a sulphur spring (to which view many philosophers inclined) had risen from the volcanic regions beneath and burst the ice asunder with such vehemence that it swept the huge and many fragments furiously apart. The mere look of the water was enough to turn one giddy. All was riot and confusion. The river was strewn with icebergs. Some of these were as broad as a bowling green and as high as a house; others no bigger than a man's hat, but most fantastically twisted. Now would come down a whole convoy of ice blocks sinking everything that stood in their way. Now, eddying and swirling like a tortured serpent, the river would seem to be hurtling itself between the fragments and tossing them from bank to bank, so that they could be heard smashing against the piers and pillars. But what was the most awful and inspiring of terror was the sight of the human creatures who had been trapped in the night and now paced their twisting and precarious islands in the utmost agony

of spirit. Whether they jumped into the flood or stayed on the
ice their doom was certain. Sometimes quite a cluster of these
poor creatures would come down together, some on their
knees, others suckling their babies. One old man seemed to be
reading aloud from a holy book. At other times, and his fate
perhaps was the most dreadful, a solitary wretch would stride
his narrow tenement alone. As they swept out to sea, some
could be heard crying vainly for help, making wild promises to
amend their ways, confessing their sins and vowing altars and
wealth if God would hear their prayers. Others were so dazed
with terror that they sat immovable and silent looking stead-
fastly before them. One crew of young watermen or post-boys,
to judge by their liveries, roared and shouted the lewdest tavern
songs, as if in bravado, and were dashed to death and sunk with
blasphemies on their lips. An old nobleman—for such his furred
gown and golden chain proclaimed him—went down not far
from where Orlando stood, calling vengeance upon the Irish
rebels, who, he cried with his last breath, had plotted this dev-
ilry. Many perished clasping some silver pot or other treasure to
their breasts; and at least a score of poor wretches were drowned
by their own cupidity, hurling themselves from the bank into the
flood rather than let a gold goblet escape them, or see before
their eyes the disappearance of some furred gown. For furniture, valuables, possessions of all sorts were carried away on the
icebergs. Among other strange sights was to be seen a cat suckling its young; a table laid sumptuously for a supper of twenty;
a couple in bed; together with an extraordinary number of cook-
ing utensils.

Dazed and astounded, Orlando could do nothing for some
time but watch the appalling race of waters as it hurled itself
past him. At last, seeming to recollect himself, he clapped spurs
to his horse and galloped hard along the river bank in the direction of the sea. Rounding a bend of the river, he came opposite

that reach where, not two days ago, the ships of the Ambassadors had seemed immovably frozen. Hastily, he made count of them all; the French; the Spanish; the Austrian; the Turk. All still floated, though the French had broken loose from her moorings, and the Turkish vessel had taken a great rent in her side and was fast filling with water. But the Russian ship was nowhere to be seen. For one moment Orlando thought it must have foundered; but, raising himself in his stirrups and shading his eyes, which had the sight of a hawk's, he could just make out the shape of a ship on the horizon. The black eagles were flying from the mast head. The ship of the Muscovite Embassy was standing out to sea.

Flinging himself from his horse, he made, in his rage, as if he would breast the flood. Standing knee deep in water he hurled at the faithless woman all the insults that have ever been the lot of her sex. Faithless, mutable, fickle, he called her; devil, adulteress, deceiver; and the swirling waters took his words, and tossed at his feet a broken pot and a little straw.

CHAPTER TWO

THE BIOGRAPHER is now faced with a difficulty which it is better perhaps to confess than to gloss over. Up to this point in telling the story of Orlando's life, documents, both private and historical, have made it possible to fulfil the first duty of a biographer, which is to plod, without looking to right or left, in the indelible footprints of truth; unenticed by flowers; regardless of shade; on and on methodically till we fall plump into the grave and write *finis* on the tombstone above our heads. But now we come to an episode which lies right across our path, so that there is no ignoring it. Yet it is dark, mysterious, and undocumented; so that there is no explaining it. Volumes might be written in interpretation of it; whole religious systems founded upon the signification of it. Our simple duty is to state the facts as far as they are known, and so let the reader make of them what he may.

In the summer of that disastrous winter which saw the frost, the flood, the deaths of many thousands, and the complete downfall of Orlando's hopes—for he was exiled from Court; in deep disgrace with the most powerful nobles of his time; the Irish house of Desmond was justly enraged; the King had already trouble enough with the Irish not to relish this further addition—in that summer Orlando retired to his great house in the country and there lived in complete solitude. One

June morning—it was Saturday the 18th—he failed to rise at
his usual hour, and when his groom went to call him he was
found fast asleep. Nor could he be awakened. He lay as if in a
trance, without perceptible breathing; and though dogs were set
to bark under his window; cymbals, drums, bones beaten perpetually in his room; a gorse bush put under his pillow; and
mustard plasters applied to his feet, still he did not wake, take
food, or show any sign of life for seven whole days. On the seventh day he woke at his usual time (a quarter before eight, precisely) and turned the whole posse of caterwauling wives and
village soothsayers out of his room; which was natural enough;
but what was strange was that he showed no consciousness of
any such trance, but dressed himself and sent for his horse as if
he had woken from a single night's slumber. Yet some change,
it was suspected, must have taken place in the chambers of his
brain, for though he was perfectly rational and seemed graver
and more sedate in his ways than before, he appeared to have
an imperfect recollection of his past life. He would listen when
people spoke of the great frost or the skating or the carnival,
but he never gave any sign, except by passing his hand across
his brow as if to wipe away some cloud, of having witnessed
them himself. When the events of the past six months were discussed, he seemed not so much distressed as puzzled, as if he
were troubled by confused memories of some time long gone
or were trying to recall stories told him by another. It was observed that if Russia was mentioned or Princesses or ships, he
would fall into a gloom of an uneasy kind and get up and look
out of the window or call one of the dogs to him, or take a knife
and carve a piece of cedar wood. But the doctors were hardly
wiser then than they are now, and after prescribing rest and ex-
ercise, starvation and nourishment, society and solitude, that he
should lie in bed all day and ride forty miles between lunch and
dinner, together with the usual sedatives and irritants, diversi-

fied, as the fancy took them, with possets of newt's slobber on rising, and draughts of peacock's gall on going to bed, they left him to himself, and gave it as their opinion that he had been asleep for a week.

But if sleep it was, of what nature, we can scarcely refrain from asking, are such sleeps as these? Are they remedial measures—trances in which the most galling memories, events that seem likely to cripple life for ever, are brushed with a dark wing which rubs their harshness off and gilds them, even the ugliest, and basest, with a lustre, an incandescence? Has the finger of death to be laid on the tumult of life from time to time lest it rend us asunder? Are we so made that we have to take death in small doses daily or we could not go on with the business of living? And then what strange powers are these that penetrate our most secret ways and change our most treasured possessions without our willing it? Had Orlando, worn out by the extremity of his suffering, died for a week, and then come to life again? And if so, of what nature is death and of what nature life? Having waited well over half an hour for an answer to these questions, and none coming, let us get on with the story.

Now Orlando gave himself up to a life of extreme solitude. His disgrace at Court and the violence of his grief were partly the reason of it, but as he made no effort to defend himself and seldom invited anyone to visit him (though he had many friends who would willingly have done so) it appeared as if to be alone in the great house of his fathers suited his temper. Solitude was his choice. How he spent his time, nobody quite knew. The servants, of whom he kept a full retinue, though much of their business was to dust empty rooms and to smooth the coverlets of beds that were never slept in, watched, in the dark of the evening, as they sat over their cakes and ale, a light passing along the galleries, through the banqueting-halls, up the staircases, into the bedrooms, and knew that their master was perambulating the house alone. None dared follow him, for the house was haunted by a great variety of ghosts, and the extent of it made it easy to lose one's way and either fall down some hidden staircase or open a door which, should the wind blow it to, would shut upon one for ever—accidents of no uncommon occurrence, as the frequent discovery of the skeletons of men and animals in attitudes of great agony made evident. Then the light would be lost altogether, and Mrs. Grimsditch, the housekeeper, would say to Mr. Dupper, the chaplain, how she hoped his Lordship had not met with some bad accident. Mr. Dupper would opine that his Lordship was on his knees, no doubt, among the tombs of his ancestors in the Chapel, which was in the Billiard Table Court, half a mile away on the south side. For he had sins on his conscience, Mr. Dupper was afraid; upon which Mrs. Grimsditch would retort, rather sharply, that so had most of us; and Mrs. Stewkley and Mrs. Field and old Nurse Carpenter would all raise their voices in his Lordship's praise; and the grooms and the stewards would swear that it was a thousand pities to see so fine a nobleman moping about the house when he might be hunting the fox or chasing the deer; and even the little laundry maids and scullery maids, the Judys and the Faiths, who were handing round the tankards and cakes would pipe up their testimony to his Lordship's gallantry; for never was there a kinder gentleman, or one more free with those little pieces of silver which serve to buy a knot of ribbon or put a posy in one's hair; until even the Blackamoor whom they called Grace Robinson by way of making a Christian woman of her, understood what they were at, and agreed that his Lordship was a handsome, pleasant, darling gentleman in the only way she could, that is to say by showing all her teeth at once in a broad grin. In short, all his serving men and women held him in high respect, and cursed the foreign Princess (but they called her by a coarser name than that) who had brought him to this pass.

But though it was probably cowardice, or love of hot ale, that led Mr. Dupper to imagine his Lordship safe among the tombs so that he need not go in search of him, it may well have been that Mr. Dupper was right. Orlando now took a strange delight in thoughts of death and decay, and, after pacing the long galleries and ballrooms with a taper in his hand, looking at picture after picture as if he sought the likeness of somebody whom he could not find, would mount into the family pew and sit for hours watching the banners stir and the moonlight waver with a bat or death's head moth to keep him company. Even this was not enough for him, but he must descend into the crypt where his ancestors lay, coffin piled upon coffin, for ten generations together. The place was so seldom visited that the rats had made free with the lead work, and now a thigh bone would catch at his cloak as he passed, or he would crack the skull of some old Sir Malise as it rolled beneath his foot. It was a ghastly sepulchre; dug deep beneath the foundations of the house as if the first Lord of the family, who had come from France with the Conqueror, had wished to testify how all pomp is built upon corruption; how the skeleton lies beneath the flesh; how we that dance and sing above must lie below; how the crimson velvet turns to dust; how the ring (here Orlando, stooping his lantern, would pick up a gold circle lacking a stone, that had rolled into a corner) loses its ruby and the eye which was so lustrous, shines no more. "Nothing remains of all these Princes," Orlando would say, indulging in some pardonable exaggeration of their rank, "except one digit," and he would take a skeleton hand in his and bend the joints this way and that. "Whose hand was it?" he went on to ask. "The right or the left? The hand of man or woman, of age or youth? Had it urged the war horse, or plied the needle? Had it plucked the rose, or grasped cold steel? Had it——" but here either his invention failed him or, what is more likely, provided him with so many instances of what a hand can do that he shrank, as his wont was, from the cardinal labour of composition, which is excision, and he put it with the other bones, thinking how there was a writer called Thomas Browne, a Doctor of Norwich, whose writing upon such subjects took his fancy amazingly.

So, taking his lantern and seeing that the bones were in order, for though romantic, he was singularly methodical and detested nothing so much as a ball of string on the floor, let alone the skull of an ancestor, he returned to that curious, moody pacing down the galleries, looking for something among the pictures, which was interrupted at length by a veritable spasm of sobbing, at the sight of a Dutch snow scene by an unknown artist. Then it seemed to him that life was not worth living any more. Forgetting the bones of his ancestors and how life is founded on a grave, he stood there shaken with sobs, all for the desire of a woman in Russian trousers, with slanting eyes, a pouting mouth, and pearls about her neck. She had gone. She had left him. He was never to see her again. And so he sobbed. And so he found his way back to his own rooms; and Mrs. Grimsditch, seeing the light in the window, put the tankard from her lips and said Praise be to God, his Lordship was safe in his room again; for she had been thinking all this while that he was foully murdered.

Orlando now drew his chair up to the table; opened the works of Sir Thomas Browne and proceeded to investigate the delicate articulation of one of the doctor's longest and most marvellously contorted cogitations.

For though these are not matters on which a biographer can profitably enlarge it is plain enough to those who have done a reader's part in making up from bare hints dropped here and there the whole boundary and circumference of a living person; can hear in what we only whisper a living voice; can see, often when we say nothing about it, exactly what he looked like, and know without a word to guide them precisely what he thought and felt and it is for readers such as these alone that we write— it is plain then to such a reader that Orlando was strangely compounded of many humours—of melancholy, of indolence, of passion, of love of solitude, to say nothing of all those contortions and subtleties of temper which were indicated on the first page, when he slashed at a dead nigger's head; cut it down; hung it chivalrously out of his reach again and then betook himself to the window-seat with a book. The taste for books was an early one. As a child he was sometimes found at midnight by a page still reading. They took his taper away, and he bred glow-worms to serve his purpose. They took the glow-worms away, and he almost burnt the house down with a tinder. To put it in a nutshell, leaving the novelist to smooth out the crumpled silk and all its implications, he was a nobleman afflicted with a love of literature. Many people of his time, still more of his rank, escaped the infection and were thus free to run or ride or make love at their own sweet will. But some were early infected by a germ said to be bred of the pollen of the asphodel and to be blown out of Greece and Italy, which was of so deadly a nature that it would shake the hand as it was raised to strike, cloud the eye as it sought its prey, and make the tongue stammer as it declared its love. It was the fatal nature of this disease to substitute a phantom for reality, so that Orlando, to whom fortune had given every gift— plate, linen, houses, men-servants, carpets, beds in profusion— had only to open a book for the whole vast accumulation to turn to mist. The nine acres of stone which were his house vanished; one hundred and fifty indoor servants disappeared; his eighty riding horses became invisible; it would take too long to count the carpets, sofas, trappings, china, plate, cruets, chafing dishes and other movables often of beaten gold, which evaporated like so much sea mist under the miasma. So it was, and Orlando would sit by himself, reading, a naked man.

The disease gained rapidly upon him now in his solitude. He would read often six hours into the night; and when they came to him for orders about the slaughtering of cattle or the harvesting of wheat, he would push away his folio and look as if he did not understand what was said to him. This was bad enough and wrung the hearts of Hall, the falconer, of Giles, the groom, of Mrs. Grimsditch, the housekeeper, of Mr. Dupper, the chaplain. A fine gentleman like that, they said, had no need of books. Let him leave books, they said, to the palsied or the dying. But worse was to come. For once the disease of reading has laid hold upon the system it weakens it so that it falls an easy prey to that other scourge which dwells in the ink pot and festers in the quill. The wretch takes to writing. And while this is bad enough in a poor man, whose only property is a chair and a table set beneath a leaky roof—for he has not much to lose, after all—the plight of a rich man, who has houses and cattle, maid-servants, asses and linen, and yet writes books, is pitiable in the extreme. The flavour of it all goes out of him; he is riddled by hot irons; gnawed by vermin. He would give every penny he has (such is the malignity of the germ) to write one little book and become famous; yet all the gold in Peru will not buy him the treasure of a well-turned line. So he falls into consumption and sickness, blows his brains out, turns his face to the wall. It matters not in what attitude they find him. He has passed through the gates of Death and known the flames of Hell.

Happily, Orlando was of a strong constitution and the disease (for reasons presently to be given) never broke him down as it has broken many of his peers. But he was deeply smitten with it, as the sequel shows. For when he had read for an hour or so in Sir Thomas Browne, and the bark of the stag and the call of the night watchman showed that it was the dead of night and all safe asleep, he crossed the room, took a silver key from his pocket and unlocked the doors of a great inlaid cabinet which stood in the corner. Within were some fifty drawers of cedar wood and upon each was a paper neatly written in Orlando's hand. He paused, as if hesitating which to open. One was inscribed "The Death of Ajax," another "The Birth of Pyramus," another "Iphigenia in Aulis," another "The Death of Hippolytus," another "Meleager," another "The Return of Odysseus,"—in fact there was scarcely a single drawer that lacked the name of some mythological personage at a crisis of his career. In each drawer lay a document of considerable size all written over in Orlando's hand. The truth was that Orlando had been afflicted thus for many years. Never had any boy begged apples as Orlando begged paper; nor sweet meats as he begged ink. Stealing away from talk and games, he had hidden himself behind curtains, in priest's holes, or in the cupboard behind his mother's bedroom which had a great hole in the floor and smelt horribly of starling's dung, with an inkhorn in one hand, a pen in another, and on his knee, a roll of paper. Thus had been written, before he was turned twenty-five, some forty-seven plays, histories, romances, poems; some in prose, some in verse; some in French, some in Italian; all romantic, and all long. One he had had printed by John Ball of the Feathers and Coronet opposite St. Paul's Cross, Cheapside; but though the sight of it gave him extreme delight, he had never dared show it even to his mother, since to write, much more to publish, was, he knew, for a nobleman an inexpiable disgrace.

Now, however, that it was the dead of night and he was alone, he chose from this repository one thick document called "Xenophila a Tragedy" or some such title, and one thin one, called simply "The Oak Tree" (this was the only monosyllabic title among the lot), and then he approached the ink horn, fingered the quill, and made other such passes as those addicted to this vice begin their rites with. But he paused.

As this pause was of extreme significance in his history, more so, indeed, than many acts which bring men to their knees and make rivers run with blood, it behoves us to ask why he paused; and to reply, after due reflection, that it was for some such reason as this. Nature, who has played so many queer tricks upon us, making us so unequally of clay and diamonds, of rainbow and granite, and stuffed them into a case, often of the most incongruous, for the poet has a butcher's face and the butcher a poet's; nature, who delights in muddle and mystery, so that even now (the first of November, 1927) we know not why we go upstairs, or why we come down again, our most daily movements are like the passage of a ship on an unknown sea, and the sailors at the mast-head ask, pointing their glasses to the horizon: Is there land or is there none? to which, if we are prophets, we make answer "Yes"; if we are truthful we say "No"; nature, who has so much to answer for besides the perhaps unwieldy length of this sentence, has further complicated her task and added to our confusion by providing not only a perfect ragbag of odds and ends within us—a piece of a policeman's trousers lying cheek by jowl with Queen Alexandra's wedding veil—but has contrived that the whole assortment shall be lightly stitched together by a single thread. Memory is the seamstress, and a capricious one at that. Memory runs her needle in and out, up and down, hither and thither. We know not what comes next, or what follows after. Thus, the most ordinary movement in the world, such as sitting down at a table and pulling the inkstand towards one, may agitate a thousand odd, disconnected fragments, now bright, now dim, hanging and bobbing and dipping and flaunting, like the underlinen of a family of fourteen on a line in a gale of wind. Instead of being a single, downright, bluff piece of work of which no man need feel ashamed, our commonest deeds are set about with a fluttering and flickering of wings, a rising and falling of lights. Thus it was that Orlando, dipping his pen in the ink, saw the mocking face of the lost Princess and asked himself a million questions instantly which were as arrows dipped in gall. Where was she; and why had she left him? Was the Ambassador her uncle or her lover? Had they plotted? Was she forced? Was she married? Was she dead? All of which so drove their venom into him that, as if to vent his agony somewhere, he plunged his quill so deep into the inkhorn that the ink spirted over the table, which act, explain it how one may (and no explanation perhaps is possible—Memory is inexplicable), at once substituted for the face of the Princess a face of a very different sort. But whose was it, he asked himself? And he had to wait, perhaps half a minute, looking at the new picture which lay on top of the old, as one lantern slide is half seen through the next, before he could say to himself, "This is the face of that rather fat, shabby man who sat in Twitchett's room ever so many years ago when old Queen Bess came here to dine; and I saw him," Orlando continued, catching at another of those little coloured rags, "sitting at the table, as I peeped in on my way downstairs, and he had the most amazing eyes," said Orlando, "that ever were, but who the devil was he?" Orlando asked, for here Memory added to the forehead and eyes, first, a coarse, grease-stained ruffle, then a brown doublet, and finally a pair of thick boots such as citizens wear in Cheapside. "Not a Nobleman; not one of us," said Orlando (which he would not have said aloud, for he was the most courteous of gentlemen; but it shows what an effect noble birth has upon the mind and incidentally how difficult it is for a nobleman to be a writer). "A poet, I dare say." By all the laws, Memory, having disturbed him sufficiently, should now have blotted the whole thing out completely, or have fetched up something so idiotic and out of keeping—like a dog chasing a cat or an old woman blowing her nose into a red cotton handkerchief—that, in despair of keeping pace with her vagaries, Orlando should have struck his pen in earnest against his paper. (For we can, if we have the resolution, turn the hussy, Memory, and all her ragtag and bobtail out of the house.) But Orlando paused. Memory still held before him the image of a shabby man with bright eyes. Still he looked; still he paused. It is these pauses that are our undoing. It is then that sedition enters the fortress and our troops rise in insurrection. Once before he had paused, and love with its horrid rout, its shawms, its cymbals, and its heads with gory locks torn from the shoulders had burst in. From love he had suffered the tortures of the damned. Now, again, he paused, and into the breach thus made, leapt Ambition, the harridan, and Poetry, the witch, and Desire of Fame, the strumpet; all joined hands and made of his heart their dancing ground. Standing upright in the solitude of his room, he vowed that he would be the first poet of his race and bring immortal lustre upon his name. He said (reciting the names and exploits of his ancestors) that Sir Boris had fought and killed the Paynim; Sir Gawain, the Turk; Sir Miles, the Pole; Sir Andrew, the Frank; Sir Richard, the Austrian; Sir Jordan, the Frenchman; and Sir Herbert, the Spaniard. But of all that killing and campaigning, that drinking and love-making, that spending and hunting and riding and eating, what remained? A skull; a finger. Whereas, he said, turning to the page of Sir Thomas Browne, which lay open upon the table—and again he paused. Like an incantation rising from all parts of the room, from the night wind and the moonlight, rolled the divine melody of those words which, lest they should outstare this page we will leave where they lie entombed, not dead, embalmed rather, so fresh is their colour, so sound their breathing—and Orlando, comparing that achievement with those of his ancestors, cried out that they and their deeds were dust and ashes, but this man and his words were immortal.

He soon perceived, however, that the battles which Sir Miles and the rest had waged against armed knights to win a kingdom, were not half so arduous as this which he now undertook to win immortality against the English language. Anyone moderately familiar with the rigours of composition will not need to be told the story in detail; how he wrote and it seemed good; read and it seemed vile; corrected and tore up; cut out; put in; was in ecstasy; in despair; had his good nights and bad mornings; snatched at ideas and lost them; saw his book plain before him and it vanished; acted his people's parts as he ate; mouthed them as he walked; now cried; now laughed; vacillated between this style and that; now preferred the heroic and pompous; next the plain and simple; now the vales of Tempe; then the fields of Kent or Cornwall; and could not decide whether he was the divinest genius or the greatest fool in the world.

It was to settle this last question that he decided, after several months of such feverish labour, to break a solitude of many years and communicate with the outer world. He had a friend in London, one Giles Isham of Norfolk, who, though of gentle birth, was acquainted with writers and could doubtless put him in touch with some member of that blessed, indeed sacred, fraternity. For, to Orlando in the state he was now in, there was a glory about a man who had written a book and had it printed, which outshone all the glories of blood and state. To his imagination it seemed as if even the bodies of those instinct with such divine thoughts must be transfigured. They must have aureoles for hair, incense for breath and roses must grow between their lips—which was certainly not true either of himself or Mr. Dupper. He could think of no greater happiness than to be allowed to sit behind a curtain and hear them talk. Even the imagination of that bold and various discourse made the memory of what he and his courtier friends used to talk about—a dog, a horse, a woman, a game of cards—seem brutish in the extreme. He bethought him with pride that he had always been called a scholar, and sneered at for his love of solitude and books. He had never been apt at pretty phrases. He would stand stock still, blush, and stride like a grenadier in a ladies' drawing-room. He had twice fallen, in sheer abstraction, from his horse. He had broken Lady Winchilsea's fan once while making a rhyme. Eagerly recalling these and other instances of his unfitness for the life of society, an ineffable hope, that all the turbulence of his youth, his clumsiness, his blushes, his long walks, and his love of the country proved that he himself belonged to the sacred race rather than to the noble — was by birth a writer, rather than an aristocrat — possessed him. For the first time since the night of the great flood he was happy.

He now commissioned Mr. Isham of Norfolk to deliver to Mr. Nicholas Greene of Clifford's Inn a document which set forth Orlando's admiration for his works (for Nick Greene was a very famous writer at that time) and his desire to make his acquaintance; which he scarcely dared ask; for he had nothing to offer in return; but if Mr. Nicholas Greene would condescend to visit him, a coach and four would be at the corner of Fetter Lane at whatever hour Mr. Greene chose to appoint, and bring him safely to Orlando's house. One may fill up the phrases which then followed; and figure Orlando's delight when, in no long time, Mr. Greene signified his acceptance of the Noble Lord's invitation; took his place in the coach and was set down in the hall to the south of the main building punctually at seven o'clock on Monday, April the twenty-first.

Many Kings, Queens, and Ambassadors had been received there; Judges had stood there in their ermine. The loveliest ladies of the land had come there; and the sternest warriors. Banners hung there which had been at Flodden and at Agincourt. There were displayed the painted coats of arms with their lions and their leopards and their coronets. There were the long tables where the gold and silver plate was stood; and there the vast fireplaces of wrought Italian marble, where nightly a whole oak tree, with its million leaves and its nests of rook and wren, was burnt to ashes. Nicholas Greene, the poet stood there now, plainly dressed in his slouched hat and black doublet, carrying in one hand a small bag.

That Orlando as he hastened to greet him was slightly disappointed was inevitable. The poet was not above middle height; was of a mean figure; was lean and stooped somewhat, and, stumbling over the mastiff on entering, the dog bit him. Moreover, Orlando for all his knowledge of mankind was puzzled where to place him. There was something about him which belonged neither to servant, squire, or noble. The head with its rounded forehead and beaked nose was fine; but the chin receded. The eyes were brilliant but the lips slobbered. It was the expression of the face as a whole, however, that was disquieting. There was none of that stately composure, which makes the faces of the nobility so pleasing to look at; nor had it anything of the dignified servility of the face of a well-trained domestic; it was a face seamed, puckered, and drawn together. Poet though he was, it seemed as if he were more used to scold than to flatter; to quarrel than to coo; to scramble than to ride; to struggle than to rest; to hate than to love. This, too, was shown by the quickness of his movements; and by something fiery and suspicious in his glance. Orlando was somewhat taken aback. But they went to dinner.

Here, Orlando, who usually took such things for granted, was, for the first time, unaccountably ashamed of the number of his servants and of the splendour of his table. Stranger still, he bethought him with pride—for the thought was generally distasteful—of that great grandmother Moll who had milked the cows. He was about somehow to allude to this humble woman and her milk-pails, when the poet forestalled him by saying that it was odd, seeing how common the name of Greene

was that the family had come over with the Conqueror and
was of the highest nobility in France. Unfortunately, they had
come down in the world and done little more than leave their
name to the royal borough of Greenwich. Further talk of the
same sort, about lost castles, coats of arms, cousins who were
baronets in the north, intermarriage with noble families in the
west, how some Greens spelt the name with an e at the end, and
others without, lasted till the venison was on the table. Then
Orlando contrived to say something of Grandmother Moll and
her cows, and had eased his heart a little of its burden by the
time the wild fowl were before them. But it was not until the
Malmsey was passing freely that Orlando dared mention what
he could not help thinking a more important matter than the
Greens or the cows; that is to say the sacred subject of poetry.
At the first mention of the word, the poet's eyes flashed fire; he
dropped the fine gentleman airs he had worn; thumped his glass
on the table, and launched into one of the longest, most intricate, most passionate, and bitterest stories that Orlando had
ever heard, save from the lips of a jilted woman, about a play of
his; another poet; and a critic. Of the nature of poetry itself, Orlando only gathered that it was harder to sell than prose, and
though the lines were shorter took longer in the writing. So the
talk went on with ramifications interminable, until Orlando ventured to hint that he had himself been so rash as to write — but
here the poet leapt from his chair. A mouse had squeaked in the
wainscot, he said. The truth was, he explained, that his nerves
were in a state where a mouse's squeak upset them for a fortnight. Doubtless the house was full of vermin, but Orlando had
not heard them. The poet then gave Orlando the full story of
his health for the past ten years or so. It had been so bad that
one could only marvel that he still lived. He had had the palsy,
the gout, the ague, the dropsy, and the three sorts of fever in
succession; added to which he had an enlarged heart, a great

spleen, and a diseased liver. But, above all, he had, he told Orlando, sensations in his spine which defied description. There was one knob about the third from the top which burnt like fire; another about the second from the bottom which was cold as ice. Sometimes he woke with a brain like lead; at others it was as if a thousand wax tapers were alight and people were throwing fireworks inside him. He could feel a rose leaf through his mattress, he said; and knew his way almost about London by the feel of the cobbles. Altogether he was a piece of machinery so finely made and curiously put together (here he raised his hand as if unconsciously and indeed, it was of the finest shape imaginable) that it confounded him to think that he had only sold five hundred copies of his poem, but that of course was largely due to the conspiracy against him. All he could say, he concluded, banging his fist upon the table, was that the art of poetry was dead in England.

How that could be with Shakespeare, Marlowe, Ben Jonson, Browne, Donne, all now writing or just having written, Orlando, reeling off the names of his favourite heroes, could not think.

Greene laughed sardonically. Shakespeare, he admitted, had written some scenes that were well enough; but he had taken them chiefly from Marlowe. Marlowe was a likely boy, but what could you say of a lad who died before he was thirty? As for Browne, he was for writing poetry in prose and people soon got tired of such conceits as that. Donne was a mountebank who wrapped up his lack of meaning in hard words. The gulls were taken in; but the style would be out of fashion twelve months hence. As for Ben Jonson—Ben Jonson was a friend of his and he never spoke ill of his friends.

No, he concluded, the great age of literature is past; the great age of literature was the Greek; the Elizabethan was inferior in every respect to the Greek. In such ages men cherished a divine ambition which he might call La Gloire (he pronounced it Glawr, so that Orlando did not at first catch his meaning). Now all young writers were in the pay of the booksellers and poured out any trash that would sell. Shakespeare was the chief offender in this way and Shakespeare was already paying the penalty. Their own age, he said, was marked by precious conceits and wild experiments—neither of which the Greeks would have tolerated for a moment. Much though it hurt him to say it—for he loved literature as he loved his life—he could see no good in the present and had no hope of the future. Here he poured himself out another glass of wine.

Orlando was shocked by these doctrines; yet could not help observing that the critic himself seemed by no means downcast. On the contrary, the more he denounced his own time, the more complacent he became. He could remember, he said, a night at the Cock Tavern in Fleet Street when Kit Marlowe was there and some others. Kit was in high feather, rather drunk, which he easily became, and in a mood to say silly things. He could see him now, brandishing his glass at the company and hiccoughing out, "Stap my vitals, Bill" (this was to Shakespeare), "there's a great wave coming and you're on the top of it," by which he meant, Greene explained, that they were trembling on the verge of a great age in English literature, and that Shakespeare was to be a poet of some importance. Happily for himself, he was killed two nights later in a drunken brawl, and so did not live to see how this prediction turned out. "Poor foolish fellow," said Greene, "to go and say a thing like that. A great age, forsooth—the Elizabethan a great age!"

"So, my dear Lord," he continued, settling himself comfortably in his chair and rubbing the wine-glass between his fingers, "we must make the best of it, cherish the past and honour those writers—there are still a few of 'em—who take antiquity for their model and write, not for pay but for Glawr." (Orlando could have wished him a better accent.) "Glawr," said Greene, "is the spur of noble minds. Had I a pension of three hundred pounds a year paid quarterly, I would live for Glawr alone. I would lie in bed every morning reading Cicero. I would imitate his style so that you couldn't tell the difference between us. That's what I call fine writing," said Greene. "That's what I call Glawr. But it's necessary to have a pension to do it."

By this time Orlando had abandoned all hope of discussing his own work with the poet; but this mattered the less as the talk now got upon the lives and characters of Shakespeare, Ben Jonson, and the rest, all of whom Greene had known intimately and about whom he had a thousand anecdotes of the most amusing kind to tell. Orlando had never laughed so much in his life. These, then, were his gods! Half were drunken and all were amorous. Most of them quarrelled with their wives; not one of them was above a lie or an intrigue of the most paltry kind. Their poetry was scribbled down on the backs of washing bills held to the heads of printer's devils at the street door. Thus Hamlet went to press; thus Lear; thus Othello. No wonder, as Greene said, that these plays show the faults they do. The rest of the time was spent in carousings and junketings in taverns and in beer gardens, when things were said that passed belief for wit, and things were done that made the utmost frolic of the courtiers seem pale in comparison. All this Greene told with a spirit that roused Orlando to the highest pitch of delight. He had a power of mimicry that brought the dead to life, and could say the finest things of books provided they were written three hundred years ago.

So time passed, and Orlando felt for his guest a strange mixture of liking and contempt, of admiration and pity, as well as something too indefinite to be called by any one name, but had something of fear in it and something of fascination. He talked incessantly about himself, yet was such good company that one could listen to the story of his ague for ever. Then he

was so witty; then he was so irreverent; then he made so free
with the names of God and Woman; then he was so full of
queer crafts and had such strange lore in his head; could make
salad in three hundred different ways; knew all that could be
known of the mixing of wines; played half-a-dozen musical in-
struments, and was the first person, and perhaps the last, to
toast cheese in the great Italian fireplace. That he did not know
a geranium from a carnation, an oak from a birch tree, a mastiff from a greyhound, a teg from a ewe, wheat from barley,
plough land from fallow; was ignorant of the rotation of the
crops; thought oranges grew under ground and turnips on trees;
preferred any townscape to any landscape;— all this and much
more amazed Orlando who had never met anybody of his kind
before. Even the maids, who despised him, tittered at his jokes,
and the men-servants, who loathed him, hung about to hear his
stories. Indeed, the house had never been so lively as now that
he was there—all of which gave Orlando a great deal to think
about, and caused him to compare this way of life with the old.
He recalled the sort of talk he had been used to about the King
of Spain's apoplexy or the mating of a bitch; he bethought him
how the day passed between the stables and the dressing closet;
he remembered how the Lords snored over their wine and
hated anybody who woke them up. He bethought him how active and valiant they were in body; how slothful and timid in
mind. Worried by these thoughts, and unable to strike a proper
balance, he came to the conclusion that he had admitted to his
house a plaguey spirit of unrest that would never suffer him to
sleep sound again.

    At the same moment, Nick Greene came to precisely the op-
posite conclusion. Lying in bed of a morning on the softest pil-
lows between the smoothest sheets and looking out of his oriel
window upon turf which, for three centuries had known neither
dandelion nor dock weed, he thought that unless he could some-

how make his escape, he should be smothered alive. Getting up and hearing the pigeons coo, dressing and hearing the fountains fall, he thought that unless he could hear the drays roar upon the cobbles of Fleet Street, he would never write another line. If this goes on much longer, he thought, hearing the footman mend the fire and spread the table with silver dishes next door, I shall fall asleep and (here he gave a prodigious yawn) sleeping die.

So he sought Orlando in his room, and explained that he had not been able to sleep a wink all night because of the silence. (Indeed, the house was surrounded by a park fifteen miles in circumference and a wall ten feet high.) Silence, he said, was of all things the most oppressive to his nerves. He would end his visit, by Orlando's leave, that very morning. Orlando felt some relief at this, yet also a great reluctance to let him go. The house, he thought, would seem dull without him. On parting (for he had never yet liked to mention the subject), he had the temerity to press his play upon the Death of Hercules upon the poet and ask his opinion of it. The poet took it; muttered something about Glawr and Cicero, which Orlando cut short by promising to pay the pension quarterly; whereupon Greene, with many protestations of affection, jumped into the coach and was gone.

The great hall had never seemed so large, so splendid, or so empty as the chariot rolled away. Orlando knew that he would never have the heart to make toasted cheese in the Italian fireplace again. He would never have the wit to crack jokes about Italian pictures; never have the skill to mix punch as it should be mixed; a thousand good quips and cranks would be lost to him. Yet what a relief to be out of the sound of that querulous voice, what a luxury to be alone once more, so he could not help reflecting, as he unloosed the mastiff which had been tied up these six weeks because it never saw the poet without biting him.

Nick Greene was set down at the corner of Fetter Lane that same afternoon, and found things going on much as he had left them. Mrs. Greene, that is to say, was giving birth to a baby in one room; Tom Fletcher was drinking gin in another. Books were tumbled all about the floor; dinner—such as it was—was set on a dressing-table where the children had been making mud pies. But this, Greene felt, was the atmosphere for writing; here he could write and write he did. The subject was made for him. A noble Lord at home. A visit to a Nobleman in the country— his new poem was to have some such title as that. Seizing the pen with which his little boy was tickling the cat's ears, and dipping it in the egg-cup which served for inkpot, Greene dashed off a very spirited satire there and then. It was so done to a turn that no one could doubt that the young Lord who was roasted was Orlando; his most private sayings and doings, his enthusiasms and follies, down to the very colour of his hair and the foreign way he had of rolling his r's were there to the life. And if there had been any doubt about it, Greene clinched the matter by introducing, with scarcely any disguise, passages from that aristocratic tragedy, the Death of Hercules, which he found as he expected, wordy and bombastic in the extreme.

The pamphlet, which ran at once into several editions, and paid the expenses of Mrs. Greene's tenth lying-in, was soon sent by friends who take care of such matters to Orlando himself. When he had read it, which he did with deadly composure from start to finish, he rang for the footman; delivered the document to him at the end of a pair of tongs; bade him drop it in the filthiest heart of the foulest midden on the estate. Then, when the man was turning to go he stopped him, "Take the swiftest horse in the stable," he said, "ride for dear life to Harwich. There embark upon a ship which you will find bound for Norway. Buy for me from the King's own kennels, the finest elk hounds of the Royal strain, male and female. Bring them back without delay. For," he murmured, scarcely above his breath as he turned to his books, "I have done with men."

The footman, who was perfectly trained in his duties, bowed and disappeared. He fulfilled his task so efficiently that he was back that day three weeks, leading in his hand a leash of the finest elk hounds, one of whom, a female, gave birth that very night under the dinner-table to a litter of eight fine puppies. Orlando had them brought to his bed-chamber.

"For," he said, patting the little brutes on the head, "I have done with men."

Nevertheless, he paid the pension quarterly.

THUS, AT THE age of thirty, or thereabouts, this young Nobleman had not only had every experience that life has to offer, but had seen the worthlessness of them all. Love and ambition, women and poets were all equally vain. Literature was a farce. The night after reading Greene's Visit to a Nobleman in the Country, he burnt in a great conflagration fifty-seven poetical works, only retaining "The Oak Tree," which was his boyish dream and very short. Two things alone remained to him in which he now put any trust; dogs and nature; an elkhound and a rose bush. The world, in all its variety, life in all its complexity had shrunk to that. A dog and a bush were the whole of it. So feeling quit of a vast mountain of illusion, and very naked in consequence, he called his hounds to him and strode through the Park.

So long had he been secluded, writing and reading, that he had half forgotten the amenities of nature, which in June can be great. When he reached that high mound whence, on fine days half of England with a slice of Wales and Scotland thrown in can be seen he flung himself under his favourite oak tree and felt that if he need never speak to another man or woman so long as he lived; if his dogs did not develop the faculty of speech; if he never met a poet or a Princess again, he might make out what years remained to him in tolerable content.

Here he came then, day after day, week after week, month after month, year after year. He saw the beech trees turn golden and the young ferns unfurl; he saw the moon sickle and then circular; he saw—but probably the reader can imagine the passage which should follow and how every tree and plant in the neighbourhood is described first green, then golden; how moons rise and suns set; how spring follows winter and autumn summer; how night succeeds day and day night; how there is first a storm and then fine weather; how things remain much as they are for two or three hundred years or so, except for a little dust and a few cobwebs which one old woman can sweep up in half an hour; a conclusion which, one cannot help feeling, might have been reached more quickly by the simple statement that "Time passed" (here the exact amount could be indicated in brackets) and nothing whatever happened.

But Time, unfortunately, though it makes animals and vegetables bloom and fade with amazing punctuality has no such simple effect upon the mind of man. The mind of man, moreover, works with equal strangeness upon the body of time. An hour, once it lodges in the queer element of the human spirit, may be stretched to fifty or a hundred times its clock length; on the other hand, an hour may be accurately represented on the timepiece of the mind by one second. This extraordinary discrepancy between time on the clock and time in the mind is less known than it should be and deserves fuller investigation. But the biographer, whose interests are, as we have said, highly restricted, must confine himself to one simple statement: when a man has reached the age of thirty, as Orlando now had, time when he is thinking becomes inordinately long; time when he is doing becomes inordinately short. Thus Orlando gave his orders and did the business of his vast estates in a flash; but directly he was alone on the mound under the oak tree, the seconds began to round and fill until it seemed as if they would never fall. They filled themselves, moreover, with the strangest variety of objects. For not only did he find himself confronted by problems which have puzzled the wisest of men, such as What is love? What friendship? What truth? but directly he came to think about them, his whole past, which seemed to him of extreme length and variety, rushed into the falling second, swelled it a dozen times its natural size, coloured it all the tints of the rainbow and filled it with all the odds and ends in the universe.

In such thinking (or by whatever name it should be called) he spent months and years of his life. It would be no exaggeration to say that he would go out after breakfast a man of thirty and come home to dinner a man of fifty-five at least. Some weeks added a century to his age, others no more than three seconds at most. Altogether, the task of estimating the length of human life (of the animals' we presume not to speak) is beyond our capacity, for directly we say that it is ages long, we are reminded that it is briefer than the fall of a rose leaf to the ground. Of the two forces which alternately, and what is more confusing still, at the same moment, dominate our unfortunate numbskulls—brevity and diuturnity—Orlando was sometimes under the influence of the elephant-footed deity, then of the gnat-winged fly. Life seemed to him of prodigious length. Yet even so, it went like a flash. But even when it stretched longest and the moments swelled biggest and he seemed to wander alone in deserts of vast eternity, there was no time for the smoothing out and deciphering of those thickly scored parchments which thirty years among men and women had rolled tight in his heart and brain. Long before he had done thinking about Love (the oak tree had put forth its leaves and shaken them to the ground a dozen times in the process) Ambition would jostle it off the field, to be replaced by Friendship or Literature. And as the first question had not been settled—What is Love?—back it would come at the least provocation or none, and hustle Books or Metaphors of What one lives for into the margin, there to wait till they saw their chance to rush into the field again. What made the process still longer was that it was profusely illustrated, not only with pictures, as that of old Queen Elizabeth, laid on her tapestry couch in rose-coloured brocade with an ivory snuff-box in her hand and a gold-hilted sword by her side, but with scents—she was strongly perfumed—and with sounds; the stags were barking in Richmond Park that winter's day. And so, the thought of love would be all ambered over with snow and winter; with log fires burning; with Russian women, gold swords and the bark of stags; with old King James' slobbering and fireworks and sacks of treasure in the holds of Elizabethan sailing ships. Every single thing, once he tried to dislodge it from its place in his mind, he found thus cumbered with other matter like the lump of glass which, after a year at the bottom of the sea, is grown about with bones and dragon-flies, and coins and the tresses of drowned women.

"Another metaphor, by Jupiter!" he would exclaim as he said this (which will show the disorderly and circuitous way in which his mind worked and explain why the oak tree flowered and faded so often before he came to any conclusion about Love). "And what's the point of it?" he would ask himself. "Why not say simply in so many words——" and then he would try to think for half an hour—or was it two years and a half?—how to say simply in so many words what love is. "A figure like that is manifestly untruthful," he argued, "for no dragon-fly, un-less under very exceptional circumstances, could live at the bot-tom of the sea. And if literature is not the Bride and Bedfellow of Truth, what is she? Confound it all," he cried, "why say Bed-fellow when one's already said Bride? Why not simply say what one means and leave it?"

So then he tried saying the grass is green and the sky is blue and so to propitiate the austere spirit of poetry whom still, though at a great distance, he could not help reverencing. "The sky is blue," he said, "the grass is green." Looking up, he saw that, on the contrary, the sky is like the veils which a thousand Madonnas have let fall from their hair; and the grass fleets and darkens like a flight of girls fleeing the embraces of hairy satyrs from enchanted woods. "Upon my word," he said (for he had fallen into the bad habit of speaking aloud), "I don't see that one's more true than another. Both are utterly false." And he despaired of being able to solve the problem of what poetry is and what truth is and fell into a deep dejection.

And here we may profit by a pause in his soliloquy to reflect how odd it was to see Orlando stretched there on his elbow on a June day and to reflect that this fine fellow with all his faculties about him and a healthy body, witness cheeks and limbs—a man who never thought twice about heading a charge or fighting a duel—should be so subject to the lethargy of thought, and rendered so susceptible by it, that when it came to a question of poetry, or his own competence in it, he was as shy as a little girl behind her mother's cottage door. In our belief, Greene's ridicule of his tragedy hurt him as much as the Princess' ridicule of his love. But to return—

Orlando went on thinking. He kept looking at the grass and at the sky and trying to bethink him what a true poet, who has his verses published in London, would say about them. Memory, meanwhile (whose habits have already been described) kept steady before his eyes the face of Nicholas Greene, as if that sardonic loose-lipped man, treacherous as he had proved himself, were the Muse in person, and it was to him that Orlando must do homage. So Orlando, that summer morning, offered him a variety of phrases, some plain, others figured, and Nick Greene kept shaking his head and sneering and muttering something about Glawr and Cicero and the death of poetry in our time. At length, starting to his feet (it was now winter and very cold) Orlando swore one of the most remarkable oaths of his lifetime, for it bound him to a servitude than which none is stricter. "I'll be blasted," he said, "if I ever write another word, or try to write another word to please Nick Greene or the Muse. Bad, good, or indifferent, I'll write, from this day forward, to please myself"; and here he made as if he were tearing a whole budget of papers across and tossing them in the face of that sneering loose-lipped man. Upon which, as a cur ducks if you stoop to shy a stone at him, Memory ducked her effigy of Nick Greene out of sight; and substituted for it—nothing whatever.

But Orlando, all the same, went on thinking. He had indeed much to think of. For when he tore the parchment across, he tore, in one rending, the scrolloping, emblazoned scroll which he had made out in his own favour in the solitude of his room appointing himself, as the King appoints Ambassadors, the first poet of his race, the first writer of his age, conferring eternal immortality upon his soul and granting his body a grave among laurels and the intangible banners of a people's reverence perpetually. Eloquent as this all was, he now tore it up and threw it in the dust-bin. "Fame," he said, "is like" (and since there was no Nick Greene to stop him, he went on to revel in images of which we will choose only one or two of the quietest) "a braided coat, which hampers the limbs; a jacket of silver which curbs the heart; a painted shield which covers a scarecrow," etc., etc. The pith of his phrases was that while fame impedes and constricts, obscurity wraps about a man like a mist; obscurity is dark, ample and free; obscurity lets the mind take its way unimpeded. Over the obscure man is poured the merciful suffusion of darkness. None knows where he goes or comes. He may seek the truth and speak it; he alone is free; he alone is truthful; he alone is at peace. And so he sank into a quiet mood, under the oak tree, the hardness of whose roots, exposed above the ground, seemed to him rather comfortable than otherwise.

Sunk for a long time in profound thoughts as to the value of obscurity, and the delight of having no name, but being like a wave which returns to the deep body of the sea; thinking how obscurity rids the mind of the irk of envy and spite; how it sets running in the veins the free waters of generosity and magna-nimity; and allows giving and taking without thanks offered or praise given; which must have been the way of all great poets, he supposed (though his knowledge of Greek was not enough to bear him out) for, he thought, Shakespeare must have writ-ten like that, and the church builders built like that, anonymously, needing no thanking or naming, but only their work in the day-time and a little ale perhaps at night—"What an admirable life this is," he thought, stretching his limbs out under the oak tree. "And why not enjoy it this very moment?" The thought struck him like a bullet. Ambition dropped like a plummet. Rid of the heart-burn of rejected love, and of vanity rebuked, and all the other stings and pricks which the nettle-bed of life had burnt upon him when ambitious of fame, but could no longer inflict upon one careless of glory, he opened his eyes, which had been wide open all the time, but had seen only thoughts, and saw, lying in the hollow beneath him, his house.

There it lay in the early sunshine of spring. It looked a town rather than a house, but a town built, not hither and thither, as this man wished or that, but circumspectly, by a single architect with one idea in his head. Courts and buildings, grey, red, plum colour, lay orderly and symmetrical; the courts were some of them oblong and some square; in this was a fountain; in that a statue; the buildings were some of them low, some pointed; here was a chapel, there a belfry; spaces of the greenest grass lay in between and clumps of cedar trees and beds of bright flowers;

all were clasped—yet so well set out was it that it seemed that every part had room to spread itself fittingly—by the roll of a massive wall; while smoke from innumerable chimneys curled perpetually into the air. This vast, yet ordered building, which could house a thousand men and perhaps two thousand horses was built, Orlando thought, by workmen whose names are unknown. Here, have lived for more centuries than I can count, the obscure generations of my own obscure family. Not one of these Richards, Johns, Annes, Elizabeths has left a token of himself behind him, yet all, working together with their spades and their needles, their love-making and their child-bearing, have left this.

Never had the house looked more noble and humane.

Why, then, had he wished to raise himself above them? For it seemed vain and arrogant in the extreme to try to better that anonymous work of creation; the labours of those vanished hands. Better was it to go unknown and leave behind you an arch, a potting shed, a wall where peaches ripen, than to burn like a meteor and leave no dust. For after all, he said, kindling as he looked at the great house on the greensward below, the unknown lords and ladies who lived there never forgot to set aside something for those who come after; for the roof that will leak; for the tree that will fall. There was always a warm corner for the old shepherd in the kitchen; always food for the hungry; always their goblets were polished, though they lay sick; and the windows were lit though they were dying. Lords though they were, they were content to go down into obscurity with the mole-catcher and the stone-mason. Obscure noblemen, forgotten builders—thus he apostrophised them with a warmth that entirely gainsaid such critics as called him cold, indifferent, slothful (the truth being that a quality often lies just on the other side of the wall from where we seek it)—thus he apostrophised his house and race in terms of the most moving eloquence; but when it came to the peroration—and what is eloquence that lacks a peroration?—he fumbled. He would have liked to have ended with a flourish to the effect that he would follow in their footsteps and add another stone to their building. Since, however, the building already covered nine acres, to add even a single stone seemed superfluous. Could one mention furniture in a peroration? Could one speak of chairs and tables and mats to lie beside people's beds? For whatever the peroration wanted that was what the house stood in need of. Leaving his speech unfinished for the moment, he strode down hill again resolved henceforward to devote himself to the furnishing of the mansion. The news—that she was to attend him instantly—brought tears to the eyes of good old Mrs. Grimsditch, now grown somewhat old. Together they perambulated the house.

The towel horse in the King's bedroom ("and that was King Jamie, my Lord," she said, hinting that it was many a day since a King had slept under their roof; but the odious Parliament days were over and there was now a Crown in England again) lacked a leg; there were no stands to the ewers in the little closet leading into the waiting room of the Duchess's page; Mr. Greene had made a stain on the carpet with his nasty pipe smoking, which she and Judy, for all their scrubbing, had never been able to wash out. Indeed, when Orlando came to reckon up the matter of furnishing with rosewood chairs and cedar wood cabinets, with silver basins, china bowls, and Persian carpets every one of the three hundred and sixty-five bedrooms which the house contained, he saw that it would be no light one; and if some thousands of pounds of his estate remained over, these would do little more than hang a few galleries with tapestry, set the dining hall with fine, carved chairs and provide mirrors of solid silver and chairs of the same metal (for which he had an inordinate passion) for the furnishing of the royal bed chambers.

He now set to work in earnest, as we can prove beyond a doubt if we look at his ledgers. Let us glance at an inventory of what he bought at this time, with the expenses totted up in the margin—but these we omit.

"To fifty pairs of Spanish blankets, ditto curtains of crimson
        and white taffeta; the valence to them of white satin em-
        broidered with crimson and white silk. . . .
"To seventy yellow satin chairs and sixty stools, suitable with
        their buckram covers to them all. . . .
"To sixty-seven walnut tree tables. . . .
"To seventeen dozen boxes containing each dozen five dozen
        of Venice glasses. . . .
"To one hundred and two mats, each thirty yards long. . . .
"To ninety-seven cushions of crimson damask laid with silver
        parchment lace and footstools of cloth of tissue and chairs
        suitable. . . .
"To fifty branches for a dozen lights apiece. . . ."

Already—it is an effect lists have upon us—we are beginning to yawn. But if we stop, it is only that the catalogue is tedious, not that it is finished. There are twenty-nine pages more
of it and the total sum disbursed ran into many thousands—
that is to say millions of our money. And if his day was spent
like this, at night again, Lord Orlando might be found reckoning out what it would cost to level a million molehills, if the men
were paid tenpence an hour; and again, how many hundred-
weight of nails at 5½d a gill were needed to repair the fence
round the park, which was fifteen miles in circumference. And
so on and so on.

The tale, we say, is tedious, for one cupboard is much like
another, and one molehill not much different from a million.
Some pleasant journeys it cost him; and some fine adventures.
As, for instance, when he set a whole city of blind women near
Bruges to stitch hangings for a silver canopied bed; and the

story of his adventure with a Moor in Venice of whom he bought (but only at the sword's point) his lacquered cabinet, might, in other hands, prove worth the telling. Nor did the work lack variety; for here would come, drawn by teams from Sussex, great trees, to be sawn across and laid along the gallery for flooring; and then a great chest from Persia, stuffed with wool and saw-dust, from which, at last, he would take a single plate, or one topaz ring.

At length, however, there was no room in the galleries for another table; no room on the tables for another cabinet; no room in the cabinet for another rose-bowl; no room in the bowl for another handful of potpourri; there was no room for anything anywhere; in short the house was furnished. In the garden snowdrops, crocuses, hyacinths, magnolias, roses, lilies, asters, the dahlia in all its varieties, pear trees and apple trees and cherry trees and mulberry trees with an enormous quantity of rare and flowering shrubs, of trees evergreen and perennial, grew so thick on each other's roots that there was no plot of earth without its bloom, and no stretch of sward without its shade. In addition, he had imported wild fowl with gay plumage; and two Malay bears, the surliness of whose manners concealed, he was certain, trusty hearts.

All now was ready; and when it was evening and the innumerable silver sconces were lit and the light airs which for ever moved about the galleries stirred the blue and green arras, so that it looked as if the huntsmen were riding and Daphne were flying; when the silver shone and lacquer glowed and wood kindled; when the carved chairs held their arms out and dolphins swam upon the walls with mermaids on their backs; when all this and much more than all this was complete and to his liking, Orlando walked through the house with his elk hounds following and felt content. He had matter now, he thought, to fill out his peroration. Perhaps it would be well to begin the speech all over again. Yet, as he paraded the galleries he felt that still something was lacking. Chairs and tables, however richly gilt and carved, sofas, resting on lions' paws with swans' necks curving under them, beds even of the softest swansdown are not by themselves enough. People sitting in them, people lying in them improve them amazingly. Accordingly Orlando now began a series of very splendid entertainments to the nobility and gentry of the neighbourhood. The three hundred and sixty-five bedrooms were full for a month at a time. Guests jostled each other on the fifty-two staircases. Three hundred servants bustled about the pantries. Banquets took place almost nightly. Thus, in a very few years, Orlando had worn the nap off his velvet, and spent the half of his fortune; but he had earned the good opinion of his neighbours, held a score of offices in the county, and was annually presented with perhaps a dozen volumes dedicated to his Lordship in rather fulsome terms by grateful poets. For though he was careful not to consort with writers at that time and kept himself always aloof from ladies of foreign blood, still, he was excessively generous both to women and to poets, and both adored him.

But when the feasting was at its height and his guests were at their revels, he was apt to take himself off to his private room alone. There when the door was shut, and he was certain of privacy, he would have out an old writing book, stitched together with silk stolen from his mother's workbox, and labelled in a round schoolboy hand, "The Oak Tree, A Poem." In this he would write till midnight chimed and long after. But as he scratched out as many lines as he wrote in, the sum of them was often, at the end of the year, rather less than at the beginning, and it looked as if in the process of writing the poem would be completely unwritten. For it is for the historian of letters to remark that he had changed his style amazingly. His floridity was chastened; his abundance curbed; the age of prose was congealing those warm fountains. The very landscape outside was less stuck about with garlands and the briars themselves were less thorned and intricate. Perhaps the senses were a little duller and honey and cream less seductive to the palate. Also that the streets were better drained and the houses better lit had its effect upon the style, it cannot be doubted.

One day he was adding a line or two with enormous labour to "The Oak Tree, A Poem" when a shadow crossed the tail of his eye. It was no shadow, he soon saw, but the figure of a very tall lady in riding hood and mantle crossing the quadrangle on which his room looked out. As this was the most private of the courts, and the lady was a stranger to him, Orlando marvelled how she had got there. Three days later the same apparition appeared again; and on Wednesday noon appeared once more. This time, Orlando was determined to follow her, nor apparently was she afraid to be found, for she slackened her steps as he came up and looked him full in the face. Any other woman thus caught in a Lord's private grounds would have been afraid; any other woman with that face, headdress, and aspect would have thrown her mantilla across her shoulders to hide it. For this lady resembled nothing so much as a hare; a hare startled, but obdurate; a hare whose timidity is overcome by an immense and foolish audacity; a hare that sits upright and glowers at its pursuer with great, bulging eyes; with ears erect but quivering, with nose, pointed, but twitching. This hare, moreover, was six feet high and wore a headdress into the bargain of some antiquated kind which made her look still taller. Thus confronted, she stared at Orlando with a stare in which timidity and audacity were most strangely combined.

First, she asked him, with a proper, but somewhat clumsy curtsey, to forgive her her intrusion. Then, rising to her full height again, which must have been something over six feet two, she went on to say—but with such a cackle of nervous laughter, so much tee-heeing and haw-hawing that Orlando thought she must have escaped from a lunatic asylum—that she was the Archduchess Harriet Griselda of Finster-Aarhorn and Scandop-Boom in the Roumanian territory. She desired above all things to make his acquaintance, she said. She had taken lodging over a baker's shop at the Park Gates. She had seen his picture and it was the image of a sister of hers who was—here she guffawed—long since dead. She was visiting the English Court. The Queen was her cousin. The King was a very good fellow but seldom went to bed sober. Here she tee-heed and hawhawed again. In short, there was nothing for it but to ask her in and give her a glass of wine.

Indoors, her manners regained the hauteur natural to a Roumanian Archduchess; and had she not shown a knowledge of wines rare in a lady, and made some observations upon firearms and the customs of sportsmen in her country, which were sensible enough, the talk would have lacked spontaneity. Jumping to her feet at last, she announced that she would call the following day, swept another prodigious curtsey and departed. The following day, Orlando rode out. The next, he turned his back; on the third he drew his curtain. On the fourth it rained, and as he could not keep a lady in the wet, nor was altogether averse to company, he invited her in and asked her opinion whether a suit of armour, which belonged to an ancestor of his, was the work of Jacobi or of Topp. He inclined to Topp. She held another opinion—it matters very little which. But it is of some importance to the course of our story that, in illustrating her argument, which had to do with the working of the tie pieces, the Archduchess Harriet took the golden shin case and fitted it to Orlando's leg.

That he had a pair of the shapeliest legs that any Nobleman has ever stood upright upon has already been said.

The Archduchess Harriet

Perhaps something in the way she fastened the ankle
buckle; or her stooping posture; or Orlando's long seclusion; or
the natural sympathy which is between the sexes; or the Bur-
gundy; or the fire—any of these causes may have been to
blame; for certainly blame there is on one side or another, when
a Nobleman of Orlando's breeding, entertaining a lady in his
house, and she his elder by many years, with a face a yard long
and staring eyes, dressed somewhat ridiculously too, in a mantle
and riding cloak though the season was warm—blame there is
when such a Nobleman is so suddenly and violently overcome
by passion of some sort that he has to leave the room.

But what sort of passion, it may well be asked, could this be?
And the answer is double-faced as Love herself. For Love—but
leaving Love out of the argument for a moment, the actual event
was this:

When the Archduchess Harriet Griselda stooped to fasten
the buckle, Orlando heard, suddenly and unaccountably, far off
the beating of Love's wings. The distant stir of that soft plumage
roused in him a thousand memories of rushing waters, of loveliness in the snow and faithlessness in the flood; and the sound
came nearer; and he blushed and trembled; and he was moved
as he had thought never to be moved again; and he was ready
to raise his hands and let the bird of beauty alight upon his
shoulders, when—horror!—a creaking sound like that the crows
make tumbling over the trees began to reverberate; the air seemed
dark with coarse black wings; voices croaked; bits of straw, twigs,
and feathers dropped; and there pitched down upon his shoulders the heaviest and foulest of the birds; which is the vulture.
Thus he rushed from the room and sent the footman to see the
Archduchess Harriet to her carriage.

For Love, to which we may now return, has two faces; one
white, the other black; two bodies; one smooth, the other hairy.
It has two hands, two feet, two tails, two, indeed, of every mem-

ber and each one is the exact opposite of the other. Yet, so strictly are they joined together that you cannot separate them. In this case, Orlando's love began her flight towards him with her white face turned, and her smooth and lovely body outwards. Nearer and nearer she came wafting before her airs of pure delight. All of a sudden (at the sight of the Archduchess presumably) she wheeled about, turned the other way round; showed herself black, hairy, brutish; and it was Lust the vulture, not Love, the Bird of Paradise that flopped, foully and disgustingly, upon his shoulders. Hence he ran; hence he fetched the footman.

But the harpy is not so easily banished as all that. Not only did the Archduchess continue to lodge at the baker's, but Orlando was haunted every day and night by phantoms of the foulest kind. Vainly, it seemed, had he furnished his house with silver and hung the walls with arras, when at any moment a dung-bedraggled fowl could settle upon his writing table. There she was, flopping about among the chairs; he saw her waddling ungracefully across the galleries. Now, she perched, top-heavy upon a fire screen. When he chased her out, back she came and pecked at the glass till she broke it.

Thus realising that his home was uninhabitable, and that steps must be taken to end the matter instantly, he did what any other young man would have done in his place, and asked King Charles to send him as Ambassador Extraordinary to Constantinople. The King was walking in Whitehall. Nell Gwyn was on his arm. She was pelting him with hazel nuts. 'Twas a thousand pities, that amorous lady sighed, that such a pair of legs should leave the country. Howbeit, the Fates were hard; she could do no more than toss one kiss over her shoulder before Orlando sailed.

CHAPTER THREE

IT IS, INDEED, highly unfortunate, and much to be regretted that at this stage of Orlando's career, when he played a most important part in the public life of his country, we have least information to go upon. We know that he discharged his duties to admiration—witness his Bath and his Dukedom. We know that he had a finger in some of the most delicate negotiations between King Charles and the Turks—to that, treaties in the vault of the Record Office bear testimony. But the revolution which broke out during his period of office, and the fire which followed, have so damaged or destroyed all those papers from which any trustworthy record could be drawn, that what we can give is lamentably incomplete. Often the paper was scorched a deep brown in the middle of the most important sentence. Just when we thought to elucidate a secret that has puzzled historians for a hundred years, there was a hole in the manuscript big enough to put your finger through. We have done our best to piece out a meagre summary from the charred fragments that remain; but often it has been necessary to speculate, to surmise, and even to make use of the imagination.

Orlando's day was passed, it would seem, somewhat in this fashion. About seven, he would rise, wrap himself in a long Turkish cloak, light a cheroot, and lean his elbows on the parapet. Thus he would stand, gazing at the city beneath him, apparently entranced. At this hour the mist would lie so thick that the domes of Santa Sofia and the rest would seem to be afloat; gradually the mist would uncover them; the bubbles would be seen to be firmly fixed; there would be the river; there the Galata Bridge; there the green turbanned pilgrims without eyes or noses, begging alms; there the pariah dogs picking up offal; there the shawled women; there the innumerable donkeys; there men on horses carrying long poles. Soon, the whole town would be astir with the cracking of whips, the beating of gongs, cryings to prayer, lashing of mules, and rattle of brass-bound wheels, while sour odours, made from bread fermenting and incense, and spice, rose even to the heights of Pera itself and seemed the very breath of the strident and multicoloured and barbaric population.

Nothing, he reflected, gazing at the view which was now sparkling in the sun, could well be less like the counties of Surrey and Kent or the towns of London and Tunbridge Wells. To the right and left rose in bald and stony prominence the inhospitable Asian mountains, to which the arid castle of a robber chief or two might hang; but parsonage there was none, nor manor house, nor cottage, nor oak, elm, violet, ivy, or wild eglantine. There were no hedges for ferns to grow on, and no fields for sheep to graze. The houses were bare and bald as eggshells. That he, who was English root and fibre, should yet exult to the depths of his heart in this wild panorama, and gaze and gaze at those passes and far heights, planning journeys there alone on foot where only the goat and shepherd had gone before; should feel a passion of affection for the bright, unseasonable flowers, love the unkempt, pariah dogs beyond even his elk hounds at home, and snuff the acrid, sharp smell of the streets eagerly into his nostrils, surprised him. He wondered if, in the season of the Crusades, one of his ancestors had taken up with a Circassian peasant woman; thought it possible; fancied a certain darkness in his complexion; and, going indoors again, withdrew to his bath.

An hour later, properly scented, curled, and anointed he would receive visits from secretaries and other high officials carrying, one after another, red boxes which yielded only to his own golden key. Within were papers of the highest importance, of which only fragments, here a flourish, there a seal firmly attached to a piece of burnt silk, now remain. Of their contents then, we cannot speak, but can only testify that Orlando was kept busy, what with his wax and seals, his various coloured ribbons which had to be diversely attached, his engrossing of titles and making of flourishes round capital letters, till luncheon came — a splendid meal of perhaps thirty courses.

After luncheon, lackeys announced that his coach and six was at the door and he went, preceded by purple Janissaries running on foot and waving great ostrich feather fans above their heads, to call upon the other ambassadors and dignitaries of state. The ceremony was always the same. On reaching the courtyard, the Janissaries struck with their fans upon the main portal, which immediately flew open revealing a large chamber, splendidly furnished. Here were seated two figures, generally of the opposite sexes. Profound bows and curtseys were exchanged. In the first room, it was permissible only to mention the weather. Having said that it was fine or wet, hot or cold, the Ambassador then passed on to the next chamber, where again, two figures rose to greet him. Here it was only permissible to compare Constantinople as a place of residence with London; and the Ambassador naturally said that he preferred Constantinople, and his hosts naturally said, though they had not seen it, that they preferred London. In the next chamber, King Charles's and the Sultan's healths had to be discussed at some length. In the next were discussed the Ambassador's health and that of his host's wife, but more briefly. In the next the Ambassador compli-

mented his host upon his furniture, and the host complimented
the Ambassador upon his dress. In the next, sweet meats were
offered, the host deploring their badness, the Ambassador ex-
tolling their goodness. The ceremony ended at length with the
smoking of a hookah and the drinking of a glass of coffee; but
though the motions of smoking and drinking were gone through
punctiliously there was neither tobacco in the pipe nor coffee in
the glass, as, had either smoke or drink been real, the human
frame would have sunk beneath the surfeit. For, no sooner had
the Ambassador despatched one such visit, than another had to
be undertaken. The same ceremonies were gone through in precisely the same order six or seven times over at the houses of
the other great officials, so that it was often late at night before
the Ambassador reached home. Though Orlando performed
these tasks to admiration and never denied that they are, perhaps, the most important part of a diplomatist's duties, he was
undoubtedly fatigued by them, and often depressed to such a
pitch of gloom that he preferred to take his dinner alone with
his dogs. To them, indeed he might be heard talking in his own
tongue. And sometimes, it is said, he would pass out of his own
gates late at night so disguised that the sentries did not know
him. Then he would mingle with the crowd on the Galata
Bridge; or stroll through the bazaars; or throw aside his shoes
and join the worshippers in the Mosques. Once, when it was
given out that he was ill of a fever, shepherds, bringing their
goats to market, reported that they had met an English Lord
on the mountain top and heard him praying to his God. This
was thought to be Orlando himself, and his prayer was, no
doubt, a poem said aloud, for it was known that he still carried
about with him, in the bosom of his cloak, a much-scored manuscript; and servants, listening at the door, heard the Ambassador chanting something in an odd, sing-song voice when he
was alone.

It is with fragments such as these that we must do our best
to make up a picture of Orlando's life and character at this time.
There exist, even to this day, rumours, legends, anecdotes of a
floating and unauthenticated kind about Orlando's life in Constantinople (we have quoted but a few of them)—which go to
prove that he possessed, now that he was in the prime of life,
the power to stir the fancy and rivet the eye which will keep a
memory green long after all that more durable qualities can do
to preserve it is forgotten. The power is a mysterious one compounded of beauty, birth, and some rarer gift, which we may call
glamour and have done with it. "A million candles," as Sasha
had said, burnt in him without his being at the trouble of lighting a single one. He moved like a stag, without any need to think
about his legs. He spoke in his ordinary voice and echo beat a
silver gong. Hence rumours gathered round him. He became
the adored of many women and some men. It was not necessary that they should speak to him or even that they should see
him; they conjured him up before them especially when the
scenery was romantic, or the sun was setting, the figure of a
noble gentleman in silk stockings. Upon the poor and unedu-
cated, he had the same power as upon the rich. Shepherds, gipsies, donkey drivers, still sing songs about the English Lord
"who dropped his emeralds in the well," which undoubtedly
refer to Orlando, who once it seems tore his jewels from him in
a moment of rage or intoxication and flung them in a fountain;
whence they were fished by a page boy. But this romantic power,
it is well known, is often associated with a nature of extreme re-
serve. Orlando seems to have made no friends. As far as is
known, he formed no attachments. A certain great lady came all
the way from England in order to be near him, and pestered
him with her attentions, but he continued to discharge his duties so indefatigably that he had not been Ambassador at the
Horn more than two years and a half before King Charles sig-

nified his intention of raising him to the highest rank in the peerage. The envious said that this was Nell Gwyn's tribute to the memory of a leg. But, as she had seen him once only, and was then busily engaged in pelting her royal master with nutshells, it is likely that it was his merits that won him his Dukedom, not his calves.

Here we must pause, for we have reached a moment of great significance in his career. For the conferring of the Dukedom was the occasion of a very famous, and indeed, much disputed incident, which we must now describe, picking our way among burnt papers and little bits of tape as best we may. It was at the end of the great fast of Ramadan that the Order of the Bath and the patent of nobility arrived in a frigate commanded by Sir Adrian Scrope; and Orlando made this the occasion for an entertainment more splendid than any that has been known before or since in Constantinople. The night was fine; the crowd immense, and the windows of the Embassy brilliantly illuminated. Again, details are lacking, for the fire had its way with all such records, and has left only tantalising fragments which leave the most important points obscure. From the diary of John Fenner Brigge, however, an English naval officer, who was among the guests, we gather that people of all nationalities "were packed like herrings in a barrel" in the courtyard. The crowd pressed so unpleasantly close that Brigge soon climbed into a Judas tree, the better to observe the proceedings. The rumour had got about among the natives (and here is additional proof of Orlando's mysterious power over the imagination) that some kind of miracle was to be performed. "Thus," writes Brigge (but his manuscript is full of burns and holes, some sentences being quite illegible) "when the rockets began to soar into the air, there was considerable uneasiness among us lest the native population . . . fraught with unpleasant consequences to all, . . . English ladies in the company, . . . I own that my hand went to my cutlass. Happily," he continues in his somewhat long-winded style, "these fears seemed, for the moment, groundless and, observing the demeanour of the natives, . . . I came to the conclusion that this demonstration of our skill in the art of pyrotechny was valuable, . . . because it impressed upon them . . . superiority of the British. . . . Indeed, the sight was one of indescribable magnificence. I found myself alternately praising the Lord that he had permitted . . . and wishing that my poor, dear mother. . . . By the Ambassador's orders, the long windows, which are so imposing a feature of Eastern architecture, for though ignorant in many ways . . . were thrown wide; and within, we could see a tableau vivant or theatrical display in which English ladies and gentlemen . . . represented a masque the work of one. . . . The words were inaudible, but the sight of so many of our countrymen and women, dressed with the highest elegance and distinction . . . moved me to emotions of which I am certainly not ashamed, though unable. . . . I was intent upon observing the astonishing conduct of Lady——— which was of a nature to fasten the eyes of all upon her, and to bring discredit upon her sex and country, when"—unfortunately a branch of the Judas tree broke, Lieutenant Brigge fell to the ground, and the rest of the entry records only his gratitude to Providence (who plays a very large part in the diary) and the exact nature of his injuries.

Happily, Miss Penelope Hartopp, daughter of the General of that name, saw the scene from inside and carries on the tale in a letter, much defaced too, which ultimately reached a female friend at Tunbridge Wells. Miss Penelope was no less lavish in her enthusiasm than the gallant officer. "Ravishing," she exclaims ten times on one page, "wondrous . . . utterly beyond description . . . gold plate . . . candelabras . . . negroes in plush breeches . . . pyramids of ice . . . fountains of negus . . . jellies

Orlando as Ambassador

made to represent His Majesty's ships . . . swans made to represent water lilies . . . birds in golden cages . . . gentlemen in slashed
crimson velvet . . . Ladies' headdresses *at least* six foot high . . .
musical boxes. . . . Mr. Peregrine said I looked *quite* lovely which
I only repeat to you, my dearest, because I know. . . . Oh! how I
longed for you all! . . . surpassing anything we have seen at the
Pantiles . . . oceans to drink . . . some gentlemen overcome . . .
Lady Betty ravishing. . . . Poor Lady Bonham made the unfortunate mistake of sitting down without a chair beneath her. . . .
Gentlemen all very gallant . . . wished a thousand times for you
and dearest Betsy. . . . But the sight of all others, the sinecure of
all eyes . . . as all admitted, for none could be so vile as to deny
it, was the Ambassador himself. Such a leg! Such a countenance!! Such princely manners!!! To see him come into the
room! To see him go out again! And something *interesting* in the
expression, which makes one feel, one scarcely knows why, that
he has *suffered!* They say a lady was the cause of it. The heartless
monster!!! How can one of our *reputed tender sex* have had the ef-
frontery!!! He is unmarried, and half the ladies in the place are
wild for love of him . . . A thousand, thousand kisses to Tom,
Gerry, Peter, and dearest Mew" [presumably her cat].

From the Gazette of the time, we gather that "as the clock
struck twelve, the Ambassador appeared on the centre Balcony
which was hung with priceless rugs. Six Turks of the Imperial
Body Guard, each over six foot in height, held torches to his
right and left. Rockets rose into the air at his appearance, and a
great shout went up from the people, which the Ambassador
acknowledged, bowing deeply, and speaking a few words of
thanks in the Turkish language, which it was one of his accom-
plishments to speak with fluency. Next, Sir Adrian Scrope, in
the full dress of a British Admiral advanced; the Ambassador
knelt on one knee; the Admiral placed the Collar of the Most
Noble Order of the Bath round his neck, then pinned the Star

to his breast; after which another gentleman of the diplomatic corps advancing in a stately manner placed on his shoulders the ducal robes, and handed him on a crimson cushion, the ducal coronet."

At length, with a gesture of extraordinary majesty and grace, first bowing profoundly, then raising himself proudly erect, Orlando took the golden circlet of strawberry leaves and placed it, with a gesture which none that saw it ever forgot, upon his brows. It was at this point that the first disturbance began. Either the people had expected a miracle—some say a shower of gold was prophesied to fall from the skies—which did not happen, or this was the signal chosen for the attack to begin; nobody seems to know; but as the coronet settled on Orlando's brows a great uproar rose. Bells began ringing; the harsh cries of the prophets were heard above the shouts of the people; many Turks fell flat to the ground and touched the earth with their foreheads. A door burst open. The natives pressed into the banqueting rooms. Women shrieked. A certain lady, who was said to be dying for love of Orlando, seized a candelabra and dashed it to the ground. What might not have happened, had it not been for the presence of Sir Adrian Scrope and a squad of British bluejackets, nobody can say. But the Admiral ordered the bugles to be sounded; a hundred bluejackets stood instantly at attention; the disorder was quelled, and quiet, at least for the time being, fell upon the scene.

So far, we are on the firm, if rather narrow, ground of ascertained truth. But nobody has ever known exactly what took place later that night. The testimony of the sentries and others seems, however, to prove that the Embassy was empty of company, and shut up for the night in the usual way by two A.M. The Ambassador was seen to go to his room, still wearing the insignia of his rank, and shut the door. Some say he locked it, which was against his custom. Others maintain that they heard music of a rustic kind, such as shepherds play, later that night in the courtyard under the Ambassador's window. A washer-woman, who was kept awake by a toothache said that she saw a man's figure, wrapped in a cloak or dressing gown, come out upon the balcony. Then, she said, a woman, much muffled, but apparently of the peasant class was drawn up by means of a rope which the man let down to her on to the balcony. There, the washer-woman said, they embraced passionately 'like lovers,' and went into the room together, drawing the curtains so that no more could be seen.

Next morning, the Duke, as we must now call him, was found by his secretaries sunk in profound slumber amid bed clothes that were much tumbled. The room was in some disor-der, his coronet having rolled on the floor, and his cloak and garter being flung all of a heap on a chair. The table was littered with papers. No suspicion was felt at first, as the fatigues of the night had been great. But when afternoon came and he still slept, a doctor was summoned. He applied remedies which had been used on the previous occasion, plasters, nettles, emetics, etc., but without success. Orlando slept on. His secretaries then thought it their duty to examine the papers on the table. Many were scribbled over with poetry, in which frequent mention was made of an oak tree. There were also various state papers and others of a private nature concerning the management of his es-tates in England. But at length they came upon a document of far greater significance. It was nothing less, indeed, than a deed of marriage, drawn up, signed, and witnessed between his Lord-ship, Orlando, Knight of the Garter, etc. etc. etc., and Rosina Pepita, a dancer, father unknown, but reputed a gipsy, mother also unknown but reputed a seller of old iron in the marketplace over against the Galata Bridge. The secretaries looked at each other in dismay. And still Orlando slept. Morning and evening they watched him, but, save that his breathing was regular and his cheeks still flushed their habitual deep rose, he gave no sign of life. Whatever science or ingenuity could do to waken him they did. But still he slept.

On the seventh day of his trance (Thursday, May the 10th) the first shot was fired of that terrible and bloody insurrection of which Lieutenant Brigge had detected the first symptoms. The Turks rose against the Sultan, set fire to the town, and put every foreigner they could find, either to the sword or to the bastinado. A few English managed to escape; but, as might have been expected, the gentlemen of the British Embassy preferred to die in defence of their red boxes, or, in extreme cases, to swallow bunches of keys rather than let them fall into the hands of the Infidel. The rioters broke into Orlando's room, but seeing him stretched to all appearance dead they left him untouched, and only robbed him of his coronet and the robes of the Garter.

And now again obscurity descends, and would indeed that it were deeper! Would, we almost have it in our hearts to exclaim, that it were so deep that we could see nothing whatever through its opacity! Would that we might here take the pen and write Finis to our work! Would that we might spare the reader what is to come and say to him in so many words, Orlando died and was buried. But here, alas, Truth, Candour, and Honesty, the austere Gods who keep watch and ward by the inkpot of the biographer, cry No! Putting their silver trumpets to their lips they demand in one blast, Truth! And again they cry Truth! and sounding yet a third time in concert they peal forth, The Truth and nothing but the Truth!

At which—Heaven be praised! for it affords us a breathing space—the doors gently open, as if a breath of the gentlest and holiest zephyr had wafted them apart, and three figures enter. First, comes our Lady of Purity; whose brows are bound with fillets of the whitest lamb's wool; whose hair is as an avalanche of the driven snow; and in whose hand reposes the white quill of a virgin goose. Following her, but with a statelier step, comes our Lady of Chastity; on whose brow is set like a turret of burning but unwasting fire a diadem of icicles; her eyes are pure stars, and her fingers, if they touch you, freeze you to the bone. Close behind her, sheltering indeed in the shadow of her more stately sisters, comes our Lady of Modesty, frailest and fairest of the three; whose face is only shown as the young moon shows when it is thin and sickle shaped and half hidden among clouds. Each advances towards the centre of the room where Orlando still lies sleeping; and with gestures at once appealing and commanding, *Our Lady of Purity* speaks first:

"I am the guardian of the sleeping fawn; the snow is dear to me; and the moon rising; and the silver sea. With my robes I cover the speckled hen's eggs and the brindled sea shell; I cover vice and poverty. On all things frail or dark or doubtful, my veil descends. Wherefore, speak not, reveal not. Spare, O spare!"

Here the trumpets peal forth.

"Purity Avaunt! Begone Purity!"

Then *Our Lady Chastity* speaks:

"I am she whose touch freezes and whose glance turns to stone. I have stayed the star in its dancing, and the wave as it falls. The highest Alps are my dwelling place; and when I walk, the lightnings flash in my hair; where my eyes fall, they kill. Rather than let Orlando wake, I will freeze him to the bone. Spare, O spare!"

Here the trumpets peal forth.

"Chastity Avaunt! Begone Chastity!"

Then *Our Lady of Modesty* speaks, so low that one can hardly hear:

"I am she that men call Modesty. Virgin I am and ever shall be. Not for me the fruitful fields and the fertile vineyard. Increase is odious to me; and when the apples burgeon or the flocks breed, I run, I run; I let my mantle fall. My hair covers my eyes. I do not see. Spare, O Spare!"

Again the trumpets peal forth:

"Modesty Avaunt! Begone Modesty!"

With gestures of grief and lamentation the three sisters now join hands and dance slowly, tossing their veils and singing as they go:

"Truth, come not out from your horrid den. Hide deeper, fearful Truth. For you flaunt in the brutal gaze of the sun things that were better unknown and undone; you unveil the shameful; the dark you make clear. Hide! Hide! Hide!"

Here they make as if to cover Orlando with their draperies. The trumpets, meanwhile, still blare forth:

"The Truth and nothing but the Truth."

At this the Sisters try to cast their veils over the mouths of the trumpets so as to muffle them, but in vain, for now all trumpets blare forth together.

"Horrid Sisters, go!"

The Sisters become distracted and wail in unison, still circling and flinging their veils up and down.

"It has not always been so! But men want us no longer; the women detest us. We go; we go. I (*Purity says this*) to the hen roost. I (*Chastity says this*) to the still unravished heights of Surrey. I (*Modesty says this*) to any cosy nook where there are curtains in plenty.

"For there, not here (all speak together joining hands and making gestures of farewell and despair towards the bed where Orlando lies sleeping) dwell still in nest and boudoir, office and lawcourt those who love us; those who honour us, virgins and city men; lawyers and doctors; those who prohibit; those who deny; those who reverence without knowing why; those who praise without understanding; the still very numerous (Heaven be praised) tribe of the respectable; who prefer to see not; desire to know not; love the darkness; those still worship us, and with reason; for we have given them Wealth, Prosperity, Comfort, Ease. To them we go, you we leave. Come, Sisters come! This is no place for us here."

They retire in haste, waving their draperies over their heads, as if to shut out something that they dare not look upon and close the door behind them.

We are, therefore, now left entirely alone in the room with the sleeping Orlando and the trumpeters. The trumpeters, ranging themselves side by side in order, blow one terrific blast:—

"THE TRUTH!"

at which Orlando woke.

He stretched himself. He rose. He stood upright in complete nakedness before us, and while the trumpets pealed Truth! Truth! Truth! we have no choice left but confess—he was a woman.

The sound of the trumpets died away and Orlando stood stark naked. No human being, since the world began, has ever looked more ravishing. His form combined in one the strength of a man and a woman's grace. As he stood there, the silver trumpets prolonged their note, as if reluctant to leave the lovely sight which their blast had called forth; and Chastity, Purity, and Modesty, inspired, no doubt, by Curiosity, peeped in at the door and threw a garment like a towel at the naked form which, unfortunately, fell short by several inches. Orlando looked himself up and down in a long looking-glass, without showing any signs of discomposure, and went, presumably, to his bath.

We may take advantage of this pause in the narrative to make certain statements. Orlando had become a woman—there is no denying it. But in every other respect, Orlando remained precisely as he had been. The change of sex, though it altered their future, did nothing whatever to alter their identity. Their faces remained, as their portraits prove, practically the same. His memory—but in future we must, for convention's sake, say 'her' for 'his,' and 'she' for 'he'—her memory then, went back through all the events of her past life without encountering any obstacle. Some slight haziness there may have been, as if a few dark drops had fallen into the clear pool of memory; certain things had become a little dimmed; but that was all. The change seemed to have been accomplished painlessly and completely and in such a way that Orlando herself showed no surprise at it. Many people, taking this into account, and holding that such a change of sex is against nature, have been at great pains to prove (1) that Orlando had always been a woman, (2) that Orlando is at this moment a man. Let biologists and psychologists determine. It is enough for us to state the simple fact; Orlando was a man till the age of thirty; when he became a woman and has remained so ever since.

But let other pens treat of sex and sexuality; we quit such odious subjects as soon as we can. Orlando had now washed, and dressed herself in those Turkish coats and trousers which can be worn indifferently by either sex; and was forced to consider her position. That it was precarious and embarrassing in the extreme must be the first thought of every reader who has followed her story with sympathy. Young, noble, beautiful, she had woken to find herself in a position than which we can conceive none more delicate for a young lady of rank. We should not have blamed her had she rung the bell, screamed, or fainted. But Orlando showed no such signs of perturbation. All her actions were deliberate in the extreme, and might indeed have been thought to show tokens of premeditation. First, she carefully examined the papers on the table; took such as seemed to be written in poetry, and secreted them in her bosom; next she called her Seleuchi hound, which had never left her bed all these days, though half famished with hunger, fed and combed him; then stuck a pair of pistols in her belt; finally wound about her

person several strings of emeralds and pearls of the finest orient
which had formed part of her Ambassadorial wardrobe. This
done, she leant out of the window, gave one low whistle, and descended the shattered and bloodstained staircase, now strewn
with the litter of waste paper baskets, treaties, despatches, seals,
sealing wax, etc., and so entered the courtyard. There, in the
shadow of a giant fig tree waited an old Gipsy on a donkey. He
led another by the bridle. Orlando swung her leg over it; and
thus, attended by a lean dog, riding a donkey, in company of a
gipsy, the Ambassador of Great Britain at the Court of the Sultan left Constantinople.

They rode for several days and nights and met with a variety of adventures, some at the hands of men, some at the
hands of nature, in all of which Orlando acquitted herself with
courage. Within a week they reached the high ground outside
Broussa which was then the chief camping ground of the gipsy
tribe to which Orlando had allied herself. Often she had looked
at those mountains from her balcony at the Embassy; often had
longed to be there; and to find oneself where one has longed to
be always, to a reflective mind, gives food for thought. For some
time, however, she was too well pleased with the change to spoil
it by thinking. The pleasure of having no documents to seal,
or sign, no flourishes to make, no calls to pay was enough. The
gipsies followed the grass; when it was grazed down, on they
moved again. She washed in streams if she washed at all; no
boxes, red, blue, or green were presented to her; there was not
a key, let alone a golden key in the whole camp; as for 'visiting,'
the word was unknown. She milked the goats; she collected
brushwood; she stole a hen's egg now and then, but always put
a coin or a pearl in place of it; she herded cattle; she stripped
vines; she trod the grape; she filled the goat-skin and drank
from it; and when she remembered how, at about this time of
day, she should have been making the motions of drinking and

smoking over an empty coffee cup and a pipe which lacked to-bacco, she laughed aloud, cut herself another hunch of bread, and begged for a puff from old Rustum's pipe, filled though it was with cow dung.

The gipsies, with whom it is obvious that she must have been in secret communication before the revolution, seem to have looked upon her as one of themselves (which is always the highest compliment a people can pay) and her dark hair and dark complexion bore out the belief that she was, by birth, one of them and had been snatched by an English Duke from a nut tree when she was a baby and taken to that barbarous land where people live in houses because they are too feeble and diseased to stand the open air. Thus, though in many ways inferior to them, they were willing to help her to become more like them; taught her their arts of cheese-making and basket-weaving, their science of stealing and bird-snaring, and were even prepared to consider letting her marry among them.

But Orlando had contracted in England some of the cus-toms or diseases (whatever you choose to consider them) which cannot, it seems, be expelled. One evening, when they were all sitting round the camp fire and the sunset was blazing over the Thessalian hills, Orlando exclaimed:

"How good to eat!"

(The gipsies have no word for 'beautiful.' This is the nearest.)

All the young men and women burst out laughing uproari-ously. The sky good to eat, indeed! The elders, however, who had seen more of foreigners than they had, became suspicious. They noticed that Orlando often sat for whole hours doing nothing whatever, except look here and then there; they would come upon her on some hill-top staring straight in front of her, no matter whether the goats were grazing or straying. They began to suspect that she had other beliefs than their own and the elder men and women thought it probable that she had fallen into the clutches of the vilest and cruelest among all the Gods, which is Nature. Nor were they far wrong. The English disease, a love of Nature, was inborn in her, and here where Nature was so much larger and more powerful than in England, she fell into its hands as she had never done before. The malady is too well known, and has been, alas, too often described to need describing afresh, save very briefly. There were mountains; there were valleys; there were streams. She climbed the mountains; roamed the valleys; sat on the banks of the streams. She likened the hills to ramparts, and the plains to the flanks of kine. She compared the flowers to enamel and the turf to Turkey rugs worn thin. Trees were withered hags, and sheep were grey boulders. Everything, in fact, was something else. She found the tarn on the mountain-top and almost threw herself in to seek the wisdom she thought lay hid there; and when, from the mountain-top, she beheld, far off, across the Sea of Marmara the plains of Greece, and made out (her eyes were admirable) the Acropolis with a white streak or two which must, she thought, be the Parthenon, her soul expanded with her eyeballs, and she prayed that she might share the majesty of the hills, know the serenity of the plains, etc., etc., as all such believers do. Then, looking down, the red hyacinth, the purple iris wrought her to cry out in ecstasy at the goodness, the beauty of nature; raising her eyes again, she beheld the eagle soaring, and imagined its raptures and made them her own. Returning home, she saluted each star, each peak, and each watch-fire as if they signalled to her alone; and at last, when she flung herself upon her mat in the gipsies' tent, she could not help bursting out again, How good to eat! How good to eat! (For it is a curious fact that though human beings have such imperfect means of communication, that they can only say 'good to eat' when they mean 'beautiful' and the other way about, they will yet endure ridicule and misunderstanding rather than keep any experience to themselves.) All the young gipsies laughed. But Rustum el Sadi, the old man who had brought Orlando out of Constantinople on his donkey, sat silent. He had a nose like a scimitar; his cheeks were furrowed as if from the age-long descent of iron hail; he was brown and keen-eyed, and as he sat tugging at his hookah he observed Orlando narrowly. He had the deepest suspicion that her God was Nature. One day, he found her in tears. Interpreting this to mean that her God had punished her, he told her that he was not surprised. He showed her the fingers of his left hand, withered by the frost; he showed her his right foot, crushed where a rock had fallen. This, he said, was what her God did to men. When she said, "But so beautiful," using the English word, he shook his head; and when she repeated it he was angry. He saw that she did not believe what he believed, and that was enough, wise and ancient as he was, to enrage him.

This difference of opinion disturbed Orlando, who had been perfectly happy until now. She began to think, was Nature beautiful or cruel; and then she asked herself what this beauty was; whether it was in things themselves, or only in herself; so she went on to the nature of reality, which led her to truth, which in its turn, led to Love, Friendship, Poetry (as in the days on the high mound at home) which meditations, since she could impart no word of them, made her long, as she had never longed before, for pen and ink.

"Oh! if only I could write!" she cried (for she had the odd conceit of those who write that words written are shared). She had no ink; and but little paper. But she made ink from berries and wine; and finding a few margins and blank spaces in the manuscript of "The Oak Tree," managed, by writing a kind of shorthand to describe the scenery in a long, blank verse poem, and to carry on a dialogue with herself about this Beauty and

Truth concisely enough. This kept her extremely happy for hours on end. But the gipsies became suspicious. First, they noticed that she was less adept than before at milking and cheese-making; next, she often hesitated before replying; and once a gipsy boy who had been asleep, woke in a terror feeling her eyes upon him. Sometimes this constraint would be felt by the whole tribe, numbering some dozens of grown men and women. It sprang from the sense they had (and their senses are very sharp and much in advance of their vocabulary) that whatever they were doing crumbled like ashes in their hands. An old woman making a basket, a boy skinning a sheep, would be singing or crooning contentedly at their work, when Orlando would come into the camp, fling herself down by the fire and gaze into the flames. She need not even look at them, and yet they felt, here is someone who doubts; (we make a rough-and-ready translation from the gipsy language) here is someone who does not do the thing for the sake of doing; nor looks for looking's sake; here is someone who believes neither in sheep-skin nor basket; but sees (here they looked apprehensively about the tent) something else. Then a vague but most unpleasant feeling would begin to work in the boy and in the old woman. They broke their withys; they cut their fingers. A great rage filled them. They wished Orlando would leave the tent and never come near them again. Yet she was of a cheerful and willing disposition, they owned; and one of her pearls was enough to buy the finest herd of goats in Broussa.

Slowly, she began to feel that there was some difference between her and the gipsies which made her hesitate sometimes to marry and settle down among them for ever. At first she tried to account for it by saying that she came of an ancient and civilised race, whereas these gipsies were an ignorant people, not much better than savages. One night when they were questioning her about England she could not help with some pride describ-

ing the house where she was born, how it had 365 bedrooms
and had been in the possession of her family for four or five
hundred years. Her ancestors were earls, or even dukes, she
added. At this she noticed again that the gipsies were uneasy;
but not angry as before when she had praised the beauty of nature. Now they were courteous, but concerned as people of fine
breeding are when a stranger has been made to reveal his low
birth or poverty. Rustum followed her out of the tent alone and
said that she need not mind if her father were a Duke, and possessed all the bedrooms and furniture that she described. They
would none of them think the worse of her for that. Then she
was seized with a shame that she had never felt before. It was
clear that Rustum and the other gipsies thought a descent of
four or five hundred years only the meanest possible. Their own
families went back at least two or three thousand years. To the
gipsy whose ancestors had built the Pyramids centuries before
Christ was born, the genealogy of Howards and Plantagenets
was no better and no worse than that of the Smiths and the
Joneses: both were negligible. Moreover, where the shepherd
boy had a lineage of such antiquity, there was nothing specially
memorable or desirable in ancient birth; vagabonds and beggars
all shared it. And then, though he was too courteous to speak
openly, it was clear that the gipsy thought that there was no
more vulgar ambition than to possess bedrooms by the hundred
(they were on top of a hill as they spoke; it was night; the mountains rose around them) when the whole earth is ours. Looked
at from the gipsy point of view, a Duke, Orlando understood,
was nothing but a profiteer or robber who snatched land and
money from people who rated these things of little worth, and
could think of nothing better to do than to build three hundred
and sixty-five bedrooms when one was enough, and none was
even better than one. She could not deny that her ancestors had
accumulated field after field; house after house; honour after

honour; yet had none of them been saints or heroes, or great benefactors of the human race. Nor could she counter the argument (Rustum was too much of a gentleman to press it, but she understood) that any man who did now what her ancestors had done three or four hundred years ago would be denounced— and by her own family most loudly—for a vulgar upstart, an adventurer, a *nouveau riche*.

She sought to answer such arguments by the familiar if oblique method of finding the Gipsy life itself rude and barbarous; and so, in a short time, much bad blood was bred between them. Indeed, such differences of opinion are enough to cause bloodshed and revolution. Towns have been sacked for less, and a million martyrs have suffered at the stake rather than yield an inch upon any of the points here debated. No passion is stronger in the breast of man than the desire to make others believe as he believes. Nothing so cuts at the root of his happiness and fills him with rage as the sense that another rates low what he prizes high. Whigs and Tories, Liberal party and Labour party—for what do they battle except their own prestige? It is not love of truth, but desire to prevail that sets quarter against quarter and makes parish desire the downfall of parish. Each seeks peace of mind and subserviency rather than the triumph of truth and the exaltation of virtue—But these moralities belong, and should be left to the historian, since they are as dull as ditch water.

"Four hundred and seventy-six bedrooms mean nothing to them," sighed Orlando.

"She prefers a sunset to a flock of goats," said the Gipsies.

What was to be done, Orlando could not think. To leave the gipsies and become once more an Ambassador seemed to her intolerable. But it was equally impossible to remain for ever where there was neither ink nor writing paper, neither reverence for the Talbots, nor respect for a multiplicity of bedrooms. So she was thinking, one fine morning on the slopes of Mount Athos, when minding her goats. And then Nature, in whom she trusted, either played her a trick or worked a miracle — again, opinions differ too much for it to be possible to say which. Orlando was gazing rather disconsolately at the steep hill-side in front of her. It was now midsummer, and if we must compare the landscape to anything it would have been to a dry bone; to a sheep's skeleton; to a gigantic skull picked white by a thousand vultures. The heat was intense and the little fig-tree under which Orlando lay only served to print patterns of fig-leaves upon her light burnous.

Suddenly, a shadow, though there was nothing to cast a shadow, appeared on the bald mountain-side opposite. It deepened quickly and soon a green hollow showed where there had been barren rock before. As she looked, the hollow deepened and widened, and a great park-like space opened in the flank of the hill. Within, she could see an undulating and grassy lawn; she could see oak trees dotted here and there; she could see the thrushes hopping among the branches. She could see the deer stepping delicately from shade to shade, and could even hear the hum of insects and the gentle sighs and shivers of a summer's day in England. After she had gazed entranced for some time, snow began falling; soon the whole landscape was covered and marked with violet shades instead of yellow sunlight. Now she saw heavy carts coming along the roads, laden with tree trunks, which they were taking, she knew, to be sawn for firewood; and then there appeared the roofs and belfries and towers and courtyards of her own home. The snow was falling steadily, and she could now hear the slither and flop which it made as it slid down the roof and fell to the ground. The smoke went up from a thousand chimneys. All was so clear and minute that she could see a daw pecking for worms in the snow. Then, gradually, the violet shadows deepened and closed over the carts and the lawns

and the great house itself. All was swallowed up. Now there was
nothing left of the grassy hollow, and instead of the green lawns
was only the blazing hill-side which a thousand vultures seemed
to have picked bare. At this, she burst into a passion of tears,
and striding back to the gipsies' camp, told them that she must
sail for England the very next day.

It was happy for her that she did so. Already the young men
had plotted her death. Honour, they said, demanded it, for she
did not think as they did. Yet they would have been sorry to cut
her throat; and welcomed the news of her departure. An English merchant ship, as luck would have it, was already under sail
in the harbour about to return to England; and Orlando, by
breaking off another pearl from her necklace not only paid her
passage but had some banknotes left over in her wallet. These
she would have liked to present to the gipsies. But they despised
wealth she knew; and she had to content herself with embraces,
which on her part were sincere.

CHAPTER FOUR

WITH SOME of the guineas left from the sale of the tenth pearl of her string, Orlando had bought herself a complete outfit of such clothes as women then wore, and it was in the dress of a young Englishwoman of rank that she now sat on the deck of the *Enamoured Lady*. It is a strange fact, but a true one that up to this moment she had scarcely given her sex a thought. Perhaps the Turkish trousers, which she had hitherto worn had done something to distract her thoughts; and the gipsy women, except in one or two important particulars, differ very little from the gipsy men. At any rate, it was not until she felt the coil of skirts about her legs and the Captain offered, with the greatest politeness, to have an awning spread for her on deck that she realised, with a start the penalties and the privileges of her position. But that start was not of the kind that might have been expected.

It was not caused, that is to say, simply and solely by the thought of her chastity and how she could preserve it. In normal circumstances a lovely young woman alone would have thought of nothing else; the whole edifice of female government is based on that foundation stone; chastity is their jewel, their centre piece, which they run mad to protect, and die when ravished of. But if one has been a man for thirty years or so, and an Ambassador into the bargain, if one has held a Queen in one's arms and one or two other ladies, if report be true, of less exalted rank, if one has married a Rosina Pepita, and so on, one does not perhaps give such a very great start about that. Orlando's start was of a very complicated kind, and not to be summed up in a trice. Nobody, indeed, ever accused her of being one of those quick wits, who run to the end of things in a minute. It took her the entire length of the voyage to moralise out the meaning of her start, and so, at her own pace, we will follow her.

"Lord," she thought, when she had recovered from her start, stretching herself out at length under her awning, "this is a pleasant, lazy way of life, to be sure. But," she thought, giving her legs a kick, "these skirts are plaguey things to have about one's heels. Yet the stuff (flowered paduasoy) is the loveliest in the world. Never have I seen my own skin (here she laid her hand on her knee) look to such advantage as now. Could I, however, leap overboard and swim in clothes like these? No! Therefore, I should have to trust to the protection of a blue-jacket. Do I object to that? Now do I?" she wondered, here encountering the first knot in the smooth skein of her argument.

Dinner came before she had untied it, and then it was the Captain himself—Captain Nicholas Benedict Bartolus, a sea-captain of distinguished aspect, who did it for her as he helped her to a slice of corned beef.

"A little of the fat, Ma'am?" he asked. "Let me cut you just the tiniest little slice the size of your finger nail." At those words, a delicious tremor ran through her frame. Birds sang; the torrents rushed. It recalled the feeling of indescribable pleasure with which she had first seen Sasha, hundreds of years ago. Then she had pursued, now she fled. Which is the greater ecstasy? The man's or the woman's? And are they not perhaps the same? No, she thought, this is the most delicious (thanking the Captain but refusing) to refuse, and see him frown. Well, she would, if he wished it, have the very thinnest, smallest shiver in the world. This was the most delicious, to yield and see him smile. "For nothing," she thought, regaining her couch on deck, and continuing the argument, "is more heavenly than to resist and to yield; to yield and to resist. Surely it throws the spirit into such a rapture that nothing else can. So that I'm not sure," she continued, "that I won't throw myself overboard, for the mere pleasure of being rescued by a blue-jacket after all."

(It must be remembered that she was like a child, entering into possession of a pleasaunce or toycupboard; her arguments would not commend themselves to mature women, who have had the run of it all their lives.)

"But what used we young fellows in the cockpit of the *Marie Rose* to say about a woman who threw herself overboard for the pleasure of being rescued by a blue-jacket?" she said. "We had a word for them. Ah! I have it. . . ." (But we must omit that word; it was disrespectful in the extreme and passing strange on a lady's lips.) "Lord! Lord!" she cried again at the conclusion of her thoughts, "must I then begin to respect the opinion of the other sex, however monstrous I think it? If I wear skirts, if I can swim, if I have to be rescued by a blue-jacket, by God!" she cried, "I must!" Upon which, a gloom fell over her. Candid by nature, and averse to all kinds of equivocation, to tell lies bored her. It seemed to her a roundabout way of going to work. Yet, she reflected, the flowered paduasoy—the pleasure of being rescued by a blue-jacket—if these were only to be obtained by roundabout ways, roundabout one must go, she supposed. She remembered how, as a young man, she had insisted that women must be obedient, chaste, scented, and exquisitely apparelled. "Now I shall have to pay in my own person for those desires," she reflected; "for women are not (judging by my own short experience of the sex) obedient, chaste, scented, and exquisitely apparelled by nature. They can only attain these graces, without which they may enjoy none of the delights of life, by the most tedious discipline. There's the hairdressing," she thought, "that alone will take an hour of my morning; there's looking in the looking-glass, another hour; there's staying and lacing; there's washing and powdering; there's changing from silk to lace and from lace to paduasoy; and there's being chaste year in year out. . . ." Here she tossed her foot impatiently, and showed an inch or two of calf. A sailor on the mast, who happened to look down at the moment, started so violently that he missed his footing and only saved himself by the skin of his teeth. "If the sight of my ankles means death to an honest fellow who, no doubt, has a wife and family to support, I must, in all humanity, keep them covered," Orlando thought. Yet her legs were among her chiefest beauties. And she fell to thinking what an odd pass we have come to when all a woman's beauty has to be kept covered, lest a sailor may fall from a mast-head. "A pox on them!" she said, realising for the first time, what, in other circumstances, she would have been taught as a child, that is to say, the sacred responsibilities of womanhood.

"And that's the last oath I shall ever be able to swear," she thought; "once I set foot on English soil. And I shall never be able to crack a man over the head, or tell him he lies in his teeth, or draw my sword and run him through the body, or sit among my peers, or wear a coronet, or walk in procession, or sentence a man to death, or lead an army, or prance down Whitehall on a charger, or wear seventy-two different medals on my breast. All I can do, once I set foot on English soil, is to pour out tea, and ask my lords how they like it. D'you take sugar? D'you take cream?" And mincing out the words, she was horrified to perceive how low an opinion she was forming of the other sex, the manly, to which it had once been her pride to belong. "To fall from a mast-head," she thought, "because you see a woman's ankles; to dress up like a Guy Fawkes and parade the streets, so that women may praise you; to deny a woman teaching lest she may laugh at you; to be the slave of the frailest chit in petticoats, and yet to go about as if you were the Lords of creation.— Heavens!" she thought, "what fools they make of us—what fools we are!" And here it would seem from some ambiguity in her terms that she was censuring both sexes equally, as if she belonged to neither; and indeed, for the time being she seemed to vacillate; she was man; she was woman; she knew the secrets, shared the weaknesses of each. It was a most bewildering and whirligig state of mind to be in. The comforts of ignorance seemed utterly denied her. She was a feather blown on the gale. Thus it is no great wonder if, as she pitted one sex against the other, and found each alternately full of the most deplorable infirmities, and was not sure to which she belonged—it was no great wonder that she was about to cry out that she would return to Turkey and become a gipsy again when the anchor fell with a great splash into the sea; the sails came tumbling on deck, and she perceived (so sunk had she been in thought, that she had seen nothing for several days) that the ship was anchored off the coast of Italy. The Captain at once sent to ask the honour of her company ashore with him in the long boat.

When she returned the next morning, she stretched herself on her couch under the awning and arranged her draperies with the greatest decorum about her ankles.

"Ignorant and poor as we are compared with the other sex," she thought, continuing the sentence which she had left unfinished the other day, "armoured with every weapon as they are, while they debar us even from a knowledge of the alphabet" (and from these opening words it is plain that something had happened during the night to give her a push towards the female sex, for she was speaking more as a woman speaks than as a man, yet with a sort of content after all) "still—they fall from the mast-head—" Here she gave a great yawn and fell asleep.

Orlando on her return to England

When she woke, the ship was sailing before a fair breeze so near the shore that towns on the cliffs' edge seemed only kept from slipping into the water by the interposition of some great rock or the twisted roots of some ancient olive tree. The scent of oranges wafted from a million trees, heavy with the fruit, reached her on deck. A score of blue dolphins, twisting their tails, leapt high now and again into the air. Stretching her arms out (arms, she had learnt already, have no such fatal effects as legs) she thanked Heaven that she was not prancing down Whitehall on a war-horse, not even sentencing a man to death. "Better is it," she thought, "to be clothed with poverty and ignorance, which are the dark garments of the female sex; better to leave the rule and discipline of the world to others; better to be quit of martial ambition, the love of power, and all the other manly desires if so one can more fully enjoy the most exalted raptures known to the human spirit, which are," she said aloud, as her habit was when deeply moved, "contemplation, solitude, love."

"Praise God that I'm a woman!" she cried, and was about to run into the extreme folly—than which none is more distressing in woman or man either—of being proud of her sex, when she paused over the singular word, which, for all we can do to put it in its place, has crept in at the end of the last sentence; Love. "Love," said Orlando. Instantly—such is its impetuosity—love took a human shape—such is its pride. For where other thoughts are content to remain abstract nothing will satisfy this one but to put on flesh and blood, mantilla and petticoats, hose and jerkin. And as all Orlando's loves had been women, now, through the culpable laggardry of the human frame to adapt itself to convention, though she herself was a woman, it was still a woman she loved; and if the consciousness of being of the same sex had any effect at all, it was to quicken and deepen those feelings which she had had as a man. For now a thousand hints and mysteries became plain to her that were then dark. Now, the obscurity, which divides the sexes and lets linger innumerable impurities in its gloom, was removed, and if there is anything in what the poet says about truth and beauty, this affection gained in beauty what it lost in falsity. At last, she cried, she knew Sasha as she was, and in the ardour of this discovery, and in the pursuit of all those treasures which were now revealed, she was so rapt and enchanted that it was as if a cannon ball had exploded at her ear when a man's voice said, "Permit me, Madam," a man's hand raised her to her feet; and the fingers of a man with a three-masted sailing ship tattooed on the middle finger pointed to the horizon.

"The cliffs of England, Ma'am," said the Captain, and he raised the hand which had pointed at the sky to the salute. Orlando now gave a second start, even more violent than the first.

"Christ Jesus!" she cried.

Happily, the sight of her native land after long absence excused both start and exclamation, or she would have been hard put to it to explain to Captain Bartolus the raging and conflicting emotions which now boiled within her. How tell him that she, who now trembled on his arm, had been a Duke and an Ambassador? How explain to him that she, who had been lapped like a lily in folds of paduasoy, had hacked heads off, and lain with loose women among treasure sacks in the holds of pirate ships on summer nights when the tulips were abloom and the bees buzzing off Wapping Old Stairs? Not even to herself could she explain the giant start she gave, as the resolute right hand of the sea-captain indicated the cliffs of the British Islands.

"To refuse and to yield," she murmured, "how delightful; to pursue and to conquer, how august; to perceive and to reason, how sublime." Not one of these words so coupled together seemed to her wrong; nevertheless, as the chalky cliffs loomed nearer, she felt culpable; dishonoured; unchaste; which, for one who had never given the matter a thought, was strange. Closer and closer they drew, till the samphire gatherers, hanging half-way down the cliff, were plain to the naked eye. And watching them, she felt, scampering up and down within her, like some derisive ghost who, in another instant will pick up her skirts and flaunt out of sight, Sasha the lost, Sasha the memory, whose reality she had proved just now so surprisingly—Sasha, she felt, mopping and mowing and making all sorts of disrespectful gestures towards the cliffs and the samphire gatherers; and when the sailors began chanting, "So good-bye and adieu to you, Ladies of Spain," the words echoed in Orlando's sad heart, and she felt that however much landing there meant comfort, meant opulence, meant consequence and state (for she would doubtless pick up some noble Prince and reign, his consort, over half Yorkshire), still, if it meant conventionality, meant slavery, meant deceit, meant denying her love, fettering her limbs, pursing her lips, and restraining her tongue, then she would turn about with the ship and set sail once more for the gipsies.

Among the hurry of these thoughts, however, there now rose, like a dome of smooth, white marble, something which, whether fact or fancy, was so impressive to her fevered imagination that she settled upon it as one has seen a swarm of vibrant dragon-flies alight, with apparent satisfaction, upon the glass bell which shelters some tender vegetable. The form of it, by the hazard of fancy, recalled that earliest, most persistent memory—the man with the big forehead in Twitchett's sitting-room, the man who sat writing, or rather looking, but certainly not at her, for he never seemed to see her poised there in all her finery, lovely boy though she must have been, she could not deny it—and whenever she thought of him, the thought spread round it, like the risen moon on turbulent waters, a sheet of silver calm. Now her hand went to her bosom (the other was still in the Captain's keeping), where the pages of her poem were hidden safe. It might have been a talisman that she kept there.

The distraction of sex, which hers was, and what it meant, subsided; she thought now only of the glory of poetry, and the great lines of Marlowe, Shakespeare, Ben Jonson, Milton began booming and reverberating, as if a golden clapper beat against a golden bell in the cathedral tower which was her mind. The truth was that the image of the marble dome which her eyes had first discovered so faintly that it suggested a poet's forehead and thus started a flock of irrelevant ideas, was no figment, but a reality; and as the ship advanced down the Thames before a favouring gale, the image with all its associations gave place to the truth, and revealed itself as nothing more and nothing less than the dome of a vast cathedral rising among a fretwork of white spires.

"St. Paul's," said Captain Bartolus, who stood by her side. "The Tower of London," he continued. "Greenwich Hospital, erected in memory of Queen Mary by her husband, his late majesty, William the Third. Westminster Abbey. The Houses of Parliament." As he spoke, each of these famous buildings rose to view. It was a fine September morning. A myriad of little water-craft plied from bank to bank. Rarely has a gayer, or more interesting, spectacle presented itself to the gaze of a returned traveller. Orlando hung over the prow, absorbed in wonder. Her eyes had been used too long to savages and nature not to be entranced by these urban glories. That, then, was the dome of St. Paul's which Mr. Wren had built during her absence. Near by, a shock of golden hair burst from a pillar—Captain Bartolus was at her side to inform her that that was the Monument; there had been a plague and a fire during her absence, he said. Do what she would to restrain them, the tears came to her eyes, until, remembering that it is becoming in a woman to weep, she let them flow. Here, she thought, had been the great carnival. Here, where the waves slapped briskly, had stood the Royal Pavilion. Here she had first met Sasha. About here (she looked down into

the sparkling waters) one had been used to see the frozen bumboat woman with her apples on her lap. All that splendour and
corruption was gone. Gone, too, was the dark night, the monstrous downpour, the violent surges of the flood. Here, where
yellow icebergs had raced circling with a crew of terror-stricken
wretches on top, floated a covey of swans, orgulous, undulant,
superb. London itself had completely changed since she had last
seen it. Then, she remembered, it had been a huddle of little
black, beetle-browed houses. The heads of rebels had grinned
on pikes at Temple Bar. The cobbled pavements had reeked of
garbage and ordure. Now, as the ship sailed past Wapping, she
caught glimpses of broad and orderly thoroughfares. Stately
coaches drawn by teams of well-fed horses stood at the doors
of houses whose bow windows, whose plate glass, whose polished knockers, testified to the wealth and modest dignity of the
dwellers within. Ladies in flowered silk (she put the Captain's
glass to her eye), walked on raised footpaths. Citizens in broi-
dered coats took snuff at street corners under lamp posts. She
caught sight of a variety of painted signs swinging in the breeze
and could form a rapid notion from what was painted on them
of the tobacco, of the stuff, of the silk, of the gold, of the silver
ware, of the gloves, of the perfumes, and of a thousand other
articles which were sold within. Nor could she do more as the
ship sailed to its anchorage by London Bridge than glance at
coffee-house windows where, on balconies, since the weather
was fine, a great number of decent citizens sat at ease, with
china dishes in front of them, clay pipes by their sides, while one
among them read from a news sheet, and was frequently interrupted by the laughter or the comments of the others. Were
these taverns, were these wits, were these poets? she asked of
Captain Bartolus, who obligingly informed her that even now—
if she turned her head a little to the left and looked along the
line of his first finger—so—they were passing the Cocoa Tree

where,—yes, there he was—one might see Mr. Addison taking his coffee; the other two gentlemen—"there, Ma'am, a little to the right of the lamp post, one of 'em humped, t'other much the same as you or me"—were Mr. Dryden and Mr. Pope.* "Sad dogs," said the Captain, by which he meant that they were Papists, "but men of parts, none the less," he added, hurrying aft to superintend the arrangements for landing.

"Addison, Dryden, Pope," Orlando repeated as if the words were an incantation. For one moment she saw the high mountains above Broussa, the next, she had set her foot upon her native shore.

BUT NOW Orlando was to learn how little the most tempestuous flutter of excitement avails against the iron countenance of the law; how harder than the stones of London Bridge it is, and than the lips of a cannon more severe. No sooner had she returned to her home in Blackfriars than she was made aware of a succession of Bow Street runners and other grave emissaries from the Law Courts that she was a party to three major suits which had been preferred against her during her absence, as well as innumerable minor litigations, some arising out of, others depending on them. The chief charges against her were (1) that she was dead, and therefore could not hold any property whatsoever; (2) that she was a woman, which amounts to much the same thing; (3) that she was an English Duke who had married one Rosina Pepita, a dancer; and had had by her three sons, which sons now declaring that their father was deceased, claimed that all his property descended to them. Such grave charges as these would, of course, take time and money to dispose of. All her estates were put in Chancery and her titles pro-

---

*The Captain must have been mistaken, as a reference to any textbook of literature will show; but the mistake was a kindly one, and so we let it stand.

nounced in abeyance while the suits were under litigation. Thus it was in a highly ambiguous condition, uncertain whether she was alive or dead, man or woman, Duke or nonentity, that she posted down to her country seat, where, pending the legal judgment, she had the Law's permission to reside in a state of incognito or incognita as the case might turn out to be.

It was a fine evening in December when she arrived and the snow was falling and the violet shadows were slanting much as she had seen them from the hill-top at Broussa. The great house lay more like a town than a house, brown and blue, rose and purple in the snow, with all its chimneys smoking busily as if inspired with a life of their own. She could not restrain a cry as she saw it there tranquil and massive, couched upon the meadows. As the yellow coach entered the park and came bowling along the drive between the trees, the red deer raised their heads as if expectantly, and it was observed that instead of showing the timidity natural to their kind, they followed the coach and stood about the courtyard when it drew up. Some tossed their antlers, others pawed the ground as the step was let down and Orlando alighted. One, it is said, actually knelt in the snow before her. She had not time to reach her hand towards the knocker before both wings of the great door were flung open, and there, with lights and torches held above their heads, were Mrs. Grimsditch, Mr. Dupper, and a whole retinue of servants come to greet her. But the orderly procession was interrupted first by the impetuosity of Canute, the elk hound, who threw himself with such ardour upon his mistress that he almost knocked her to the ground; next, by the agitation of Mrs. Grimsditch, who, making as if to curtsey, was overcome with emotion and could do no more than gasp Milord! Milady! Milady! Milord! until Orlando comforted her with a hearty kiss upon both her cheeks. After that, Mr. Dupper began to read from a parchment, but the dogs barking, the huntsmen winding their horns, and the stags, who had come into the courtyard in the confusion, baying the moon, not much progress was made, and the company dispersed within after crowding about their Mistress, and testifying in every way to their great joy at her return.

No one showed an instant's suspicion that Orlando was not the Orlando they had known. If any doubt there was in the human mind the action of the deer and the dogs would have been enough to dispell it, for the dumb creatures, as is well known, are far better judges both of identity and character than we are. Moreover, said Mrs. Grimsditch, over her dish of china tea to Mr. Dupper that night, if her Lord was a Lady now, she had never seen a lovelier one, nor was there a penny piece to choose between them; one was as well favoured as the other; they were as like as two peaches on one branch; which, said Mrs. Grimsditch, becoming confidential, she had always had her suspicions (here she nodded her head very mysteriously) which it was no surprise to her (here she nodded her head very knowingly) and for her part, a very great comfort; for what with the towels wanting mending and the curtains in the chaplain's parlour being moth-eaten round the fringes, it was time they had a Mistress among them.

"And some little masters and mistresses to come after her," Mr. Dupper added, being privileged by virtue of his holy office to speak his mind on such delicate matters as these.

So, while the old servants gossiped in the servants' hall, Orlando took a silver candle in her hand and roamed once more through the halls, the galleries, the courts, the bedrooms; saw loom down at her again the dark visage of this Lord Keeper, that Lord Chamberlain among her ancestors; sat now in this chair of state, now reclined on that canopy of delight; observed the arras, how it swayed; watched the huntsmen riding and Daphne flying; bathed her hand, as she had loved to do as a child, in the yellow pool of light which the moonlight made

falling through the heraldic Leopard in the window; slid along
the polished planks of the gallery, the other side of which was
rough timber; touched this silk, that satin; fancied the carved
dolphins swam; brushed her hair with King James' silver brush;
buried her face in the pot pourri, which was made as the Conqueror had taught them many hundred years ago and from the
same roses; looked at the garden and imagined the sleeping crocuses, the dormant dahlias; saw the frail nymphs gleaming white
in the snow and the great yew hedges, thick as a house, black
behind them; saw the orangeries and the giant medlars;—all
this she saw, and each sight and sound, rudely as we write it down,
filled her heart with such a lust and balm of joy, that at length,
tired out, she entered the Chapel and sank into the old red arm-
chair in which her ancestors used to hear service. There she lit
a cheroot ('twas a habit she had brought back from the East)
and opened the prayer book.

It was a little book bound in velvet, stitched with gold, which
had been held by Mary Queen of Scots on the scaffold, and the
eye of faith could detect a brownish stain, said to be made of a
drop of the Royal blood. But what pious thoughts it roused in
Orlando, what evil passions it soothed asleep, who dare say, seeing that of all communions, this with the deity is the most in-
scrutable? Novelist, poet, historian all falter with their hand on
that door; nor does the believer himself enlighten us, for is he
more ready to die than other people, or more eager to share his
goods? Does he not keep as many maids and carriage horses as
the rest? and yet with it all, holds a faith he says which should
make goods a vanity and death desirable. In the Queen's prayer
book, along with the blood-stain, was also a lock of hair and a
crumb of pastry; Orlando now added to these keepsakes a flake
of tobacco, and so, reading and smoking, was moved by the humane jumble of them all—the hair, the pastry, the blood-stain,
the tobacco—to such a mood of contemplation as gave her a

reverent air suitable in the circumstances, though she had, it is said, no traffic with the usual God. Nothing, however, can be more arrogant, though nothing is commoner than to assume that of Gods there is only one, and of religions none but the speaker's. Orlando, it seemed, had a faith of her own. With all the religious ardour in the world, she now reflected upon her sins and the imperfections that had crept into her spiritual state. The letter S, she reflected, is the serpent in the Poet's Eden. Do what she would there were still too many of these sinful reptiles in the first stanzas of "The Oak Tree." But 'S' was nothing, in her opinion, compared with the termination 'ing.' The present participle is the Devil himself, she thought (now that we are in the place for believing in Devils). To evade such temptations is the first duty of the poet, she concluded, for as the ear is the antechamber to the soul, poetry can adulterate and destroy more surely than lust or gunpowder. The poet's then in the highest office of all, she continued. His words reach where others fall short. A silly song of Shakespeare's has done more for the poor and the wicked than all the preachers and philanthropists in the world. No time, no devotion, can be too great, therefore, which makes the vehicle of our message less distorting. We must shape our words till they are the thinnest integument for our thoughts. Thoughts are divine. Thus it is obvious that she was back in the confines of her own religion which time had only strengthened in her absence, and was rapidly acquiring the intolerance of belief.

"I am growing up," she thought, taking her taper at last. "I am losing some illusions," she said, shutting Queen Mary's book, "perhaps to acquire others," and she descended among the tombs where the bones of her ancestors lay.

But even the bones of her ancestors, Sir Miles, Sir Gervase, and the rest, had lost something of their sanctity since Rustum el Sadi had waved his hand that night in the Asian mountains. Somehow the fact that only three or four hundred years ago these skeletons had been men with their way to make in the world like any modern upstart, and that they had made it by acquiring houses and offices, garters and ribbands, as any other upstart does, while poets, perhaps, and men of great mind and breeding had preferred the quietude of the country, for which choice they paid the penalty by extreme poverty, and now hawked broadsheets in the Strand, or herded sheep in the fields, filled her with remorse. She thought of the Egyptian pyramids and what bones lie beneath them as she stood in the crypt; and the vast, empty hills which lie above the Sea of Marmara seemed, for the moment, a finer dwelling-place than this many-roomed mansion in which no bed lacked its quilt and no silver dish its silver cover.

"I am growing up," she thought, taking her taper. "I am losing my illusions, perhaps to acquire new ones," and she paced down the long gallery to her bedroom. It was a disagreeable process, and a troublesome. But it was interesting, amazingly, she thought, stretching her legs out to her log fire (for no sailor was present), and she reviewed, as if it were an avenue of great edifices, the progress of her own self along her own past.

How she had loved sound when she was a boy, and thought the volley of tumultuous syllables from the lips the finest of all poetry. Then—it was the effect of Sasha and her disillusionment perhaps,—into this high frenzy was let fall some black drop, which turned her rhapsody to sluggishness. Slowly there had opened within her something intricate and many-chambered, which one must take a torch to explore, in prose not verse; and she remembered how passionately she had studied that doctor at Norwich, Browne, whose book was at her hand there. She had formed here in solitude after her affair with Greene, or tried to form, for Heaven knows, these growths are age-long in coming, a spirit capable of resistance. "I will write," she had said, "what I enjoy writing"; and so had scratched out twenty-six volumes.

Yet still for all her travels and adventures and profound think-
ings and turnings this way and that, she was only in process of
fabrication. What the future might bring, Heaven only knew.
Change was incessant, and change perhaps would never cease.
High battlements of thought; habits that had seemed durable as
stone went down like shadows at the touch of another mind and
left a naked sky and fresh stars twinkling in it. Here she went to
the window, and in spite of the cold could not help unlatching
it. She leant out into the damp night air. She heard a fox bark in
the woods, and the clutter of a pheasant trailing through the
branches. She heard the snow slither and flop from the roof to
the ground. "By my life," she exclaimed, "this is a thousand
times better than Turkey. Rustum," she cried, as if she were ar-
guing with the gipsy (and in this new power of bearing an argument in mind and continuing it with someone who was not
there to contradict she showed again the development of her
soul) "you were wrong. This is better than Turkey. Hair, pastry,
tobacco — of what odds and ends are we compounded," she
said (thinking of Queen Mary's prayer book). "What a phantasmagoria the mind is and meeting-place of dissemblables. At one
moment we deplore our birth and state and aspire to an ascetic
exaltation; the next we are overcome by the smell of some old
garden path and weep to hear the thrushes sing." And so bewil-
dered as usual by the multitude of things which call for explanation and imprint their message without leaving any hint as to
their meaning upon the mind, she threw her cheroot out of the
window and went to bed.

Next morning, in pursuance of these thoughts, she had out
her pen and paper, and started afresh upon "The Oak Tree," for
to have ink and paper in plenty when one has made do with
berries and margins is a delight not to be conceived. Thus she
was now striking out a phrase in the depths of despair, now in

the heights of ecstasy writing one in, when a shadow darkened the page. She hastily hid her manuscript.

As her window gave on to the most central of the courts, as she had given orders that she would see no one, as she knew no one and was herself legally unknown, she was first surprised at the shadow, then indignant at it, then (when she looked up and saw what caused it) overcome with merriment. For it was a familiar shadow, a grotesque shadow, the shadow of no less a personage than the Archduchess Harriet Griselda of Finster-Aarhorn and Scand-op-Boom in the Roumanian territory. She was loping across the court in her old black riding-habit and mantle as before. Not a hair of her head was changed. This then was the woman who had chased her from England! This was the eyrie of that obscene vulture—this the fatal fowl herself! At the thought that she had fled all the way to Turkey to avoid her seductions (now become excessively flat), Orlando laughed aloud. There was something inexpressibly comic in the sight. She resembled, as Orlando had thought before, nothing so much as a monstrous hare. She had the staring eyes, the lank cheeks, the high headdress of that animal. She stopped now, much as a hare sits erect in the corn when thinking itself unobserved, and stared at Orlando, who stared back at her from the window. After they had stared like this for a certain time, there was nothing for it but to ask her in, and soon the two ladies were exchanging compliments while the Archduchess struck the snow from her mantle.

"A plague on women," said Orlando to herself, going to the cupboard to fetch a glass of wine, "they never leave one a moment's peace. A more ferreting, inquisiting, busybodying set of people don't exist. It was to escape this Maypole that I left England, and now"—here she turned to present the Archduchess with the salver, and behold—in her place stood a tall gentleman in black. A heap of clothes lay in the fender. She was alone with a man.

Recalled thus suddenly to a consciousness of her sex, which she had completely forgotten, and of his, which was now remote enough to be equally upsetting, Orlando felt seized with faintness.

"La!" she cried, putting her hand to her side, "how you frighten me!"

"Gentle creature," cried the Archduchess, falling on one knee and at the same time pressing a cordial to Orlando's lips, "forgive me for the deceit I have practised on you!"

Orlando sipped the wine and the Archduke knelt and kissed her hand.

In short, they acted the parts of man and woman for ten minutes with great vigour and then fell into natural discourse. The Archduchess (but she must in future be known as the Archduke) told his story—that he was a man and always had been one; that he had seen a portrait of Orlando and fallen hopelessly in love with him; that to compass his ends, he had dressed as a woman and lodged at the Baker's shop; that he was desolated when he fled to Turkey; that he had heard of her change and hastened to offer his services (here he teed and heed intolerably). For to him, said the Archduke Harry, she was and would ever be the Pink, the Pearl, the Perfection of her sex. The three p's would have been more persuasive if they had not been interspersed with tee-hees and haw-haws of the strangest kind. "If this is love," said Orlando to herself, looking at the Archduke on the other side of the fender, and now from the woman's point of view, "there is something highly ridiculous about it."

Falling on his knees, the Archduke Harry made the most passionate declaration of his suit. He told her that he had something like twenty million ducats in a strong box at his castle. He had more acres than any nobleman in England. The shooting was excellent: he could promise her a mixed bag of ptarmigan and grouse such as no English moor, or Scotch either, could rival. True, the pheasants had suffered from the gape in his absence, and the does had slipped their young, but that could be put right, and would be with her help when they lived in Roumania together.

As he spoke, enormous tears formed in his rather prominent eyes and ran down the sandy tracts of his long and lanky cheeks.

That men cry as frequently and as unreasonably as women, Orlando knew from her own experience as a man; but she was beginning to be aware that women should be shocked when men display emotion in their presence, and so, shocked she was.

The Archduke apologised. He commanded himself sufficiently to say that he would leave her now, but would return on the following day for his answer.

That was a Tuesday. He came on Wednesday; he came on Thursday; he came on Friday; and he came on Saturday. It is true that each visit began, continued, or concluded with a declaration of love, but in between there was much room for silence. They sat on either side of the fireplace and sometimes the Archduke knocked over the fire irons and Orlando picked them up again. Then the Archduke would bethink him how he had shot an elk in Sweden, and Orlando would ask, was it a very big elk, and the Archduke would say that it was not as big as the reindeer which he shot in Norway; and Orlando would ask, had he ever shot a tiger, and the Archduke would say he had shot an albatross, and Orlando would say (half hiding her yawn) was an albatross as big as an elephant, and the Archduke would say—something very sensible, no doubt, but Orlando heard it not, for she was looking at her writing table, out of the window, at the door. Upon which the Archduke would say, "I adore you," at the

very same moment that Orlando said "Look, it's beginning to
rain," at which they were both much embarrassed, and blushed
scarlet, and could neither of them think what to say next. Indeed,
Orlando was at her wit's end what to talk about and had she not
bethought her of a game called Fly Loo, at which great sums of
money can be lost with very little expense of spirit, she would
have had to marry him, she supposed; for how else to get rid of
him she knew not. By this device, however, and it was a simple
one, needing only three lumps of sugar and a sufficiency of flies,
the embarrassment of conversation was overcome and the necessity of marriage avoided. For now, the Archduke would bet her
five hundred pounds to a tester that a fly would settle on this
lump and not on that. Thus, they would have occupation for a
whole morning watching the flies (who were naturally sluggish at
this season and often spent an hour or so circling round the ceiling) until at length, some fine blue bottle made his choice and the
match was won. Many hundreds of pounds changed hands between them at this game, which the Archduke, who was a born
gambler, swore was every bit as good as horse racing, and vowed
he could play at for ever. But Orlando soon began to weary.

"What's the good of being a fine young woman in the prime
of life," she asked, "if I have to pass all my mornings watching
blue bottles with an Archduke?"

She began to detest the sight of sugar; flies made her dizzy.
Some way out of the difficulty there must be, she supposed, but
she was still awkward in the arts of her sex, and as she could no
longer knock a man over the head or run him through the body
with a rapier, she could think of no better method than this. She
caught a blue bottle, gently pressed the life out of it (it was half
dead already, or her kindness for the dumb creatures would not
have permitted it) and secured it by a drop of gum arabic to a
lump of sugar. While the Archduke was gazing at the ceiling,
she deftly substituted this lump for the one she had laid her

money on, and crying, "Loo Loo!" declared that she had won her bet. Her reckoning was that the Archduke, with all his knowledge of sport and horseracing would detect the fraud and, as to cheat at Loo is the most heinous of crimes, and men have been banished from the society of mankind to that of apes in the tropics for ever because of it, she calculated that he would be manly enough to refuse to have anything further to do with her. But she misjudged the simplicity of the amiable nobleman. He was no nice judge of flies. A dead fly looked to him much the same as a living one. She played the trick twenty times on him and he paid her over £17,250 (which is about £40,885: 6: 8 of our own money) before Orlando cheated so grossly that even he could be deceived no longer. When he realised the truth at last, a painful scene ensued. The Archduke rose to his full height. He coloured scarlet. Tears rolled down his cheeks one by one. That she had won a fortune from him was nothing—she was welcome to it; that she had deceived him was something—it hurt him to think her capable of it; but that she had cheated at Loo was everything. To love a woman who cheated at play was, he said, impossible. Here he broke down completely. Happily, he said, recovering slightly, there were no witnesses. She was, after all, only a woman, he said. In short, he was preparing in the chivalry of his heart to forgive her and had bent to ask her pardon for the violence of his language, when she cut the matter short, as he stooped his proud head, by dropping a small toad between his skin and his shirt.

In justice to her, it must be said that she would infinitely have preferred a rapier. Toads are clammy things to conceal about one's person a whole morning. But if rapiers are forbidden, one must have recourse to toads. Moreover toads and laughter between them sometimes do what cold steel cannot. She laughed. The Archduke blushed. She laughed. The Archduke cursed. She laughed. The Archduke slammed the door.

"Heaven be praised!" cried Orlando still laughing. She heard the sound of chariot wheels driven at a furious pace down the courtyard. She heard them rattle along the road. Fainter and fainter the sound became. Now it faded away altogether.

"I am alone," said Orlando, aloud since there was no one to hear.

That silence is more profound after noise still wants the confirmation of science. But that loneliness is more apparent directly after one has been made love to, many women would take their oath. As the sound of the Archduke's chariot wheels died away, Orlando felt drawing further from her and further from her an Archduke (she did not mind that) a fortune (she did not mind that) a title (she did not mind that) the safety and circumstance of married life (she did not mind that) but life she heard going from her, and a lover. "Life and a lover," she murmured; and going to her writing-table she dipped her pen in the ink and wrote:

"Life and a lover"—a line which did not scan and made no sense with what went before—something about the proper way of dipping sheep to avoid the scab. Reading it over she blushed and repeated,

"Life and a lover." Then laying her pen aside she went into her bedroom, stood in front of her mirror, and arranged her pearls about her neck. Then since pearls do not show to advantage against a morning gown of sprigged cotton, she changed to a dove grey taffeta; thence to one of peach bloom; thence to a wine coloured brocade. Perhaps a dash of powder was needed, and if her hair were disposed—so—about her brow, it might become her. Then she slipped her feet into pointed slippers, and drew an emerald ring upon her finger. "Now," she said when all was ready and lit the silver sconces on either side of the mirror. What woman would not have kindled to see what Orlando saw then burning in the snow—for all about the looking glass were snowy lawns, and she was like a fire, a burning bush, and the candle flames about her head were silver leaves; or again, the glass was green water, and she a mermaid, slung with pearls, a siren in a cave, singing so that oarsmen leant from their boats and fell down, down to embrace her; so dark, so bright, so hard, so soft, was she, so astonishingly seductive that it was a thousand pities that there was no one there to put it in plain English, and say outright "Damn it Madam, you are loveliness incarnate," which was the truth. Even Orlando (who had no conceit of her person) knew it, for she smiled the involuntary smile which women smile when their own beauty, which seems not their own, forms like a drop falling or a fountain rising and confronts them all of a sudden in the glass—this smile she smiled and then she listened for a moment and heard only the leaves blowing and the sparrows twittering, and then she sighed, "Life, a lover," and then she turned on her heel with extraordinary rapidity; whipped her pearls from her neck, stripped the satins from her back, stood erect in her neat black silk knickerbockers of an ordinary nobleman, and rang the bell. When the servant came, she told him to order a coach and six to be in readiness instantly. She was summoned by urgent affairs to London. Within an hour of the Archduke's departure, off she drove.

AND AS SHE drove, we may seize the opportunity, since the landscape was of a simple English kind which needs no description, to draw the reader's attention more particularly than we could at the moment to one or two remarks which have slipped in here and there in the course of the narrative. For example, it may have been observed that Orlando hid her manuscripts when interrupted. Next, that she looked long and intently in the glass; and now, as she drove to London, one might notice her starting and suppressing a cry when the horses galloped faster than she liked. Her modesty as to her writing, her vanity as to her person, her fears for her safety all seem to hint that what was said a short time ago about there being no change in Orlando the man and Orlando the woman, was ceasing to be altogether true. She was becoming a little more modest, as women are, of her brains, and a little more vain, as women are, of her person. Certain susceptibilities were asserting themselves, and others were diminishing. The change of clothes had, some philosophers will say, much to do with it. Vain trifles as they seem, clothes have, they say, more important offices than merely to keep us warm. They change our view of the world and the world's view of us. For example, when Captain Bartolus saw Orlando's skirt, he had an awning stretched for her immediately, pressed her to take another slice of beef, and invited her to go ashore with him in the long boat. These compliments would certainly not have been paid her had her skirts, instead of flowing, been cut tight to her legs in the fashion of breeches. And when we are paid compliments, it behoves us to make some return. Orlando curtseyed; she complied; she flattered the good man's humours as she would not have done had his neat breeches been a woman's skirts, and his braided coat a woman's satin bodice. Thus, there is much to support the view that it is clothes that wear us and not we them; we may make them take the mould of arm or breast, but they mould our hearts, our brains, our tongues to their liking. So, having now worn skirts for a considerable time, a certain change was visible in Orlando, which is to be found even in her face. If we compare the picture of Orlando as a man with that of Orlando as a woman we shall see that though both are undoubtedly one and the same person, there are certain changes. The man has his hand free to seize his sword; the woman must use hers to keep the satins from slipping from her shoulders. The man looks the world full in the face, as if it were made for his uses and fashioned to his liking. The woman takes a sidelong glance at it, full of subtlety, even of suspicion. Had they both worn the same clothes, it is possible that their outlook might have been the same too.

That is the view of some philosophers and wise ones, but on the whole, we incline to another. The difference between the sexes is, happily, one of great profundity. Clothes are but a symbol of something hid deep beneath. It was a change in Orlando herself that dictated her choice of a woman's dress and of a woman's sex. And perhaps in this she was only expressing rather more openly than usual—openness indeed was the soul of her nature—something that happens to most people without being thus plainly expressed. For here again, we come to a dilemma. Different though the sexes are, they intermix. In every human being a vacillation from one sex to the other takes place, and often it is only the clothes that keep the male or female likeness, while underneath the sex is the very opposite of what it is above. Of the complications and confusions which thus result every one has had experience; but here we leave the general question and note only the odd effect it had in the particular case of Orlando herself.

For it was this mixture in her of man and woman, one being uppermost and then the other, that often gave her conduct an unexpected turn. The curious of her own sex would argue how, for example, if Orlando was a woman, did she never take more than ten minutes to dress? And were not her clothes chosen rather at random, and sometimes worn rather shabby? And then they would say, still, she has none of the formality of a man, or a man's love of power. She is excessively tender-hearted. She could not endure to see a donkey beaten or a kitten drowned. Yet again, they noted, she detested household matters, was up at dawn and out among the fields in summer before the sun had risen. No farmer knew more about the crops than she did. She could drink with the best and liked games of hazard. She rode well and drove six horses at a gallop over London Bridge. Yet again, though bold and active as a man, it was remarked that the sight of another in danger brought on the most womanly palpitations. She would burst into tears on slight provocation. She was unversed in geography, found mathematics intolerable, and held some caprices which are more common among women than men, as for instance, that to travel south is to travel down hill. Whether, then, Orlando was most man or woman, it is difficult to say and cannot now be decided. For her coach was now rattling over the cobbles. She had reached her home in the city. The steps were being let down; the iron gates were being opened. She was entering her father's house at Blackfriar's which, though fashion was fast deserting that end of the town, was still a pleasant, roomy mansion, with gardens running down to the river, and a pleasant grove of nut trees to walk in.

Here she took up her lodging and began instantly to look about her for what she had come in search of—that is to say, life and a lover. About the first there might be some doubt; the second she found without the least difficulty two days after her arrival. It was a Tuesday that she came to town. On Thursday she went for a walk in the Mall, as was then the habit of persons of quality. She had not made more than a turn or two of the avenue before she was observed by a little knot of vulgar people who go there to spy upon their betters. As she came past them, a common woman carrying a child at her breast stepped forward, peered familiarly into Orlando's face, and cried out, "Lawk upon us, if it ain't the Lady Orlando!" Her companions came crowding round, and Orlando found herself in a moment the centre of a mob of staring citizens and tradesmen's wives, all eager to gaze upon the heroine of the celebrated law suit. Such was the interest that the case excited in the minds of the common people. She might, indeed, have found herself gravely discommoded by the pressure of the crowd—she had forgotten that ladies are not supposed to walk in public places alone—had not a tall gentleman at once stepped forward and offered her the protection of his arm. It was the Archduke. She was overcome with distress and yet with some amusement at the sight. Not only had this magnanimous nobleman forgiven her, but in order to show that he took her levity with the toad in good part, he had procured a jewel made in the shape of that reptile which he pressed upon her with a repetition of his suit as he handed her to her coach.

What with the crowd, what with the Duke, what with the jewel, she drove home in the vilest temper imaginable. Was it impossible then to go for a walk without being half suffocated, presented with a toad set in emeralds, and asked in marriage by an Archduke? She took a kinder view of the case next day when she found on her breakfast table half a dozen billets from some of the greatest ladies in the land—Lady Suffolk, Lady Salisbury, Lady Chesterfield, Lady Tavistock, and others who reminded her in the politest manner of old alliances between their families and her own, and desired the honour of her acquaintance. Next day, which was a Saturday, many of these great ladies waited on her in person. On Tuesday, about noon, their footmen brought cards of invitation to various routs, dinners, and assemblies in the near future; so that Orlando was launched without delay, and with some splash and foam at that, upon the waters of London society.

To give a truthful account of London society at that or indeed at any other time, is beyond the powers of the biographer or the historian. Only those who have little need of the truth, and no respect for it—the poets and the novelists—can be trusted to do it, for this is one of the cases where the truth does not exist. Nothing exists. The whole thing is a miasma—a mirage. To make our meaning plain—Orlando could come home from one of these routs at three or four in the morning with cheeks like a Christmas tree and eyes like stars. She would untie a lace, pace the room a score of times, untie another lace, stop, and pace the room again. Often the sun would be blazing over Southwark chimneys before she could persuade herself to get into bed, and there she would lie, pitching and tossing, laughing and sighing for an hour or longer before she slept at last. And what was all this stir about? Society. And what had society said or done to throw a reasonable lady into such excitement? In plain language, nothing. Rack her memory as she would, next day Orlando could never remember a single word to magnify into the name something. Lord O. had been gallant. Lord A. polite. The Marquis of C. charming. Mr. M. amusing. But when she tried to recollect in what their gallantry, politeness, charm, or wit had consisted, she was bound to suppose her memory at fault, for she could not name a thing. It was the same always. Nothing remained over the next day, yet the excitement of the moment was intense. Thus we are forced to conclude that society is one of those brews such as skilled housekeepers serve hot about Christmas time, whose flavour depends upon the proper mixing and stirring of a dozen different ingredients. Take one out, and it is in itself insipid. Take away Lord O., Lord A., Lord C., or Mr. M. and separately each is nothing. Stir them all together and they combine to give off the most intoxicating of flavours, the most seductive of scents. Yet this intoxication, this seductiveness, entirely evade our analysis. At one and the same time therefore, society is everything and society is nothing. Society is the most powerful concoction in the world and society has no existence whatsoever. Such monsters the poets and the novelists alone can deal with; with such something-nothings their works are stuffed out to prodigious size; and to them with the best will in the world we are content to leave it.

Following the example of our predecessors, therefore, we will only say that society in the reign of Queen Anne was of unparalleled brilliance. To have the entry there was the aim of every well bred person. The graces were supreme. Fathers instructed their sons, mothers their daughters. No education was complete for either sex which did not include the science of deportment, the art of bowing and curtseying, the management of the sword and the fan, the care of the teeth, the conduct of the leg, the flexibility of the knee, the proper methods of entering and leaving the room, with a thousand etceteras, such as will immediately suggest themselves to anybody who has himself been in society. Since Orlando had won the praise of Queen Elizabeth for the way she handed a bowl of rose water as a boy, it must be supposed that she was sufficiently expert to pass muster. Yet it is true that there was an absent mindedness about her which sometimes made her clumsy; she was apt to think of poetry when she should have been thinking of taffeta; her walk was a little too much of a stride for a woman, perhaps, and her gestures, being abrupt, might endanger a cup of tea on occasion.

Whether this slight disability was enough to counterbalance the splendour of her bearing, or whether she inherited a drop too much of that black humour which ran in the veins of all her race, certain it is that she had not been in the world more than a score of times before she might have been heard to ask herself, had there been anybody but her spaniel Pippin to hear her, "What the devil is the matter with me?" The occasion was Tuesday, the 16th of June, 1712; she had just returned from a great ball at Arlington House; the dawn was in the sky, and she was pulling off her stockings. "I don't care if I never meet another soul as long as I live," cried Orlando, bursting into tears. Lovers she had in plenty, but life, which is after all of some importance in its way, escaped her. "Is this," she asked — but there was none to answer, "is this what people call life?" The spaniel raised her forepaw in token of sympathy. The spaniel licked Orlando with her tongue. Orlando stroked the spaniel with her hand. Orlando kissed the spaniel with her lips. In short, there

was the truest sympathy between them that can be between a
dog and its mistress, and yet, it cannot be denied that the dumb-
ness of animals is a great impediment to the refinements of intercourse. They wag their tails; they bow the front part of the
body and elevate the hind; they roll, they jump, they paw, they
whine, they bark, they slobber; they have all sorts of ceremonies
and artifices of their own, but the whole thing is of no avail,
since speak they cannot. Such was her quarrel, she thought, setting the dog gently on to the floor, with the great people at Arlington House. They too, wag their tails, bow, roll, jump, paw,
and slobber, but talk they cannot. "All these months that I've
been out in the world," said Orlando, pitching one stocking
across the room, "I've heard nothing but what Pippin might
have said. I'm cold. I'm happy. I'm hungry. I've caught a mouse.
I've buried a bone. Please kiss my nose." And it was not enough.

How, in so short a time, she had passed from intoxication
to disgust we will only seek to explain by supposing that this
mysterious composition which we call society, is nothing absolutely good or bad in itself, but has a spirit in it, volatile but po-
tent, which either makes you drunk when you think it, as
Orlando thought it, delightful, or gives you a headache when
you think it, as Orlando thought it, repulsive. That the faculty
of speech has much to do with it either way, we take leave to
doubt. Often a dumb hour is the most ravishing of all; brilliant
wit can be tedious beyond description. But to the poets we leave
it, and so on with our story.

Orlando threw the second stocking after the first and went
to bed dismally enough, determined that she would forswear society for ever. But again as it turned out, she was too hasty in
coming to her conclusions. For the very next morning she woke
to find, among the usual cards of invitation upon her table, one
from a certain great Lady, the Countess of R. Having determined over night that she would never go into society again, we

can only explain Orlando's behaviour—she sent a messenger hot foot to R—— House to say that she would attend her Ladyship with all the pleasure in the world—by the fact that she was still suffering from the poison of three honeyed words dropped into her ear on the deck of the *Enamoured Lady* by Captain Nicholas Benedict Bartolus as they sailed down the Thames. Addison, Dryden, Pope, he had said, pointing to the Cocoa Tree, and Addison, Dryden, Pope had chimed in her head like an incantation ever since. Who can credit such folly? but so it was. All her experience with Nick Greene had taught her nothing. Such names still exercised over her the most powerful fascination. Something, perhaps, we must believe in, and as Orlando, we have said, had no belief in the usual divinities she bestowed her credulity upon great men—yet with a distinction. Admirals, soldiers, statesmen, moved her not at all. But the very thought of a great writer stirred her to such a pitch of belief that she almost believed him to be invisible. Her instinct was a sound one. One can only believe entirely, perhaps, in what one cannot see. The little glimpse she had of the poets from the deck of the ship was of the nature of a vision. That the cup was china, or the gazette paper, she doubted. When Lord O. said one day that he had dined with Dryden the night before, she flatly disbelieved him. Now, the Lady R.'s reception room had the reputation of being the antechamber to the presence room of genius; it was the place where men and women met to swing censers and chant hymns to the bust of genius in a niche in the wall. Sometimes the God himself vouchsafed his presence for a moment. Intellect alone admitted the suppliant, and nothing (so the report ran) was said inside that was not witty.

It was thus with great trepidation that Orlando entered the room. She found a company already assembled in a semicircle round the fire. Lady R., an oldish lady, of dark complexion, with a black lace mantilla on her head, was seated in a great arm chair in the centre. Thus being somewhat deaf, she could control the conversation on both sides of her. On both sides of her sat men and women of the highest distinction. Every man, it was said, had been a Prime Minister and every woman, it was whispered, had been the mistress of a king. Certain it is that all were brilliant, and all were famous. Orlando took her seat with a deep reverence in silence. . . . After three hours, she curtseyed profoundly and left.

But what, the reader may ask with some exasperation, happened in between? In three hours, such a company must have said the wittiest, the profoundest, the most interesting things in the world. So it would seem indeed. But the fact appears to be that they said nothing. It is a curious characteristic which they share with all the most brilliant societies that the world has known. Old Madame du Deffand and her friends talked for fifty years without stopping. And of it all, what remains? Perhaps three witty sayings. So that we are at liberty to suppose either that nothing was said, or that nothing witty was said, or that the fraction of three witty sayings lasted eighteen thousand two hundred and fifty nights, which does not leave a liberal allowance of wit for any one of them.

The truth would seem to be—if we dare use such a word in such a connection—that all these groups of people lie under an enchantment. The hostess is our modern Sibyl. She is a witch who lays her guests under a spell. In this house they think themselves happy; in that witty; in a third profound. It is all an illusion (which is nothing against it, for illusions are the most valuable and necessary of all things, and she who can create one is among the world's greatest benefactors), but as it is notorious that illusions are shattered by conflict with reality, so no real happiness, no real wit, no real profundity are tolerated where the illusion prevails. This serves to explain why Madame du Deffand said no more than three witty things in the course of fifty years. Had she said more, her circle would have been destroyed. The witticism, as it left her lips, bowled over the current conversation as a cannon ball lays low the violets and the daisies. When she made her famous 'mot de Saint Denis' the very grass was singed. Disillusionment and desolation followed. Not a word was uttered. "Spare us another such, for Heaven's sake, Madame!" her friends cried with one accord. And she obeyed. For almost seventeen years she said nothing memorable and all went well. The beautiful counterpane of illusion lay unbroken on her circle as it lay unbroken on the circle of Lady R. The guests thought that they were happy, thought that they were witty, thought that they were profound, and, as they thought this, other people thought it still more strongly; and so it got about that nothing was more delightful than one of Lady R.'s assemblies; everyone envied those who were admitted; those who were admitted envied themselves because other people envied them; and so there seemed no end to it—except that which we have now to relate.

For about the third time Orlando went there a certain incident occurred. She was still under the illusion that she was listening to the most brilliant epigrams in the world, though, as a matter of fact, old General C. was only saying, at some length, how the gout had left his left leg and gone to his right, while Mr. L. interrupted when any proper name was mentioned, "R.? Oh! I know Billy R. as well as I know myself. S.? My dearest friend. T.? Stayed with him a fortnight in Yorkshire"—which, such is the force of illusion, sounded like the wittiest repartee, the most searching comment upon human life and kept the company in a roar; when the door opened and a little gentleman entered whose name Orlando did not catch. Soon a curiously disagreeable sensation came over her. To judge from their faces, the rest began to feel it as well. One gentleman said there was a draught. The Marchioness of C. feared a cat must be under the sofa. It was as if their eyes were being slowly opened after a pleasant dream and nothing met them but a cheap wash-stand and a dirty counterpane. It was as if the fumes of some delicious wine were slowly leaving them. Still the General talked and still Mr. L. remembered. But it became more and more apparent how red the General's neck was, how bald Mr. L.'s head was. As for what they said—nothing more tedious and trivial could be imagined. Everybody fidgeted and those who had fans, yawned behind them. At last Lady R. rapped with hers upon the arm of her great chair. Both gentlemen stopped talking.

Then the little gentleman said,

He said next,

He said finally,*

Here, it cannot be denied, was true wit, true wisdom, true profundity. The company was thrown into complete dismay. One such saying was bad enough; but three, one after another, on the same evening! No society could survive it.

"Mr. Pope," said old Lady R. in a voice trembling with sarcastic fury, "you are pleased to be witty." Mr. Pope flushed red. Nobody spoke a word. They sat in dead silence some twenty minutes. Then, one by one, they rose and slunk from the room. That they would ever come back after such an experience was doubtful. Link boys could be heard calling their coaches all down South Audley Street. Doors were slammed and carriages drove off. Orlando found herself near Mr. Pope on the staircase. His lean and misshapen frame was shaken by a variety of emotions. Darts of malice, rage, triumph, wit, and terror (he was shaking like a leaf) shot from his eyes. He looked like some squat reptile set with a burning topaz in its forehead. At the same time, the strangest tempest of emotion seized now upon

*These sayings are too well known to require repetition, and besides, they are all to be found in his published works.

the luckless Orlando. A disillusionment so complete as that inflicted not an hour ago leaves the mind rocking from side to side. Everything appears ten times more bare and stark than before. It is a moment fraught with the highest danger for the human spirit. Women turn nuns and men priests in such moments. In such moments, rich men sign away their wealth; and happy men cut their throats with carving knives. Orlando would have done all willingly, but there was a rasher thing still for her to do, and this she did. She invited Mr. Pope to come home with her.

For if it is rash to walk into a lion's den unarmed, rash to navigate the Atlantic in a rowing boat, rash to stand on one foot on the top of St. Paul's, it is still more rash to go home alone with a poet. A poet is Atlantic and lion in one. While one drowns us the other gnaws us. If we survive the teeth, we succumb to the waves. A man who can destroy illusions is both beast and flood. Illusions are to the soul what atmosphere is to the earth. Roll up that tender air and the plant dies, the colour fades. The earth we walk on is a parched cinder. It is marl we tread and fiery cobbles scorch our feet. By the truth we are undone. Life is a dream. 'Tis waking that kills us. He who robs us of our dreams robs us of our life—(and so on for six pages if you will, but the style is tedious and may well be dropped).

On this showing, however, Orlando should have been a heap of cinders by the time the chariot drew up at her house in Blackfriars. That she was still flesh and blood, though certainly exhausted, is entirely due to a fact to which we drew attention earlier in the narrative. The less we see the more we believe. Now the streets that lie between Mayfair and Blackfriars were at that time very imperfectly lit. True, the lighting was a great improvement upon that of the Elizabethan age. Then the benighted traveller had to trust to the stars or the red flame of some night watchman to save him from the gravel pits at Park Lane or the oak woods where swine rooted in the Tottenham

Court Road. But even so it wanted much of our modern effi-
ciency. Lamp posts lit with oil-lamps occurred every two hundred yards or so, but between lay a considerable stretch of pitch
darkness. Thus for ten minutes Orlando and Mr. Pope would be
in blackness; and then for about half a minute again in the light.
A very strange state of mind was thus bred in Orlando. As the
light faded, she began to feel steal over her the most delicious
balm. "This is indeed a very great honour for a young woman,
to be driving with Mr. Pope," she began to think, looking at the
outline of his nose. "I am the most blessed of my sex. Half an
inch from me — indeed, I feel the knot of his knee ribbons
pressing against my thigh — is the greatest wit in her Majesty's
dominions. Future ages will think of us with curiosity and envy
me with fury." Here came the lamp post again. "What a foolish
wretch I am!" she thought. "There is no such thing as fame and
glory. Ages to come will never cast a thought on me or on Mr.
Pope either. What's an 'age,' indeed? What are we?" and their
progress through Berkeley Square seemed the groping of two
blind ants, momentarily thrown together without interest or
concern in common, across a blackened desert. She shivered.
But here again was darkness. Her illusion revived. "How noble
his brow is," she thought (mistaking a hump on a cushion for
Mr. Pope's forehead in the darkness). "What a weight of genius
lives in it! What wit, wisdom and truth — what a wealth of all
those jewels, indeed, for which people are ready to barter their
lives! Yours is the only light that burns for ever. But for you the
human pilgrimage would be performed in utter darkness"; (here
the coach gave a great lurch as it fell into a rut in Park Lane)
"without genius we should be upset and undone. Most august,
most lucid of beams," — thus she was apostrophising the hump
on the cushion when they drove beneath one of the street lamps
in Berkeley Square and she realised her mistake. Mr. Pope had a
forehead no bigger than another man's. "Wretched man," she

thought, "how you have deceived me! I took that hump for your forehead. When one sees you plain, how ignoble, how despicable you are! Deformed and weakly, there is nothing to venerate in you, much to pity, most to despise."

Again they were in darkness and her anger became modified directly she could see nothing but the poet's knees.

"But it is I that am a wretch," she reflected, once they were in complete obscurity again, "for base as you may be, am I not still baser? It is you who nourish and protect me, you who scare the wild beast, frighten the savage, make me clothes of the silk worm's wool, and carpets of the sheep's. If I want to worship have you not provided me with an image of yourself and set it in the sky? Are not evidences of your care everywhere? How humble, how grateful, how docile, should I not be, therefore? Let it be all my joy to serve, honour, and obey you."

Here they reached the big lamp post at the corner of what is now Piccadilly Circus. The light blazed in her eyes, and she saw, besides some degraded creatures of her own sex, two wretched pigmies on a stark desert land. Both were naked, solitary, and defenceless. The one was powerless to help the other. Each had enough to do to look after itself. Looking Mr. Pope full in the face, "It is equally vain," she thought, "for you to think you can protect me, or for me to think I can worship you. The light of truth beats upon us without shadow, and the light of truth is damnably unbecoming to us both."

All this time, of course, they went on talking agreeably, as people of birth and education use, about the Queen's temper and the Prime Minister's gout, while the coach went from light to darkness down the Haymarket, along the Strand, up Fleet Street and reached, at length, her house in Blackfriars. For some time the dark spaces between the lamps had been becoming brighter and the lamps themselves less bright—that is to say, the sun was rising, and it was in the equable but confused light of a summer's morning in which everything is seen but nothing is seen distinctly that they alighted, Mr. Pope handing Orlando from her carriage and Orlando curtseying Mr. Pope to precede her into her mansion with the most scrupulous attention to the rites of the Graces.

From the foregoing passage, however, it must not be supposed that genius (but the disease is now stamped out in the British Isles, the late Lord Tennyson, it is said, being the last person to suffer from it) is constantly alight, for then we should see everything plain and perhaps should be scorched to death in the process. Rather it resembles the lighthouse in its working, which sends one ray and then no more for a time; save that genius is much more capricious in its manifestations and may flash six or seven beams in quick succession (as Mr. Pope did that night) and then lapse into darkness for a year or for ever. To steer by its beams is therefore impossible, and when the dark spell is on them men of genius are, it is said, much like other people.

It was happy for Orlando, though at first disappointing, that this should be so, for she now began to live much in the company of men of genius, yet after all they were not much different from other people. Addison, Pope, Swift, proved, she found, to be fond of tea. They liked arbours. They collected little bits of coloured glass. They adored grottoes. Rank was not distasteful to them. Praise was delightful. They wore plum-coloured suits one day and grey another. Mr. Swift had a fine malacca cane. Mr. Addison scented his handkerchiefs. Mr. Pope suffered with his head. A piece of gossip did not come amiss. Nor were they without their jealousies. (We are jotting down a few reflections that came to Orlando higgledy-piggledy.) At first, she was annoyed with herself for noticing such trifles, and kept a book in which to write down their memorable sayings, but the page remained empty. All the same, her spirits revived, and she took to tearing up her cards of invitation to great parties; kept her evenings free; began to look forward to Mr. Pope's visit, to Mr. Addison's, to Mr. Swift's—and so on and so on. If the reader will here refer to the *Rape of the Lock,* to the *Spectator,* to *Gulliver's Travels,* he will understand precisely what these mysterious words may mean. Indeed, biographers and critics might save themselves all their labours if readers would only take this advice. For when we read:

> Whether the Nymph shall break Diana's Law,
> Or some frail China Jar receive a Flaw,
> Or stain her Honour, or her new Brocade,
> Forget her Pray'rs,—or miss a Masquerade,
> Or lose her heart, or Necklace, at a Ball

—we know as if we heard him how Mr. Pope's tongue flickered like a lizard's, how his eyes flashed, how his hand trembled, how he loved, how he lied, how he suffered. In short, every secret of a writer's soul, every experience of his life, every quality of his mind is written large in his works, yet we require critics to explain the one and biographers to expound the other. That time hangs heavy on people's hands is the only explanation of the monstrous growth.

So, now that we have read a line or two of the *Rape of the Lock,* we know exactly why Orlando was so much amused and so much frightened and so very bright-cheeked and bright-eyed that afternoon.

Mrs. Nelly then knocked at the door to say that Mr. Addison waited on her Ladyship. At this, Mr. Pope got up with a wry smile, made his congee, and limped off. In came Mr. Addison. Let us, as he takes his seat, read the following passage from the *Spectator*.

"I consider woman as a beautiful, romantic animal, that may be adorned with furs and feathers, pearls and diamonds, ores and silks. The lynx shall cast its skin at her feet to make her a tippet, the peacock, parrot and swan shall pay contributions to her muff; the sea shall be searched for shells, and the rocks for gems, and every part of nature furnish out its share towards the embellishment of a creature that is the most consummate work of it. All this, I shall indulge them in, but as for the petticoat I have been speaking of, I neither can, nor will allow it."

We hold that gentleman, cocked hat and all, in the hollow of our hands. Look once more into the crystal. Is he not clear to the very wrinkle in his stocking? Does not every ripple and curve of his wit lie exposed before us, and his benignity and his timidity and his urbanity and the fact that he would marry a Countess and die very respectably in the end? All is clear. And when Mr. Addison has said his say, there is a terrific rap at the door, and Mr. Swift, who had these arbitrary ways with him, walks in unannounced. One moment, where is *Gulliver's Travels?* Here it is! Let us read a passage from the voyage to the Houyhnhnms:

"I enjoyed perfect Health of Body and Tranquillity of Mind; I did not find the Treachery or Inconstancy of a Friend, nor the Injuries of a secret or open Enemy. I had no occasion of bribing, flattering or pimping, to procure the Favour of any great Man or of his Minion. I wanted no Fence against Fraud or Oppression; Here was neither Physician to destroy my Body, nor Lawyer to ruin my Fortune; No Informer to watch my Words, and Actions, or forge Accusations against me for Hire: Here were no Gibers, Censurers, Backbiters, Pickpockets, Highwaymen, House-breakers, Attorneys, Bawds, Buffoons, Gamesters, Politicians, Wits, splenetick tedious Talkers. . . ."

But stop, stop your iron pelt of words, lest you flay us all alive, and yourself too! Nothing can be plainer than that violent man. He is so coarse and yet so clean; so brutal, yet so kind;

scorns the whole world, yet talks baby language to a girl, and
will die, can we doubt it, in a madhouse.

So Orlando poured out tea for them all; and sometimes
when the weather was fine, she carried them down to the country with her, and feasted them royally in the Round Parlour,
which she had hung with their pictures all in a circle, so that Mr.
Pope could not say that Mr. Addison came before him, or the
other way about. They were very witty, too (but their wit is all
in their books) and taught her the most important part of style,
which is the natural run of the voice in speaking—a quality
which none that has not heard it can imitate, not Greene even,
with all his skill; for it is born of the air, and breaks like a wave
on the furniture and rolls and fades away, and is never to be re-
captured, least of all by those who prick up their ears, half a century later, and try. They taught her this, merely by the cadence
of their voices in speech; so that her style changed somewhat,
and she wrote some very pleasant, witty verses and characters
in prose. And so she lavished her wine on them and put bank
notes, which they took very kindly, beneath their plates at dinner, and accepted their dedications, and thought herself highly
honoured by the exchange.

Thus time ran on, and Orlando could often be heard saying
to herself with an emphasis which might, perhaps, make the
hearer a little suspicious, "Upon my soul, what a life this is!"
(For she was still in search of that commodity.) But circumstances soon forced her to consider the matter more narrowly.
One day she was pouring out tea for Mr. Pope while as anyone
can tell from the verses quoted above he sat very bright-eyed,
observant and all crumpled up in a chair by her side.

"Lord," she thought, as she raised the sugar tongs, "how
women in ages to come will envy me! And yet——" she paused;
for Mr. Pope needed her attention. And yet—let us finish her

thought for her—when anybody says "How future ages will
envy me," it is safe to say that they are extremely uneasy at the
present moment. Was this life quite so exciting, quite so flattering, quite so glorious as it sounds when the memoir writer has
done his work upon it? For one thing, Orlando had a positive
hatred of tea; for another, the intellect, divine as it is, and all
worshipful, has a habit of lodging in the most seedy of carcases,
and often, alas, acts the cannibal among the other faculties so
that often, where the Mind is biggest, the Heart, the Senses,
Magnanimity, Charity, Tolerance, Kindliness, and the rest of
them scarcely have room to breathe. Then the high opinion
poets have of themselves; then the low one they have of others;
then the enmities, injuries, envies, and repartees in which they
are constantly engaged; then the volubility with which they impart them; then the rapacity with which they demand sympathy
for them; all this, one may whisper, lest the wits may overhear
us, makes pouring out tea a more precarious and, indeed, arduous occupation than is generally allowed. Added to which (we
whisper again lest the women may overhear us), there is a little
secret which men share among them; Lord Chesterfield whispered it to his son with strict injunctions to secrecy, "Women
are but children of a larger growth. . . . A man of sense only
trifles with them, plays with them, humours and flatters them,"
which, since children always hear what they are not meant to,
and sometimes, even, grow up, may have somehow leaked out,
so that the whole ceremony of pouring out tea is a curious one.
A woman knows very well that, though a wit sends her his
poems, praises her judgment, solicits her criticism, and drinks
her tea, this by no means signifies that he respects her opinions,
admires her understanding, or will refuse, though the rapier is
denied him, to run her through the body with his pen. All this,
we say, whisper it as low as we can, may have leaked out by now;
so that even with the cream jug suspended and the sugar tongs

distended the ladies may fidget a little, look out of the window
a little, yawn a little, and so let the sugar fall with a great plop—
as Orlando did now—into Mr. Pope's tea. Never was any mor-
tal so ready to suspect an insult or so quick to avenge one as Mr.
Pope. He turned to Orlando and presented her instantly with
the rough draught of a certain famous line in the "Characters of
Women." Much polish was afterwards bestowed on it, but even
in the original it was striking enough. Orlando received it with
a curtsey. Mr. Pope left her with a bow. Orlando, to cool her
cheeks, for really she felt as if the little man had struck her,
strolled in the nut grove at the bottom of the garden. Soon the
cool breezes did their work. To her amazement she found that
she was hugely relieved to find herself alone. She watched the
merry boatloads rowing up the river. No doubt the sight put her
in mind of one or two incidents in her past life. She sat herself
down in profound meditation beneath a willow tree. There she
sat till the stars were in the sky. Then she rose, turned, and went
into the house, where she sought her bedroom and locked the
door. Now she opened a cupboard in which hung still many of
the clothes she had worn as a young man of fashion, and from
among them she chose a black velvet suit richly trimmed with
Venetian lace. It was a little out of fashion, indeed, but it fitted
her to perfection and dressed in it she looked the very figure of
a noble Lord. She took a turn or two before the mirror to make
sure that her petticoats had not lost her the freedom of her legs,
and then let herself secretly out of doors.

It was a fine night early in April. A myriad stars mingling
with the light of a sickle moon, which again was enforced by
the street lamps, made a light infinitely becoming to the human
countenance and to the architecture of Mr. Wren. Everything appeared in its tenderest form, yet, just as it seemed on the point
of dissolution, some drop of silver sharpened it to animation.
Thus it was that talk should be, thought Orlando (indulging in

foolish reverie); that society should be, that friendship should
be, that love should be. For, Heaven knows why, just as we have
lost faith in human intercourse some random collocation of
barns and trees or a haystack and a waggon presents us with
so perfect a symbol of what is unattainable that we begin the
search again.

She entered Leicester Square as she made these observations. The buildings had an airy yet formal symmetry not theirs
by day. The canopy of the sky seemed most dexterously washed
in to fill up the outline of roof and chimney. A young woman
who sat dejectedly with one arm drooping by her side, the other
reposing in her lap, on a seat beneath a plane tree in the middle
of the square seemed the very figure of grace, simplicity, and
desolation. Orlando swept her hat off to her in the manner of
a gallant paying his addresses to a lady of fashion in a public
place. The young woman raised her head. It was of the most exquisite shapeliness. The young woman raised her eyes. Orlando
saw them to be of a lustre such as is sometimes seen on teapots
but rarely in a human face. Through this silver glaze the girl
looked up at him (for a man he was to her) appealing, hoping,
trembling, fearing. She rose; she accepted his arm. For—need
we stress the point?—she was of the tribe which nightly bur-
nishes their wares, and sets them in order on the common
counter to wait the highest bidder. She led Orlando to the room
in Gerrard Street which was her lodging. To feel her hanging
lightly yet like a suppliant on her arm, roused in Orlando all the
feelings which become a man. She looked, she felt, she talked
like one. Yet, having been so lately a woman herself, she suspected that the girl's timidity and her hesitating answers and the
very fumbling with the key in the latch and the fold of her cloak
and the droop of her wrist were all put on to gratify her masculinity. Upstairs they went, and the pains which the poor creature had been at to decorate her room and hide the fact that she

had no other deceived Orlando not a moment. The deception roused her scorn; the truth roused her pity. One thing showing through the other bred the oddest assortment of feeling, so that she did not know whether to laugh or to cry. Meanwhile Nell, as the girl called herself, unbuttoned her gloves; carefully concealed the left hand thumb which wanted mending; then drew behind a screen, where, perhaps, she rouged her cheeks, arranged her clothes, fixed a new kerchief round her neck—all the time prattling as women do, to amuse her lover, though Orlando could have sworn, from the tone of her voice, that her thoughts were elsewhere. When all was ready, out she came, prepared—but here Orlando could stand it no longer. In the strangest torment of anger, merriment, and pity she flung off all disguise and admitted herself a woman.

At this, Nell burst into such a roar of laughter as might have been heard across the way.

"Well, my dear," she said, when she had somewhat recovered, "I'm by no means sorry to hear it. For the plain Dunstable of the matter is" (and it was remarkable how soon on discovering that they were of the same sex, her manner changed and she dropped her plaintive, appealing ways) "the plain Dunstable of the matter is, that I'm not in the mood for the society of the other sex to-night. Indeed, I'm in the devil of a fix." Whereupon, drawing up the fire and stirring a bowl of Punch, she told Orlando the whole story of her life. Since it is Orlando's life that engages us at present, we need not relate the adventures of the other lady, but it is certain that Orlando had never known the hours speed faster or more merrily, though Mistress Nell had not a particle of wit about her, and when the name of Mr. Pope came up in talk asked innocently if he were connected with the perruque maker of that name in Jermyn Street. Yet, to Orlando, such is the charm of ease and the seduction of beauty, this poor girl's talk, larded though it was with the commonest expressions of the street corners tasted like wine after the fine phrases she had been used to, and she was forced to the conclusion that there was something in the sneer of Mr. Pope, in the condescension of Mr. Addison, and in the secret of Lord Chesterfield which took away her relish for the society of wits, deeply though she must continue to respect their works.

These poor creatures, she ascertained, for Nell brought Prue, and Prue Kitty, and Kitty Rose, had a society of their own of which they now elected her a member. Each would tell the story of the adventures which had landed her in her present way of life. Several were the natural daughters of earls and one was a good deal nearer than she should have been to the King's person. None was too wretched or too poor but to have some ring or handkerchief in her pocket which stood her in lieu of pedigree. So they would draw round the Punch bowl which Orlando made it her business to furnish generously, and many were the fine tales they told and many the amusing observations they made for it cannot be denied that when women get together— but hist—they are always careful to see that the doors are shut and that not a word of it gets into print. All they desire is—but hist again—is that not a man's step on the stair? All they desire, we were about to say when the gentleman took the very words out of our mouths. Women have no desires, says this gentleman, coming into Nell's parlour; only affectations. Without desires (she has served him and he is gone) their conversation cannot be of the slightest interest to anyone. "It is well known," says Mr. S. W., "that when they lack the stimulus of the other sex, women can find nothing to say to each other. When they are alone, they do not talk; they scratch." And since they cannot talk together and scratching cannot continue without interruption and it is well known (Mr. T. R. has proved it) "that women are incapable of any feeling of affection for their own sex and hold each other in the greatest aversion," what can we suppose that women do when they seek out each other's society?

As that is not a question that can engage the attention of a sensible man, let us, who enjoy the immunity of all biographers and historians from any sex whatever, pass it over, and merely state that Orlando professed great enjoyment in the society of her own sex, and leave it to the gentlemen to prove, as they are very fond of doing, that this is impossible.

But to give an exact and particular account of Orlando's life at this time becomes more and more out of the question. As we peer and grope in the ill-lit, ill-paved, ill-ventilated courtyards that lay about Gerrard Street and Drury Lane at that time, we seem now to catch sight of her and then again to lose it. What makes the task of identification still more difficult is that she found it convenient at this time to change frequently from one set of clothes to another. Thus she often occurs in contemporary memoirs as "Lord" So-and-so, who was in fact her cousin; her bounty is ascribed to him, and it is he who is said to have written the poems that were really hers. She had, it seems, no difficulty in sustaining the different parts, for her sex changed far more frequently than those who have worn only one set of clothing can conceive; nor can there be any doubt that she reaped a twofold harvest by this device; the pleasures of life were increased and its experiences multiplied. From the probity of breeches she turned to the seductiveness of petticoats and enjoyed the love of both sexes equally.

So then one may sketch her spending her morning in a China robe of ambiguous gender among her books; then receiving a client or two (for she had many scores of suppliants) in the same garment; then she would take a turn in the garden and clip the nut trees—for which knee breeches were convenient; then she would change into a flowered taffeta which best suited a drive to Richmond and a proposal of marriage from some great nobleman; and so back again to town, where she would don a snuff-coloured gown like a lawyer's and visit the courts to hear how her cases were doing — for her fortune was wasting hourly and the suits seemed no nearer consummation than they had been a hundred years ago; and so, finally, when night came, she would more often than not become a nobleman complete from head to toe and walk the streets in search of adventure.

Returning from some of these junketings — of which there were many stories told at the time, as, that she fought a duel, served on one of the King's ships as a captain, was seen to dance naked on a balcony, and fled with a certain lady to the Low Countries where the lady's husband followed them (but of the truth or otherwise of these stories, we express no opinion), returning from whatever her occupation may have been, she made a point sometimes of passing beneath the windows of a coffee house, where she could see the wits without being seen, and thus could fancy from their gestures what wise, witty, or spiteful things they were saying without hearing a word of them which was perhaps an advantage; and once she stood half an hour watching three shadows on the blind drinking tea together in a house in Bolt Court.

Never was any play so absorbing. She wanted to cry out, Bravo! Bravo! For, to be sure, what a fine drama it was — what a page torn from the thickest volume of human life! There was the little shadow with the pouting lips, fidgeting this way and that on his chair, uneasy, petulant, officious; there was the bent female shadow, crooking a finger in the cup to feel how deep the tea was, for she was blind; and there was the Roman-looking rolling shadow in the big arm-chair — he who twisted his fingers so oddly and jerked his head from side to side and swallowed down the tea in such vast gulps. Dr. Johnson, Mr. Boswell, and Mrs. Williams, those were the shadows' names. So absorbed was she in the sight, that she forgot to think how other ages would have envied her, though it seems probable that on this occasion they would. She was content to gaze and gaze. At length Mr. Boswell rose. He saluted the old woman with tart asperity. But with what humility did he not abase himself before the great rolling shadow, who now rose to its full height and rocking somewhat as he stood there rolled out the most magnificent phrases that have ever left human lips; so Orlando thought them, though she never heard a word that any of the three shadows said as they sat there drinking tea.

At length she came home one night after one of these saunterings and mounted to her bedroom. She took off her laced coat and stood there in shirt and breeches looking out of the window. There was something stirring in the air which forbade her to go to bed. A white haze lay over the town, for it was a frosty night in midwinter and a magnificent vista lay all round her. She could see St. Paul's, the Tower, Westminster Abbey, with all the spires and domes of the city churches, the smooth bulk of its banks, the opulent and ample curves of its halls and meeting-places. On the north rose the smooth, shorn heights of Hampstead, and in the west the streets and squares of Mayfair shone out in one clear radiance. Upon this serene and orderly prospect the stars looked down, glittering, positive, hard, from a cloudless sky. In the extreme clearness of the atmosphere the line of every roof, the cowl of every chimney was perceptible. Even the cobbles in the streets showed distinct one from another; and Orlando could not help comparing this orderly scene with the irregular and huddled purlieus which had been the city of London in the reign of Queen Elizabeth. Then, she remembered, the city, if such one could call it, lay crowded, a mere huddle and conglomeration of houses, under her windows at Blackfriars. The stars reflected themselves in deep pits of stagnant water which lay in the middle of the streets. A black shadow at the corner where the wine shop used to stand was as likely as not, the corpse of a murdered man. She could remember the cries of many a one wounded in such night brawlings, when she was a little boy, held to the diamond-paned window in her nurse's arms. Troops of ruffians, men and women, unspeakably interlaced, lurched down the streets, trolling out wild songs with jewels flashing in their ears, and knives gleaming in their fists. On such a night as this the impermeable tangle of the forests on Highgate and Hampstead would be outlined, writhing in contorted intricacy against the sky. Here and there, on one of the hills which rose above London, was a stark gallows tree, with a corpse nailed to rot or parch on its cross; for danger and insecurity, lust and violence, poetry and filth swarmed over the tortuous Elizabethan highways and buzzed and stank—Orlando could remember even now the smell of them on a hot night—in the little rooms and narrow pathways of the city. Now—she leant out of her window—all was light, order, and serenity. There was the faint rattle of a coach on the cobbles. She heard the far-away cry of the night watchman—"Just twelve o'clock on a frosty morning." No sooner had the words left his lips than the first stroke of midnight sounded. Orlando then for the first time noticed a small cloud gathered behind the dome of St. Paul's. As the stroke sounded, the cloud increased, and she saw it darken and spread with extraordinary speed. At the same time a light breeze rose and by the time the sixth stroke of midnight had struck the whole of the eastern sky was covered with an irregular moving darkness, though the sky to the west and north stayed clear as ever. Then the cloud spread north. Height upon height above the city was engulfed by it. Only Mayfair, with all its lights, burnt more brilliantly than ever by contrast. With the eighth stroke, some hurrying tatters of cloud sprawled over Piccadilly. They seemed to mass themselves and to advance with extraordinary rapidity towards the west end. As the ninth, tenth and eleventh strokes struck, a huge blackness sprawled over the whole of London. With the twelfth stroke of midnight, the darkness was complete. A turbulent welter of cloud covered the city. All was dark; all was doubt; all was confusion. The Eighteenth century was over; the Nineteenth century had begun.

CHAPTER FIVE

THIS GREAT cloud which hung, not only over London, but over the whole of the British Isles on the first day of the nineteenth century stayed, or rather, did not stay, for it was buffeted about constantly by blustering gales, long enough to have extraordinary consequences upon those who lived beneath its shadow. A change seemed to have come over the climate of England. Rain fell frequently, but only in fitful gusts, which were no sooner over than they began again. The sun shone, of course, but it was so girt about with clouds and the air was so saturated with water, that its beams were discoloured and purples, oranges, and reds of a dull sort took the place of the more positive landscapes of the eighteenth century. Under this bruised and sullen canopy the green of the cabbages was less intense, and the white of the snow was muddied. But what was worse, damp now began to make its way into every house — damp, which is the most insidious of all enemies, for while the sun can be shut out by blinds, and the frost roasted by a hot fire, damp steals in while we sleep; damp is silent, imperceptible, ubiquitous. Damp swells the wood, furs the kettle, rusts the iron, rots the stone. So gradual is the process, that it is not until we pick up some chest of drawers, or coal scuttle, and the whole thing drops to pieces in our hands, that we suspect even that the disease is at work.

Thus, stealthily, and imperceptibly, none marking the exact day or hour of the change, the constitution of England was altered and nobody knew it. Everywhere the effects were felt. The hardy country gentleman, who had sat down gladly to a meal of ale and beef in a room designed, perhaps by the brothers Adam, with classic dignity, now felt chilly. Rugs appeared, beards were grown and trousers fastened tight under the instep. The chill which he felt in his legs he soon transferred to his house; furniture was muffled; walls and tables were covered too. Then a change of diet became essential. The muffin was invented and the crumpet. Coffee supplanted the after-dinner port, and, as coffee led to a drawing-room in which to drink it, and a drawing-room to glass cases, and glass cases to artificial flowers, and artificial flowers to mantelpieces, and mantelpieces to pianofortes, and pianofortes to drawing-room ballads, and drawing-room ballads (skipping a stage or two) to innumerable little dogs, mats, and antimacassars, the home—which had become extremely important—was completely altered.

Outside the house—it was another effect of the damp—ivy grew in unparalleled profusion. Houses that had been of bare stone were smothered in greenery. No garden, however formal its original design, lacked a shrubbery, a wilderness, a maze. What light penetrated to the bedrooms where children were born was naturally of an obfusc green and what light penetrated to the drawing-rooms where grown men and women lived came through curtains of brown and purple plush. But the change did not stop at outward things. The damp struck within. Men felt the chill in their hearts; the damp in their minds. In a desperate effort to snuggle their feelings into some sort of warmth one subterfuge was tried after another. Love, birth, and death were all swaddled in a variety of fine phrases. The sexes drew further and further apart. No open conversation was tolerated. Evasions and concealments were sedulously practised on both sides. And just as the ivy and the evergreen rioted in the damp earth outside, so did the same fertility show itself within⸢The life of the average woman was a succession of child-births. She married at nineteen and had fifteen or eighteen children by the time she was thirty; for twins abounded.⸥Thus the British Empire came into existence; and thus—for there is no stopping damp; it gets into the inkpot as it gets into the wood-work—sentences swelled, adjectives multiplied, lyrics became epics, and little trifles that had been essays a column long were now encyclopaedias in ten or twenty volumes. But Eusebius Chubb shall be our witness to the effect this all had upon the mind of a sensitive man who could do nothing to stop it. There is a passage towards the end of his memoirs where he describes how, after writing thirty-five folio pages one morning 'all about nothing' he screwed the lid on his inkpot and went for a turn in his garden. Soon he found himself involved in the shrubbery. Innumerable leaves creaked and glistened above his head. He seemed to himself "to crush the mould of a million more under his feet." Thick smoke exuded from a damp bonfire at the end of the garden. He reflected that no fire on earth could ever hope to consume that vast vegetable encumbrance. Wherever he looked, vegetation was rampant. Cucumbers "came scrolloping across the grass to his feet." Giant cauliflowers towered deck above deck till they rivalled, to his disordered imagination, the elm trees themselves. Hens laid incessantly eggs of no special tint. Then, remembering with a sigh his own fecundity and his poor wife Jane, now in the throes of her fifteenth confinement indoors, how, he asked himself, could he blame the fowls? He looked upwards into the sky. Did not heaven itself, or that great frontispiece of heaven, which is the sky, indicate the assent, in-deed, the instigation of the heavenly hierarchy? For there, win-ter or summer, year in year out, the clouds turned and tumbled,

like whales, he pondered, or elephants rather; but no, there was
no escaping the simile which was pressed upon him from a
thousand airy acres; the whole sky itself as it spread wide above
the British Isles was nothing but a vast feather bed; and the
undistinguished fecundity of the garden, the bedroom and the
henroost was copied there. He went indoors, wrote the passage
quoted above, laid his head in a gas oven, and when they found
him later he was past revival.

While this went on in every part of England, it was all very
well for Orlando to mew herself in her house at Blackfriars and
pretend that the climate was the same; that one could still say
what one liked and wear knee-breeches or skirts as the fancy
took one. Even she, at length, was forced to acknowledge that
times were changed. One afternoon in the early part of the century she was driving through St. James' Park in her old panelled
coach when one of those sunbeams, which occasionally, though
not often, managed to come to earth, struggled through, mar-
bling the clouds with strange prismatic colours as it passed. Such
a sight was sufficiently strange after the clear and uniform skies
of the eighteenth century to cause her to pull the window down
and look at it. The puce and flamingo clouds made her think
with a pleasurable anguish, which proves that she was insensibly
afflicted with the damp already, of dolphins dying in Ionian seas.
But what was her surprise when, as it struck the earth, the sun-
beam seemed to call forth, or to light up, a pyramid, hecatomb,
or trophy (for it had something of a banquet-table air)—a conglomeration at any rate of the most heterogeneous and ill-
assorted objects, piled higgledy-piggledy in a vast mound where
the statue of Queen Victoria now stands! Draped about a vast
cross of fretted and floriated gold were widow's weeds and bridal
veils; hooked on to other excrescences were crystal palaces,
bassinettes, military helmets, memorial wreaths, trousers, whiskers,

wedding cakes, cannon, Christmas trees, telescopes, extinct monsters, globes, maps, elephants and mathematical-instruments—
the whole supported like a gigantic coat of arms on the right
side by a female figure clothed in flowing white; on the left, by a
portly gentleman wearing a frock-coat and sponge-bag trousers.
The incongruity of the objects, the association of the fully
clothed and the partly draped, the garishness of the different
colours and their plaid-like juxtapositions afflicted Orlando with
the most profound dismay. She had never, in all her life, seen
anything at once so indecent, so hideous, and so monumental.
It might, and indeed it must be, the effect of the sun on the
water-logged air; it would vanish with the first breeze that blew;
but for all that, it looked, as she drove past, as if it were destined
to endure for ever. Nothing, she felt, sinking back into the corner of her coach, no wind, rain, sun, or thunder, could ever demolish that garish erection. Only the noses would mottle and
the trumpets would rust; but there they would remain, pointing
east, west, south, and north, eternally. She looked back as her
coach swept up Constitution Hill. Yes, there it was, still beam-
ing placidly in a light which—she pulled her watch out of her
fob—was, of course, the light of twelve o'clock mid-day. None
other could be so prosaic, so matter of fact, so impervious to
any hint of dawn or sunset, so seemingly calculated to last for
ever. She was determined not to look again. Already she felt the
tides of her blood run sluggishly. But what was more peculiar,
a blush, vivid and singular, overspread her cheeks as she passed
Buckingham Palace and her eyes seemed forced by a superior
power down upon her knees. Suddenly she saw with a start that
she was wearing black breeches. She never ceased blushing till
she had reached her country house, which, considering the time
it takes four horses to trot thirty miles, will be taken, we hope,
as a signal proof of her chastity.

Once there, she followed what had now become the most imperious need of her nature and wrapped herself as well as she could in a damask quilt which she snatched from her bed. She explained to the Widow Bartholomew (who had succeeded good old Grimsditch as housekeeper) that she felt chilly.

"So do we all, m'lady," said the Widow, heaving a profound sigh. "The walls is sweating," she said, with a curious, lugubrious complacency, and sure enough, she had only to lay her hand on the oak panels for the fingerprints to be marked there. The ivy had grown so profusely that many windows were now sealed up. The kitchen was so dark that they could scarcely tell a kettle from a cullender. A poor black cat had been mistaken for coals and shovelled on the fire. Most of the maids were already wearing three or four red-flannel petticoats, though the month was August.

"But is it true, m'lady," the good woman asked, hugging herself, while the golden crucifix heaved on her bosom, "that the Queen, bless her, is wearing a what d'you call it, a———," the good woman hesitated and blushed.

"A crinoline," Orlando helped her out (for the word had reached Blackfriars). Mrs. Bartholomew nodded. The tears were already running down her cheeks, but as she wept she smiled. For it was pleasant to weep. Were they not all of them weak women? wearing crinolines the better to conceal the fact; the great fact; the only fact; but, nevertheless, the deplorable fact; which every modest woman did her best to deny until denial was impossible; the fact that she was about to bear a child? to bear fifteen or twenty children indeed, so that most of a modest woman's life was spent, after all, in denying what, on one day at least of every year, was made obvious.

"The muffins is keepin' 'ot," said Mrs. Bartholomew, mopping up her tears, "in the liberry."

And wrapped in a damask bed quilt, to a dish of muffins Orlando now sat down.

"The muffins is keepin' 'ot in the liberry"—Orlando minced out the horrid Cockney phrase in Mrs. Bartholomew's refined Cockney accents as she drank—but not, she detested the mild fluid—her tea. It was in this very room, she remembered, that Queen Elizabeth had stood astride the fireplace with a flagon of beer in her hand, which she suddenly dashed on the table when Lord Burghley tactlessly used the imperative instead of the subjunctive. "Little man, little man,"—Orlando could hear her say—"is 'must' a word to be addressed to princes?" And down came the flagon on the table: there was the mark of it still.

But when Orlando leapt to her feet, as the mere thought of that great Queen commanded, the bed quilt tripped her up, and she fell back in her arm-chair with a curse. To-morrow she would have to buy twenty yards or more of black bombazine, she supposed, to make a skirt. And then (here she blushed), she would have to buy a crinoline, and then (here she blushed) a bassinette, and then another crinoline, and so on.... The blushes came and went with the most exquisite iteration of modesty and shame imaginable. One might see the spirit of the age blowing, now hot, now cold, upon her cheeks. And if the spirit of the age blew a little unequally, the crinoline being blushed for before the husband, her ambiguous position must excuse her (even her sex was still in dispute) and the irregular life she had lived before.

At length the colour on her cheeks resumed its stability and it seemed as if the spirit of the age—if such indeed it were—lay dormant for a time. Then Orlando felt in the bosom of her shirt as if for some locket or relic of lost affection, and drew out no such thing, but a roll of paper, sea-stained, blood-stained, travel-stained—the manuscript of her poem, "The Oak Tree." She had carried this about with her for so many years now, and in such hazardous circumstances, that many of the pages were stained, some were torn, while the straits she had been in for writing paper when with the gipsies, had forced her to overscore the margins and cross the lines till the manuscript looked like a piece of darning most conscientiously carried out. She turned back to the first page and read the date, 1586, written in her own boyish hand. She had been working at it for close on three hundred years now. It was time to make an end. And so she began turning and dipping and reading and skipping and thinking as she read how very little she had changed all these years. She had been a gloomy boy, in love with death, as boys are; and then she had been amorous and florid; and then she had been sprightly and satirical; and sometimes she had tried prose and sometimes she had tried the drama. Yet through all these changes she had remained, she reflected, fundamentally the same. She had the same brooding meditative temper, the same love of animals and nature, the same passion for the country and the seasons.

"After all," she thought, getting up and going to the window, "nothing has changed. The house, the garden are precisely as they were. Not a chair has been moved, not a trinket sold. There are the same walks, the same lawns, the same trees, and the same pool, with, I dare say, the same carp in it. True, Queen Victoria is on the throne and not Queen Elizabeth, but what difference. . . ."

No sooner had the thought taken shape, than, as if to rebuke it, the door was flung wide, and in marched Basket, the butler, followed by Bartholomew, the housekeeper, to clear away tea. Orlando, who had just dipped her pen in the ink, and was about to indite some reflection upon the eternity of all things, was much annoyed to be impeded by a blot, which spread and meandered round her pen. It was some infirmity of the quill, she supposed; it was split or dirty. She dipped it again. The blot increased. She tried to go on with what she was saying; no words came. Next she tried to decorate the blot with wings and whiskers, till it became a round-headed monster, something between a bat and a wombat. But as for writing poetry with Basket and Bartholomew in the room, it was impossible. No sooner had she said "Impossible" than, to her astonishment and alarm, the pen began to curve and caracole with the smoothest possible fluency. Her page was written in the neatest sloping Italian hand with the most insipid verse she had ever read in her life:

> I am myself but a vile link
>   Amid life's weary chain,
> But I have spoken hallow'd words,
>   Oh, do not say in vain!

> Will the young maiden, when her tears,
>   Alone in moonlight shine,
> Tears for the absent and the loved,
>   Murmur——

she wrote without a stop as Bartholomew and Basket grunted and groaned about the room, mending the fire, picking up the muffins.

Again she dipped her pen and off it went—

> She was so changed, the soft carnation cloud
> Once mantling o'er her cheek like that which eve
> Hangs o'er the sky, glowing with roseate hue,
> Had faded into paleness, broken by
> Bright burning blushes, torches of the tomb,

but here, by an abrupt movement she spilt the ink over the page and blotted it from human sight she hoped for ever. She was all of a quiver, all of a stew. Nothing more repulsive could be imagined than to feel the ink flowing thus in cascades of involuntary inspiration. What had happened to her? Was it the damp, was it Bartholomew, was it Basket, what was it? she demanded. But the room was empty. No one answered her, unless the dripping of the rain in the ivy could be taken for an answer.

Meanwhile, she became conscious, as she stood at the window, of an extraordinary tingling and vibration all over her, as if she were made of a thousand wires upon which some breeze or errant fingers were playing scales. Now her toes tingled; now her marrow. She had the queerest sensations about the thigh bones. Her hairs seemed to erect themselves. Her arms sang and twanged as the telegraph wires would be singing and twanging in twenty years or so. But all this agitation seemed at length to concentrate in her hands; and then in one hand, and then in one finger of that hand, and then finally to contract itself so that it made a ring of quivering sensibility about the second finger of the left hand. And when she raised it to see what caused this agitation, she saw nothing—nothing but the vast solitary emerald which Queen Elizabeth had given her. And was that not enough? she asked. It was of the finest water. It was worth ten thousand pounds at least. The vibration seemed, in the oddest way (but remember we are dealing with some of the darkest manifestations of the human soul) to say No, that is not enough; and, further, to assume a note of interrogation, as though they were asking, what did it mean, this hiatus, this strange oversight? till poor Orlando felt positively ashamed of the second finger of her left hand without in the least knowing why. At this moment, Bartholomew came in to ask which dress she should lay out for dinner, and Orlando, whose senses were much quickened, instantly glanced at Bartholomew's left hand, and instantly perceived what she had never noticed before—a thick ring of rather jaundiced yellow circling the second finger where her own was bare.

"Let me look at your ring, Bartholomew," she said, stretching her hand to take it.

At this, Bartholomew made as if she had been struck in the breast by a rogue. She started back a pace or two, clenched her hand and flung it away from her with a gesture that was noble in the extreme. ["No," she said, with resolute dignity, her Ladyship might look if she pleased, but as for taking off her wedding ring, not the Archbishop nor the Pope nor Queen Victoria on her throne could force her to do that. Her Thomas had put it on her finger twenty-five years, six months, three weeks ago; she had slept in it; worked in it; washed in it; prayed in it; and proposed to be buried in it. In fact, Orlando understood her to say, but her voice was much broken with emotion, that it was by the gleam on her wedding ring that she would be assigned her station among the angels and its lustre would be tarnished for ever if she let it out of her keeping for a second.]

"Heaven help us," said Orlando, standing at the window and watching the pigeons at their pranks. "What a world we live in! What a world to be sure." Its complexities amazed her. It now seemed to her that the whole world was ringed with gold. She went in to dinner. Wedding rings abounded. She went to church. Wedding rings were everywhere. She drove out. Gold, or pinchbeck, thin, thick, plain, smooth, they glowed dully on every hand. Rings filled the jewellers' shops, not the flashing pastes and diamonds of Orlando's recollection, but simple bands without a stone in them. At the same time, she began to notice a new habit among the town people. In the old days, one would meet a boy trifling with a girl under a hawthorn hedge frequently enough. Orlando had flicked many a couple with the tip of her whip and laughed and passed on. Now, all that was changed. Couples trudged and plodded in the middle of the road indissolubly linked together. The woman's right hand was invariably passed through the man's left and her fingers were firmly gripped by his. Often it was not till the horses' noses were on them that they budged, and then, though they moved it was all in one piece, heavily, to the side of the road. Orlando could only suppose that some new discovery had been made about the race; they were somehow stuck together, couple after couple, but who had made it, and when, she could not guess. It did not seem to be Nature. She looked at the doves and the rabbits and the elk hounds and she could not see that Nature had changed her ways or mended them, since the time of Elizabeth at least. There was no indissoluble alliance among the brutes that she could see. Could it be Queen Victoria then, or Lord Melbourne? Was it from them that the great discovery of marriage proceeded? Yet the Queen, she pondered, was said to be fond of dogs, and Lord Melbourne, she had heard, was said to be fond of women. It was strange—it was distasteful; indeed, there was something in this indissolubility of bodies which was repugnant to her sense of decency and sanitation. Her ruminations, however, were accompanied by such a tingling and twangling of the afflicted finger that she could scarcely keep her ideas in order. They were languishing and ogling like a housemaid's fancies. They made her blush. There was nothing for it but to buy one of those ugly bands and wear it like the rest. This she did, slipping it, overcome with shame, upon her finger in the shadow of a curtain; but without avail. The tingling persisted more violently, more indignantly than ever. She did not sleep a wink that night. Next morning when she took up the pen to write, either she could think of nothing, and the pen made one large lachrymose blot after another, or it ambled off, more alarmingly still into mellifluous fluencies about early death and corruption, which were worse than no thinking at all. For it would seem—her case proved it—that we write, not with the fingers, but with the whole person. The nerve which controls the pen winds itself about every fibre of our being, threads the heart, pierces the liver. Though the seat of her trouble seemed to be the left finger, she could feel herself poisoned through and through, and was forced at length to consider the most desperate of remedies, which was to yield completely and submissively to the spirit of the age, and take a husband.

That this was much against her natural temperament, has been sufficiently made plain. When the sound of the Archduke's chariot wheels died away, the cry that rose to her lips was "Life! A Lover!" not "Life! A Husband!" and it was in pursuit of this aim that she had gone to town and run about the world as has been shown in the previous chapter. Such is the indomitable nature of the spirit of the age however, that it batters down anyone who tries to make stand against it far more effectually than those who bend its own way. Orlando had inclined herself naturally to the Elizabethan spirit, to the Restoration spirit, to the spirit of the eighteenth century, and had in consequence scarcely been aware of the change from one age to the other. But the spirit of the nineteenth century was antipathetic to her in the extreme, and thus it took her and broke her, and she was aware of her defeat at its hands as she had never been before. For it is probable that the human spirit has its place in time assigned to it; some are born of this age, some of that; and now that Orlando was grown a woman, a year or two past thirty indeed, the lines of her character were fixed, and to bend them the wrong way was intolerable.

So she stood mournfully at the drawing-room window (Bartholomew had so christened the library) dragged down by the weight of the crinoline which she had submissively adopted. It was heavier and more drab than any dress she had yet worn. None had ever so impeded her movements. No longer could she stride through the garden with her dogs, or run lightly to the high mound and fling herself beneath the oak tree. Her skirts collected damp leaves and straw. The plumed hat tossed on the breeze. The thin shoes were quickly soaked and mud-caked. Her muscles had lost their pliancy. She had become nervous lest there should be robbers behind the wainscot and afraid, for the first time in her life, of ghosts in the corridors. All these things inclined her, step by step, to submit to the new discovery, whether Queen Victoria's or another's, that each man and each woman has another allotted to it for life, whom it supports, by whom it is supported, till death them do part. It would be a comfort, she felt, to lean; to sit down; yes, to lie down; never, never, never to get up again. Thus did the spirit work upon her, for all her past pride, and as she came sloping down the scale of emotion to this lowly and unaccustomed lodging place, those twanglings and tinglings which had been so captious and so interrogative modulated into the sweetest melodies, till it seemed as if angels were plucking harp-strings with white fingers and her whole being was pervaded by a seraphic harmony.

But whom could she lean upon? She asked that question of the wild autumn winds. For it was now October, and wet as usual. Not the Archduke; he had married a very great lady and had hunted hares in Roumania these many years now; nor Mr. M.; he was become a Catholic; nor the Marquis of C.; he made sacks in Botany Bay; nor the Lord O.; he had long been food for fishes. One way or another, all her old cronies were gone now, and the Nells and the Kits of Drury Lane, much though she favoured them, scarcely did to lean upon.

"Whom," she asked, casting her eyes upon the revolving clouds, clasping her hands, as she knelt on the window-sill, and looking the very image of appealing womanhood as she did so, "can I lean upon?" Her words formed themselves, her hands clasped themselves, involuntarily, just as her pen had written of its own accord. It was not Orlando who spoke, but the spirit of the age. But whichever it was, nobody answered it. The rooks were tumbling pell mell among the violet clouds of autumn.

The rain had stopped at last and there was an iridescence in the sky which tempted her to put on her plumed hat and her little stringed shoes and stroll out before dinner.

"Everyone is mated except myself," she mused, as she trailed disconsolately across the courtyard. There were the rooks; Canute and Pippin even—transitory as their alliances were, still each this evening seemed to have a partner. "Whereas, I, who am mistress of it all," Orlando thought, glancing as she passed at the innumerable emblazoned windows of the hall, "am single, am mateless, am alone."

Such thoughts had never entered her head before. Now they bore her down unescapably. Instead of thrusting the gate open, she tapped with a gloved hand for the porter to unfasten it for her. One must lean on someone, she thought, if it is only on a porter; and half wished to stay behind and help him to grill his chop on a bucket of fiery coals, but was too timid to ask it. So she strayed out into the park alone, faltering at first and apprehensive lest there might be poachers or game keepers or even errand-boys to marvel that a great lady should walk alone.

At every step she glanced nervously lest some male form should be hiding behind a furze bush or some savage cow be lowering its horns to toss her. But there were only the rooks flaunting in the sky. A steel-blue plume from one of them fell among the heather. She loved wild birds' feathers. She had used to collect them as a boy. She picked it up and stuck it in her hat. The air blew upon her spirit somewhat and revived it. As the rooks went whirling and wheeling above her head and feather after feather fell gleaming through the purplish air, she followed them, her long cloak floating behind her, over the moor, up the hill. She had not walked so far for years. Six feathers had she picked from the grass and drawn between her finger tips and pressed to her lips to feel their smooth, glinting plumage, when she saw, gleaming on the hill-side, a silver pool, mysterious as

Orlando about the year 1840

the lake into which Sir Bedivere flung the sword of Arthur. A single feather quivered in the air and fell into the middle of it. Then, some strange ecstasy came over her. Some wild notion she had of following the birds to the rim of the world and flinging herself on the spongy turf and there drinking forgetfulness, while the rooks' hoarse laughter sounded over her. She quickened her pace; she ran; she tripped; the tough heather roots flung her to the ground. Her ankle was broken. She could not rise. But there she lay content. The scent of the bog myrtle and the meadow-sweet was in her nostrils. The rooks' hoarse laughter was in her ears. "I have found my mate," she murmured. "It is the moor. I am nature's bride," she whispered, giving herself in rapture to the cold embraces of the grass as she lay folded in her cloak in the hollow by the pool. "Here will I lie. (A feather fell upon her brow.) I have found a greener laurel than the bay. My forehead will be cool always. These are wild birds' feathers—the owls, the nightjars. I shall dream wild dreams. My hands shall wear no wedding ring," she continued, slipping it from her finger. "The roots shall twine about them. Ah!" she sighed, pressing her head luxuriously on its spongy pillow, "I have sought happiness through many ages and not found it; fame and missed it; love and not known it; life—and behold, death is better. I have known many men and many women," she continued; "none have I understood. It is better that I should lie at peace here with only the sky above me—as the gipsy told me years ago. That was in Turkey." And she looked straight up into the marvellous golden foam into which the clouds had churned themselves, and saw next moment a track in it, and camels passing in single file through the rocky desert among clouds of red dust; and then, when the camels had passed, there were only mountains, very high and full of clefts and with pinnacles of rock, and she fancied she heard goat bells ringing in their passes, and in their folds were fields of irises and gentians.

So the sky changed and her eyes slowly lowered themselves down and down till they came to the rain-darkened earth and saw the great hump of the South Downs, flowing in one wave along the coast; and where the land parted, there was the sea, the sea with ships passing; and she fancied she heard a gun far out at sea, and thought at first, "That's the Armada," and then she thought, "No, it's Nelson," and then remembered how those wars were over and the ships were busy merchant ships; and the sails on the winding river were those of pleasure boats. She saw, too, cattle sprinkled on the dark fields, sheep and cows, and she saw the lights coming here and there in farm-house windows, and lanterns moving among the cattle as the shepherd went his rounds and the cowman; and then the lights went out and the stars rose and tangled themselves about the sky. Indeed, she was falling asleep with the wet feathers on her face and her ear pressed to the ground when she heard, deep within, some hammer on an anvil, or was it a heart beating? Tick-tock, tick-tock, so it hammered, so it beat, the anvil, or the heart in the middle of the earth; until, as she listened, she thought it changed to the trot of a horse's hoofs; one, two, three, four, she counted; then she heard a stumble; then, as it came nearer and nearer, she could hear the crack of a twig and the suck of the wet bog in its hoofs. The horse was almost on her. She sat upright. Towering dark against the yellow-slashed sky of dawn, with the plovers rising and falling about him, she saw a man on horseback. He started. The horse stopped.

"Madam," the man cried, leaping to the ground, "you're hurt!"

"I'm dead, Sir!" she replied.

A FEW MINUTES later, they became engaged.

The morning after as they sat at breakfast, he told her his name. It was Marmaduke Bonthrop Shelmerdine, Esquire.

"I knew it!" she said, for there was something romantic and chivalrous, passionate, melancholy, yet determined about him which went with the wild, dark-plumed name — a name which had in her mind, the steel blue gleam of rooks' wings, the hoarse laughter of their caws, the snake-like twisting descent of their feathers in a silver pool, and a thousand other things besides, which will be described presently.

"Mine is Orlando," she said. He had guessed it. For if you see a ship in full sail coming with the sun on it proudly sweeping across the Mediterranean from the South Seas, one says at once, "Orlando," he explained.

In fact, though their acquaintance had been so short, they had guessed, as always happens between lovers, everything of any importance about each other in two seconds at the utmost, and it now remained only to fill in such unimportant details as what they were called; where they lived; and whether they were beggars or people of substance. He had a castle in the Hebrides, but it was ruined, he told her. Gannets feasted in the banqueting hall. He had been a soldier and a sailor, and had explored the East. He was on his way now to join his brig at Falmouth, but the wind had fallen and it was only when the gale blew from the South-west that he could put out to sea. Orlando looked hastily out of the breakfast room window at the gilt leopard on the weather vane. Mercifully his tail pointed due east and was steady as a rock. "Oh! Shel, don't leave me!" she cried. "I'm passionately in love with you," she said. No sooner had the words left her mouth than an awful suspicion rushed into both their minds simultaneously.

"You're a woman, Shel!" she cried.

"You're a man, Orlando!" he cried.

Never was there such a scene of protestation and demonstration as then took place since the world began. When it was over and they were seated again she asked him, what was this talk of a South-west gale? Where was he bound for?

"For the Horn," he said briefly, and blushed. (For a man had to blush as a woman had, only at rather different things.) It was only by dint of great pressure on her side and the use of much intuition that she gathered that his life was spent in the most desperate and splendid of adventures—which is to voyage round Cape Horn in the teeth of a gale. Masts had been snapped off; sails torn to ribbons (she had to drag the admission from him). Sometimes the ship had sunk, and he had been left the only survivor on a raft with a biscuit.

"It's about all a fellow can do nowadays," he said sheepishly, and helped himself to great spoonfuls of strawberry jam. The vision which she had thereupon of this boy (for he was little more) sucking peppermints, for which he had a passion, while the masts snapped and the stars reeled and he roared brief orders to cut this adrift, to stow that overboard, brought the tears to her eyes, tears, she noted, of a finer flavour than any she had cried before. "I am a woman," she thought, "a real woman, at last." She thanked Bonthrop from the bottom of her heart for having given her this rare and unexpected delight. Had she not been lame in the left foot, she would have sat upon his knee.

"Shel, my darling," she began again, "tell me . . ." and so they talked two hours or more, perhaps about Cape Horn, perhaps not, and really it would profit little to write down what they said, for they knew each other so well that they could say anything they liked, which is tantamount to saying nothing, or saying such stupid, prosy things, as how to cook an omelette, or where to buy the best boots in London, which have no lustre taken from their setting, yet are positively of amazing beauty within it. For it has come about, by the wise economy of nature, that our modern spirit can almost dispense with language; the commonest expressions do, since no expressions do; hence the most ordinary conversation is often the most poetic, and the most poetic is precisely that which cannot be written down. For which reasons we leave a great blank here, which must be taken to indicate that the space is filled to repletion.

After some days more of this kind of talk,

"Orlando, my dearest," Shel was beginning, when there was a scuffling outside, and Basket the butler entered with the information that there was a couple of Peelers downstairs with a warrant from the Queen.

"Show 'em up," said Shelmerdine briefly, as if on his own quarter deck taking up, by instinct, a stand with his hands behind him in front of the fireplace. Two officers in bottle green uniforms with truncheons at their hips then entered the room and stood at attention. Formalities being over, they gave into Orlando's own hands, as their commission was, a legal document of some very impressive sort, judging by the blobs of sealing wax, the ribbons, the oaths, and the signatures, which were all of the highest importance.

Orlando ran her eyes through it and then, using the first finger of her right hand as pointer, read out the following facts as being most germane to the matter.

"The lawsuits are settled," she read out ... "some in my favour, as for example ... others not. Turkish marriage annulled (I was ambassador in Constantinople, Shel," she explained). "Children pronounced illegitimate (they said I had three sons by

Pepita, a Spanish dancer). So they don't inherit, which is all to the good. . . . Sex? Ah! what about sex? My sex," she read out with some solemnity, "is pronounced indisputably, and beyond the shadow of a doubt (what I was telling you a moment ago, Shel?) Female. The estates which are now desequestrated in perpetuity descend and are tailed and entailed upon the heirs male of my body, or in default of marriage"—but here she grew impatient with this legal verbiage, and said, "but there won't be any default of marriage, nor of heirs either, so the rest can be taken as read." Whereupon she appended her own signature beneath Lord Palmerston's and entered from that moment into the undisturbed possession of her titles, her house, and her estate—which were now so much shrunk, for the cost of the lawsuits had been prodigious, that though she was infinitely noble again, she was also excessively poor.

When the result of the lawsuit was made known (and rumour flew much quicker than the telegraph which has supplanted it), the whole town was filled with rejoicings.

[Horses were put into carriages for the sole purpose of being taken out. Empty barouches and landaus were trundled up and down the High Street incessantly. Addresses were read from the Bull. Replies were made from the Stag. The town was illuminated. Gold caskets were securely sealed in glass cases. Coins were well and duly laid under stones. Hospitals were founded. Rat and Sparrow clubs were inaugurated. Turkish women by the dozen were burnt in effigy in the market place, together with scores of peasant boys with the label "I am a base Pretender," lolling from their mouths. The Queen's cream-coloured ponies were soon seen trotting up the avenue with a command to Orlando to dine and sleep at the Castle, that very same night. Her table, as on a previous occasion, was snowed under with invitations from the Countess of R., Lady Q., Lady Palmerston, the Marchioness of P., Mrs. W. E. Gladstone, and others, beseeching the pleasure of her company, reminding her of ancient alliances between their family and her own, etc.]—all of which is properly enclosed in square brackets, as above, for the good reason that a parenthesis it was without any importance in Orlando's life. She skipped it, to get on with the text. For when the bonfires were blazing in the market place, she was in the dark woods with Shelmerdine alone. So fine was the weather that the trees stretched their branches motionless above them, and if a leaf fell, it fell, spotted red and gold, so slowly that one could watch it for half an hour fluttering and falling till it came to rest at last, on Orlando's foot.

"Tell me, Mar," she would say (and here it must be explained, that when she called him by the first syllable of his first name, she was in a dreamy, amorous, acquiescent mood, domestic, languid a little, as if spiced logs were burning, and it was evening, yet not time to dress, and a thought wet perhaps outside, enough to make the leaves glisten, but a nightingale might be singing even so among the azaleas, two or three dogs barking at distant farms, a cock crowing—all of which the reader should imagine in her voice)—"Tell me, Mar," she would say, "about Cape Horn." Then Shelmerdine would make a little model on the ground of the Cape with twigs and dead leaves and an empty snail shell or two.

"Here's the north," he would say. "There's the south. The wind's coming from hereabouts. Now the Brig is sailing due west; we've just lowered the top-boom mizzen; and so you see—here, where this bit of grass is, she enters the current which you'll find marked—where's my map and compasses, Bo'sun?—Ah! thanks, that'll do, where the snail shell is. The current catches her on the starboard side, so we must rig the jib boom or we shall be carried to the larboard, which is where that beech leaf is,—for you must understand my dear—" and so he would go on, and she would listen to every word; interpreting

them rightly, so as to see, that is to say, without his having to tell
her, the phosphorescence on the waves, the icicles clanking in
the shrouds; how he went to the top of the mast in a gale; there
reflected on the destiny of man; came down again; had a whisky
and soda; went on shore; was trapped by a black woman; re-
pented; reasoned it out; read Pascal; determined to write philosophy; bought a monkey; debated the true end of life; decided in
favour of Cape Horn, and so on. All this and a thousand other
things she understood him to say and so when she replied, Yes,
negresses are seductive, aren't they? he having told her that the
supply of biscuits now gave out, he was surprised and delighted
to find how well she had taken his meaning.

"Are you positive you aren't a man?" he would ask anxiously, and she would echo,

"Can it be possible you're not a woman?" and then they
must put it to the proof without more ado. For each was so surprised at the quickness of the other's sympathy, and it was to
each such a revelation that a woman could be as tolerant and free-
spoken as a man, and a man as strange and subtle as a woman,
that they had to put the matter to the proof at once.

And so they would go on talking or rather, understanding,
which has become the main art of speech in an age when words
are growing daily so scanty in comparison with ideas that "the
biscuits ran out" has to stand for kissing a negress in the dark
when one has just read Bishop Berkeley's philosophy for the
tenth time. (And from this it follows that only the most profound masters of style can tell the truth, and when one meets
a simple one-syllable writer, one may conclude, without any
doubt at all, that the poor man is lying.)

So they would talk; and then, when her feet were fairly covered with spotted autumn leaves, Orlando would rise and stroll
away into the heart of the woods in solitude, leaving Bonthrop
sitting there among the snail shells, making models of Cape

Horn. "Bonthrop," she would say, "I'm off," and when she called him by his second name, "Bonthrop," it should signify to the reader that she was in a solitary mood, felt them both as specks on a desert, was desirous only of meeting death by herself, for people die daily, die at dinner tables, or like this, out of doors in the autumn woods; and with the bonfires blazing and Lady Palmerston or Lady Derby asking her out every night to dinner, the desire for death would overcome her, and so saying "Bonthrop," she said in effect, "I'm dead," and pushed her way as a spirit might through the spectre-pale beech trees, and so oared herself deep into solitude as if the little flicker of noise and movement were over and she were free now to take her way—all of which the reader should hear in her voice when she said "Bonthrop"; and should also add, the better to illumine the word, that for him too, the word signified, mystically, separation and isolation and the disembodied pacing the deck of his brig in unfathomable seas.

After some hours of death, suddenly a jay shrieked "Shelmerdine," and stooping, she picked one of those autumn crocuses which to some people signify that very word, and put it with the jay's feather that came tumbling blue through the beech woods, in her breast. Then she called "Shelmerdine" and the word went shooting this way and that way through the woods and struck him where he sat, making models out of snail shells in the grass. He saw her, and heard her coming to him with the crocus and the jay's feather in her breast, and cried "Orlando," which meant (and it must be remembered that when bright colours like blue and yellow mix themselves in our thoughts, some of it rubs off on our words) first the bowing and swaying of bracken as if something were breaking through, which proved to be a ship in full sail, heaving and tossing a little dreamily, rather as if she had a whole year of summer days to make her voyage in; and so the ship bears down, heaving this way, heaving that way, nobly, indolently and rides over the crest of this wave and sinks into the hollow of that one, and so, suddenly stands over you (who are in a little cockle shell of a boat, looking up at her) with all her sails quivering and then behold, they drop all of a heap on deck—as Orlando dropped now into the grass beside him.

Eight or nine days had been spent thus, but on the tenth, which was the 26th of October, Orlando was lying in the bracken, while Shelmerdine recited Shelley (whose entire works he had by heart), when a leaf which had started to fall slowly enough from a tree top whipped briskly across Orlando's foot. A second leaf followed and then a third. Orlando shivered and turned pale. It was the wind. Shelmerdine—but it would be more proper now to call him Bonthrop—leapt to his feet.

"The wind!" he cried.

Together they ran through the woods, the wind plastering them with leaves as they ran, to the great court and through it and the little courts, frightened servants leaving their brooms, their saucepans, to follow after till they reached the Chapel and there a scattering of lights was lit as fast as could be, one knocking over this bench, another snuffing out that taper. Bells were rung. People were summoned. At length there was Mr. Dupper catching at the ends of his white tie and asking where was the prayer book. And they thrust Queen Mary's prayer book in his hands and he searched hastily fluttering the pages, and said, "Marmaduke Bonthrop Shelmerdine, and Lady Orlando, kneel down"; and they knelt down, and now they were bright and now they were dark as the light and shadow came flying helter skelter through the painted windows; and among the banging of innumerable doors and a sound like brass pots beating, the organ sounded, its growl coming loud and faint alternately, and Mr. Dupper, who was grown a very old man, tried now to raise his voice above the uproar and could not be heard and then all was quiet for a moment, and one word—it might be "the jaws of

Marmaduke Bonthrop Shelmerdine, Esquire

death"—rang out clear, while all the estate servants kept pressing in with rakes and whips still in their hands to listen, and some sang aloud and others prayed and now a bird was dashed against the pane, and now there was a clap of thunder, so that no one heard the word Obey spoken or saw, except as a golden flash, the ring pass from hand to hand. All was movement and confusion. And up they rose with the organ booming and the lightning playing and the rain pouring and the Lady Orlando, with her ring on her finger, went out into the court in her thin dress and held the swinging stirrup, for the horse was bitted and bridled and the foam was still on his flank, for her husband to mount, which he did with one bound and the horse leapt forward and Orlando, standing there, cried out Marmaduke Bonthrop Shelmerdine! and he answered her Orlando! and the words went dashing and circling like wild hawks together among the belfries and higher and higher, further and further, faster and faster, they circled, till they crashed and fell in a shower of fragments to the ground; and she went in.

CHAPTER SIX

ORLANDO WENT indoors. It was completely still. It was very silent. There was the ink pot: there was the pen; there was the manuscript of her poem, broken off in the middle of a tribute to eternity. She had been about to say, when Basket and Bartholomew interrupted with the tea things, nothing changes. And then, in the space of three seconds and a half, everything had changed—she had broken her ankle, fallen in love, married Shelmerdine.

There was the wedding ring on her finger to prove it. It was true that she had put it there herself before she met Shelmerdine, but that had proved worse than useless. She now turned the ring round and round, with superstitious reverence, taking care that it should not slip past the finger joint.

"The wedding ring has to be put on the second finger of the left hand," she said, like a child cautiously repeating its lesson, "for it to be of any use at all."

She spoke thus, aloud and rather more pompously than was her wont, as if she wished someone whose good opinion she desired to overhear her. Indeed, she had in mind, now that she was at last able to collect her thoughts, the effect that her behaviour would have had upon the spirit of the age. She was extremely anxious to be informed whether the steps she had taken in the matter of getting engaged to Shelmerdine and marrying him met with its approval. She was certainly feeling more her-self. Her finger had not tingled once, or nothing to count, since that night on the moor. Yet, she could not deny that she had her doubts. She was married, true; but if one's husband was always sailing round Cape Horn, was it marriage? If one liked him, was it marriage? If one liked other people, was it marriage? And fi-nally, if one still wished, more than anything in the whole world, to write poetry, was it marriage? She had her doubts.

But she would put it to the test. She looked at the ring. She looked at the ink pot. Did she dare? No, she did not. But she must. No, she could not. What should she do then? Faint, if possible. But she had never felt better in her life.

"Hang it all!" she cried, with a touch of her old spirit. "Here goes!"

And she plunged her pen neck deep in the ink. To her enor-mous surprise, there was no explosion. She drew the nib out. It was wet, but not dripping. She wrote. The words were a little long in coming, but come they did. Ah! but did they make sense? she wondered, a panic coming over her lest it might have been at some of its involuntary pranks again. She read,

> And then I came to a field where the springing grass,
> Was dulled by the hanging cups of fritillaries,
> Sullen and foreign-looking, the snaky flower,
> Scarfed in dull purple, like Egyptian girls—

At this point she felt that power (remember we are dealing with the most obscure manifestations of the human spirit) which had been reading over her shoulder, tell her to stop. Grass, the power seemed to say, going back with a ruler such as governesses use to the beginning, is all right; the hanging cups of fritillaries—ad-mirable; the snaky flower—a thought strong from a lady's pen, perhaps, but Wordsworth, no doubt, sanctions it; but—girls?

Are girls necessary? You have a husband at the Cape, you say? Ah, well, that'll do.

And so the spirit passed on.

Orlando now performed in spirit (for all this took place in spirit) a deep obeisance to the spirit of her age, such as—to compare great things with small—a traveller, conscious that he has a bundle of cigars in the corner of his suit case, makes to the customs officer who has obligingly made a scribble of white chalk on the lid. For she was extremely doubtful whether, if the spirit had examined the contents of her mind carefully, it would not have found something highly contraband for which she would have had to pay the full fine. She had only escaped by the skin of her teeth. She had just managed, by some dexterous deference to the spirit of the age, by putting on a ring and finding a man on a moor, by loving nature and being no satirist, cynic, or psychologist—any one of which goods would have been discovered at once—to pass its examination successfully. And she heaved a deep sigh of relief, as, indeed, well she might, for the transaction between a writer and the spirit of the age is one of infinite delicacy, and upon a nice arrangement between the two the whole fortune of his works depend. Orlando had so ordered it that she was in an extremely happy position; she need neither fight her age, nor submit to it; she was of it, yet remained herself. Now, therefore, she could write, and write she did. She wrote. She wrote. She wrote.

It was now November. After November, comes December. Then January, February, March, and April. After April comes May. June, July, August follow. Next is September. Then October, and so, behold, here we are back at November again, with a whole year accomplished.

This method of writing biography, though it has its merits, is a little bare, perhaps, and the reader, if we go on with it, may complain that he could recite the calendar for himself and so save his pocket whatever sum the publisher may think proper to charge for this book. But what can the biographer do when his subject has put him in the predicament in which Orlando has now put us? Life, it has been agreed by everyone whose opinion is worth consulting, is the only fit subject for novelist or biographer; life, the same authorities have decided, has nothing whatever to do with sitting still in a chair and thinking. Thought and life are as the poles asunder. Therefore—since sitting in a chair and thinking is precisely what Orlando is doing now—there is nothing for it but to recite the calendar, tell one's beads, blow one's nose, stir the fire, look out of the window, until she has done. Orlando sat so still that you could have heard a pin drop. Would, indeed, that a pin had dropped! That would have been life of a kind. Or if a butterfly had fluttered through the window and settled on her chair, one could write about that. Or suppose she had got up and killed a wasp. Then, at once, we could out with our pens and write. For there would be blood shed, if only the blood of a wasp. And if killing a wasp is the merest trifle compared with killing a man, still it is a fitter subject for novelist or biographer than this mere wool-gathering; this thinking; this sitting in a chair day in, day out, with a cigarette and a sheet of paper and a pen and an ink pot. If only subjects, we might complain (for our patience is wearing thin), had more consideration for their biographers! What is more irritating than to see one's subject, on whom one has lavished so much time and trouble, slipping out of one's grasp altogether and indulging—witness her sighs and gasps, her flushing, her palings, her eyes now bright as lamps, now haggard as dawns—what is more humiliating than to see all this dumb show of emotion and excitement gone through before our eyes when we know that what causes it—thought and imagination—are of no importance whatsoever?

But Orlando was a woman—Lord Palmerston had just
proved it. And when we are writing the life of a woman, we may,
it is agreed, waive our demand for action, and substitute love instead. Love, the poet has said, is woman's whole existence. And
if we look for a moment at Orlando writing at her table, we
must admit that never was there a woman more fitted for that
calling. Surely, since she is a woman, and a beautiful woman, and
a woman in the prime of life, she will soon give over this pre-
tence of writing and thinking and begin to think, at least of a
gamekeeper (and as long as she thinks of a man, nobody objects
to a woman thinking). And then she will write him a little note
(and as long as she writes little notes nobody objects to a woman
writing either) and make an assignation for Sunday dusk; and
Sunday dusk will come; and the gamekeeper will whistle under
the window—all of which is, of course, the very stuff of life and
the only possible subject for fiction. Surely Orlando must have
done one of these things? Alas,—a thousand times, alas, Orlando did none of them. Must it then be admitted that Orlando
was one of those monsters of iniquity who do not love? She was
kind to dogs, faithful to friends, generosity itself to a dozen
starving poets, had a passion for poetry. But love—as the male
novelists define it—and who, after all, speak with greater authority?—has nothing whatever to do with kindness, fidelity,
generosity, or poetry. Love is slipping off one's petticoat and—
But we all know what love is. Did Orlando do that? Truth compels us to say no, she did not. If then, the subject of one's biography will neither love nor kill, but will only think and imagine,
we may conclude that he or she is no better than a corpse and
so leave her.

The only resource now left us is to look out of the window.
There were sparrows; there were starlings; there were a number
of doves, and one or two rooks, all occupied after their fashion.
One finds a worm, another a snail. One flutters to a branch; an-

other takes a little run on the turf. Then a servant crosses the courtyard, wearing a green baize apron. Presumably he is engaged on some intrigue with one of the maids in the pantry, but as no visible proof is offered us, in the courtyard, we can but hope for the best and leave it. Clouds pass, thin or thick, with some disturbance of the colour of the grass beneath. The sun dial registers the hour in its usual cryptic way. One's mind begins tossing up a question or two, idly, vainly, about this same life. Life, it sings, or croons rather, like a kettle on a hob, Life, life, what art thou? Light or darkness, the baize apron of the under footman or the shadow of the starling on the grass?

Let us go, then, exploring, this summer morning, when all are adoring the plum blossom and the bee. And humming and hawing, let us ask of the starling (who is a more sociable bird than the lark) what he may think on the brink of the dust bin, whence he picks among the sticks combings of scullion's hair. What's life, we ask, leaning on the farmyard gate; Life, Life, Life! cries the bird, as if he had heard, and knew precisely, what we meant by this bothering prying habit of ours of asking questions indoors and out and peeping and picking at daisies as the way is of writers when they don't know what to say next. Then they come here, says the bird, and ask me what life is; Life, Life, Life!

We trudge on then by the moor path, to the high brow of the wine-blue purple-dark hill, and fling ourselves down there, and dream there and see there a grasshopper, carting back to his home in the hollow, a straw. And he says (if sawings like his can be given a name so sacred and tender) Life's labour, or so we interpret the whirr of his dust-choked gullet. And the ant agrees and the bees, but if we lie here long enough to ask the moths, when they come at evening, stealing among the paler heather bells, they will breathe in our ears such wild nonsense as one hears from telegraph wires in snow storms; tee hee, haw haw, Laughter, Laughter! the moths say.

Having asked then of man and of bird and the insects, for fish, men tell us, who have lived in green caves, solitary for years to hear them speak, never, never say, and so perhaps know what life is—having asked them all and grown no wiser, but only older and colder (for did we not pray once in a way to wrap up in a book something so hard, so rare, one could swear it was life's meaning?) back we must go and say straight out to the reader who waits a tiptoe to hear what life is—Alas, we don't know.

AT THIS MOMENT, but only just in time to save the book from extinction, Orlando pushed away her chair, stretched her arms, dropped her pen, came to the window, and exclaimed, "Done!"

She was almost felled to the ground by the extraordinary sight which now met her eyes. There was the garden and some birds. The world was going on as usual. All the time she was writing the world had continued.

"And if I were dead, it would be just the same!" she exclaimed.

Such was the intensity of her feelings that she could even imagine that she had suffered dissolution, and perhaps some faintness actually attacked her. For a moment she stood looking at the fair, indifferent spectacle with staring eyes. At length she was revived in a singular way. The manuscript which reposed above her heart began shuffling and beating as if it were a living thing, and, what was still odder, and showed how fine a sympathy was between them, Orlando, by inclining her head, could make out what it was that it was saying. It wanted to be read. It must be read. It would die in her bosom if it were not read. For the first time in her life she turned with violence against nature. Elk hounds and rose bushes were about her in profusion. But elk hounds and rose bushes can none of them read. It is a lamentable oversight on the part of Providence which had never struck her before. Human beings alone have this power. Human beings had become necessary. She rang the bell. She ordered the carriage to take her to London at once.

"There's just time to catch the eleven forty-five, M'Lady," said Basket. Orlando had not yet realised the invention of the steam engine, but such was her absorption in the sufferings of a being, who, though not herself, yet entirely depended on her, that she saw a railway train for the first time, took her seat in a railway carriage, and had the rug arranged about her knees without giving a thought to "that stupendous invention, which had (the historians say) completely changed the face of Europe in the past twenty years" (as, indeed, happens much more frequently than historians suppose). She noticed only that it was extremely smutty; rattled horribly; and the windows stuck. Lost in thought, she was whirled up to London in something less than an hour and stood on the platform at Charing Cross, not knowing where to go.

The old house at Blackfriars, where she had spent so many pleasant days in the eighteenth century, was now sold, part to the Salvation Army, part to an umbrella factory. She had bought another in Mayfair which was sanitary, convenient, and in the heart of the fashionable world, but was it in Mayfair that her poem would be relieved of its desire? Pray God, she thought, remembering the brightness of their ladyships' eyes and the symmetry of their lordships' legs, "they haven't taken to reading there." For that would be a thousand pities. Then there was Lady R.'s. The same sort of talk would be going on there still, she had no doubt. The gout might have shifted from the General's left leg to his right, perhaps. Mr. L. might have stayed ten days with R. instead of T. Then Mr. Pope would come in. Oh! but Mr. Pope was dead. Who were the wits now, she wondered—but that was not a question one could put to a porter, and so she moved on. Her ears were now distracted by the jingling of

innumerable bells on the heads of innumerable horses. Fleets of
the strangest little boxes on wheels were drawn up by the pavement. She walked out into the Strand. There the uproar was
even worse. Vehicles of all sizes, drawn by blood horses and by
dray horses, conveying one solitary dowager or crowded to the
top by whiskered men in silk hats were inextricably mixed. Carriages, carts, and omnibuses seemed to her eyes, so long used to
the look of a plain sheet of foolscap, alarmingly at loggerheads;
and to her ears, attuned to a pen scratching, the uproar of the
street sounded violently and hideously cacophonous. Every inch
of the pavement was crowded. Streams of people, threading in
and out between their own bodies and the lurching and lumber-
ing traffic with incredible agility, poured incessantly east and
west. Along the edge of the pavement stood men, holding out
trays of toys, and bawled. At corners, women sat beside great
baskets of spring flowers and bawled. Boys running in and out
of the horses' noses, holding printed sheets to their bodies,
bawled too, Disaster! Disaster! At first Orlando supposed that
she had arrived at some moment of national crisis; but whether
it was happy or tragic, she could not tell. She looked anxiously
at people's faces. But that confused her still more. Here would
come by a man sunk in despair, muttering to himself as if he
knew some terrible sorrow. Past him would nudge a fat, jolly-
faced fellow, shouldering his way along as if it were a festival for
all the world. Indeed, she came to the conclusion that there was
neither rhyme nor reason in any of it. Each man and each
woman was bent on his own affairs. And where was she to go?

She walked on without thinking, up one street and down
another, by vast windows piled with handbags, and mirrors, and
dressing gowns, and flowers, and fishing rods, and luncheon
baskets; while stuff of every hue and pattern, thickness or thin-
ness, was looped and festooned and ballooned across and across.
Sometimes she passed down avenues of sedate mansions, soberly

numbered 'one,' 'two,' 'three,' and so on right up to two or three hundred, each the copy of the other, with two pillars and six steps and a pair of curtains neatly drawn and family luncheons laid on tables, and a parrot looking out of one window and a man servant out of another, until her mind was dizzied with the monotony. Then she came to great open squares with black, shiny, tightly-buttoned statues of fat men in the middle, and war horses prancing, and columns rising and fountains falling and pigeons fluttering. So she walked and walked along pavements between houses until she felt very hungry, and something fluttering above her heart rebuked her with having forgotten all about it. It was her manuscript, "The Oak Tree."

She was confounded at her own neglect. She stopped dead where she stood. No coach was in sight. The street, which was wide and handsome, was singularly empty. Only one elderly gentleman was approaching. There was something vaguely familiar to her in his walk. As he came nearer, she felt certain that she had met him at some time or other before. But when? But where? Could it be that this gentleman, so neat, so portly, so prosperous, with a cane in his hand and a flower in his button hole, with a pink, plump face, and combed white moustaches, could it be, Yes, by jove, it was!— her old, her very old friend, Nick Greene!

At the same time he looked at her; remembered her; recognized her. "The Lady Orlando!" he cried, sweeping his silk hat almost in the dust.

"Sir Nicholas!" she exclaimed. For she was made aware intuitively by something in his bearing that the scurrilous penny-a-liner, who had lampooned her and many another in the time of Queen Elizabeth, was now risen in the world and become certainly a Knight and doubtless a dozen other fine things into the bargain.

With another bow, he acknowledged that her conclusion was correct; he was a Knight; he was a Litt.D.; he was a Professor.

He was the author of a score of volumes. He was, in short, the most influential critic of the Victorian age.

A violent tumult of emotion besieged her at meeting the man who had caused her, years ago, so much pain. Could this be the plaguey, restless fellow who had burnt holes in her carpets, and toasted cheese in the Italian fireplace and told such merry stories of Marlowe and the rest that they had seen the sun rise nine nights out of ten? He was now sprucely dressed in a grey morning suit, had a pink flower in his button hole, and grey suede gloves to match. But even as she marvelled, he made another profound bow, and asked her whether she would honour him by lunching with him? The bow was a thought overdone perhaps, but the imitation of fine breeding was creditable. She followed him, wondering, into a superb restaurant, all red plush, white table cloths, and silver cruets, as unlike as could be the old tavern or coffee house with its sanded floor, its wooden benches, its bowls of punch and chocolate, and its broadsheets and spittoons. He laid his gloves neatly on the table beside him. Still she could hardly believe that he was the same man. His nails were clean; where they used to be an inch long. His chin was shaved; where a black beard used to sprout. He wore gold sleeve links; where his ragged linen used to dip in the broth. It was not, indeed, until he had ordered the wine, which he did with a care that reminded her of his taste in Malmsey long ago, that she was convinced he was the same man. "Ah!" he said, heaving a little sigh, which was yet comfortable enough, "Ah! my dear lady, the great days of literature are over. Marlowe, Shakespeare, Ben Jonson—those were the giants. Dryden, Pope, Addison—those were the heroes. All, all are dead now. And whom have they left us? Tennyson, Browning, Carlyle!"—he threw an immense amount of scorn into his voice. "The truth of it is," he said, pouring himself a glass of wine, "that all our young writers are in the pay of booksellers. They turn out any trash that serves to pay their tailor's bills. It is an age," he said, helping himself to hors d'œuvres, "marked by precious conceits and wild experiments—none of which the Elizabethans would have tolerated for an instant."

"No, my dear lady," he continued, passing with approval the turbot au gratin, which the waiter exhibited for his sanction, "the great days are over. We live in degenerate times. We must cherish the past; honour those writers—there are still a few left of 'em—who take antiquity for their model and write, not for pay but——" Here Orlando almost shouted "Glawr!" Indeed she could have sworn that she had heard him say the very same things three hundred years ago. The names were different, of course, but the spirit was the same. Nick Greene had not changed, for all his knighthood. And yet, some change there was. For while he ran on about taking Addison as one's model (it had been Cicero once, she thought) and lying in bed of a morning (which she was proud to think her pension paid quarterly enabled him to do) rolling the best works of the best authors round and round on one's tongue for an hour, at least, before setting pen to paper, so that the vulgarity of the present time and the deplorable condition of our native tongue (he had lived long in America, she believed) might be purified—while he ran on in much the same way that Greene had run on three hundred years ago, she had time to ask herself, how was it then that he had changed? He had grown plump; but he was a man verging on seventy. He had grown sleek: literature had been a prosperous pursuit evidently, but somehow the old restless, uneasy vivacity had gone. His stories, brilliant as they were, were no longer quite so free and easy. He mentioned, it is true, "my dear friend Pope," or "my illustrious friend, Addison" every other second, but he had an air of respectability about him, which was depressing, and he preferred, it seemed, to enlighten her about the doings and sayings of her own blood relations rather than tell her, as he used to do, scandal about the poets.

Orlando was unaccountably disappointed. She had thought of literature all these years (her seclusion, her rank, her sex must be her excuse) as something wild as the wind, hot as fire, swift as lightning; something errant, incalculable, abrupt, and behold, literature was an elderly gentleman in a grey suit talking about duchesses. The violence of her disillusionment was such that some hook or button fastening the upper part of her dress burst open, and out upon the table fell "The Oak Tree," a poem.

"A manuscript!" said Sir Nicholas, putting on his gold pince nez. "How interesting, how excessively interesting! Permit me to look at it." And once more, after an interval of some three hundred years Nicholas Greene took Orlando's poem, and laying it down among the coffee cups and the liqueur glasses began to read it. But now his verdict was very different from what it had been then. It reminded him, he said as he turned over the pages, of Addison's *Cato*. It compared favourably with Thomson's *Seasons*. There was no trace in it, he was thankful to say, of the modern spirit. It was composed with a regard to truth, to nature, to the dictates of the human heart, which was rare indeed, in these days of unscrupulous eccentricity. It must, of course, be published instantly.

Really Orlando did not know what he meant. She had always carried her manuscripts about with her in the bosom of her dress. The idea tickled Sir Nicholas considerably.

"But what about Royalties?" he asked.

Orlando's mind flew to Buckingham Palace and some dusky potentates who happened to be staying there.

Sir Nicholas was highly diverted. He explained that he was alluding to the fact that Messrs. —— (here he mentioned a well known firm of publishers) would be delighted, if he wrote them a line, to put the book on their list. He could probably arrange for a royalty of ten per cent on all copies up to two thousand; after that it would be fifteen. As for the reviewers, he would himself write a line to Mr. —— who was the most influential; then a compliment—say a little puff of her own poems—addressed to the wife of the editor of the —— never did any harm. He would call ——. So he ran on. Orlando understood nothing of all this, and from old experience did not altogether trust his good nature, but there was nothing for it but to submit to what was evidently his wish and the fervent desire of the poem itself. So Sir Nicholas made the blood-stained packet into a neat parcel; flattened it into his breast pocket, lest it should disturb the set of his coat; and with many compliments on both sides, they parted.

Orlando walked up the street. Now that the poem was gone,—and she felt a bare place in her breast where she had been used to carry it—she had nothing to do but reflect upon whatever she liked—the extraordinary chances it might be of the human lot. Here she was in St. James' Street; a married woman; with a ring on her finger; where there had been a coffee house once there was now a Restaurant; it was about half past three in the afternoon; the sun was shining; there were three pigeons; a mongrel terrier dog; two hansom cabs and a barouche landau. What then, was Life? The thought popped into her head violently, irrelevantly (unless old Greene were somehow the cause of it). And it may be taken as a comment, adverse or favourable, as the reader chooses to consider it upon her relations with her husband (who was at the Horn), that whenever anything popped violently into her head, she went straight to the nearest telegraph office and wired to him. There was one, as it happened, close at hand. "My God Shel," she wired; "life literature Greene toady—" here she dropped into a cypher language which they had invented between them so that

a whole spiritual state of the utmost complexity might be conveyed in a word or two without the telegraph clerk being any
the wiser, and added the words "Rattigan Glumphoboo," which
summed it up precisely. For not only had the events of the
morning made a deep impression on her, but it cannot have
escaped the reader's attention that Orlando was growing up—
which is not necessarily growing better—and "Rattigan Glumphoboo" described a very complicated spiritual state—which if
the reader puts all his intelligence at our service he may discover
for himself.

There could be no answer to her telegram for some hours;
indeed, it was probable, she thought, glancing at the sky, where
the upper clouds raced swiftly past, that there was a gale at Cape
Horn, so that her husband would be at the mast head, as likely
as not, or cutting away some tattered spar, or even alone in a
boat with a biscuit. And so, leaving the post office, she turned
to beguile herself into the next shop, which was a shop so common in our day that it needs no description, yet, to her eyes,
strange in the extreme; a shop where they sold books. All her
life long Orlando had known manuscripts; had held in her
hands the rough brown sheets on which Spenser had written in
his little crabbed hand; she had seen Shakespeare's script and
Milton's. She owned, indeed, a fair number of quartos and fo-
lios often with a sonnet in her praise in them and sometimes a
lock of hair. But these innumerable little volumes, bright, identical, ephemeral, for they seemed bound in cardboard and
printed on tissue paper, surprised her infinitely. The whole
works of Shakespeare cost half a crown and could be put in your
pocket. One could hardly read them, indeed, the print was so
small, but it was a marvel, none the less. 'Works'—the works of
every writer she had known or heard of and many more
stretched from end to end of the long shelves. On tables and
chairs, more 'works' were piled and tumbled, and these she saw,

turning a page or two, were often works about other works by
Sir Nicholas and a score of others whom, in her ignorance, she
supposed, since they were bound and printed, to be very great
writers too. So she gave an astounding order to the bookseller
to send her everything of any importance in the shop and left.

She turned into Hyde Park, which she had known of old
(beneath that cleft tree, she remembered, the Duke of Hamilton fell run through the body by Lord Mohun) and her lips,
which are often to blame in the matter, began framing the
words of her telegram into a senseless singsong; life literature
Greene toady, Rattigan Glumphoboo; so that several park keepers looked at her with suspicion and were only brought to a
favourable opinion of her sanity by noticing the pearl necklace
which she wore. She had carried off a sheaf of papers and critical journals from the book shop, and at length, flinging herself
on her elbow beneath a tree, she spread these pages round her
and did her best to fathom the noble art of prose composition
as these masters practised it. For still the old credulity was alive
in her; even the blurred type of a weekly newspaper had some
sanctity in her eyes. So she read, lying on her elbow, an article
by Sir Nicholas on the collected works of a man she had once
known—John Donne. But she had pitched herself, without
knowing it, not far from the Serpentine. The barking of a thousand dogs sounded in her ears. Carriage wheels rushed cease-
lessly in a circle round her. Leaves sighed overhead. Now and
again a braided skirt and a pair of tight scarlet trousers crossed
the grass within a few steps of her. Once a gigantic rubber ball
bounced on the newspaper. Violets, oranges, reds, and blues
broke through the interstices of the leaves and sparkled in the
emerald on her finger. She was distracted between the two. She
looked at the paper and looked up; she looked at the sky and
looked down. Life? Literature? One to be made into the other?
But how monstrously difficult! For—here came by a pair of

tight scarlet trousers—how would Addison have put that? Here
came two dogs dancing on their hind legs. How would Lamb
have described that? For reading Sir Nicholas and his friends
(as she did in the intervals of looking about her), she somehow
got the impression—here she rose and walked—they made one
feel—it was an extremely uncomfortable feeling—one must
never, never say what one thought. (She stood on the banks of
the Serpentine. It was a bronze colour; spider-thin boats were
skimming from side to side.) They made one feel, she continued, that one must always, always write like somebody else. (The
tears formed themselves in her eyes.) For really, she thought,
pushing a little boat off with her toe, I don't think I could (here
the whole of Sir Nicholas' article came before her as articles do,
ten minutes after they are read, with the look of his room, his
head, his cat, his writing table, and the time of the day thrown
in), I don't think I could, she continued, considering the article
from this point of view, sit in a study, no, it's not a study, it's a
mouldy kind of drawing-room, all day long, and talk to pretty
young men, and tell them little anecdotes, which they mustn't
repeat, about what Tupper said about Smiles; and then, she continued, weeping bitterly, they're all so manly; and then, I do detest Duchesses; and I don't like cake; and though I'm spiteful
enough, I could never learn to be as spiteful as all that, so how
can I be a critic and write the best English prose of my time?
Damn it all! she exclaimed, launching a penny steamer so vigor-
ously that the poor little boat almost sank in the bronze coloured
waves.

Now, the truth is that when one has been in a state of mind
(as nurses call it)—and the tears still stood in Orlando's eyes—
the thing one is looking at becomes, not itself, but another
thing, which is bigger and much more important and yet remains the same thing. If one looks at the Serpentine in this state
of mind, the waves soon become just as big as the waves on the

Atlantic; the toy boats become indistinguishable from ocean lin-
ers. So Orlando mistook the toy boat for her husband's brig;
and the wave she had made with her toe for a mountain of water
off Cape Horn; and as she watched the toy boat climb the
ripple, she thought she saw Bonthrop's ship climb up and up a
glassy wall; up and up it went, and a white crest with a thousand
deaths in it arched over it; and through the thousand deaths it
went and disappeared—'It's sunk!' she cried out in an agony—
and then, behold, there it was again sailing along safe and sound
among the ducks on the other side of the Atlantic.

"Ecstasy!" she cried. "Ecstasy! Where's the post office?" she
wondered. "For I must wire at once to Shel and tell him. . . ."
And repeating "A toy boat on the Serpentine," and "Ecstasy," alternately, for the thoughts were interchangeable and meant exactly the same thing, she hurried towards Park Lane.

"A toy boat, a toy boat, a toy boat," she repeated, thus
enforcing upon herself the fact that it is not articles by Nick
Greene on John Donne nor eight-hour bills nor covenants nor
factory acts that matter; it's something useless, sudden, violent;
something that costs a life; red, blue, purple; a spirt; a splash;
like those hyacinths (she was passing a fine bed of them); free
from taint, dependence, soilure of humanity or care for one's
kind; something rash, ridiculous, "like my hyacinth, husband I
mean, Bonthrop: that's what it is—a toy boat on the Serpentine, it's ecstasy—ecstasy." Thus she spoke aloud, waiting for
the carriages to pass at Stanhope Gate, for the consequence of
not living with one's husband, except when the wind is sunk, is
that one talks nonsense aloud in Park Lane. It would no doubt
have been different had she lived all the year round with him as
Queen Victoria recommended. As it was the thought of him
would come upon her in a flash. She found it absolutely necessary to speak to him instantly. She did not care in the least what
nonsense it might make, or what dislocation it might inflict on

the narrative. Nick Greene's article had plunged her in the depths of despair; the toyboat had raised her to the heights of joy. So she repeated: "Ecstasy, ecstasy," as she stood waiting to cross.

But the traffic was heavy that spring afternoon, and kept her standing there, repeating ecstasy, ecstasy, or a toy boat on the Serpentine, while the wealth and power of England, sat, as if sculptured, in hat and cloak, in four-in-hand, victoria and barouche landau. It was as if a golden river had coagulated and massed itself in golden blocks across Park Lane. The ladies held card-cases between their fingers; the gentlemen balanced gold-mounted canes between their knees. She stood there gazing, admiring, awe-struck. One thought only disturbed her, a thought familiar to all who behold great elephants, or whales of an incredible magnitude, and that is how do these leviathans to whom obviously stress, change, and activity are repugnant, propagate their kind? Perhaps, Orlando thought, looking at the stately, still faces, their time of propagation is over; this is the fruit; this is the consummation. What she now beheld was the triumph of an age. Portly and splendid there they sat. But now, the policeman let fall his hand; the stream became liquid; the massive conglomeration of splendid objects moved, dispersed and disappeared into Piccadilly.

So she crossed Park Lane and went to her house in Curzon Street where, when the meadow-sweet blew there, she could re-member curlew calling and one very old man with a gun.

SHE COULD remember, she thought, stepping across the thresh-old of her house, how Lord Chesterfield had said—but her memory was checked. Her discreet eighteenth-century hall, where she could see Lord Chesterfield putting his hat down here and his coat down there with an elegance of deportment which it was a pleasure to watch, was now completely littered with parcels. While she had been sitting in Hyde Park the bookseller had delivered her order, and the house was crammed—there were parcels slipping down the staircase—with the whole of Victorian literature done up in grey paper and neatly tied with string. She carried as many of these packets as she could to her room, ordered footmen to bring the others, and, rapidly cutting innumerable strings, was soon surrounded by innumerable volumes.

Accustomed to the little literatures of the sixteenth, seventeenth, and eighteenth centuries, Orlando was appalled by the consequences of her order. For, of course, to the Victorians themselves Victorian literature meant not merely four great names separate and distinct but four great names sunk and embedded in a mass of Alexander Smiths, Dixons, Blacks, Milmans, Buckles, Taines, Paynes, Tuppers, Jamesons—all vocal, clamorous, prominent, and requiring as much attention as anybody else. Orlando's reverence for print had a tough job set before it, but drawing her chair to the window to get the benefit of what light might filter between the high houses of Mayfair, she tried to come to a conclusion.

And now it is clear that there are only two ways of coming to a conclusion upon Victorian literature—one is to write it out in sixty volumes octavo, the other is to squeeze it into six lines of the length of this one. Of the two courses, economy, since time runs short, leads us to choose the second; and so we proceed. Orlando then came to the conclusion (opening half-a-dozen books) that it was very odd that there was not a single dedication to a nobleman among them; next (turning over a vast pile of memoirs) that several of these writers had family trees half as high as her own; next, that it would be impolitic in the extreme to wrap a ten-pound note round the sugar tongs when Miss Christina Rossetti came to tea; next (here were half-a-dozen invitations to celebrate centenaries by dining) that literature since it ate all these dinners must be growing very corpulent;

next (she was invited to a score of lectures upon the Influence of this upon that; the Classical revival; the Romantic survival, and other titles of the same engaging kind) that literature since it listened to all these lectures must be growing very dry; next (here she attended a reception given by a peeress) that literature since it wore all these fur tippets must be growing very respectable; next (here she visited Carlyle's sound-proof room at Chelsea) that genius since it needed all this coddling must be growing very delicate; and so at last she reached her final conclusion, which was of the highest importance but which, as we have already much overpassed our limit of six lines, we must omit.

Orlando, having come to this conclusion, stood looking out of the window for a considerable space of time. For, when anybody comes to a conclusion it is as if they had tossed the ball over the net and must wait for the unseen antagonist to return it to them. What would be sent her next from the colourless sky above Chesterfield House, she wondered? And with her hands clasped, she stood for a considerable space of time wondering. Suddenly she started—and here we could only wish that, as on a former occasion, Purity, Chastity, and Modesty would push the door ajar and provide, at least, a breathing space in which we could think how to wrap up what now has to be told delicately, as a biographer should. But no! Having thrown their white garment at the naked Orlando and seen it fall short by several inches, these ladies had given up all intercourse with her these many years; and were now otherwise engaged. Is nothing, then, going to happen this pale March morning to mitigate, to veil, to cover, to conceal, to shroud this undeniable event whatever it may be? For after giving that sudden, violent start, Orlando—but Heaven be praised, at this very moment there struck up outside one of these frail, reedy, fluty, jerky, old-fashioned barrel-organs which are still sometimes played by Italian organ-grinders in back streets. Let us accept the intervention, humble though it is, as if it were the music of the spheres, and allow it, with all its gasps and groans, to fill this page with sound until the moment comes which it is impossible to deny is coming; which the footman has seen coming and the maid-servant; and the reader will have to see too; for Orlando herself is clearly unable to ignore it any longer—let the barrel-organ sound and transport us on thought, which is no more than a little boat, when music sounds, tossing on the waves; on thought, which is, of all carriers, the most clumsy, the most erratic, over the roof tops and the back gardens where washing is hanging to—what is this place? Do you recognise the Green and in the middle the steeple, and the gates with a lion couchant on either side? Oh yes, it is Kew! Well, Kew will do. So here then we are at Kew, and I will show you to-day (the second of March) under the plum tree, a grape hyacinth, and a crocus, and a bud, too, on the almond tree; so that to walk there is to be thinking of bulbs, hairy and red, thrust into the earth in October; flowering now; and to be dreaming of more than can rightly be said, and to be taking from its case a cigarette or cigar even, and to be flinging a cloak under (as the rhyme requires) an oak, and there to sit, waiting the kingfisher, which, it is said, was seen once to cross in the evening from bank to bank.

Wait! Wait! The kingfisher comes; the kingfisher comes not.

Behold, meanwhile, the factory chimneys, and their smoke; behold the city clerks flashing by in their outrigger. Behold the old lady taking her dog for a walk and the servant girl wearing her new hat for the first time not at the right angle. Behold them all. Though Heaven has mercifully decreed that the secrets of all hearts are hidden so that we are lured on for ever to suspect something, perhaps, that does not exist; still through our cigarette smoke, we see blaze up and salute the splendid fulfilment of natural desires for a hat, for a boat, for a rat in a ditch; as once one saw blazing—such silly hops and skips the mind takes when

it slops like this all over the saucer and the barrel-organ plays—
saw blazing a fire in a field against minarets near Constantinople.

Hail! natural desire! Hail! happiness! divine happiness! and
pleasure of all sorts, flowers and wine, though one fades and the
other intoxicates; and half-crown tickets out of London on Sun-
days, and singing in a dark chapel hymns about death, and anything, anything that interrupts and confounds the tapping of
typewriters and filing of letters and forging of links and chains,
binding the Empire together. Hail even the crude, red bows on
shop girls' lips (as if Cupid, very clumsily, dipped his thumb in
red ink and scrawled a token in passing). Hail, happiness! kingfisher flashing from bank to bank, and all fulfilment of natural
desire, whether it is what the male novelist says it is; or prayer;
or denial; hail! in whatever form it comes, and may there be
more forms, and stranger. For dark flows the stream—would it
were true, as the rhyme hints "like a dream"—but duller and
worser than that is our usual lot; without dreams, but alive,
smug, fluent, habitual, under trees whose shade of an olive
green drowns the blue of the wing of the vanishing bird when
he darts of a sudden from bank to bank.

Hail, happiness, then, and after happiness, hail not those
dreams which bloat the sharp image as spotted mirrors do the
face in a country-inn parlour; dreams which splinter the whole
and tear us asunder and wound us and split us apart in the night
when we would sleep; but sleep, sleep, so deep that all shapes
are ground to dust of infinite softness, water of dimness in-
scrutable, and there, folded, shrouded, like a mummy, like a
moth, prone let us lie on the sand at the bottom of sleep.

But wait! but wait! we are not going, this time, visiting the
blind land. Blue, like a match struck right in the ball of the in-
nermost eye, he flys, burns, bursts the seal of sleep; the kingfisher; so that now floods back refluent like a tide, the red, thick
stream of life again; bubbling, dripping; and we rise, and our

eyes (for how handy a rhyme is to pass us safe over the awkward transition from death to life) fall on——(here the barrel-organ stops playing abruptly).

"It's a very fine boy, M'Lady," said Mrs. Banting, the midwife. In other words Orlando was safely delivered of a son on Thursday, March the 20th, at three o'clock in the morning.

ONCE MORE Orlando stood at the window, but let the reader take courage; nothing of the same sort is going to happen today, which is not, by any means, the same day. No——for if we look out of the window, as Orlando was doing at the moment, we shall see that Park Lane itself has considerably changed. Indeed one might stand there ten minutes or more, as Orlando stood now, without seeing a single barouche landau. "Look at that!" she exclaimed, some days later when an absurd truncated carriage without any horses began to glide about of its own accord. A carriage without any horses indeed! She was called away just as she said that, but came back again after a time and had another look out of the window. It was odd sort of weather nowadays. The sky itself, she could not help thinking had changed. It was no longer so thick, so watery, so prismatic now that King Edward——see, there he was, stepping out of his neat brougham to go and visit a certain lady opposite——had succeeded Queen Victoria. The clouds had shrunk to a thin gauze; the sky seemed made of metal, which in hot weather tarnished verdigris, copper colour or orange as metal does in a fog. It was a little alarming——this shrinkage. Everything seemed to have shrunk. Driving past Buckingham Palace last night, there was not a trace of that vast erection which she had thought everlasting; top hats, widows' weeds, trumpets, telescopes, wreaths, all had vanished and left not a stain, not a puddle even, on the pavement. But it was now——after another interval she had come back again to her favourite station in the window——now, in the evening, that the change was most remarkable. Look at the lights in the houses! At a touch, a whole room was lit; hundreds of rooms were lit; and one was precisely the same as the other. One could see everything in the little square-shaped boxes; there was no privacy; none of those lingering shadows and odd corners that there used to be; none of those women in aprons carrying wobbly lamps which they put down carefully on this table and on that. At a touch, the whole room was bright. And the sky was bright all night long; and the pavements were bright; everything was bright. She came back again at mid-day. How narrow women had grown lately! They looked like stalks of corn, straight, shining, identical. And men's faces were as bare as the palm of one's hand. The dryness of the atmosphere brought out the colour in everything and seemed to stiffen the muscles of the cheeks. It was harder to cry now. People were much gayer. Water was hot in two seconds. Ivy had perished or been scraped off houses. Vegetables were less fertile; families were much smaller. Curtains and covers had been frizzled up and the walls were bare so that new brilliantly coloured pictures of real things like streets, umbrellas, apples, were hung in frames, or painted upon the wood. There was something definite and distinct about the age, which reminded her of the eighteenth century, except that there was a distraction, a desperation—as she was thinking this, the immensely long tunnel in which she seemed to have been travelling for hundreds of years widened; the light poured in; her thoughts became mysteriously tightened and strung up as if a piano tuner had put his key in her back and stretched the nerves very taut; at the same time her hearing quickened; she could hear every whisper and crackle in the room so that the clock ticking on the mantelpiece beat like a hammer. And so for some seconds the light went on becoming brighter and brighter, and she saw everything more and more clearly and the clock ticked louder and louder until there was a terrific explosion right in her ear. Orlando leapt as if she had been violently struck on the head. Ten times she was struck. In fact it was ten o'clock in the morning. It was the eleventh of October. It was 1928. It was the present moment.

No one need wonder that Orlando started, pressed her hand to her heart, and turned pale. For what more terrifying revelation can there be than that it is the present moment? That we survive the shock at all is only possible because the past shelters us on one side, the future on another. But we have no time now for reflections; Orlando was terribly late already. She ran downstairs, jumped into her motor car, pressed the self-starter and was off. Vast blue blocks of building rose into the air; the red cowls of chimneys were spotted irregularly across the sky; the road shone like silver-headed nails; omnibuses bore down upon her with sculptured white-faced drivers; she noticed sponges, bird-cages, boxes of green American cloth. But she did not allow these sights to sink into her mind even the fraction of an inch as she crossed the narrow plank of the present, lest she should fall into the raging torrent beneath. "Why don't you look where you're going to? . . . Put your hand out can't you?"—that was all she said sharply, as if the words were jerked out of her. For the streets were immensely crowded; people crossed without looking where they were going. People buzzed and hummed round the plate-glass windows within which one could see a glow of red, a blaze of yellow, as if they were bees, Orlando thought—but her thought that they were bees was violently snipped off and she saw, regaining perspective with one flick of her eye, that they were bodies. "Why don't you look where you're going?" she snapped out.

At last, however, she drew up at Marshall & Snelgrove's and went into the shop. Shade and scent enveloped her. The present fell from her like drops of scalding water. Light swayed up and down like thin stuffs puffed out by a summer breeze. She

took a list from her bag and began reading in a curious stiff
voice at first as if she were holding the words—boy's boots,
bath salts, sardines—under a tap of many-coloured water. She
watched them change as the light fell on them. Bath and boots
became blunt, obtuse; sardines serrated itself like a saw. So she
stood in the ground-floor department of Messrs. Marshall &
Snelgrove; looked this way and that; snuffed this smell and
that and thus wasted some seconds. Then she got into the lift,
for the good reason that the door stood open; and was shot
smoothly upwards. The very fabric of life now, she thought as
she rose, is magic. In the eighteenth century, we knew how
everything was done; but here I rise through the air; I listen to
voices in America; I see men flying—but how it's done, I can't
even begin to wonder. So my belief in magic returns. Now the
lift gave a little jerk as it stopped at the first floor; and she had
a vision of innumerable coloured stuffs flaunting in a breeze
from which came distinct, strange smells; and each time the lift
stopped and flung its doors open, there was another slice of the
world displayed with all the smells of that world clinging to it.
She was reminded of the river off Wapping in the time of Elizabeth, where the treasure ships and the merchant ships used to
anchor. How richly and curiously they had smelt! How well she
remembered the feel of rough rubies running through her fingers when she dabbled them in a treasure sack! And then lying
with Sukey—or whatever her name was—and having Cumberland's lantern flashed on them! The Cumberlands had a house
in Portland Place now and she had lunched with them the other
day and ventured a little joke with the old man about almshouses in the Sheen Road. He had winked. But here as the lift
could go no higher, she must get out—Heaven knows into
what 'department' as they called it. She stood still to consult her
shopping list, but was blessed if she could see, as the list bade
her, bath salts, or boy's boots anywhere about. And indeed, she

was about to descend again, without buying anything, but was saved from that outrage by saying aloud automatically the last item on her list; which happened to be "sheets for a double bed."

"Sheets for a double bed," she said to a man at a counter and, by a dispensation of Providence, it was sheets that the man at that particular counter happened to sell. For Grimsditch, no, Grimsditch was dead; Bartholomew, no, Bartholomew was dead; Louise then—Louise had come to her in a great taking the other day, for she had found a hole in the bottom of the sheet in the royal bed. Many kings and queens had slept there, Elizabeth; James; Charles; George; Victoria; Edward; no wonder the sheet had a hole in it. But Louise was positive she knew who had done it. It was the Prince Consort.

"Sale bosch!" she said (for there had been another war; this time against the Germans).

"Sheets for a double bed," Orlando repeated dreamily, for a double bed with a silver counterpane in a room fitted in a taste which she now thought perhaps a little vulgar—all in silver; but she had furnished it when she had a passion for that metal. While the man went to get sheets for a double bed, she took out a little looking-glass and a powder puff. Women were not nearly as roundabout in their ways, she thought, powdering herself with the greatest unconcern, as they had been when she herself first turned woman and lay on the deck of the *Enamoured Lady*. She gave her nose the right tint deliberately. She never touched her cheeks. Honestly, though she was now thirty-six, she scarcely looked a day older. She looked just as pouting, as sulky, as handsome, as rosy (like a million-candled Christmas tree, Sasha had said) as she had done that day on the ice, when the Thames was frozen and they had gone skating——

"The best Irish linen, Ma'am," said the shopman, spreading the sheets on the counter,—and they had met an old woman picking up sticks. Here, as she was fingering the linen abstractedly, one of the swing-doors between the departments opened and let through, perhaps from the fancy-goods department, a whiff of scent, waxen, tinted as if from pink candles, and the scent curved like a shell round a figure—was it a boy's or was it a girl's—furred, pearled, in Russian trousers—young, slender, seductive—a girl, by God! but faithless, faithless!

"Faithless!" cried Orlando (the man had gone) and all the shop seemed to pitch and toss with yellow water and far off she saw the masts of the Russian ship standing out to sea, and then, miraculously (perhaps the door opened again) the conch which the scent had made became a platform, a dais, off which stepped a fat, furred woman, marvellously well preserved, seductive, diademed, a Grand Duke's mistress; she who, leaning over the banks of the Volga, eating sandwiches, had watched men drown; and began walking down the shop toward her.

"Oh, Sasha!" Orlando cried. Really, she was shocked that she should have come to this; she had grown so fat; so lethargic; and she bowed her head over the linen so that this apparition of a grey woman in fur, and a girl in Russian trousers with all these smells of wax candles, white flowers and Russian sailors that it brought with it might pass behind her back unseen.

"Any napkins, towels, dusters to-day, Ma'am?" the shopman persisted. And it is enormously to the credit of the shopping list, which Orlando now consulted, that she was able to reply with every appearance of composure, that there was only one thing in the world she wanted and that was bath salts; which was in another department.

But descending in the lift again—so insidious is the repetition of any scene—she was again sunk far beneath the present moment; and thought when the lift bumped on the ground, that she heard a pot broken against a river bank. As for finding the right department, whatever it might be, she stood engrossed among the handbags, deaf to the suggestions of all the polite,

black, combed, sprightly, shop assistants, who descending as
they did equally and some of them, perhaps, as proudly, even
from such depths of the past as she did, chose to let down the
impervious screen of the present so that to-day they appeared
shop assistants in Marshall and Snelgrove's merely. Orlando
stood there hesitating. Through the great glass doors she could
see the traffic in Oxford Street. Omnibus seemed to pile itself
upon omnibus and then to jerk itself apart. So the ice blocks had
pitched and tossed that day on the Thames. An old nobleman
in furred slippers had sat astride one of them. There he went—
she could see him now—calling down maledictions upon the
Irish rebels. He had sunk there, where her car stood.

"Time has passed over me," she thought, trying to collect
herself; "this is the oncome of middle age. How strange it is!
Nothing is any longer one thing. I take up a handbag and I think
of an old bumboat woman frozen in the ice. Someone lights a
pink candle and I see a girl in Russian trousers. When I step out
of doors—as I do now," here she stepped on to the pavement
of Oxford Street, "what is it that I taste? Little herbs. I hear goat
bells. I see mountains. Turkey? India? Persia?" Her eyes filled
with tears.

That Orlando had gone a little too far from the present moment will, perhaps, strike the reader who sees her now preparing to get into her motor car with her eyes full of tears and
visions of Persian mountains. And indeed, it cannot be denied
that the most successful practitioners of the art of life, often unknown people by the way, somehow contrive to synchronise the
sixty or seventy different times which beat simultaneously in
every normal human system so that when eleven strikes, all the
rest chime in unison, and the present is neither a violent disrup-
tion nor completely forgotten in the past. Of them we can justly
say that they live precisely the sixty-eight or seventy-two years
allotted them on the tombstone. Of the rest, some we know to

be dead, though they walk among us; some are not yet born, though they go through the forms of life; others are hundreds of years old though they call themselves thirty-six. The true length of a person's life, whatever the *Dictionary of National Biography* may say, is always a matter of dispute. Indeed it is a difficult business—this time-keeping; nothing more quickly disorders it than contact with any of the arts; and it may have been her love of poetry that was to blame for making Orlando lose her shopping list and start home without the sardines, the bath salts, or the boots. Now as she stood with her hand on the door of her motor car, the present again struck her on the head. Eleven times she was violently assaulted.

"Confound it all!" she cried, for it is a great shock to the nervous system, hearing a clock strike—so much so that for some time now there is nothing to be said of her save that she frowned slightly, changed her gears admirably, and cried out, as before, "Look where you're going!" "Don't you know your own mind?" "Why didn't you say so then?" while the motor car shot, swung, squeezed, and slid, for she was an expert driver, down Regent Street, down Haymarket, down Northumberland Avenue, over Westminster Bridge, to the left, straight on, to the right, straight on again. . . .

The old Kent Road was very crowded on Thursday, the eleventh of October, 1928. People spilt off the pavement. There were women with shopping bags. Children ran out. There were sales at drapers' shops. Streets widened and narrowed. Long vistas steadily shrunk together. Here was a market. Here a funeral. Here a procession with banners upon which was written in great letters "Ra—Un," but what else? Meat was very red. Butchers stood at the door. Women almost had their heels sliced off. Amor Vin— that was over a porch. A woman looked out of a bedroom window, profoundly contemplative, and very still. Applejohn and Applebed, Undert—. Nothing could be seen whole or read from start to finish. What was seen begun—like two friends starting to meet each other across the street—was never seen ended. After twenty minutes the body and mind were like scraps of torn paper tumbling from a sack and, indeed, the process of motoring fast out of London so much resembles the chopping up small of body and mind, which precedes un-consciousness and perhaps death itself that it is an open ques-tion in what sense Orlando can be said to have existed at the present moment. Indeed we should have given her over for a person entirely disassembled were it not that here, at last, one green screen was held out on the right, against which the little bits of paper fell more slowly; and then another was held out on the left so that one could see the separate scraps now turning over by themselves in the air; and then green screens were held continuously on either side, so that her mind regained the illu-sion of holding things within itself and she saw a cottage, a farmyard and four cows, all precisely life-size.

When this happened, Orlando heaved a sigh of relief, lit a cigarette, and puffed for a minute or two in silence. Then she called hesitatingly, as if the person she wanted might not be there, "Orlando?" For if there are (at a venture) seventy-six dif-ferent times all ticking in the mind at once, how many different people are there not—Heaven help us—all having lodgment at one time or another in the human spirit? Some say two thou-sand and fifty-two. So that it is the most usual thing in the world for a person to say, directly they are alone, Orlando? (if that is one's name) meaning by that, Come, come! I'm sick to death of this particular self. I want another. Hence, the astonishing changes we see in our friends. But it is not altogether plain sail-ing, either, for though one may say, as Orlando said (being out in the country and needing another self presumably) Orlando? still the Orlando she needs may not come; these selves of which we are built up, one on top of another, as plates are piled on a waiter's hand, have attachments elsewhere, sympathies, little constitutions and rights of their own, call them what you will (and for many of these things there is no name) so that one will only come if it is raining, another in a room with green curtains, another when Mrs. Jones is not there, another if you can promise it a glass of wine—and so on; for everybody can multiply from his own experience the different terms which his different selves have made with him—and some are too wildly ridiculous to be mentioned in print at all.

So Orlando, at the turn by the barn, called "Orlando?" with a note of interrogation in her voice and waited. Orlando did not come.

"All right then," Orlando said, with the good humour people practise on these occasions; and tried another. For she had a great variety of selves to call upon, far more than we have been able to find room for, since a biography is considered complete if it merely accounts for six or seven selves, whereas a person may well have as many thousand. Choosing then, only those selves we have found room for, Orlando may now have called on the boy who cut the nigger's head down; the boy who strung it up again; the boy who sat on the hill; the boy who saw the poet; the boy who handed the Queen the bowl of rose water; or she may have called upon the young man who fell in love with Sasha; or upon the Courtier; or upon the Ambassador; or upon the Soldier; or upon the Traveller; or she may have wanted the woman to come to her; the Gipsy; the Fine Lady; the Hermit; the girl in love with life; the Patroness of Letters; the woman who called Mar (meaning hot baths and evening fires) or Shelmerdine (meaning crocuses in autumn woods) or Bonthrop (meaning the death we die daily) or all three together—which meant more things than we have space to write out—all these selves were different and she may have called upon any one of them.

Perhaps; but what appeared certain (for we are now in the region of 'perhaps' and 'appears') was that the one she needed most kept aloof, for she was, to hear her talk, changing her selves as quickly as she drove—there was a new one at every corner—as happens when, for some unaccountable reason, the conscious self, which is the uppermost, and has the power to desire, wishes to be nothing but one self. This is what some people call the true self, and it is, they say, compact of all the selves we have it in us to be; commanded and locked up by the Captain self, the Key self, which amalgamates and controls them all. Orlando was certainly seeking this self as the reader can judge from overhearing her talk as she drove (and if it is rambling talk, disconnected, trivial, dull, and sometimes unintelligible, it is the reader's fault for listening to a lady talking to herself; we only copy her words as she spoke them, adding in brackets which self in our opinion is speaking, but in this we may well be wrong).

"What then? Who then?" she said. "Thirty-six; in a motor car; a woman. Yes, but a million other things as well. A snob am I? The garter in the hall? The leopards? My ancestors? Proud of them? Yes! Greedy, luxurious, vicious? Am I? (here a new self came in). Don't care a damn if I am. Truthful? I think so. Generous? Oh, but that don't count (here a new self came in). Lying in bed of a morning on fine linen; listening to the pigeons; silver dishes; wine; maids; footmen. Spoilt? Perhaps (here another self came in). My books (here she mentioned fifty classical titles; which represented, so we think, the early romantic works that she tore up). Facile, glib, romantic. But (here another self came in) a duffer, a fumbler. More clumsy I couldn't be. And—and—(here she hesitated for a word and if we suggest 'Love' we may be wrong, but certainly she laughed and blushed and then cried out) a toad set in emeralds! Harry the Archduke! Bluebottles on the ceiling! (here another self came in). But Nell,

Kit, Sasha? (she was sunk in gloom: tears actually shaped themselves and she had long given over crying). Trees, she said. (She
was passing a clump. Here another self came in.) I love trees,
trees growing there a thousand years. And barns (she passed a
tumbledown barn at the edge of the road). And sheep dogs
(here one came trotting across the road. She carefully avoided
it). And the night. But people (here another self came in).
People? (She repeated it as a question.) Chattering, spiteful, always telling lies. (Here she turned into the High Street of her
native town which was crowded, for it was market day, with
farmers, and shepherds, and old women with hens in baskets.)
Peasants I like. I understand crops. But (here another self came
skipping over the top of her mind like the beam from a lighthouse). Fame! (She laughed.) Fame! Seven editions. A prize.
Photographs in the evening papers (here she alluded to the
'Oak Tree' and 'The Burdett Coutts' Memorial Prize which she
had won; and we must here snatch time to remark how discom-
posing it is for her biographer that this culmination and peroration should be dashed from us on a laugh casually like this; but
the truth is that when we write of a woman, everything is out of
place — culminations and perorations; the accent never falls
where it does with a man). "Fame!" she repeated. "A poet — a
charlatan; both every morning as regularly as the post comes in.
To dine, to meet; to meet, to dine; fame — fame!" (She had here
to slow down to pass through the crowd of market people. But
no one noticed her. A porpoise in a fishmonger's shop attracted
far more attention than a lady who had won a prize and might,
had she chosen, have worn three coronets one on top of another on her brow.) Driving very slowly she now hummed as if
it were part of an old song, "With my guineas I'll buy flowering
trees, flowering trees, flowering trees and walk among my flowering trees and tell my sons what fame is." So she hummed, and
now all her words began to sag here and there (another self

came in) like a barbaric necklace of heavy beads. "And walk among my flowering trees," she sang, "and see the moon rise slow, the waggons go . . ." Here she stopped short, and looked ahead of her intently at the bonnet of the car in profound meditation.

"He sat at Twitchett's table," she mused, "with a dirty ruff on. . . . Was it old Mr. Baker come to measure the timber? Or was it Sh—p—re?" (for when we speak names we deeply reverence to ourselves we never speak them whole). She gazed for ten minutes ahead of her, letting the car come almost to a standstill.

"Haunted!" she cried, suddenly pressing the accelerator. "Haunted! ever since I was a child. There flies the wild goose. It flies past the window out to sea. Up I jumped (she gripped the steering wheel tighter) and stretched after it. But the goose flies too fast. I've seen it, here — there — there — England, Persia, Italy. Always it flies fast out to sea and always I fling after it words like nets (here she flung her hand out) which shrivel as I've seen nets shrivel drawn on deck with only sea-weed in them. And sometimes there's an inch of silver — six words — in the bottom of the net. But never the great fish who lives in the coral groves." Here she bent her head, pondering deeply.

And it was at this moment, when she had ceased to call "Orlando" and was deep in thoughts of something else that the Orlando whom she had called came of its own accord; as was proved by the change that now came over her as she passed through the lodge gates into the park.

The whole of her darkened and settled, as when some foil whose addition makes the round and solidity of a surface is added to it, and the shallow becomes deep and the near distant; and all is contained as water is contained by the sides of a well. So she was now darkened, stilled, and become, with the addition of this Orlando, what is called, rightly or wrongly, a single

self, a real self. And she fell silent. For it is probable that when
people talk aloud, the selves (of which there may be more than
two thousand) are conscious of disseverment, and are trying to
communicate but when communication is established there is
nothing more to be said.

Masterfully, swiftly, she drove up the curving drive between
the elms and oaks through the falling turf of the park whose fall
was so gentle that had it been water it would have spread the
beach with a smooth green tide. Planted here and in solemn
groups were beech trees and oak trees. The deer stepped among
them, one white as snow, another with its head on one side, for
some wire netting had caught in its horns. All this, the trees,
deer, and turf, she observed with the greatest satisfaction as if
her mind had become a fluid that flowed round things and
enclosed them completely. Next minute she drew up in the
courtyard, where, for so many hundred years she had come, on
horseback or in coach and six, with men riding before or coming after; where plumes had tossed, torches flashed, and the
same flowering trees that let their leaves drop now had shaken
their blossoms. Now she was alone. The autumn leaves were
falling. The porter opened the great gates. "Morning, James,"
she said, "there're some things in the car. Will you bring 'em in?"
words of no beauty, interest, or significance in themselves, it will
be conceded, but now so plumped out with meaning that they
fell like ripe nuts from a tree, and proved that when the shriv-
elled skin of the ordinary is stuffed out with meaning it satisfies
the senses amazingly. This was true indeed of every movement
and action now, usual though they were; so that to see Orlando
change her skirt for a pair of whipcord breeches, and leather
jacket, which she did in less than three minutes, was to be ravished with the beauty of movement as if Madame Lopokova
were using her highest art. Then she strode into the dining-
room where her old friends Dryden, Pope, Swift, Addison re-

garded her demurely at first as who should say Here's the prize winner! but when they reflected that two hundred guineas was in question, they nodded their heads approvingly. Two hundred guineas, they seemed to say; two hundred guineas are not to be sniffed at. She cut herself a slice of bread and ham, clapped the two together and began to eat, striding up and down the room, thus shedding her company habits in a second, without thinking. After five or six such turns, she tossed off a glass of red Spanish wine, and, filling another which she carried in her hand, strode down the long corridor and through a dozen drawing-rooms and so began a perambulation of the house, attended by such elk hounds and spaniels as chose to follow her.

This, too, was all in the day's routine. As soon would she come home and leave her own grandmother without a kiss as come back and leave the house unvisited. She fancied that the rooms brightened as she came in; stirred, opened their eyes as if they had been dozing in her absence. She fancied, too, that, hundreds and thousands of times as she had seen them, they never looked the same twice, as if so long a life as theirs had been had stored in them a myriad moods which changed with winter and summer, bright weather and dark and her own fortunes and the people's characters who visited them. Polite, they always were to strangers, but a little weary; with her, they were entirely open and at their ease. Why not indeed? They had known each other close on four centuries now. They had nothing to conceal. She knew their sorrows and joys. She knew what age each part of them was and its little secrets—a hidden drawer, a concealed cupboard, or some deficiency perhaps, such as a part made up, or added later. They, too, knew her in all her moods and changes. She had hidden nothing from them; had come to them as child, as man, crying and dancing, brooding and gay. In this window-seat, she had written her first verses; in that chapel, she had been married. And she would be buried here, she reflected, kneeling on the window-sill in the long gallery and sipping her Spanish wine. Though she could hardly fancy it, the body of the heraldic leopard would be making yellow pools on the floor the day they lowered her to lie among her ancestors. She, who believed in no immortality, could not help feeling that her soul would come and go for ever with the reds on the panels and the greens on the sofa. For the room— she had strolled into the Ambassador's bedroom—shone like a shell that has lain at the bottom of the sea for centuries and has been crusted over and painted a million tints by the water; it was rose and yellow, green and sand-coloured. It was frail as a shell, as iridescent and as empty. No Ambassador would ever sleep there again. Ah, but she knew where the heart of the house still beat. Gently opening a door, she stood on the threshold so that (as she fancied) the room could not see her and watched the tapestry rising and falling on the eternal faint breeze which never failed to move it. Still the hunter rode; still Daphne flew. The heart still beat, she thought, however faint, however far withdrawn; the frail indomitable heart of the immense building.

Now, calling her troop of dogs to her she passed down the gallery whose floor was laid with oak trees sawn across. Rows of chairs with all their velvets faded stood ranged against the wall holding their arms out for Elizabeth, for James, for Shakespeare it might be, for Cecil, who never came. The sight made her gloomy. She unhooked the rope that fenced them off. She sat on the Queen's chair; she opened a manuscript book lying on Lady Betty's table; she stirred her fingers in the aged rose leaves; she brushed her short hair with King James' silver brushes; she bounced up and down upon his bed (but no King would ever sleep there again, for all Louise's new sheets) and pressed her cheek against the worn silver counterpane that lay upon it. But everywhere were little lavender bags to keep the moth out and printed notices, "Please do not touch," which, though she had put them there herself, seemed to rebuke her. The house was no longer hers entirely, she sighed. It belonged to time now; to history; was past the touch and control of the living. Never would beer be spilt here any more, she thought (she was in the bedroom that had been old Nick Greene's) or holes burnt in the carpet. Never two hundred servants come running and brawling down the corridors with warming pans and great branches for the great fireplaces. Never would ale be brewed and candles made and saddles fashioned and stone shaped in the workshops outside the house. Hammers and mallets were silent now. Chairs and beds were empty; tankards of silver and gold were locked in glass cases. The great wings of silence beat up and down the empty house.

So she sat at the end of the gallery with her dogs couched round her, in Queen Elizabeth's hard armchair. The gallery stretched far away to a point where the light almost failed. It was as a tunnel bored deep into the past. As her eyes peered down it, she could see people laughing and talking; the great men she had known; Dryden, Swift, and Pope; and statesmen in colloquy; and lovers dallying in the window-seats; and people eating and drinking at the long tables; and the wood smoke curling round their heads and making them sneeze and cough. Still further down, she saw sets of splendid dancers formed for the quadrille. A fluty, frail, but nevertheless stately music began to play. An organ boomed. A coffin was borne into the chapel. A marriage procession came out of it. Armed men with helmets left for the wars. They brought banners back from Flodden and Poitiers and stuck them on the wall. The long gallery filled itself thus, and still peering further, she thought she could make out at the very end, beyond the Elizabethans and the Tudors, some one older, further, darker, a cowled figure, monastic, severe, a monk, who went with his hands clasped, and a book in them murmuring—

Orlando at the present time

Like thunder, the stable clock struck four. Never did any earthquake so demolish a whole town. The gallery and all its occupants fell to powder. Her own face, that had been dark and sombre as she gazed, was lit as by an explosion of gunpowder. In this same light everything near her showed with extreme distinctness. She saw two flies circling round and noticed the blue sheen on their bodies; she saw a knot in the wood where her foot was, and her dog's ear twitching. At the same time, she heard a bough creaking in the garden, a sheep coughing in the park, a swift screaming past the window. Her own body quivered and tingled as if suddenly stood naked in a hard frost. Yet, she kept, as she had not done when the clock struck ten in London, complete composure (for she was now one and entire, and presented, it may be a larger surface to the shock of time). She rose, but without precipitation, called her dogs, and went firmly but with great alertness of movement down the staircase and out into the garden. Here the shadows of the plants were miraculously distinct. She noticed the separate grains of earth in the flower beds as if she had a microscope stuck to her eye. She saw the intricacy of the twigs of every tree. Each blade of grass was distinct and the markings of veins and petals. She saw Stubbs, the gardener, coming along the path, and every button on his gaiters; she saw Betty and Prince, the cart horses, and never had she marked so clearly the white star on Betty's forehead, and the three long hairs that fell down below the rest on Prince's tail. Out in the quadrangle the old grey walls of the house looked like a scraped new photograph; she heard the loud speaker condensing on the terrace a dance tune that people were listening to in the red velvet opera house at Vienna. Braced and strung up by the present moment she was also strangely afraid, as if every time the gulf of time gaped and let a second through some unknown danger might come with it. The tension was too relentless and too rigorous to be endured long without discomfort.

She walked more briskly than she liked, as if her legs were moved for her, through the garden and out into the park. Here she forced herself by a great effort, to stop by the carpenter's shop, and to stand stock-still watching Joe Stubbs fashion a cart wheel. She was standing with her eye fixed on his hand when the quarter struck. It hurtled through her like a meteor, so hot that no fingers can hold it. She saw with disgusting vividness that the thumb on Joe's right hand was without a finger nail and there was a raised saucer of pink flesh where the nail should have been. The sight was so repulsive that she felt faint for a moment, but in that moment's darkness, when her eyelids flickered, she was relieved of the pressure of the present. There was something strange in the shadow that the flicker of her eyes cast, something which (as anyone can test for himself by looking now at the sky), is always absent from the present—whence its terror, its nondescript character—something one trembles to pin through the body with a name and call beauty, for it has no body, is as a shadow without substance or quality of its own, yet has the power to change whatever it adds itself to. This shadow now while she flickered her eye in her faintness in the carpenter's shop stole out, and attaching itself to the innumerable sights she had been receiving, composed them into something tolerable, comprehensible. Yes, she thought, heaving a deep sigh of relief, as she turned from the carpenter's shop to climb the hill, I can begin to live again. I am by the Serpentine, she thought, the little boat is climbing through the white arch of a thousand deaths. I am about to understand. . . .

Those were her words, spoken quite distinctly, but we cannot conceal the fact that she was now a very indifferent witness to the truth of what was before her and might easily have mistaken a sheep for a cow, or an old man called Smith for one who was called Jones and was no relation of his whatever. For the shadow of faintness which the thumb without a nail had cast had deepened now, at the back of her brain (which is the part furthest from sight) into a pool where things dwell in darkness so deep that what they are we scarcely know. She now looked down into this pool or sea in which everything is reflected— and, indeed, some say that all our most violent passions, and art and religion are the reflections which we see in the dark hollow at the back of the head when the visible world is obscured for the time. She looked there now, long, deeply, profoundly, and immediately the ferny path up the hill along which she was walking became not entirely a path, but partly the Serpentine; the hawthorn bushes were partly ladies and gentlemen sitting with card cases and gold-mounted canes; the sheep were partly tall Mayfair houses; everything was partly something else, and each gained an odd moving power from this union of itself and something not itself so that with this mixture of truth and false-hood her mind became like a forest in which things moved; lights and shadows changed, and one thing became another. Ex-cept when Canute, the elk hound, chased a rabbit and so re-minded her that it must be about half past four—it was indeed twenty-three minutes to six—she forgot the time.

The ferny path led, with many turns and windings, higher and higher to the oak tree, which stood on the top. The tree had grown bigger, sturdier, and more knotted since she had known it, somewhere about the year 1588, but it was still in the prime of life. The little sharply frilled leaves were still fluttering thickly on its branches. Flinging herself on the ground, she felt the bones of the tree running out like ribs from a spine this way and that beneath her. She liked to think that she was riding the back of the world. She liked to attach herself to something hard. As she flung herself down a little square book bound in red cloth fell from the breast of her leather jacket—her poem The Oak Tree. "I should have brought a trowel," she reflected. The earth was so shallow over the roots that it seemed doubtful if she could do as she meant and bury the book here. Besides the dogs would dig it up. No luck ever attends these symbolical celebrations, she thought. Perhaps it would be as well then to do without them. She had a little speech on the tip of her tongue which she meant to speak over the book as she buried it. (It was a copy of the first edition, signed by author and artist.) "I bury this as a tribute," she was going to have said, "a return to the land of what the land has given me," but Lord! once one began mouthing words aloud, how silly they sounded! She was reminded of old Greene getting upon a platform the other day, comparing her with Milton (save for his blindness) and handing her a cheque for two hundred guineas. She had thought then of the oak tree here on its hill, and what has that got to do with this, she had wondered? What has praise and fame to do with poetry? What has seven editions (the book had already gone into no less) got to do with the value of it? Was not writing poetry a secret transaction, a voice answering a voice? So that all this chatter and praise, and blame and meeting people who admired one and meeting people who did not admire one was as ill suited as could be to the thing itself—a voice answering a voice. What could have been more secret, she thought, more slow, and like the intercourse of lovers, than the stammering answer she had made all these years to the old crooning song of the woods, and the farms and the brown horses standing at the gate, neck to neck, and the smithy and the kitchen and the fields, so laboriously bearing wheat, turnips, grass, and the gardens blowing irises and fritillaries?

So she let her book lie unburied and dishevelled on the ground, and watched the vast view, varied like an ocean floor this evening with the sun lightening it and the shadows darkening it. There was a village with a church tower among elm trees; a grey-domed manor house in a park, a spark of light burning on some glass-house, a farmyard with yellow corn stacks. The fields were marked with black tree clumps, and beyond the fields stretched long woodlands, and there was the gleam of a river, and then hills again. In the far distance Snowdon's crags broke white among the clouds; she saw the far Scottish hills and the wild tides that swirl about the Hebrides. She listened for the sound of gun-firing out at sea. No — only the wind blew. There was no war to-day. Drake had gone; Nelson had gone. "And that," she thought, letting her eyes, which had been looking at these far distances, drop once more to the land beneath her, "was my land once: that Castle between the downs was mine; and all that moor running almost to the sea was mine." Here the landscape (it must have been some trick of the fading light) shook itself, heaped itself, let all this encumbrance of houses, castles, and woods slide off its tent-shaped sides. The bare mountains of Turkey were before her. It was blazing noon. She looked straight at the baked hill-side. Goats cropped the sandy tufts at her feet. An eagle soared above her. The raucous voice of old Rustum, the gipsy, croaked in her ears, "What is your antiquity and your race, and your possessions compared with this? What do you need with four hundred bedrooms and silver lids on all your dishes, and housemaids dusting?"

At this moment some church clock chimed in the valley. The tent-like landscape collapsed and fell. The present showered down upon her head once more, but now that the light was fading, gentlier than before, calling into view nothing detailed, nothing small, but only misty fields, lamps in cottage windows, the slumbering bulk of a wood, and a fan-shaped light pushing the darkness before it along some lane. Whether it had struck nine, ten, or eleven, she could not say. Night had come — night that she loved of all times, night in which the reflections in the dark pool of the mind shine more clearly than by day. It was not necessary to faint now in order to look deep into the darkness where things shape themselves and to see in the pool of the mind now Shakespeare, now a girl in Russian trousers, now a toy boat on the Serpentine, and then the Atlantic itself, where it storms in great waves past Cape Horn. There was her husband's brig, rising to the top of the wave! Up, it went, and up and up. The white arch of a thousand deaths rose before it. Oh rash, oh ridiculous man, always sailing, so uselessly, round Cape Horn in the teeth of a gale! But the brig was through the arch and out on the other side; it was safe at last!

"Ecstasy!" she cried, "ecstasy!" And then the wind sank, the waters grew calm; and she saw the waves rippling peacefully in the moonlight.

"Marmaduke Bonthrop Shelmerdine!" she cried, standing by the oak tree.

The beautiful, glittering name fell out of the sky like a steel blue feather. She watched it fall, turning and twisting like a slow falling arrow that cleaves the deep air beautifully. He was coming, as he always came, in moments of dead calm; when the wave rippled and the spotted leaves fell slowly over her foot in the autumn woods; when the leopard was still; the moon was on the waters, and nothing moved between sky and sea. It was then that he came.

All was still now. It was near midnight. The moon rose slowly over the weald. Its light raised a phantom castle upon earth. There stood the great house with all its windows robed in silver. Of wall or substance there was none. All was phantom. All was still. All was lit as for the coming of a dead Queen. Gazing below her, Orlando saw dark plumes tossing in the courtyard, and torches flickering and shadows kneeling. A Queen once more stepped from her chariot.

"The house is at your service, Ma'am," she cried, curtseying deeply. "Nothing has been changed. The dead Lord, my father, shall lead you in."

Immediately, the first stroke of midnight sounded. The cold breeze of the present brushed her face with its little breath of fear. She looked anxiously into the sky. It was dark with clouds now. The wind roared in her ears. But in the roar of the wind she heard the roar of an aeroplane coming nearer and nearer.

"Here! Shel, here!" she cried, baring her breast to the moon (which now showed bright) so that her pearls glowed like the eggs of some vast moon-spider. The aeroplane rushed out of the clouds and stood over her head. It hovered above her. Her pearls burnt like a phosphorescent flare in the darkness.

And as Shelmerdine, now grown a fine sea captain, hale, fresh-coloured, and alert, leapt to the ground, there sprang up over his head a single wild bird.

"It is the goose!" Orlando cried. "The wild goose. . . ."

And the twelfth stroke of midnight sounded; the twelfth stroke of midnight, Thursday, the eleventh of October, Nineteen Hundred and Twenty-eight.

INDEX

Notes to *Orlando: A Biography*

These notes include references to three annotated editions of *Orlando*: *Orlando*, notes by Sandra M. Gilbert (London: Penguin, 1995); *Orlando*, edited by Rachel Bowlby (Oxford: Oxford University Press, 1998); *Orlando*, edited by J. H. Stape (Oxford: Blackwell, 1998). References to Vita Sackville-West's *Knole and the Sackvilles* (London: Heinemann, 1922) are noted as *Knole*. Vita Sackville-West will herself be represented by the initials VSW.

Preface

Defoe [5]   Daniel Defoe (1660–1731), writer of political pamphlets, conduct books, "secret histories," and novels that defined and exemplified English realism, including *Moll Flanders* (1722) and *Robinson Crusoe* (1719).

Sir Thomas Browne [5]   Browne (1605–1682) was a distinguished physician and author of *Religio Medici* (1643), *Vulgar Errors* (1646), and *Hydriotaphia, or Urn Burial* (1658), three of the oddest works in English literature.

Sterne [5]   Laurence Sterne (1713–1768), clergyman and English writer born in Ireland; author of *The Life and Opinions of Tristram Shandy* (1760–67).

Sir Walter Scott [5]   Scottish poet and novelist (1771–1832), enormously popular in his day, one of the inventors of the historical novel and a great favorite of Woolf's father, Sir Leslie Stephen.

Lord Macaulay [5]   Thomas Babington Macaulay (1800–1859), a politician who helped abolish the slave trade in the East Indies, was an essayist and historian who wrote the immensely popular and influential *History of England* (1849–61); Macaulay's historical prose was one of Woolf's early passions.

Emily Brontë [5]   Romantic poet and author (1818–1848) of a single and unique masterwork, the novel *Wuthering Heights* (1847).

De Quincey [5]   Thomas De Quincey (1785–1859), essayist and autobiographer about whom Woolf wrote in her essay "Impassioned Prose" (*Granite and Rainbow* 1958. New York: Harcourt Brace Jovanovich, 1975: 32–40).

Walter Pater [5]   Walter Horatio Pater (1839–1894), aesthete, essayist, and author of one novel, *Marius the Epicurean* (1885).

Mr. C. P. Sanger [5]   Charles Percy Sanger (1871–1930), a statistician and barrister who edited a standard work on wills, is cited for his knowledge of the law of property. In 1926 he wrote an article on the structure of Emily Brontë's *Wuthering Heights,* often reprinted, that worked out the chronology of its interlacing narratives. Perhaps this is why he is the first of Woolf's living influences to be named in this time-defying novel.

Mr. Sydney-Turner [5]   Saxon Sydney-Turner (1880–1962), a career civil servant in the treasury, was a friend of Woolf's brother Thoby Stephen and of her husband, Leonard Woolf, and a member of the Bloomsbury Group.

Mr. Arthur Waley [5]   Arthur David Waley (1889–1966), noted translator and authority on Japanese and Chinese literature, lived in Bloomsbury and was a friend of Roger Fry (see page 249). Woolf had reviewed his translation of *The Tale of Genji* by Murasaki Shikibu for *Vogue* in 1925.

Madame Lopokova (Mrs. J. M. Keynes) [5] Lydia Vasilievna Lopokova (1892–1981) was a Russian ballerina, at times partnered (famously) with Nijinsky, in Diaghilev's modern dance company, the Ballets Russes. She married the economist John Maynard Keynes (see page 251) in 1925.

Mr. Roger Fry [5]   Roger Eliot Fry (1866–1934) was a painter, art critic, and Slade Professor of Fine Arts at Cambridge. His writings include *Vision and Design* (1920), *Transformations* (1926), and *Cézanne* (1927). Woolf's biography of him, *Roger Fry* (1940), was a thoroughly conventional one.

my nephew Mr. Julian Bell [5]   Julian Heward Bell (1908–1937), son of Vanessa Bell, Woolf's sister, was an undergraduate at Cambridge at the time Woolf was writing *Orlando*. A promising poet, he was to die in the Spanish Civil War.

Miss M. K. Snowdon [5]   Margaret Kemplay "Snow" Snowden (ca. 1878–1966) was a painter and old friend of Vanessa Bell, herself a painter. Snowden's "vain" researches in the archives of Harrogate and Cheltenham were at least in places where she happened to live. Woolf was particularly interested in Snowden's accounts of Cheltenham tea parties and anecdotes about the "fallen pride" of the local families experiencing social decline (see *Letters* 3: 447).

Mr. Angus Davidson [5]   Angus Henry Gordon Davidson (1898–1980), translator and biographer, managed the Hogarth Press from 1924 to 1927.

Mrs. Cartwright [5]   Employed at the Hogarth Press from 1925 to 1930.

Miss Janet Case [5]   Janet Elizabeth Case (1862–1937), classical scholar who tutored Woolf in Greek and became a lifelong friend.

Lord Berners [5]   Gerald Hugh Tyrwhitt-Wilson (1883–1950), four-teenth Baron Berners, was a composer, painter, novelist, and known eccentric.

Mr. Francis Birrell [5]   Francis Locker Birrell (1889–1935) was a journalist who ran a bookshop in the heart of Bloomsbury with David Garnett.

my brother, Dr. Adrian Stephen [5]   Adrian Leslie Stephen (1883–1948), Woolf's younger brother, was a physician and psychoanalyst.

Mr. F. L. Lucas [5]   Frank Laurence Lucas (1894–1967), classical scholar and poet, several of whose works were published by the Hogarth Press.

Mr. and Mrs. Desmond Maccarthy [5]   Charles Otto Desmond Mac-Carthy (1877–1952) was a journalist who in 1920 became literary editor of the *New Statesman,* where he wrote a weekly column under the pen name Affable Hawk. Mary Josefa "Molly" Mac-Carthy (née Warre-Cornish, 1882–1953) was a novelist. She is thought to have coined the term *Bloomsberries* to describe the loose society of friends living in the Bloomsbury area of Lon-don. In 1920 she organized the Memoir Club, for which Woolf was to produce some of her finest autobiographical writings.

my brother-in-law, Mr. Clive Bell [5]   Arthur Clive Heward Bell (1881–1964) was an art critic who married Woolf's sister, Vanessa, in 1907. He wrote *Art* (1914) and *Since Cézanne* (1922); his work *Civilization* appeared the same year as *Orlando.*

Mr. G. H. Rylands [5]   George Humphrey Wolferstan "Dadie" Ry-lands (1902–1999), literary scholar, theater director, and teacher. A good friend of Virginia and Leonard Woolf, he worked at the Hogarth Press for six months in 1924.

Lady Colefax [5]   Sibyl Sophie Colefax (1874–1950), London hostess.

Miss Nellie Boxall [5]   Boxall (ca. 1877–1962) was the Woolfs' cook and housekeeper and was frequently invoked when Woolf was pondering "the great servant question" in her diaries and letters.

Mr. J. M. Keynes [5]   John Maynard Keynes (1883–1946), economist and author of the influential *Economic Consequences of the Peace* (1919).

Miss Violet Dickinson [5]   Violet Mary Dickinson (1865–1948), Woolf's close friend who played an important part in Woolf's early years as a writer and looked after her following her father's death.

Hon. Edward Sackville West [5]   Edward Charles "Eddy" Sackville West (1901–1965; fifth baron, 1962), writer and music critic, was VSW's first cousin. On his father's death in 1962, he inherited Knole.

Mr. and Mrs. St. John Hutchinson [5–6]   St. John "Jack" (1884–1942), liberal barrister and politician, and Mary Hutchinson (1889–1977) were patrons of the arts.

Mr. Duncan Grant [6]   Duncan James Corrowr Grant (1885–1978), a decorative artist and painter, was the partner of Vanessa Bell and the father of her daughter, Angelica (1918–).

Mr. and Mrs. Stephen Tomlin [6]   Stephen Tomlin (1901–1937) was a sculptor; his 1931 bust of Woolf is still in the garden at Monk's House. Julia Frances Tomlin (née Strachey, 1901–1979) was a writer whose first novel, *Cheerful Weather for the Wedding,* was published by the Hogarth Press in 1932.

Mr. and Lady Ottoline Morrell [6]   Lady Ottoline Violet Anne Morrell (née Cavendish-Bentinck, 1873–1938) was a flamboyant and much-parodied literary hostess whose celebrated home, Garsington Manor in Oxfordshire, was a country retreat for many

English writers, artists, and intellectuals. Woolf was to write her obituary for the *Times* and composed, with the help of T. S. Eliot, her memorial tablet.

my mother-in-law, Mrs. Sidney Woolf [6]   Marie Bathilde DeJongh Woolf (1850–1939), Leonard's mother.

Mr. Osbert Sitwell [6]   Sir Francis Osbert Sacheverell Sitwell (1892–1969), poet, novelist, travel writer, and author of a five-volume autobiography.

Madame Jacques Raverat [6]   Gwendolyn Mary "Gwen" Raverat (née Darwin, 1885–1957), artist who worked in many media, including book illustrations and theater design, but was most known for her wood engravings.

Colonel Cory Bell [6]   Lieutenant Colonel William Cory Bell (1875–1961), Clive Bell's older brother, was a soldier and politician.

Miss Valerie Taylor [6]   Taylor (1902–1988) was a stage actress with whom Clive Bell was involved, and was for a time infatuated with VSW.

Mr. J. T. Sheppard [6]   John Tressider "Jack" Sheppard (1881–1968), influential classical scholar and charismatic teacher at King's College, Cambridge University.

Mr. and Mrs. T. S. Eliot [6]   Thomas Stearns Eliot (1888–1965), poet, critic, editor, and publisher whose *The Waste Land* (1922) was one of the landmarks of modern poetry. Vivienne (known as Vivien) Haigh-Wood (1888–1947), a writer and his troubled wife.

Miss Ethel Sands [6]   Sands (1873–1962) was an American-born painter and hostess. Woolf met Arnold Bennett at Sands's home.

Miss Nan Hudson [6]   Anna Hope "Nan" Hudson (1886–1957), American painter and Ethel Sands's life companion.

Mr. Quentin Bell [6]   Quentin Claudian Bell (1910–1996), son of Vanessa Bell, an art historian, potter, and writer who would publish an important two-volume biography of his aunt in 1972.

Mr. Raymond Mortimer [6]   Charles Raymond Bell Mortimer (1895–1980), literary journalist, editor, and art critic who wrote an important and lively column for the *New Statesman,* whose staff he joined at Woolf's suggestion.

Miss Emphie Case [6]   Euphemia "Emphie" Case, older sister of Janet Case.

Lady Gerald Wellesley [6]   Dorothy Violet "Dottie" Wellesley, later Duchess of Wellington (née Ashton, 1885–1956), poet and one of VSW's lovers. VSW wrote the main body of the entry for Wellesley in the *Dictionary of National Biography.*

Mr. Lytton Strachey [6]   Giles Lytton Strachey (1880–1932), biographer and literary reviewer whose urbane, witty, and often critical treatment of his subjects revolutionized the art of biography. His works include *Eminent Victorians* (1918) and *Queen Victoria* (1921), arguably his masterpiece. Woolf dedicated her first collection of critical essays, *The Common Reader* (1925), to him. His *Elizabeth and Essex* (1928) appeared the same year as *Orlando.*

the Viscountess Cecil [6]   Eleanor "Nelly" Cecil (née Lambton, 1868–1959), wife of Lord Robert Cecil, Viscount of Chelwood, encouraged Woolf when she was just beginning as a writer. In 1908 she collaborated with Woolf in a review column called "The Book on the Table" that appeared in the *Cornhill Magazine* (Lee 161).

Miss Hope Mirrlees [6]   Helen Hope Mirrlees (1887–1978), British translator, novelist, and poet most noted for her strange and influential fantasy novel *Lud-in-the-Mist* (1926). Her long poem *Paris* was published by the Hogarth Press in 1919.

Mr. E. M. Forster [6]   Edward Morgan Forster (1879–1970), essayist, short-story writer, and novelist, among whose works are *Howards End* (1910) and *A Passage to India* (1924). He was a member of the Bloomsbury Group.

Hon. Harold Nicolson [6]   Harold George Nicolson (1886–1968), diplomat, politician, and writer, was VSW's husband.

my sister, Vanessa Bell [6]   Vanessa (née Stephen, 1879–1961), painter.

Miss Angelica Bell [6]   Helen Vanessa Angelica Bell (b. 1918), an artist, was the daughter of Vanessa Bell and Duncan Grant (although she and most others were led to believe that Clive Bell was her father). She was to write of her childhood in *Deceived with Kindness* (1984). The service she performed was posing for the illustration of "The Russian Princess as a Child."

my husband [6]   Leonard Sidney Woolf (1880–1969), novelist, journalist, writer of political essays and a five-volume autobiography, and, with his wife, cofounder of the Hogarth Press.

a gentleman in America [6]   A fictitious person, perhaps compounded from Woolf's many correspondents.

Illustrations

Orlando as a Boy [Frontispiece]   The "Orlando" pictured here is the Honorable Edward Sackville, son of Edward, fourth Earl of Dorset, in a portrait (ca. 1640) by Cornelius Nuie that forms part of the collection of paintings at Knole. The painting is actually a double portrait, the other subject being the fourth Earl of Dorset's other son, Richard, Lord Buckhurst. It was Richard who was to succeed his father, so at the outset Woolf seems to have chosen a portrait insinuating that inheritance of Knole is by no means secure for her hero/heroine. The Honorable Edward Sackville was killed in the English Civil War. VSW confessed that "I know nothing of this Edward Sackville except that he was knighted at an early age, was reported to be 'a good chymist,'" and, as she illustrates with quotations, was celebrated in verse obituaries for his moral excellence (*Knole* 106).

The Russian Princess as a Child [41]   Photograph of nine-year-old Angelica Bell, dressed in Russian costume, taken by her mother, Vanessa, in the spring of 1928 expressly for *Orlando*.

The Archduchess Harriet [85]   Portrait of Mary, fourth Countess of Dorset (née Curzon, 1568–1645), by Marcus Gheeraerts, in the Knole collection. VSW notes that she was, like her husband, "another staunch figure: severe, uncompromising, but impeccable" (*Knole* 84). She was governess to the children of Charles I.

Orlando as Ambassador [95]   Portrait of Lionel Sackville, seventh Earl and the first Duke of Dorset (1688–1765) by Rosalba Carriera in the Knole collection. Woolf chose to picture Orlando the diplomat as a man VSW dutifully describes as a "personage of some solidity: weighty, Georgian solidity" (*Knole* 152). VSW observes that "[u]nlike his predecessors or their descendants, he was neither an ambassador, a poet, nor a patron of art or letters—'I have not,' he wrote, 'genius sufficient for works of *mere imagination*'—but first a soldier and then a statesman, both disastrously" (*Knole* 156). He was a particular disaster as Lord Lieutenant of Ireland. VSW confesses that he remained for her "a public character, not a relation" (*Knole* 157). Knowing his views on the works of "mere imagination," Woolf places his portrait just before Orlando's metamorphosis into a woman, a transformation that rebukes his low estimation of the power of imagination.

Orlando on her return to England [118]   A lovely portrait but an anachronism. This illustration is a 1927 studio photograph of

VSW by Lenare, who specialized in society portraits. It was Woolf who insisted that VSW pose to evoke the pictorial manner of Sir Peter Lely, the portrait painter who was court painter for the court of Charles I, the Protectorate and the Restoration.

Orlando about the year 1840 [181]   Photograph of VSW by Vanessa Bell and Duncan Grant in their London studio in 1927.

Marmaduke Bonthrop Shelmerdine, Esquire [192]   Portrait of an unknown man from the collection at VSW's estate in Sissinghurst Castle, Kent.

Orlando at the present time [234]   Photograph of VSW at her home, Long Barn, Weald, Kent, taken expressly for the book by Leonard Woolf in 1928.

Text

Moor [11]   North African Muslim of mixed Arab and Berber descent. Orlando first appears to us imitating one of his literary namesakes, Orlando Furioso, the hero of Ludovico Ariosto's epic of the same name (1532). That the shrunken head is said to be one of the relics inherited from Orlando's father, who "struck it from the shoulders of a vast Pagan" while waging ruthless war in the "barbarian fields of Africa," is the first of the novel's many historical and moral ironies.

fields of asphodel [11]   Orlando's "fathers" roamed, it seems, in actual fields of asphodel, a lilylike plant that the ancients believed to be the favorite food of the dead and so planted them near graves. In Greek myth, the fields of asphodel are a region in Hades where the shades of the dead who are neither virtuous nor evil wander among lesser spirits. In early English poetry, however, asphodels can refer to daffodils, a symbol of chivalry.

Africa or France [11]   Orlando's "fathers" are off subduing the Moors in the fields of Africa or helping fight the war against France.

arras [12]   A tapestry, usually woven with scenic or pictorial designs, that is hung on the wall.

coronets [12]   A coronet is a small crown worn by a prince or someone of high rank; hence Orlando's ancestors were noble since their arrival (as invaders) in England.

heraldic leopard [12]   In the highly codified language of heraldry, the leopard symbolizes a valiant and hardy warrior.

"Æthelbert: A Tragedy in Five Acts" [13]   Orlando's drama may represent Aethelbert (560–616), King of Kent and the first Christian king of Anglo-Saxon England, whose code of laws is the first existing document preserved in the Anglo-Saxon vernacular. But Orlando probably is writing about Aethelbert, King of East Anglia (779–794), who ascended to the throne at a very young age and was soon thereafter murdered by his rival, Offa, King of Mercia, who coveted his territories. He was later canonized. Legend has it that Aethelbert, victim to just the kind of "horrid plots" in which Orlando is fluent, was beheaded, a fate which imaginatively intrigues the young Orlando, who begins the book by slicing at the head of a Moor.

jerkins [14]   Loose-fitting, sleeveless, often belted hip-length coat or jacket worn by men in the sixteenth and seventeenth centuries.

Snowden [15]   The highest mountain in Wales, with six ridges (hence its serrated edges). Woolf spells it incorrectly here, but correctly (Snowdon) on page 239.

The Queen had come. [16]   Queen Elizabeth visited Knole in 1573.

breeches . . . double dahlias [16]   Orlando's dress is typical of his time and class. *Breeches* are knee-length pants that fit snugly at their lower edges; a *waistcoat* is a heavily ornamented, sleeveless garment worn under a close-fitting jacket known as a *doublet*; a *rosette* is a dress ornament made of ribbons in the shape of a rose, but in this instance enlarged to the size of not one but two dahlias. Orlando, so splendidly attired as he goes to greet the queen, is contrasted to the unkempt Shakespeare, as described below.

rather fat, rather shabby man [17]   This unprepossessing, unnamed figure is identified in the index as Shakespeare, said to have visited Knole, a legend Nigel Nicolson, VSW's son, denied (Bowlby 319).

hodden [17]   Coarse, undyed woolen cloth.

waxworks at the Abbey [18]   Life-size wax figures of English monarchs dating to the time of Henry VIII and including Elizabeth I, Charles II, Queen Anne, and William and Mary, displayed in the East Cloister of Westminster Abbey, the site of the royal tombs. Since they were made while their models were still alive or newly dead, the waxworks are not only lifelike but historically reliable human images. Woolf mocks the idea of such fidelity by singling out the one feature that proves waxworks cannot be trusted—the waxwork queen's eyes are always wide open, something only a wax image can manage. Woolf's essay "Waxworks at the Abbey" was published in the *New Republic* in April 1928.

the gift of the great monastic house . . . Orlando's father [18]   Knole was never a great monastic house, but it did belong to Archbishop Thomas Cranmer, who, as VSW writes, "was compelled—quite amicably, but nevertheless compelled—to present it to Henry

VIII, whose fancy it had taken" (*Knole* 8). Knole remained a Crown property until Elizabeth presented it to her cousin Thomas Sackville in June 1566. VSW reports but does not confirm the tradition that "the Queen bestowed Knole upon him because she wished to have him nearer to her court and councils . . ." (*Knole* 39). This tradition supports Woolf's representation of the queen as inordinately fond of Orlando.

Whitehall [19]   Whitehall Palace, built in the thirteenth and redesigned in the sixteenth century, has served as the seat of government from the time of King Henry VIII.

named him her Treasurer and Steward [19]   Thomas Sackville was appointed lord high treasurer in 1594 and lord high steward in 1601. Initially, lord high steward was largely a ceremonial post, but it grew into a position of considerable power. The lord high steward presided over the trial of peers. Thomas Sackville presided over the trial of the Earl of Essex.

jewelled order of the Garter [19]   The Order of the Garter, the oldest order of knighthood, was founded in 1348 by Edward III as a reward for loyalty and military merit. Its patron saint is Saint George, also the patron saint of soldiers and of England, and its motto is *"Honi Soit Qui Mal Y Pense"* (Shame on him who thinks this evil).

sent him to Scotland . . . to the unhappy Queen [19]   It was Thomas Sackville who brought the news to Mary, Queen of Scots that Parliament had sentenced her to death.

Polish wars [19]   The Livonian War (1558–82) pitted Russia, the invader, against Sweden and Denmark. England did not directly participate in the Polish Wars but did provide Russia with gunpowder. This is the first hint of an English-Russian connection that will soon figure importantly in Orlando's love life.

huzzas [19]   Shouts of triumph.

Richmond [20]   Richmond was the royal residence, rebuilt after a fire in 1498, until Henry VIII moved to Hampton Court. Queen Elizabeth died there.

Doris, Chloris, Delia, or Diana [21]   Conventional poetic names chosen, as Woolf suggests, for their rhymes, euphony, or mythological association.

Some grains of the Kentish or Sussex . . . came to him from Normandy [21] Orlando's genetic ancestry is a hardy mixture of the "brown earth"—the rich loam of Kent, proverbially the garden of England, and Sussex—and the "blue blood" inherited from his "Sackville" ancestors who came from Normandy, France (*Knole* 29–30).

Wapping Old Stairs [22]   Stairs leading up from the Thames where small ships and fishing boats used to dock; located near the Tower of London, this is where Orlando might find and consort with "low company."

Azores [22]   An island chain in the mid-Atlantic, colonized by Portugal, that served as a stopover point for treasure-laden ships returning from the New World.

Indies [22]   Coveted lands in southeastern Asia including India, Indochina, Malaya, and the Malay Archipelago.

Earl of Cumberland [23]   George Clifford, third Earl of Cumberland, was a flamboyant courtier who as a young man was the queen's champion in tournament jousts. A naval commander who played an important part in the defeat of the Spanish Armada, he was the first governor of the East India Company. His daughter, Anne Clifford, married Richard Sackville, the third Earl of Dorset. Her character and her writings are shrewdly pre-

sented in VSW's account of Knole during the reign of James I
(*Knole* 49—78).

Spanish ventures [23]   Naval raids and skirmishes against Spain for
control of the sea trade. The Earl of Cumberland was enriched
by his years of buccaneering, but his extravagant habits led him
to sell off many of his lands.

alms houses . . . in the Sheen Road [23]   There are in fact almshouses
on Sheen Road, Richmond, but since they were not built until
1834, Cumberland could not have financed them. When a reader
wrote Woolf noting this historical error, Woolf replied in a letter dated August 27, 1932: "[Mrs. Woolf] cannot recollect that
she had any authority for saying that Lord Cumberland founded
almshouses; she thinks it probable that having some recollection of old almshouses in that neighbourhood, she fathered
them upon Lord Cumberland on the spur of the moment"
(cited in Gilbert 237). An almshouse is a privately financed
house for the poor.

beer gardens [24]   A place of popular Elizabethan entertainments.

skittle alleys [24]   Skittles is a bowling game with nine wooden pins
set up at one end of an alley.

King James [24]   James I of England and James VI of Scotland
(1566—1625) ascended the throne in 1603 and ruled until his
death.

Clorinda, Favilla, Euphrosyne [24]   As the context implies, conven-
tional female names in Elizabethan poetry: *Euphrosyne,* which
means "mirth" or "joy" in Greek and is one of the Three
Graces, was the name of the ship that Woolf's first heroine,
Rachel Vinrace, sails on her fateful voyage to South America in
The Voyage Out. It was also the title of a collection of verse by

Clive Bell, Saxon Sydney-Turner, Lytton Strachey, Leonard Woolf, and others that was privately published in 1905.

Somersetshire [24]   Mainly agricultural county in the southwest of England.

address in horsemanship [24]   Skill or dexterity in riding.

drugget [24]   Coarse woolen fabric.

Irish Desmonds [25]   Irish family that rebelled against English attempts to infringe and curtail their local authority from the 1560s through 1570s.

virginals [25]   Small harpsichord placed on a table or held in the lap to be played.

covenants, jointures . . . tenements [25]   Legal agreements for contracting a marriage, especially among landed or wealthy parties. A covenant is a sealed legal contract of consent or mutual agreement; a jointure is the legal arrangement by which a husband settles an estate on his wife for her use after his death in exchange for her dower; *messuages* refers to a house and adjacent land; tenements, in common law, may include any kind of permanent property or possession, such as lands, houses, rents, commons, an office, a franchise, even a peerage.

Great Frost [25]   The Great Frost of 1608. Woolf takes most of her details from Thomas Dekker's pamphlet "The Great Frost. Cold doings in London, except it be at the Lottery. With News out of the Country. A familiar talk between a Countrywoman and a Citizen . . . ," which formed part of Edward Arber's nineteenth-century anthology *English Garner: Ingatherings of our History and Literature.*

Norwich [25]   Principal city of East Anglia, known for its trade in cattle, grain, and wool.

Derbyshire [26]   Region located in the north midlands of England.

The Court was at Greenwich [26]   Known as the royal borough, Greenwich is a city on the Thames that once housed the royal court. It was the birthplace of Henry VIII and his daughters, Elizabeth and Mary. It is now, of course, more commonly known as the site of the prime meridian, which regulates world time.

stories of the north-west passage [26]   The Northwest Passage was a hypothetical route that would connect the Atlantic and the Pacific coasts of North America through Canada. The British in particular hoped it would offer a safer sea route to the Orient than those around Cape Horn and the Cape of Good Hope, which exposed their ships to possible Spanish or Portuguese attack.

Spanish Armada [26]   The Spanish Armada was defeated in 1588 by a British naval force under the command of Sir Francis Drake.

wherry boat [27]   A passenger barge or long, narrow, light boat, sharp at both ends, for fast rowing or sailing.

bumboat [27]   A boat used for conveying provisions, fruit, etc., for sale, to vessels lying in port or offshore, called *bum* after its clumsy shape and appearance.

farthingales [27]   A hoop skirt or hoop petticoat, or other light, elastic material, used to extend the petticoat.

coranto and lavolta [27]   Popular dances in the Renaissance. The coranto was a court dance; the lavolta, a peasant dance reputed to be obscene. *Volta* means turning and the lavolta is thought to be an ancestor of the waltz. Both dances originated in Italy, were introduced into France by Catherine de Medici, and were adapted by the English. In "The Elizabethan Lumber Room," Woolf mentions the lavolta as one of the characteristic "extravagances" of Elizabethan culture.

quadrille [27]   A "set" dance composed of four couples performing a series of dance figures, the most common of which is
called the "Flirtation" figure, in which a man dances with a set
of women in turn.

minuet [27]   A slow and graceful court dance that consists of a
salute to the partner, a high step, and a balance.

Muscovite [27]   A native or inhabitant of Muscovy, the English
name for ancient Russia; hence, a Russian.

Lord Francis Vere . . . Earl of Moray [29]   Attendants at the court
of James I: Francis Vere (ca. 1560–1609) was commander in
chief of the British forces in the Netherlands during the wars
for independence from Spain; James Stewart, the third Earl of
Moray (1581?–1638), illegitimate son of James IV of Scotland,
accompanied James VI to England when he came to assume
the throne and was a member of the Privy Chamber (Stape
198).

Je crois . . . [29]   "I think I met a gentleman of your family in
Poland last summer." These French sentences were translated
by VSW from Woolf's original English at Woolf's request (*Letters of Vita Sackville-West to Virginia Woolf* 268).

La beauté . . . [29]   "The ladies of the English court ravish me with
their beauty. Never have I seen so graceful a lady as your queen
or so fine a headdress as she wears."

trulls [30]   Harlots.

puling [30]   Whimpering.

une grande perche mal fagotée [30]   Dismissive description of the decorative maypole as "a badly dressed tall pole."

George Villiers [30]   Villiers (1592–1628) was a courtier and royal favorite who was named first Duke of Buckingham (1617) and later lord high admiral.

Blackamoor [31]   A black-skinned African.

Tower [32]   The Tower of London was a fortress and prison where several monarchs died or were executed. In 1603 James I turned it into a museum to house the royal jewels.

Beefeaters [32]   Guards at the Tower of London; yeomen of the king's guard.

the Heads on Temple Bar [32]   Temple Bar is a stone gateway marking the point where Fleet Street becomes the Strand at the westernmost part of the City of London. The heads, as noted soon after, are the heads of rebels executed for treason.

Royal Exchange [32]   The central marketplace of London and of British industry.

osiers [33]   A form of willow used in the making of baskets.

the philosopher . . . Anabaptist [34]   Robert Burton in *The Anatomy of Melancholy* (1621). Burton was in fact an Anglican and would not have considered the Anabaptists, who rejected infant baptism and the Lutheran justification by faith, as the true church.

orgulous [35]   Proud; haughty.

canary [37]   Wine made in the Canary Islands; also called sack.

this day sennight [37]   In a week's time; a sennight was seven nights and days.

sacking [38]   Coarse cloth out of which bags are made.

fretted cross at Charing [39]   One of the nine memorial crosses that King Edward I erected in memory of his wife, Eleanor of

Castile. *Charing,* which means "bend in the river," is the name of a district of central London in the city of Westminster.

St. Paul's [39]   Known as Old St. Paul's, this was actually the third church to be built at Ludgate Hill, the first of which was built in the seventh century and dedicated by King Aethelbert of Kent. The cathedral of Old St. Paul's was not completed until 1313, but by the sixteenth century it was decaying. It was to be rebuilt, magnificently, by Sir Christopher Wren after the Great Fire of London in 1666 (see the note to page 122).

cressets [40]   Open receptacles filled with grease or oil to be burned as a beacon.

cony catchers [42]   Literally, rabbit catchers; Elizabethan slang for cheat or swindler.

whimples [42]   Female headdress that covers the head and neck, leaving only the face exposed.

ostlers [42]   Stableboys.

dishclout [42]   Dishcloth.

Punch and Judy show [42]   A puppet show featuring the quarrelsome couple Punch and Judy. Punch, whose name is derived from the character of Punchinello in Italian *commedia dell'arte,* was especially combative and bullying.

the frenzy of the Moor [42]   Shakespeare's Othello, consumed with a fatal jealousy of his wife, Desdemona.

Methinks it should be now . . . Should yawn [43]   From Shakespeare's *Othello,* act 5, scene 2.

Jour de ma vie! [43]   The motto of the Sackvilles, literally "Day of my life!"; idiomatically, "Light of my life!"

Blackfriars [43]   A district of London south of the Thames, noted for its theaters.

purlieus [44]   Originally, the ground near a royal forest that had been unlawfully added to it; hence, any outer portion or adjacent land.

trolling their ditties [44]   Singing songs in a loud and merry voice.

stories of Drake, Hawkins, and Grenville [44]   Stories recounting the legendary exploits of English sea adventurers. Sir Francis Drake (1540–1596) was one of the greatest English naval heroes and privateers; his raids on the Spanish Main earned him the nickname of *El Draque,* "The Dragon," from the Spanish. Drake and his crew were the first Englishmen to circumnavigate the globe, claiming a portion of California for Elizabeth along the way. He was vice admiral of the fleet that defeated the Spanish Armada. Sir John Hawkins (1532–1595), Drake's cousin, was a famous pirate. Sir Richard Grenville (1542–1591), cousin to Sir Walter Raleigh, was a naval commander whose most legendary exploit was the loss of both his ship, the *Revenge,* and his life defending the Azores against the Spanish.

Thames off Wapping [46]   The banks of the River Thames off Wapping, the district of London where boatmen docked.

watermen [47]   Figures who make their living on the docks; watermen are boatmen for hire in harbors, in distinction from a seaman, who is engaged to sail on the high seas.

post-boys [47]   Boys who ride a post-horse; couriers.

Irish rebels [47]   The Irish were constantly agitating against British colonial rule, but Woolf's point here is how paranoid the nobleman, presumably an absentee landlord, had become in thinking that a natural catastrophe was the fiendish work of Irish insurgents.

possets [51]   A drink made of hot milk, but here composed of the slobber from a newt (a small lizard).

Mrs. Grimsditch, the housekeeper . . . Mr. Dupper [52]   The names of these characters, including "the Blackamoor whom they called Grace Robinson," mentioned on the same page, are the actual names of the servants employed at Knole during the early seventeenth century, as listed in *Knole,* 78–81. Not so the Judys and Faiths mentioned soon after.

the first Lord . . . come from France with the Conqueror [53]   Herbrand de Sauqueville was a contemporary of William the Conqueror and joined him in the Norman invasion of 1066. He became Lord of Fawley in 1070.

Thomas Browne, a Doctor of Norwich, whose writing upon such subjects [54] For Browne, see the notes to the preface. The work that absorbs him is most likely *Hydriotaphia, or Urn Burial; or, a Discourse of the Sepulchral Urns, lately found in Norfolk. Together with the Garden of Cyrus, or the quincuncial Lozenge, or Net-Work Plantations of the Ancients, artificially, naturally, mystically, considered. With sundry Observations.*

folio [56]   A large sheet of paper folded once in the middle, making two leaves or four pages of a book or manuscript.

"Death of Ajax" . . . "Return of Odysseus" [57]   Mythological personages whose exploits demand dramatic treatment. Ajax was a heroic Greek warrior in the Trojan War who went mad and killed himself when the armor of the dead Achilles was awarded to Odysseus rather than to himself. Pyramus was a mythological figure not famous for his birth but for his ill-fated love for Thisbe. He killed himself when he mistakenly believed Thisbe

to be dead. Agamemnon sacrificed his daughter Iphigenia at Aulis to secure the favor of the gods before he set sail for Troy. A famed horseman, Hippolytus, son of the Greek king Theseus, rejected the advances of his stepmother, Phaedra, who, after falsely accusing him of violating her, hanged herself. In answer to Theseus's appeal for vengeance, the sea god Poseidon raised a sea monster to frighten Hippolytus's horses, which in their panic dragged him to death. Meleager, lover of the fierce huntress Atalanta, killed the boar ravaging Caledonia, but soon quarreled with and then killed his uncles over the pelt he awarded her. Angered, his mother threw a log on the fire, which she had been warned would bring his death once it had been consumed, and so Meleager perished at his mother's hand. The return of Odysseus to Ithaca after twenty years of fighting the Trojan War and wandering through the known Mediterranean world is the culminating episode of his odyssey.

priest's holes [57]   Hiding places for Catholic priests to escape the persecutions of the Reformation.

Xenophila [57]   Woolf's own verbal concoction suggesting a lover (*phila*) of the foreign (*xeno*).

rainbow and granite [58]   In one of the many instances of self-quotation that pepper this droll literary fantasy, Woolf playfully alludes to her own image for the unstable combinations of fancy and fact that can defeat the biographer's re-creation of living character. The image appears in her essay "The New Biography," written just before she began writing *Orlando*: "Nor can we name the biographer whose art is subtle and bold enough to present that queer amalgamation of dream and reality, that perpetual marriage of granite and rainbow."

(the first of November, 1927) [58]   Presumably the actual day the page is being written.

Queen Bess [59]   Popular, affectionate name for Queen Elizabeth.

Cheapside [59]   Street and market district of London and site of the Mermaid Tavern, gathering place for Elizabethan dramatists like Shakespeare.

shawms [60]   Double-reed wind instrument, forerunner of the oboe.

Paynim [60]   A non-Christian, especially a Muslim.

Sir Boris . . . Sir Jordan [60]   VSW notes "a long monotonous list of Sir Jordans, Sir Andrews, Sir Edwards, Sir Richards, carrying on through the Crusades, the French wars, and the wars of the Roses" (*Knole* 30).

the vales of Tempe . . . Kent or Cornwall [61]   Woolf is playing off two kinds of poetic landscapes: the classical Greek Vale of Tempe, a valley between Mounts Olympus and Ossa in Thessaly, said to be sacred to Apollo and celebrated in Virgil's *Georgics,* against the native regions of Kent, popularly known as the Garden of England and the setting for Chaucer's *Canterbury Tales,* and Cornwall, the setting of Arthurian legend.

Giles Isham of Norfolk [61]   Isham (1903–1976), a Shakespearean actor, was Woolf's, not Elizabethan Orlando's, contemporary.

grenadier [62]   A member of the British Grenadier Guards, the first regiment of the royal household infantry.

Lady Winchilsea's fan [62]   Anne Finch, Countess of Winchilsea (1661–1720), was a poet invoked by Woolf as an example of a female imagination that "had no chance of showing itself for the fine distinguished gift it was" in *A Room of One's Own* (60). Her adornment may have been intended as an allusion to Oscar Wilde's *Lady Windermere's Fan* (1892), but if so, it would be a deliberate anachronism.

Mr. Nicholas Greene of Clifford's Inn [62]   Greene, the only character outside the household servants to live as long as Orlando, was modeled partly on Robert Greene (ca. 1558–1592), the Elizabethan dramatist, pamphleteer, and writer of prose romances, and partly on the Edwardian literary critic, biographer, and memoirist Edmund Gosse (1849–1928). Here, Woolf is spoofing Greene's literary habit of describing himself as "from Norwich" on his title pages. Clifford's Inn is one of the Inns of Chancery, where law students resided. Greene, reputed to be the first English literary celebrity due to the popularity of his writing and his conscious crafting of a public persona, is satirized in *A Room of One's Own* as the actor-manager who seduces Shakespeare's talented, unsung (and imaginary) sister, Judith.

a coach and four [62]   A coach pulled by four horses.

at Flodden and at Agincourt [62]   The banners on Flodden field commemorate the English victory over James IV of Scotland in 1513 and those at Agincourt the defeat of the French army by the English army of Henry V in 1415.

baronets [64]   Hereditary title of honor reserved for commoners, ranking immediately below the barons and above all orders of knighthood except the Garter.

Malmsey [64]   Strong sweet wine.

dropsy [64]   Fluid collecting in the body; an old-fashioned name for edema.

Marlowe . . . Donne [65]   All preeminent poets and prose stylists of their day. Christopher "Kit" Marlowe (1564–1593) was a dramatist most noted for *Tamburlaine, Dr. Faustus,* and his untimely death. Ben Jonson (1572–1637), Shakespeare's main rival, was a writer of tragedies, "humour" comedies, and masques. John Donne (1572–1631) was a writer of love poems, sermons, religious poetry, elegies, and sonnets, and was dean of St. Paul's Cathedral.

mountebank [65]   Originally, a quack who mounted a bench or stage to attract customers for his patent medicines; an itinerant entertainer and charlatan.

Cock Tavern in Fleet Street [66]   Called the Cock Alehouse in Marlowe's time.

Stap my vitals . . . [66]   According to the OED, stap is an "affected pronunciation of STOP v., in the phrase stap my vitals, used as an exclamation of surprise, anger, etc., or as an asseveration." It became a common exclamation in Restoration comedy.

Marlowe . . . killed . . . in a drunken brawl [66]   Legend has it that Marlowe was killed in a drunken brawl, but the facts of his death are unconfirmed and speculation persists that he was murdered for his heretical beliefs or as a consequence of his work as a spy.

Cicero [67]   Marcus Tullius Cicero (106–43 B.C.) was an orator and statesman of ancient Rome whose speeches, treatises on rhetoric, and philosophical works were important literary models for Renaissance authors.

printer's devils [67]   Apprentice or errand boy in a printing shop.

junketings [67]   Expeditions for pleasure.

teg [68]   A sheep that is two years old, ready to be sheared for the first time.

oriel window [68]   A bay window.

cranks [69]   An often humorous turn of phrase, often used precisely as Woolf does here, in the phrase "quips and cranks," after Milton's line "Quips, and cranks and wanton wiles," in "L'Allegro" (line 25).

Fetter Lane [69]   A street in central London; the political philosopher Thomas Hobbes resided there.

Death of Hercules [70]   Legendary hero of extraordinary strength famed for performing twelve seemingly impossible labors demanded by the Argive king Eurystheus. His death was particularly agonizing, hence liable to the "wordy and bombastic" treatment Greene gives it. Mythology recounts how Hercules' wife gave him a robe smeared with the blood of one of his victims, Nessus, in the deluded belief that it would restore his love for her. The robe stuck to Hercules' skin as it burst into flames. In agony, he built a huge pyre atop Mount Oite and had it set afire.

lying-in [70]   Period of labor and childbirth.

midden [70]   Dung heap; manure.

Harwich [70]   Port town in east central England.

"Time passed" (here the exact amount could be indicated in brackets) [72]   Woolf has fun parodying herself in this self-amused reference to "Time Passes," the second part of *To the Lighthouse,* in which all the human events are recorded in brackets.

diuturnity [73]   Of long duration; of rare usage. Compare the neologism *scrolloping* Woolf creates soon after sporting with this deliberate archaism (76).

deserts of vast eternity [73]   From Andrew Marvell's poem "To his Coy Mistress":

> But at my back I always hear
> Time's winged chariot hurrying near.
> And Yonder all before us lie
> Deserts of vast eternity.

King James' slobbering [74] Macaulay describes the king in his *History of England* as "stammering, slobbering, shedding unmanly tears."

whole budget of papers [76] A bundle of papers.

scrolloping [76] Woolf's coinage, acknowledged and explained in the OED: "fanciful portmanteau formation by Virginia Woolf, prob. combining SCROLL sb., LOLLOP v., etc.] Characterized by or possessing heavy, florid ornament. Also *transf.* and as *pres. ppl.,* proceeding involutions, rambling." All the OED examples for this strange word come from Woolf: Hers is obviously a neologism that did not strike the literary fancy.

peroration [78] In rhetoric, the concluding part of a speech or essay.

odious Parliament days . . . a Crown in England again [79] The period of the so-called Long Parliament, 1640–1660, during which England was embroiled in civil wars. Charles I was beheaded in 1649 and a republican Commonwealth (1649–1653) established under Oliver Cromwell. The monarchy was restored in 1660 with the ascent of Charles II to the throne.

the matter of furnishing . . . three hundred and sixty-five bedrooms which the house contained [79] The furnishings of the opulent Sackville estate are itemized here according to the description of the household in *Knole,* 15. Knole was reputed to have 365 bedrooms, one for each day of the year.

To fifty pairs . . . [80] In her family history, VSW is surprisingly candid—and amusing—in reproducing the inventories for banquets and for furnishing Knole that illustrate the extravagances of her ancestors. See *Knole* 95–6.

buckram [80] A coarse cotton fabric stiffened with glue.

5½d [80]   Five and a half pence (*pence* is the plural of *penny*).

Bruges [80]   City in Belgium, often called the Venice of the North; the first book in English ever printed was published in Bruges by William Caxton.

sward [81]   Surface layer of grass or grass roots.

Daphne . . . flying [81]   In Greek mythology, Daphne was a dryad who took flight to escape the sexual advances of Apollo. She appealed to the river god Peneus to help her; he took pity on her and turned her into a laurel tree, which subsequently became sacred to Apollo. The story is recounted in Ovid's *Metamorphoses*.

Archduchess Harriet Griselda of Finster-Aarhorn [84]   Woolf's male model for this imposing figure was Henry George Charles "Harry" Lascelles (1882–1947), sixth Earl of Harewood, who courted VSW.

Roumanian territory [84]   During this period, the territory was part of the Ottoman Empire.

work of Jacobi or of Topp [84]   The English Jacobi (1560–1590) and the Austrian Jacob Topp (1530–1597) both made armor for Thomas Sackville. They are explicitly mentioned in *Knole* (99).

tie pieces [84]   Leather straps that attach the armor to the body.

shin case [84]   Armor plate fitted over the lower leg.

King Charles [87]   Charles II (1630–1685), monarch of the Restoration, reigned from 1660 to 1685.

Nell Gwyn [87]   Gwyn (1650–1687) was an actress and mistress of Charles II. She was also a mistress of Richard Sackville, and VSW gives a shrewd account of her character in *Knole* (122–27).

his Bath [88]   An order of knighthood, so called because of the ritual bathing that preceded investiture. Here Woolf implants another historical irony: Orlando receives public acclaim for his performance as a knight of the Bath at the beginning of the reign of Charles II, who will discontinue the practice. The knighthood was revived by King George I in 1725.

Santa Sofia . . . Galata Bridge [89] The masterpiece of Byzantine architecture, the Church (or Hagia) of Santa Sofia (Greek, holy wisdom) was built by the Emperor Justinian in the sixth century and was converted to a mosque when the Turks conquered Constantinople in 1453. The Galata Bridge, the oldest bridge in Istanbul, built over the harbor (the Golden Horn of the Bosporus Straits), also dates to the Turkish conquest of the city.

heights of Pera [89] Pera was a flourishing trade colony, noted for its magnificent view of the city from its high ground. It was ruled by the Republic of Genoa, a gift from Byzantium in exchange for its support of the Empire after the Fourth Crusade, and was conquered by the Turks, along with Constantinople, in 1453. Woolf had commented on the view during her own trip to Constantinople in 1906 (Stape 204).

Tunbridge Wells [89] City along the southeast border of Kent, not far from Knole.

the Crusades [89] Series of wars undertaken by European Christians between the eleventh and fourteenth centuries to recover the Holy Land from the Muslims.

Circassian [89] A native or inhabitant of Circassia, in the northern Caucasus.

engrossing of titles [90] Writing in a large, clear hand, often for the final form of a legal document.

Janissaries [90] Soldiers of the Turkish infantry who serve as the sultan's guard and form the main part of the standing army.

Sultan's healths [90] The sultan was the ruler of the Ottoman Empire.

the Horn [92] A headland of extreme southern Chile in the Tierra del Fuego archipelago, noted for its treacherous sailing conditions.

Sir Adrian Scrope [93] Scrope (1601–1660) was one of the signatories of the death warrant of Charles I. After the restoration of the monarchy, he was tried and found guilty of regicide and subsequently was hanged, drawn, and quartered. If this is indeed the historical personage Woolf wishes to invoke, she risks either anachronism or another miraculous tampering with the natural order of things. A few pages later, she has Scrope, alive and well and commissioned in Turkey, quell the disorder that erupts when the crown of the Noble Order of the Bath is placed (by him) on Orlando's shoulders.

Judas tree [93] A small tree native to the eastern Mediterranean that bears purple flowers. It takes its name from the popular legend that Judas Iscariot hanged himself from such a tree.

tableau vivant [94] A scene presented by costumed actors who remain silent and motionless as if in a picture.

negus [94] A sweet drink concocted by Colonel Francis Negus (d. 1732) made from port or sherry mixed with hot water, lemon juice, sugar, and nutmeg.

Pantiles [96] Formerly known as the Walks and the (Royal) Parade, the Pantiles is a fashionable walk in Tunbridge Wells, so called for the curved tiles, normally used for roofing, used for pavement.

sinecure [96] In the only extant corrected proof of the novel (housed at the Mortimer Rare Book Room, William Allan Neilson Library of Smith College), this nonsensical phrase remains uncorrected by Woolf. In all English editions, the phrase is "cynosure of all eyes." Although the latter phrase makes sense and is probably what Woolf intended, as the phrase is written in the margin of her holograph draft of the novel (Stuart Nelson Clarke, *Virginia Woolf* Orlando: *The Holograph Draft* [London: S. N. Clarke, 1993]: 103), it is possible that the American edition's malapropism indicates Woolf's gentle satire at Miss Hartopp's expense.

British bluejackets [97]   British sailors in the Royal Navy (after the color of their jackets).

Rosina Pepita [98]   Josefa Pepita (1830–1871) was the name of VSW's maternal grandmother, a Spanish dancer who indeed never married VSW's grandfather, Juan Antonio de Oliva. VSW wrote a biography of her, simply titled *Pepita* (1937).

bastinado [99]   A form of torture in the Ottoman Empire in which the soles of the feet are beaten with sticks or clubs.

red boxes [99]   Cases for official papers.

fillets [99]   Headbands, here made of whitest lamb's wool.

Avaunt! [100]   Away!

Horrid Sisters [101]   Virtuous counterparts of the Weird Sisters of *Macbeth*. As Bowlby notes: "As in the play—Lady Macbeth's 'Unsex me here'—their appearance precedes a disturbance of sexual identity; but here, they try in vain to prevent the change in Orlando which so threatens their loudly capitalized values" (Bowlby 326).

still unravished heights of Surrey [101]   Woolf's coy allusion to Keats's famous line in "Ode on a Grecian Urn": "Thou still unravish'd bride of quietness." Surrey is the social habitat of the "tribe of the respectable" who "prefer to see not; desire to know not." The Sisters would rather retire to these unsullied precincts than face the truth of Orlando's metamorphosis into a woman.

But let other pens treat of sex and sexuality [103]   Compare to "Let other pens dwell on guilt and misery," Jane Austen, *Mansfield Park,* chapter 48.

Seleuchi hound [103]   Woolf is giving her idiosyncratic spelling of saluki hound, a tall slender dog with a short, silky coat and fringes of hair on the ears, back of the legs, and tail. Of Persian origin, the saluki may be the oldest domesticated breed of dog.

Broussa [104]   City in northwest Turkey and, according to Nigel Nicolson, the only city outside Europe Woolf ever visited (Bowlby 327).

old Rustum's pipe [105]   Rustum, the leader of the gypsy tribe, might take his name from the legendary hero Rustam, the Hercules of Persian mythology. Stape suggests Matthew Arnold's "Sohrab and Rustum" (1853), a retelling of one episode in the life of Rustum (205). The poem recounts the tragic series of mistakes that leads Rustum to slay his own son, Sohrab.

Thessalian hills [105]   Hills in northern Greece.

kine [106]   Oxen.

Sea of Marmara [106]   Sea in northwest Turkey connecting Europe and Asia. On the east it connects to the Black Sea through the Bosporus and on the west to the Aegean Sea (part of the Mediterranean Sea) through the Dardanelles. Istanbul (formerly Constantinople) is located at the entrance of the Bosporus into the Sea of Marmara, which takes its name from an island famed for its marble (marmara).

the gipsy language [108]   The mother tongue of the gypsy is Romany, an Indo-European language with Sanskrit roots.

withys [108]   Long, flexible twigs; a rope made of such twigs.

the genealogy of Howards and Plantagenets [109]   Two of the most famous and important English noble and royal families. The Howards could trace their descent from the time of William the Conqueror; two of Henry VIII's wives, Anne Boleyn and Catherine Howard, were Howards. The Plantagenets were a line of English kings from Henry II to Richard III (1154–1485).

Whigs and Tories, Liberal party and Labour party [110]   Opposing political parties during two different eras of British political history. The Whigs and Tories were rival parties from the late seventeenth to mid-nineteenth century. The parties were formed during the Exclusion Crisis (1678–81), when the Whigs supported and the Tories opposed excluding James II and James VII from the British throne. Each party took its name from terms of insult: *Whig* is a word adapted from the Scottish term for horse thieves, and was applied to those opposed to the succession of James II to the throne. *Tory* is an Irish name for "outlaw." The Tories generally came from the landed gentry and were Church of England, the Whigs from the commercial and monied classes and tended to be Dissenters. The Liberal Party grew out of the Whig Party and was one of the two dominant political parties in England from the mid-nineteenth century to the early 1920s. The Labour Party emerged in the late nineteenth century to represent, as its name suggests, working-class constituencies.

the Talbots [110]   A distinguished English family.

Mount Athos [111]   Mount Athos, or Hagion Oros (i.e., Holy Mountain), overlooking the Aegean Sea in northern Greece, has been a monastic spiritual center for Christian Orthodox ascetic life since 1054. Women are forbidden to enter its grounds.

burnous [111]   A long woolen cloak with a hood worn by Arabs and Berbers.

paduasoy [114]   A rich, corded silk fabric, popular with both sexes in the eighteenth century.

pleasaunce [115]   Garden grounds featuring shady walks, ornamental water fountains, and statuary.

dress up like a Guy Fawkes [116]   To put on a gaudy, showy outfit, so called after the custom of dressing up like a "guy," an effigy made of old clothes that is traditionally burned or paraded in wheelbarrows on November 5, Guy Fawkes Day. This popular holiday commemorates the failure of the notorious Gunpowder Plot to assassinate King James I and all the members of the Parliament. The conspirators, led by the Roman Catholic Fawkes (1570–1606), planned to blow up the House of Lords on the opening of the 1605 Parliament, a day when the king, a Protestant, would be in residence. Their plot was exposed and they were executed for treason. Woolf's astonishment at the lengths to which men will array themselves to attract sexual as well as social attention increased rather than diminished over time, and forms the basis of her satiric look at the lavish costumes worn for public ceremonies in *Three Guineas.*

whirligig [117]   A spinning toy; hence, a mind that is spinning, here in the newfound realization of how easily men make fools of themselves in their relations with women.

long boat [117]   Largest boat of a sailing vessel.

what the poet says about truth and beauty [120]   The famous lines from Keats's "Ode on a Grecian Urn" (1820):

> Beauty is truth, truth beauty—that is all
> Ye know on earth, and all ye need to know.

Keats has not been born, however, at the time that Orlando makes her famous discovery, another of Woolf's playful anachronisms.

the samphire gatherers, hanging half-way down the cliff [121]   Samphire is a succulent, aromatic plant with shiny leaves that is used in making pickles. It grows freely on rocks by the seashore, which can make gathering it somewhat hazardous, a possibility Shakespeare dramatizes in his description of the white cliffs of Dover in *King Lear* (act 4, scene 6):

> Half way down
> Hangs one that gathers samphire; dreadful trade!

Orlando is looking at those very cliffs as the novel echoes these lines.

mopping and mowing [121]   Grimacing.

So good-bye and adieu to you, Ladies of Spain [121]   The second line of a traditional sea shanty, or song, whose first verse runs:

> Farewell and adieu to you fair Spanish ladies,
> Farewell and adieu to you ladies of Spain;
> For we're under orders for to sail to old England,
> And we may never see you fair ladies again.

Queen Mary by her husband, his late majesty, William the Third [122]   Queen Mary (1662-1694) ruled jointly with her husband and first cousin, William of Orange (1650-1702), who became William III. William and Mary, as they were called in popular histories, ascended the throne after the Glorious Revolution that deposed King James II, Mary's unpopular Catholic father.

They reigned jointly from 1689 until Mary's death by smallpox, at which time her husband became sole ruler of England. Greenwich Hospital, a royal charity for sailors and their dependents, was designed by Sir Christopher Wren, mentioned below. It was begun in 1696, according to instructions of Queen Mary, who had been moved by the sorry state of sailors returning from the Battle of La Hogue in 1692, and completed in 1715.

St. Paul's [122]   The St. Paul's that Orlando admires is the fourth and still standing cathedral built by Sir Christopher Wren after the third cathedral was destroyed in the London fire of 1666. Completed in 1708, it is the only Renaissance cathedral in England. Its magnificent dome, inspired by St. Peter's Basilica in Rome, has made it a London landmark.

Mr. Wren [122]   Sir Christopher Wren (1632–1723), who was also a mathematician and astronomer, was the architect responsible for building many of the "urban glories" that so entrance Orlando on her return to a transformed London. Wren was a dominant force in rebuilding the city after the Great Fire of 1666 decimated the city. He designed fifty-one London churches to replace eighty-seven destroyed in the Great Fire, as well as such distinguished secular buildings as the Royal Greenwich Observatory and the Wren Library of Trinity College, Cambridge.

the Monument [122]   The Monument, the popular name for the Monument to the Great Fire of London, is located at the northern end of London Bridge. Designed by Christopher Wren and Robert Hooke, the Monument is a Doric fluted tower topped by a gilded urn out of which issue tongues of fire. The urn has a hinged lid that covers a shaft that contains a zenith telescope. At the time of its construction (1661–67), it was the tallest freestanding stone tower in the world.

beetle-browed [123]   A furrowed brow suggesting either a worried or a scowling expression, so named after the high, prominent head casings of the beetle.

Captain's glass [123]   His telescope.

London Bridge [123]   London Bridge, which has existed in its present site in some form or another since Roman times, was the only bridge over the Thames until the opening of Westminster Bridge in 1750.

the Cocoa Tree [123]   A chocolate house where Tories gathered.

Mr. Addison [124]   Joseph Addison (1672–1719) was a politician and writer, who, with his friend Richard Steele, founded the *Spectator*, a distinguished literary magazine that first appeared on March 1, 1711.

Mr. Dryden [124]   John Dryden (1631–1700) was a poet, satirist, literary critic, and playwright who first gained attention with his poem *Astraea Redux*, commemorating the accession of Charles II to the throne. He was England's poet laureate from 1668 to 1689, when James II was deposed in the Glorious Revolution. His best known works include *Absalom and Achitophel* (1681) and the satiric *MacFlecknoe* (1682), an attack on the poet Thomas Shadwell, who would later succeed him as poet laureate. His *Marriage à la Mode* (1672) ushered in the witty reign of Restoration comedy.

Mr. Pope [124]   Alexander Pope (1688–1744) was a poet, satirist, and translator (most notably of Homer's *Iliad* and *Odyssey*) who ranks with the greatest poets of any age. He is the "humped" figure the captain points out to Orlando, his disfigurement the result of a form of spinal tuberculosis that left him a hunchback and a mere four and a half feet tall.

they were Papists [124]   *Papist* is a pejorative term for Roman Catholic. It was coined during the English Reformation to deride those who supported papal authority over the Anglican Church. Dryden, whose *Religio Laici* (1682) expressed a Protestant layman's creed, converted to Roman Catholicism in 1686. *The Hind and the Panther* (1687), an animal fable that casts the Catholic Church as the hind and the Church of England as the panther, reflected his conversion. Pope was born a Catholic.

Bow Street runners [124]   Policemen, so called because of the street near Covent Garden where the main police court is located.

in Chancery [124]   Orlando's estates are being held by the court of Chancery until their ownership is legally determined. It will take more than two hundred years for this case to be determined. Woolf is recalling Dickens's satire on Chancery in *Bleak House,* in which the ongoing case of Jarndyce and Jarndyce is "in Chancery" apparently until the last vestige of the contested estate is consumed in legal and human costs. Unlike the common courts, which were bound by legal precedent, the High Court of Chancery gave power to the lord chancellor to determine cases according to perceived equity or fairness rather than according to the strict letter of the law.

*The Captain must have been mistaken, as a reference to any textbook of literature will show [124]   Those who prefer their references close at hand need only look at the notes above to see that Pope could not be seen in the company of the adult Dryden, since he was born twelve years before Dryden died. None of these figures could be found at any time at the Tory Cocoa Tree, but rather at Will's, the gathering place for writers and intellectuals, or at the Kit-Kat Club, a club Addison helped found, which catered to prominent Whig politicians and writers.

Lord Keeper [126]   An officer of the British Crown entrusted with the Great Seal of England.

Lord Chamberlain [126]   A hereditary, ceremonial office whose duties include attending and dressing the sovereign on his coronation and the care of the Palace of Westminster and the Houses of Parliament on state occasions.

It was a little book . . . which had been held by Mary Queen of Scots [127] This keepsake was given to Thomas Sackville by the doomed queen, who was grateful for the tact he displayed in telling her that she had been condemned to death (*Knole* 47).

integument [128]   A natural covering or membrane.

ribbands [129]   Ribbons worn as decoration.

broadsheets [129]   A broadsheet is a newspaper printed on a large piece of paper, usually on one side; also called *broadside*.

that doctor at Norwich, Browne [129]   Sir Thomas Browne, whose book *Urn Burial* Orlando had been reading there.

dissemblables [130]   Unlike, dissimilar, various. Woolf's is the only modern usage the OED gives for this Gallicism.

the gape [133]   A disease in birds and poultry caused by gape-worms, which obstruct their breathing.

does had slipped their young [133]   Gave birth prematurely, said of animals.

expense of spirit [134]   "The expense of spirit in a waste of shame / Is lust in action." Shakespeare, Sonnet 129.

dipping sheep [136]   Dipping sheep in a chemical to protect them against parasites, like the scab.

sprigged cotton [136]   Cotton cloth ornamented with a small twig design.

a siren in a cave [137]   A Siren is a sea nymph, usually represented as having a woman's head and the body of a bird. In Greek mythology, the Sirens were said to inhabit an island surrounded by dangerous rocks. Their singing was so enchanting that all sailors who heard them forgot their danger and were shipwrecked on their shores. Jason and the Argonauts were saved from them by the music of Orpheus, whose songs were lovelier. Cunning Odysseus, who wanted to hear their enchanting song, stopped up the ears of his crew and had himself tied securely to a mast.

so dark, so bright, so hard, so soft, was she [137]   An allusion and strategic rewriting of lines taken from Ben Jonson's "A Celebration of Charis" (1640): "O so white, O so soft, O so sweet is she!" Orlando is celebrating what is dark and hard rather than white and soft in her otherwise sweet appearance.

knickerbockers [137]   Full trousers gathered and banded just below the knee.

the Mall [140]   A fashionable promenade in St. James's Park, first laid out in 1660.

billets [141]   Short notes or letters, from the French.

Lady Suffolk, Lady Salisbury . . . and others who reminded her in the politest manner of old alliances between their families and her own [141] Henrietta Hobart (1681–1767), afterward Mrs. Howard and Countess of Suffolk, became the mistress of George II. She cultivated the society of men of letters and corresponded with many of them, including Jonathan Swift. Frances Bennett, Lady Salisbury, was the wife of the fourth Earl of Salisbury. Lady

Chesterfield, born Elizabeth Savile (d. 1708), was the mother of the fourth Earl of Chesterfield, noted for his fine manners and his letters to his son. Elizabeth Howland, Lady Tavistock (d. 1724), was the wife of the fourth Duke of Bedford, whose subsidiary title, created in 1694, is the Marquess of Tavistock.

routs [141]   Fashionable evening gatherings.

Southwark [142]   A district of London located on the southern bank of the Thames where the roads to London converged. It was thus famous for its inns.

reign of Queen Anne [142]   Anne (1665–1714), daughter of James II, reigned from 1702 to 1714. She was the last Stuart monarch and the first to rule over Great Britain (created when the Act of Union joined Scotland to England and Wales in 1707). The "unparalleled brilliance" of her reign was exemplified in the works of Swift, Pope, Addison, and Defoe, as well as in the scientific treatises of Sir Isaac Newton and the philosophy of George Berkeley.

Old Madame du Deffand [146]   Marie de Vichy-Chamrond, Marquise du Deffand (1697–1780), French woman of letters, in whose salon (1753–80) gathered many of the most brilliant figures of the French Enlightenment, including Voltaire, Montesquieu, and D'Alembert, was reputed to be among the most brilliant women of her time. Her much admired correspondence reveals a wit and an intelligence impressive on their own terms (see note on page 289).

our modern Sibyl [146]   A pun on the name of society hostess Sibyl Colefax, acknowledged in the preface, playing on the Sibyl as a prophetic female figure. The modern Sibyl has lost her oracular power to speak the truth and has become instead an enchantress who weaves illusions that have no relation to real happiness, real wit, real profundity.

mot de Saint Denis [147]   A witticism for which Madame du Deffand was justly famous. Her *mot* concerns the legendary martyrdom of Saint Denis, the first bishop of Paris and patron saint of France, who was beheaded on the city's highest hill, thereafter called Montmartre (the hill of the martyr). According to the *Golden Legend,* a thirteenth-century collection of saints' lives by Jacobus de Voragine, the bishop picked up his head and walked several miles preaching a sermon. On hearing Cardinal de Polignac's recounting the story of Saint Denis's miraculous walk, Madame du Deffand remarked: *"La distance n'y fait rien; il n'y a que le premier pas qui coute"* ("The distance is nothing; it is the first step that is hard"). The *mot* takes on a special piquancy in a book that begins with a mock beheading. It also belies the claim, made by Orlando's biographer, that Madame du Deffand's reputation for wit was another of her well-spun illusions.

Link boys [148]   Boys hired to carry torches (links) to light the way along the streets at night.

South Audley Street [148]   A street in Mayfair, a fashionable London district.

It is marl . . . [149]   A somewhat irreverent jumble of literary and religious quotations. Compare to Milton's *Paradise Lost* (1667): "His spear . . . / He walkt with to support uneasie steps / Over the burning Marle . . ." (book 1, lines 292–96); Saint John 8:32, "And ye shall know the truth and the truth shall make you free"; *Life Is a Dream (La vida es sueño,* 1635) is the title of a play by Pedro Calderón de la Barca.

Park Lane [149]   Fashionable address since the eighteenth century, Park Lane, a half-mile street running between Hyde Park Corner and Marble Arch, is the site of such imposing mansions as Dorchester House and the Duke of Westminster's Grosvenor House.

Tottenham Court Road [149–50]   A commercial street in central London.

Berkeley Square [150]   Town square in the west end of London, originally laid out in the mid-eighteenth century. The surrounding London plane trees, planted in 1789, are among the oldest in central London.

the big lamp post at the corner of what is now Piccadilly Circus [151]   The big lamppost lights up Piccadilly Street, named after the collars made famous by a local tailor, Robert Baker. The Circus (which refers to a circular open space at a street junction) was not created until 1819. Today it is the hub of the theater district in central London.

the Queen's temper [151]   Queen Anne was reported to be a dull and stubborn woman on bad terms with her sister, Mary, who preceded her to the throne. She reigned at a time when political parties had not yet consolidated their power, so that the queen, who could and did shift her favors, had great political power.

the Prime Minister's gout [151]   Sir Robert Walpole (1676–1745) is regarded as England's first prime minister. His actual title was first lord of the treasury and chancellor of the exchequer, a position he held from 1715 to 1717, upon the accession of King George I, and from 1721 to 1742, under George II. He was a much satirized figure and counted Pope as one of his enemies.

the Haymarket [151]   The Haymarket, which runs from Piccadilly Circus to Pall Mall, has been a theater district since the seventeenth century. Haymarket was also a major area of prostitution.

the Strand [151]   A London street that follows the curve of the Thames River, connecting Trafalgar Square to Fleet Street and ending at Temple Bar, the westernmost boundary of the city of London. The name comes from the Old English word for "shore" or "riverbank." At this point, the street would run right along the river itself. The Thames Embankment was not built until the nineteenth century.

late Lord Tennyson [152]   Another example of Woolf's deliberately jumbled chronology and send-up of the pompous, untroubled pronouncements common to many literary histories. The "late" poet who Orlando's biographer claims was the last English writer to be afflicted by the disease of genius was Alfred, Lord Tennyson (1809–1892), an English poet famed for the mellifluous verse of such works as *Maud* and *The Idylls of the King*. The first English poet to be raised to the peerage, he served as poet laureate from 1850 until his death. His reputation was not high among the moderns, however. Joyce satirized him as "Lawn Tennyson," and Woolf used passages from his "Charge of the Light Brigade" to spoof Victorian heroic bombast in *To the Lighthouse*.

malacca cane [152]   Cane made from the rattan palms of India and Sri Lanka, which are noted for their long stems.

Whether the Nymph . . . at a Ball [153]   As the biographer notes, a passage from Pope's "The Rape of the Lock" (1714), canto 2, lines 105–9.

made his congee [153]   To take leave with a formal bow, as if asking permission to do so, from the French *prendre conge*.

I consider woman as a beautiful . . . [153]   Not in fact from Addison's *Spectator*, but from the *Tatler*, no. 116, January 5, 1710.

tippet [154]   A shoulder covering or cape made of wool with long ends hanging in front.

marry a Countess and die very respectably in the end [154]   Addison married the Countess of Warwick in 1716, died a member of Parliament, and was buried in Westminster Abbey. His last years, however respectable, were not happy. His wife was an imperious woman, his stepson a rake who was unpleasant to him, he fell out with his good friend Richard Steele, with whom he co-founded the *Spectator,* and he was derided by Pope.

I enjoyed perfect Health of Body and Tranquillity of Mind . . . [154]   From Swift's satiric account of Gulliver's voyage to the land of the Houyhnhnms, a breed of horses more rational than men that has fashioned a near-utopian society. *Gulliver's Travels* (1726), part IV, chapter 10.

talks baby language to a girl, and will die, can we doubt it, in a madhouse [155]   The dearest woman in Swift's life was Esther Johnson (b. 1681), known as Stella, to whom he dedicated his *Journal to Stella* (1710–13). Swift first met her when she was eight and some passages in the *Journal* imitate her speech as a child. Woolf herself dedicated an essay to the *Journal,* "Swift's Journal to Stella" (1925). Stella, who some speculate secretly married Swift in 1714, died in 1728, leaving Swift bereft. From 1738 until his death, the mental degeneration he had feared all his life became more pronounced. He died after a long period of mental paralysis and was buried next to Stella. He left most of his fortune to found a hospital for idiots and lunatics.

Round Parlour, which she had hung with their pictures all in a circle [155]   Called the Poet's Parlour at Knole, the walls of the parlor were indeed hung with portraits of Charles Sackville's literary friends, including Dryden, Thomas Hobbes, William Congreve, John Locke, William Wycherley, and Pope (*Knole* 151).

put bank notes, which they took very kindly, beneath their plates [155]   VSW reports that Dryden found a hundred-pound note hidden under his plate after dining with Charles Sackville (*Knole* 149).

Lord Chesterfield whispered it to his son [156]   Philip Dormer Stanhope (1694–1773), fourth Earl of Chesterfield, was a British statesman famed for his oratory, and a man of letters. His *Letters to His Son* (1774) were published by his widow after his death. Woolf quotes here an excerpt from the letter of September 5, 1748, which shows the sexually cynical, calculating side of his nature. The letter concludes that "but for solid reasoning good sense, I never in my life knew one that had it, or who reasoned or acted consequentially for four and twenty hours together."

a certain famous line in the "Characters of Women" [157]   The famous, much quoted line, itself a quotation, comes from Pope's "Of the Characters of Women" (1735), which begins: "Nothing so true as what you once let fall, / 'Most Women have no Characters at all.'" Woolf cites the line in *A Room of One's Own* (29).

Leicester Square [158]   A square in the West End of London, north of Trafalgar Square and east of Piccadilly Circus, that at the time was known for its female and male prostitutes. In the place of the plane tree where Orlando meets "the poor creature," Nell, now stands a statue of William Shakespeare.

Gerrard Street [158]   Located in the Soho district of London, Gerrard Street, built from 1677 to 1685, was initially distinguished by its aristocratic inhabitants. By the mid-eighteenth century, when Orlando visits Nell's room, it was better known for its taverns and coffeehouses. It is now known for its Chinese restaurants and is often identified as London's Chinatown.

the plain Dunstable of the matter is . . . [159]   Proverbial for a direct or plain path, after the road from London to Dunstable, notable for stretches of even and direct road.

perruque [159]   A man's wig commonly worn in the seventeenth and eighteenth centuries, usually powdered and gathered at the back of the neck with a ribbon; also spelled *peruke* and sometimes called a periwig.

Jermyn Street [159]   Street in central London, running parallel to Piccadilly Circus. Its proximity to the Royal Court made it a highly desirable residential district. It was particularly popular with bachelors since there were many gentlemen's clubs in the neighborhood. Catering to male clients led to a busy trade in tailors, wine merchants, and most especially shirt makers, for which Jermyn Street is still famous today.

Several were the natural daughters of earls [160]   Illegitimate daughters. Thomas Sackville, the sixth Earl of Dorset, made provisions for three natural daughters in his will (*Knole* 142), but Woolf is also alluding to the known fact that VSW's mother, Victoria Sackville (1862–1936), was illegitimate, the daughter of a gypsy.

Drury Lane [161]   A street in Covent Garden noted for its theaters, especially the Drury Lane Theatre. After the first building burned in 1672, the theater was rebuilt by Christopher Wren in 1674.

fled with a certain lady to the Low Countries [162]   In 1920 VSW fled with Violet Trefusis to France, not to the Low Countries. They were tracked down and reclaimed by their husbands. The Low Countries is the name given to the kingdoms of Holland and Belgium, and the grand duchy of Luxembourg.

a house in Bolt Court [162]   A house off Gough Square belonging to Dr. Johnson (see below). He was to die there.

Dr. Johnson, Mr. Boswell, and Mrs. Williams [162]   Samuel Johnson (1709–1784), a lexicographer (*Dictionary of the English Language*), biographer, and the leading literary critic and scholar of his time. James Boswell (1740–1795), Johnson's friend and his biographer (the monumental *Life of Samuel Johnson*). Ann Williams (1706–1783), poet and member of the Johnson household.

heights of Hampstead [163]   Hampstead is a suburb of London initially noted for its medicinal wells. North and east of Hampstead, and separating it from Highgate (see below), are the heights of Hampstead Heath, London's largest ancient park.

Mayfair [163] Originally a fairground and now a fashionable district in West London.

cowl [163] A hood-shaped covering that helps increase the draft of a chimney.

Highgate [164] A village north of London, so called because it is the highest point in London.

the brothers Adam [167] An eighteenth-century family business of Scottish architects and furniture designers formed by brothers Robert (1728–1792) and James (1730–1794). Although the project almost bankrupted their firm, the Adelphi development with its terraced houses on the banks of the Thames (1768–72) was one of their first important public buildings in London. Woolf singles them out for the "classic dignity" of their designs, which will contrast to the ornate Victorian interiors to come.

crumpet [167] A cake with a flat top and spongy texture often served with butter, jam, honey, or cheese. The muffin is an English muffin, a cake like the crumpet except that it is split and toasted while the crumpet is toasted whole. Woolf is calling attention to the way a change in diet helped entrench a new ideology of family and fireside, the domestic rituals of the hearth.

antimacassars [167] An antimacassar is a cloth placed over the backs or arms of chairs to protect them from the hair oil (made of macassar oil) used by Victorian men. These cloths began to be known as antimacassars around 1850.

obfusc [167] Woolf's verbal invention, the first of two in this chapter. It is either a truncation of *obfuscation,* or a playful fusion of *obfuscation* and *subfusc,* a dark-hued color or piece of clothing.

Eusebius Chubb [168]   An imaginary character. In inventing this
name, Woolf may have wished to set up a subliminal connection
between the orthodox Chubb, whose surname in Middle English connoted a stupid or indolent person, and the spiritual associations of Eusebius, which means "most pious" and is the
name of several prominent saints, including that of a fourth-
century historian of the Christian church.

mew herself in her house [169]   To confine herself to her house.

Ionian seas [169]   Part of the Mediterranean Sea, lying between
Greece, Italy, and Sicily; in ancient times, considered part of the
Adriatic.

hecatomb [169]   A large-scale ritual sacrifice.

vast mound where the statue of Queen Victoria now stands [169]   The
Queen Victoria Memorial, erected in 1911, stands in front of
Buckingham Palace. The monument features a large statue of
the queen that faces the Mall, who is flanked on three sides by
the statues of the Angel of Justice, the Angel of Truth, and the
figure of Charity. A statue of Victory tops the monument, a
symbol of Britannia's rule.

crystal palaces [169]   The Crystal Palace was an iron and glass building erected in 1851 in Hyde Park to house the Great Exhibition
of the Works of Industry of all Nations, organized by Prince Albert, Queen Victoria's consort, as a tribute to Victorian indus-
trial technology and design.

frock-coat and sponge-bag trousers [170]   Common male attire in the
nineteenth century. A frock coat is a man's dress coat with knee-
length skirts or panels front and back. Sponge-bag trousers are
named after the fabric once used to make bags for carrying bath
supplies like sponges.

Constitution Hill [170]   Road in Westminster that connects the Mall just before Buckingham Palace to Hyde Park Corner. It runs through the gardens of the palace.

Buckingham Palace [170]   The main residence of the royal family.

cullender [171]   A colander.

crinoline [171] A stiffened petticoat made of horsehair and cotton or linen, later a wire accessory to hold the skirt in a rounded, billowy shape. Although highly fashionable, the crinoline did have its detractors, who claimed that its cagelike structure restricted women's mobility by making it difficult for them to move through doors, walk easily, or even sit down. Made of highly flammable material, crinolines were also very dangerous. The crinoline reached the height of its popularity in 1850.

Lord Burghley [172]   Robert Cecil (1563–1612), Lord Burghley, served as a minister to Elizabeth I. His tactless use of "the imperative rather than the subjunctive" in telling the queen to go to bed, as related below, is a famous anecdote. The queen twice addresses him as "little man," referring to his slight stature. In less angry moods she called him "my elf" and—especially to his chagrin—"my pygmy."

bombazine [172]   A corded or twilled fabric made of silk or worsted wool that was often used for mourning clothes.

Queen Victoria is on the throne [173]   Queen Victoria (1819–1901) was on the throne longer than any other English monarch. She was queen of the United Kingdom of Great Britain and Ireland from 1837 and empress of India from 1877 until her death.

caracole [174]   A turning movement, from the maneuver on horseback involving a half turn to the left or right, from the Spanish *caracol*, or "spiral."

I am myself... Murmur [174]   This insipid verse is taken, as Stape discovered, from Letitia Elizabeth Landon's "The Lines of Life," in *The Venetian Bracelet and Other Poems* (1829). Landon is also quoted, only to have lines blotted, in the excerpt that follows. Stape notes that both quotations are from D. E. Enfield's *L. E. L., A Mystery of the Thirties,* published by the Hogarth Press in 1928 (Stape 211).

pinchbeck [176]   An alloy of brass invented by Christopher Pinchbeck, a London clockmaker, that closely resembles, and so might serve as a cheap substitute for, gold.

Lord Melbourne [177]   William Lamb (1779–1848), second Viscount Melbourne, was a Whig statesman and prime minister in 1834 and from 1835 to 1841. He was prime minister when Victoria became queen at the age of eighteen and became her trusted mentor and adviser.

twangling [177]   Twitching or throbbing, as if in pain. The very thought of a wedding ring on her finger physically upsets Orlando's nervous system.

the Archduke; he had married a very great lady [179]   Lord Lascelles married Princess Mary, George V's daughter, in 1922.

he made sacks in Botany Bay [179]   Transported to Australia for criminal activities; Botany Bay was the popular name for the Australian penal colony.

Canute and Pippin [180]   The names of VSW's dogs.

Sir Bedivere flung the sword of Arthur [182]   Sir Bedivere, one of King Arthur's oldest companions at the Round Table, throws the sword Excalibur back to the Lady in the Lake at the request of the dying king.

bog myrtle [182]   A flowering shrub that typically grows in peat bogs.

I have found my mate . . . It is the moor [182]   Orlando's "strange ecstasy" is a sane parody of Catherine Earnshaw's mad effusions in Emily Brontë's *Wuthering Heights,* chapter XII.

a greener laurel than the bay [182]   The bay laurel, sacred to Apollo, Greek god of poetry, music, and prophecy, was used to crown the heads of poets and heroes. It has since become a symbol of poetic achievement, a symbolism preserved in the honorary post of poet laureate.

nightjars [182]   Medium-size nocturnal birds, known as nighthawks in North America.

the South Downs [183]   Chalk countryside in southern England.

Nelson [183]   Horatio Nelson (1758–1805) was a naval commander of British forces during the Napoleonic Wars. He defeated the French but also lost his life in the Battle of Trafalgar. A monument in his honor, Nelson's Column, stands in the center of Trafalgar Square in London.

He had a castle in the Hebrides [184]   The Hebrides are islands off the west coast of Scotland. Bowlby glosses this as an allusion to the Scottish origins of Harold Nicolson's family (Bowlby 335).

Gannets [184]   Large seabirds who would normally feed off the waters of the Hebrides, not in the abandoned banqueting halls of its absentee lord.

For the Horn [185]   Cape Horn. Rounding the Horn was one of the great challenges for the sea adventurer.

a great blank here [186]   The biographer may be responding to the modern spirit capable of dispensing with language, but Woolf herself is alluding to the blank page filled to repletion in Laurence Sterne's *Tristram Shandy.* Sterne, who is acknowledged in the preface but is not named in the book or in the index, makes his presence felt by the literary freedoms he inspires in Woolf.

Peelers [186]   Policemen, named after Sir Robert Peel (1788–1850), British politician who, as home secretary, created the first London police force in 1829. The policemen are also called bobbies after his first name.

The lawsuits are settled [186]   Orlando's legal troubles reflect the protracted lawsuit over the inheritance of Knole that culminated in a highly publicized trial in 1909 to 1910. The lawsuit was settled in favor of Vita and her mother.

estates which are now desequestrated in perpetuity descend and are tailed [187]   Legal jargon that means estates that were previously confiscated or sequestrated are returned to the legally determined owners and now can be inherited through established lines of succession.

Lord Palmerston [187]   Henry John Temple, third Viscount Palmerston (1784–1865), prime minister from 1855 to 1858 and from 1859 to 1865.

barouches and landaus [187]   Fashionable horse-drawn vehicles of the nineteenth century. A barouche was a four-wheeled carriage with a collapsible hood and a box seat in front for the driver. A landau was a luxurious open carriage that takes its name from the city in Germany where it originated.

the Bull . . . the Stag [187]   Actual pubs operating at that time in Sevenoaks, the town in Kent where Knole is located.

Rat and Sparrow clubs [187]   Clubs formed to exterminate rats and cull birds.

base Pretender [187]   Originally, any claimant to a throne that is already occupied. Here, someone making a fraudulent claim to an estate or inheritance.

Mrs. W. E. Gladstone [187]   The wife of William Ewart Gladstone (1809–1898), who was the dominant Liberal politician of his time. He served as prime minister of England four times (1868–74, 1880–85, 1886, and 1892–94), during which he enacted educational and parliamentary reforms and supported Irish home rule. He epitomized the moralistic tone of Victorian society and was much disliked by the queen he served.

Mar [188]   VSW's pet name, used by her mother and husband.

top-boom mizzen . . . larboard [188]   A robust parody of nautical terms. A top boom mizzen is the topmost spar holding the sail on the third mast from the bow of a ship. Starboard is the righthand side of a ship. The jib boom is a continuation of a spar extending from the bow or head of a ship. Larboard is the port or left side of the ship.

read Pascal [189]   Blaise Pascal (1632–1662) was a French philosopher and moralist most noted for the meditative *Pensées* that a repentant Shel reads in his search for moral reason after his encounter with a black woman.

Bishop Berkeley's philosophy [189]   George Berkeley (1685–1753) was an Anglo-Irish clergyman and philosopher whose idealist philosophy is epitomized in his maxim *"esse est percipi"*—to be is to be perceived (with its corollary that what is not perceived does not exist).

Lady Derby [190]   VSW's great-aunt, Mary, Countess of Derby (1824–1900). Lady Derby had been the kindest relative to VSW's mother, Victoria, who was illegitimate, when she came to England after her mother's death.

bracken [190]   A thicket of tall ferns.

Shelley [191]   Percy Bysshe Shelley (1792–1822) was a Romantic poet. One of his most famous and anthologized poems, "Ode to the West Wind" (1819), with its reference to dead leaves and an inspiriting wind, may be alluded to in Bonthrop's (as the biographer now insists we call him) cry, "The wind!"

And then I came to a field [195]   A direct quotation from the "Spring" section of VSW's poem *The Land* (1926).

fritillaries [195]   Perennial plants with bell-shaped flowers.

tell one's beads [197]   To pray using the rosary.

Love, the poet has said, is woman's whole existence [198]   "Man's love is of his life a thing apart / 'Tis woman's whole existence." The poet is Lord Byron, who offered this opinion in *Don Juan,* canto I, stanza 194 (1819).

a gamekeeper . . . under the window [198]   I had always thought this was an allusion to the gamekeeper, Mellors, in D. H. Lawrence's *Lady Chatterley's Lover,* but Stape points out that the first draft of this passage was written before Lawrence's novel was privately published in Florence in July 1928 (Stape 233).

baize apron [199]   Baize is a coarse woolen cloth, usually green or red in color and most often used to cover gaming tables.

scullion [199]   A kitchen servant assigned the most menial tasks.

Salvation Army [201]   The Salvation Army was founded in London by William Booth in 1865 as a Christian Revival Association. The Army initially set out to convert and minister to alcoholics, drug addicts, and prostitutes.

plain sheet of foolscap [202]   Foolscap—so named after its fool's cap and bells watermark common since the fifteenth century—is a large sheet of paper, 17 x 13½ inches.

penny-a-liner [203]   A nonstaff contributor to a local newspaper; the name derives from the custom of paying a penny for each line of news.

Litt.D. [203]   *Litterarum doctor* (doctor of letters).

morning suit [204]   Formal daywear for men that, despite its name, may be worn until five in the afternoon.

Tennyson, Browning, Carlyle [204]   Literary giants, whatever scorn Greene heaps upon them. Robert Browning (1812–1889), prolific Victorian poet and husband of Elizabeth Barrett, was most known for his dramatic monologues. Thomas Carlyle (1795–1881) was an influential historian, social critic, essayist, and Victorian sage.

Addison's Cato [206]   Joseph Addison's *Cato, a Tragedy* (1713). The play was immensely popular, especially in the American colonies, and became an inspirational text during the American Revolution. George Washington had it read to his troops at Valley Forge.

Thomson's Seasons [206]   James Thomson's famous poem *The Seasons* (1726–30), whose structure, one book per season, is a model for VSW's poem *The Land*.

dusky potentates [206]   There is no apparent reason Orlando's mind should fly to Buckingham Palace and imagine potentates staying there. Perhaps Woolf is playfully alluding to her own "dusky" role in the Dreadnought Hoax of 1910, in which, along with her brother Adrian Stephen, Duncan Grant, and others, she darkened her skin and put on a turban and oriental garb to impersonate a delegation of Abyssinian royals come to review the warship HMS *Dreadnought,* the flagship of the Royal Navy in port at Weymouth. The hoax was highly publicized at the time and incensed the embarrassed Royal Navy.

hansom cabs [207]   Two-wheeled, horse-drawn covered carriages with a driver's seat before and behind the passenger's cab.

Spenser [208]   Edmund Spenser (1552–1599), English poet and poet laureate. His pastoral lyric poem *The Shepheardes Calendar* (1579) might have been especially treasured by Orlando, whose poem is also organized according to the natural cycle of the seasons. He is most known, however, for his allegorical epic poem *The Faerie Queen* (1596).

quartos [208]   A quarto describes the size of a book whose pages are folded twice to make four leaves.

Duke of Hamilton fell run through the body by Lord Mohun [209]   James Douglas (b. 1658), fourth Duke of Hamilton, was killed in a duel with Charles, Lord Mohun (b. 1675?), that took place in Hyde Park on November 15, 1712. The duel, in which Lord Mohun also lost his life, is recounted by William Makepeace Thackeray in his historical novel *Henry Esmond* (1852), part III, chapters 5 and 6.

the Serpentine [209]   A lake in Hyde Park created in 1730 by order of Queen Caroline, wife of George II, so called after its curved, snakelike shape.

Lamb [210]   Charles Lamb (1775–1834), poet and essayist best known for his retelling, along with his sister Mary, *Tales from Shakespeare* (1807), and for his essays, published under his pen name, *Essays of Elia* (1823).

what Tupper said about Smiles [210]   Whatever Tupper said was likely to be expressed in a bromide. Martin Farquhar Tupper (1810–1889), a prolific poet of maxims in verse, was the author of *Proverbial Philosophy* (1838). Samuel Smiles (1812–1904), Scottish reformer and, like Tupper, a prolific author, was best known for his biographies and tracts advocating the virtues of self-help, most popularly in the book *Self-Help* (1859).

Nick Greene on John Donne [211]   For Greene's modern literary incarnation, Woolf draws on the life of Edmund Gosse, who in 1899 had published an edition of *The Life and Letters of John Donne*.

eight-hour bills nor covenants nor factory acts [211]   Legislation of extreme importance to Labour after the nine-day General Strike "in defense of [coal]miners' wages and hours" called by the Trades Union Congress in May 1926. In 1928 there was a government move to repeal the Eight Hours Act, a cornerstone of the labor and trade union movements. The covenants discussed here do not concern the legalities of marriage but the contracts that made sympathetic strikes illegal. A Factories Bill proposed in 1927 was eventually postponed.

Stanhope Gate [211]   Street between Park Lane and South Audley Street in fashionable Mayfair. Old Jolyon Forsyte, one of the few endearing Forsytes in John Galsworthy's generational saga, lives in Stanhope Gate, as recounted in the opening chapter of the first volume of *The Forsyte Saga, The Man of Property* (1906).

four-in-hand . . . victoria [212]   The four-in-hand, as the name suggests, is an imposing carriage pulled by a team of four horses driven by one man. A victoria is a light, low-riding, four-wheeled carriage for two, with a folding top and an elevated driver's seat in front.

Curzon Street [212]   A small street behind Park Lane in Mayfair.

meadow-sweet [212]   An herb with clusters of delicate white blossoms that grows in damp meadows.

curlew [212]   A wading bird with a long curved bill and brown plumage.

Alexander Smiths . . . Jamesons [213]   Woolf's roll call of these writers clamoring for her attention includes, with the exception of Hippolyte Taine (1828–1893), the influential French literary critic and historian, names of fairly undistinguished writers who flourished in the nineteenth century. Although her examples seem deliberately chosen for their common names—Smith, Black, Dixon—that in the plural suggest a generic rather than a distinctive and individual literary style, she refers to actual writers. Alexander Smith (1830–1867), Scottish poet and essayist; Richard Watson Dixon (1833–1900), historian and poet; William Black (1841–1898), Scottish journalist and novelist; Henry Hart Milman (1791–1868), historian and playwright; Henry Thomas Buckle (1821–1862), historian; James Payne (1830–1898), novelist; Tupper, see note to page 210; Anna Brownell Jameson (1794–1860), Irish travel writer and essayist.

octavo [213]   A book whose pages are made by folding a sheet of paper three times to form eight leaves.

Miss Christina Rossetti [213]   Christina Georgina Rossetti (1830–1894), poet, most notably of *Goblin Market and Other Poems* (1862).

Carlyle's sound-proof room at Chelsea [214]   Carlyle's attic study was equipped with double walls to ensure quiet.

Chesterfield House [214]   Eighteenth-century residence of Lord Chesterfield, on the corner of Curzon and South Audley streets.

lion couchant [215]   Heraldic position, with the lion lying down with head raised; symbol of Britannia.

Kew [215]   The Green marks the entrance to Kew Gardens, officially the Royal Botanic Gardens, located in the southwest London district of Kew. The steeple Orlando recognizes crowns the Chinese pagoda. *Kew Gardens* (1919) is one of Woolf's first experimental short stories.

half-crown tickets [216]   Cheap tickets; a half crown is worth only two shillings and sixpence.

refluent [216]   Flowing back; ebbing.

King Edward [217]   Edward VII (1841–1910) reigned from 1901 to 1910, the year, Virginia Woolf famously asserted in "Mr. Bennett and Mrs. Brown" (1924), "human character changed."

brougham [217]   A closed four-wheeled carriage with an open driver's seat in front.

a certain lady opposite [217]   Edward VII's mistress, Alice Keppel (1869–1947), the mother of Violet Trefusis. A contemporary note: Her great-granddaughter is Camilla Parker Bowles, who married Prince Charles in 2005.

Marshall & Snelgrove's [219]   A major department store at the time, founded in 1848.

Portland Place [220]   An elegant, wide street in the Marylebone district of London, near Regent's Park, Portland Place was initially laid out by the Adam Brothers (see note to page 167) and contains many of their elegant terraced houses.

Prince Consort. "Sale bosch!" [221]   Louise is referring to Prince Albert (1819–1861), Queen Victoria's husband. The recent world war that pitted England and France against Germany inspires her vilification of the prince consort, who was German, as a "Sale bosch," a French slur meaning "filthy Hun."

Dictionary of National Biography [224]   The standard reference
work on notable British figures. Woolf's father, Leslie Stephen,
established the *Dictionary* in 1882 and edited it until 1891. The
biographer's jab at the *Dictionary*'s convention of recording, as
many of these notes do, a person's life span within parentheses,
is a measure of the freedom Woolf felt in writing this irreverent
work. She had already satirized her father's project in *To the
Lighthouse,* when she represented Mr. Ramsay, a character based
on her father, as a methodical thinker plodding his way through
the great alphabet of thought, finding himself stuck on *Q* and
despairing of ever reaching *R.*

Regent Street . . . old Kent Road [224]   Orlando's route home. Regent's Street, named after the prince regent (later George IV),
was initially built as a royal route from Carleton House to Regent's Park. It runs past Piccadilly and Oxford Circus. Northumberland Avenue runs along the Strand. Westminster Bridge,
spanning the Thames, connects Westminster to Lambeth. The
Old Kent Road, which once was a Roman road, is traditionally
one of the poor districts. That may explain the urban sights Orlando takes in as she makes her way along the thoroughfare —
a market, an undertaker, and, most strikingly, a procession with
banners whose wording she can't quite make out. Orlando's
journey across space also takes her to the heart of the present,
Thursday, the eleventh of October, 1928.

Ra—Un . . . Amor Vin— . . . Undert—. [224]   Woolf often commented on how experience seemed cut off or cut short in
modern times. Here she typographically represents this percep-
tion. Still, the wording on the banners raises a real question
about what is being said. Gilbert has suggested that the banners read "Rally of the Unemployed" or "Rally against Un-
employment" (Gilbert 262–63). The Old Kent Road would be
a fitting gathering spot for such a demonstration. A famous

music hall song reflecting the situation and sentiments of London's urban poor was "Knocked 'em in the Old Kent Road." Amor Vin— is easily completed as the Latin tag *Amor Vincit Omnia,* Love Conquers All, an inspiring maxim likely to grace a parlor sampler—or a porch. And however grim, there is no reason to doubt that "Undert—" advertises that Applejohn and Applebed are undertakers.

duffer [227]   A dull, incompetent person.

High Street of her native town [228]   High Street is a common name for the main street of a British town.

A prize. [228]   VSW won the 1927 Hawthornden Prize for *The Land.*

'The Burdett Coutts' Memorial Prize [228]   Angela Georgina Burdett-Coutts (1814–1906), in her time reputed to be the wealthiest woman in England, was a noted philanthropist. Among the projects she sponsored were low-income housing, gin mills for Nigeria, soup kitchens, temperance societies, and drinking fountains for dogs, but, as the quotation marks suggest, she never established nor inspired a literary prize in her memory.

as if Madame Lopokova were using her highest art [230]   Changing her clothes with balletic grace. See the note to the preface, page 249.

the Ambassador's bedroom . . . Rows of chairs . . . Lady Betty's table . . . King James' silver brushes [232]   A final tribute to the lavish accommodations and furnishings at Knole.

Cecil [232]   William Cecil (1520–1598), first Baron Burghley, was an English statesman and chief adviser to Elizabeth I. He persuaded her to have Mary, Queen of Scots executed.

Flodden and Poitiers [233]   On Flodden, see the note to page 62 above. The Battle of Poitiers, fought on September 19, 1356, was the second of three major English victories against France in the Hundred Years' War.

Tudors [233]   Henry VII was the first and Elizabeth I the last of the Tudor monarchs of England.

weald [240]   Woodland.

Suggestions for Further Reading:
Virginia Woolf

Editions

The Complete Shorter Fiction. Edited by Susan Dick. 2nd ed. San Diego: Harcourt, 1989.

The Diary of Virginia Woolf. Edited by Anne Olivier Bell. 5 vols. New York: Harcourt, 1977–84.

The Essays of Virginia Woolf. Edited by Andrew McNeillie. 6 vols. [in progress]. San Diego: Harcourt Brace Jovanovich, 1986–.

The Letters of Virginia Woolf. Edited by Nigel Nicolson and Joanne Trautmann. 6 vols. New York: Harcourt Brace Jovanovich, 1975–80.

Moments of Being. Edited by Jeanne Schulkind. San Diego: Harcourt, 1985.

A Passionate Apprentice: The Early Journals, 1897–1909. Edited by Mitchell A. Leaska. San Diego: Harcourt, 1990.

Biographies and Reference Works

Briggs, Julia. *Virginia Woolf: An Inner Life*. San Diego: Harcourt, 2005.

Hussey, Mark. *Virginia Woolf A to Z: A Comprehensive Reference for Students, Teachers, and Common Readers to Her Life, Works, and Critical Reception*. New York: Facts on File, 1995.

Kirkpatrick, B. J., and Stuart N. Clarke. *A Bibliography of Virginia Woolf*. 4th ed. Oxford: Clarendon, 1997.

Lee, Hermione. *Virginia Woolf*. New York: Knopf, 1996.

Marder, Herbert. *The Measure of Life: Virginia Woolf's Last Years.* Ithaca, NY: Cornell University Press, 2000.

Poole, Roger. *The Unknown Virginia Woolf.* 4th ed. Cambridge: Cambridge University Press, 1995.

Reid, Panthea. *Art and Affection: A Life of Virginia Woolf.* New York: Oxford University Press, 1996.

General Criticism

Abel, Elizabeth. *Virginia Woolf and the Fictions of Psychoanalysis.* Chicago: University of Chicago Press, 1989.

Bazin, Nancy Topping. *Virginia Woolf and the Androgynous Vision.* New Brunswick, NJ: Rutgers University Press, 1973.

Beer, Gillian. *Virginia Woolf: The Common Ground.* Ann Arbor: University of Michigan Press, 1996.

Cuddy-Keane, Melba. *Virginia Woolf, the Intellectual, and the Public Sphere.* Cambridge: Cambridge University Press, 2003.

DiBattista, Maria. *Virginia Woolf's Major Novels: The Fables of Anon.* New Haven, CT: Yale University Press, 1980.

Fleishman, Avrom. *Virginia Woolf: A Critical Reading.* Baltimore: Johns Hopkins University Press, 1975.

Froula, Christine. *Virginia Woolf and the Bloomsbury Avant-Garde: War, Civilization, Modernity.* New York: Columbia University Press, 2005.

Guiguet, Jean. *Virginia Woolf and Her Works.* New York: Harcourt Brace Jovanovich, 1965.

Harper, Howard. *Between Language and Silence: The Novels of Virginia Woolf.* Baton Rouge: Louisiana State University Press, 1982.

Hussey, Mark. *The Singing of the Real World: The Philosophy of Virginia Woolf's Fiction.* Columbus: Ohio State University Press, 1986.

———, ed. *Virginia Woolf and War: Fiction, Reality and Myth.* Syracuse, NY: Syracuse University Press, 1991.

Majumdar, Robin, and Allen McLaurin, eds. *Virginia Woolf: The Critical Heritage.* Boston: Routledge, 1975.

Marcus, Jane. *Art and Anger: Reading Like a Woman.* Columbus: Ohio State University Press, 1988.

———, ed. *New Feminist Essays on Virginia Woolf.* Lincoln: University of Nebraska Press, 1981.

———, ed. *Virginia Woolf: A Feminist Slant.* Lincoln: University of Nebraska Press, 1983.

———, ed. *Virginia Woolf and Bloomsbury: A Centenary Celebration.* Bloomington: Indiana University Press, 1987.

———. *Virginia Woolf and the Languages of Patriarchy.* Bloomington: Indiana University Press, 1987.

McLaurin, Allen. *Virginia Woolf: The Echoes Enslaved.* Cambridge: Cambridge University Press, 1973.

McNees, Eleanor, ed. *Virginia Woolf: Critical Assessments.* 4 vols. New York: Routledge, 1994.

Minow-Pinkney, Makiko. *Virginia Woolf and the Problem of the Subject: Feminine Writing in the Major Novels.* New Brunswick, NJ: Rutgers University Press, 1987.

Phillips, Kathy J. *Virginia Woolf Against Empire.* Knoxville: University of Tennessee Press, 1994.

Roe, Sue, and Susan Sellers, eds. *The Cambridge Companion to Virginia Woolf.* Cambridge: Cambridge University Press, 2000.

Ruotolo, Lucio. *The Interrupted Moment: A View of Virginia Woolf's Novels.* Stanford, CA: Stanford University Press, 1986.

Silver, Brenda R. *Virginia Woolf Icon.* Chicago: University of Chicago Press, 1999.

Zwerdling, Alex. *Virginia Woolf and the Real World.* Berkeley: University of California Press, 1986.

SUGGESTIONS FOR FURTHER READING:
Orlando: A Biography

(in addition to the works cited in the introduction)

Baldanza, Frank O. "*Orlando* and the Sackvilles." *PMLA* 70.1 (March 1955): 274–79.

Brown, Carolyn. "Feminist Literary Strategies in the Postmodern Condition." In *From My Guy to Sci-Fi: Genre and Women's Writing in the Postmodern World.* Edited by Helen Carr, 112–34. London: Pandora Press, 1989.

Fox, Alice. *Virginia Woolf and the Literature of the English Renaissance.* Oxford: Clarendon Press, 1990.

Graham, J. W. "The 'Caricature Value' of Parody and Fantasy in *Orlando.*" *University of Toronto Quarterly* 30.4 (July 1961): 345–65.

Knopp, Sherron E. "'If I Saw You Would You Kiss Me?': Sapphism and the Subversiveness of Virginia Woolf's *Orlando.*" *PMLA* 103.1 (January 1988): 24–33.

Lawrence, Karen R. "Woolf's Voyages Out." In *Penelope Voyages: Women and Travel in the British Literary Tradition,* 154–206. Ithaca, NY: Cornell University Press, 1994.

Little, Judy. "(En)gendering Laughter: Woolf's *Orlando* as Contraband in the Age of Joyce." *Women's Studies* 15.1–3 (1988): 179–91.

Love, Jean O. "*Orlando* and its Genesis: Venturing and Experimenting in Art, Love, and Sex." In *Virginia Woolf: Revaluation and Continuity.* Edited by Ralph Freedman, 189–218. Berkeley: University of California Press, 1980.

Moore, Madeline. "*Orlando*: An Imaginative Answer." In *The Short Season Between Two Silences: The Mystical and the Political in the Novels of Virginia Woolf,* 93–115. Boston: George Allen and Unwin, 1984.

Nord, Deborah Epstein. "Androgyny, Writing and Place in *Orlando* and *A Room of One's Own.*" In *Woolf Across Cultures.* Edited by Natalya Reinhold, 227–34. New York: Pace University Press, 2004.

Raitt, Suzanne. *Vita and Virginia: The Work and Friendship of V. Sackville-West and Virginia Woolf.* Oxford: Clarendon Press, 1993.

Schaffer, Talia. "Posing *Orlando.*" In *Sexual Artifice.* Edited by Ann Kibbey, Kayann Short, and Abouali Farmanfarmaian, 26–63. New York: New York University Press, 1994.

Scott, Alison M. "'Tantalising fragments': The Proofs of Virginia Woolf's *Orlando.*" *Papers of the Bibliographical Society of America* 88.3 (1994): 279–351.

Squier, Susan. "Tradition and Revision in Woolf's *Orlando*: Defoe and 'The Jessamy Brides.'" *Women's Studies* 12.2 (1986): 167–77.

Trautmann, Joanne. *Jessamy Brides: The Friendship of Virginia Woolf and V. Sackville West.* Penn State Studies No. 36. University Park: Pennsylvania State University Press, 1973.

Wilson, J. J. "Why Is *Orlando* Difficult?" In *New Feminist Essays on Virginia Woolf.* Edited by Jane Marcus, 170–84. London: Macmillan, 1981.